RUTHLESS GAME

RUTHLESS GAME

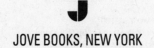

CHRISTINE FEEHAN

JOVE BOOKS, NEW YORK

THE BERKLEY PUBLISHING GROUP
Published by the Penguin Group
Penguin Group (USA) Inc.
375 Hudson Street, New York, New York 10014, USA
Penguin Group (Canada), 90 Eglinton Avenue East, Suite 700, Toronto, Ontario M4P 2Y3, Canada
(a division of Pearson Penguin Canada Inc.)
Penguin Books Ltd., 80 Strand, London WC2R 0RL, England
Penguin Group Ireland, 25 St. Stephen's Green, Dublin 2, Ireland (a division of Penguin Books Ltd.)
Penguin Group (Australia), 250 Camberwell Road, Camberwell, Victoria 3124, Australia
(a division of Pearson Australia Group Pty. Ltd.)
Penguin Books India Pvt. Ltd., 11 Community Centre, Panchsheel Park, New Delhi—110 017, India
Penguin Group (NZ), 67 Apollo Drive, Rosedale, North Shore 0632, New Zealand
(a division of Pearson New Zealand Ltd.)
Penguin Books (South Africa) (Pty.) Ltd., 24 Sturdee Avenue, Rosebank, Johannesburg 2196,
South Africa

Penguin Books Ltd., Registered Offices: 80 Strand, London WC2R 0RL, England

This is a work of fiction. Names, characters, places, and incidents either are the product of the author's imagination or are used fictitiously, and any resemblance to actual persons, living or dead, business establishments, events, or locales is entirely coincidental. The publisher does not have control over and does not have any responsibility for author or third-party websites or their content.

RUTHLESS GAME

A Jove Book / published by arrangement with the author

ISBN: 978-1-61129-010-3

JOVE®
Jove Books are published by The Berkley Publishing Group,
a division of Penguin Group (USA) Inc.,
375 Hudson Street, New York, New York 10014.
JOVE® is a registered trademark of Penguin Group (USA) Inc.
The "J" design is a trademark of Penguin Group (USA) Inc.

PRINTED IN THE UNITED STATES OF AMERICA

For Mike and Margo Anthony

For My Readers

Be sure to go to http://www.christinefeehan.com/ members/ to sign up for my *private* book announcement list and download the *free* e-book of *Dark Desserts*. Join my community and get firsthand news, enter the book discussions, ask your questions, and chat with me. Please feel free to email me at Christine@christine feehan.com. I would love to hear from you.

Acknowledgments

As always when writing a book, I have several people to thank: Morey Sparks, for information on weapons; Jack, for answering questions regarding weapons; and of course, Brian Feehan, who always drops everything to work out tough fight scenes. Manda, thank you for going above and beyond, working late nights and weekends when I needed you to get the book finished. Domini, as always, you make the book so much better! I appreciate you all so much!

The GhostWalker Symbol Details

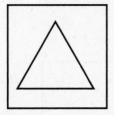

SIGNIFIES
shadow

SIGNIFIES
protection against
evil forces

SIGNIFIES
the Greek letter *psi,* which is
used by parapsychology
researchers to signify ESP or
other psychic abilities

SIGNIFIES
qualities of a knight—
loyalty, generosity,
courage, and honor

SIGNIFIES
shadow knights who protect
against evil forces using
psychic powers, courage,
and honor

nox noctis est nostri

The GhostWalker Creed

We are the GhostWalkers, we live in the shadows
The sea, the earth, and the air are our domain
No fallen comrade will be left behind
We are loyalty and honor bound
We are invisible to our enemies
and we destroy them where we find them
We believe in justice and we protect our country
and those unable to protect themselves
What goes unseen, unheard, and unknown
are GhostWalkers
There is honor in the shadows and it is us
We move in complete silence whether
in jungle or desert
We walk among our enemy unseen and unheard
Striking without sound and scatter to the winds
before they have knowledge of our existence
We gather information and wait with endless patience
for that perfect moment to deliver swift justice
We are both merciful and merciless
We are relentless and implacable in our resolve
We are the GhostWalkers and the night is ours

CHAPTER 1

The lone coyote trotted across the desert on the outskirts of the city. Bold, he nosed close to the trash scattered along the edges of the sand. The night air was cool, but the sand was still warm from the hot day's sun. He padded along, nose to the ground, sniffing around the back of a long structure until he came to an alleyway. Someone coughed, and a bottle smashed against the side of the building. The coyote whirled and ran. He'd been shot at many times coming in too close to these particular buildings, but the food was unusually plentiful. Still, he didn't want to take a chance, not when there were so many men walking around so late at night.

The coyote reluctantly slunk away from the banquet, edged out to a pile of boulders, and hunched down, waiting for things to settle a little more before he made another try. In the distant desert, he heard a muffled sound, like the beating of large wings, and he turned his head toward the sky, cowering closer to the rock.

The helicopter came in fast and low, running without

lights and in eerie silence. Ropes dropped from the open doors, and five men descended fast and, in one smooth, coordinated motion, began sprinting across the desert with unprecedented speed. Seconds later the helicopter was gone, and the coyote surged to his feet, ready to run as the men, nothing more than shadows, raced toward him. There was no sound, not even the thud of boots on sand. The wind carried their scents, and as they approached, their bodies were more defined, appearing as a single dark entity with ten glowing eyes.

The coyote took a few steps one way and then, as the men split apart, running no more than two feet from one another in perfect unison, he stepped in the other direction, whirled, tail down, and then stopped, confused. The men rushed by like the wind, not so much as hesitating, yet those strange eyes flashed over the animal as he cowered, obviously seeing him, although he was in the darker shadow of the rocks.

Javier, you're on. Just take a look. Hear what I'm saying? A look. No one dies yet. Mack McKinley, leader of GhostWalker Team Three, sent his first man into the hot zone. The unique GhostWalker unit he led had no need of radios. They were all telepathic.

I'm hurt, boss. Laughter spilled into Mack's mind. *Why would you ever think someone might die?*

Mack sent Javier Enderman a stern warning look. Javier could see easily in the darkness, even when he chose not to. He looked like a kid with his dark black eyes and innocent, boyish face—one of his greatest assets. Everyone always underestimated him, if they ever actually saw him.

Urban warfare was a unique art. Every citizen in a hot zone could potentially be innocent—or an enemy. It took special men and women with nerves of steel to be able to function in such a high-stress situation. His GhostWalker unit was comprised of such individuals, all highly trained and with very special, unique psychic gifts.

Mack and the others dropped to their bellies, disappearing into the sand just feet from the first building at the edge of the city. Javier jogged with absolute confidence right up to the structure and into the alley. As he got closer to the buildings, his solid form simply disappeared, blending completely with his surroundings.

I think our informant is on to something. We've got a major force here, Mack, Javier reported. *Guns on the roof, stairways, tucked in the alleys. I see several at the windows in the building across the street. Big op here.*

Can you find a way to blend in without having to kill anyone? We aren't supposed to be here. Get in, get out with the package, and no one the wiser.

Javier sighed heavily. *You know, boss, you're maligning my character. Of course I can find a way to blend. No faith.*

Mack's gut tightened. Javier was an accomplished assassin despite his youthful, innocent appearance. He was highly skilled with explosives and a maniac when it came to computers. Highly intelligent, he followed one person, and that was Mack. Javier could usually find a group of teens and simply join them, but the kids in this part of the city were most likely paid to report strangers. He refrained from telling Javier to be careful, knowing the man wouldn't appreciate his caution, but they'd been raised on the streets together. Javier was more than a teammate—he was family, and Mack looked after family.

These men had followed him into hell, and Mack felt responsible for them. They had all thought psychic enhancement was an exciting program, one that would allow them the best ability to save lives and serve their country—and maybe it would have been, had it not been run by a madman who had not only enhanced their psychic abilities but had also changed their DNA, adding the animal enhancements he thought would make them all supersoldiers.

There was Gideon Carpenter, a man who would be their savior in any crisis. He had eyes like a hawk, could shoot the wings off a fly with hands as steady as a rock. He would protect them from great distances, and so far, Mack had never known him to miss. Before he could get into position, they would need to have information and the rooftop of his choice cleared.

Ethan Myers lay on his belly, eyes locked on the structures ahead, his body streamlined for climbing. The man could go up a building like a spider, clear the rooftop, and be gone before anyone ever knew he'd been there. He waited, coiled to react, as steady as they came.

Mack glanced to the man on his right. Kane Cannon was the fifth man making up their team of rescuers. Kane had always been with him, from the streets of Chicago, college, every type of Special Forces training available to them as well as the GhostWalker experiments and additional field training. Kane always guarded his back, and he knew exactly what Mack was thinking. He shifted his weight subtly, telling Mack he was ready. He was invaluable, a man who literally could see through walls and into buildings. He could lay out the position of the enemy in seconds.

Our informant should be in the third apartment, bottom floor, corner building, Mack sent telepathically to his team. *You're up, Kane. Make certain she's alone. Sergeant Major is sure the information could not have been obtained by anyone other than a GhostWalker. This is an unknown and could be a trap.*

Kane shoved upward with his hands, and his feet went smoothly under him in a practiced move. He ran low, muscles warm and fluid, sending him across the open feet of desert to the entrance of the alley Javier had gone through. Smells assailed him: urine and alcohol mixed with cooked meat. He slipped inside the dark shadow of the alley and instantly became part of it. He moved, shrouded in silence, knife in hand, as he approached the street.

The scent of death was strong. Dim light spilled a foot into the alley from the street. He crouched low and carefully searched out the darker shadows. A body lay crumpled against the base of the building, in the darkest spot. Kane crouched beside him. An automatic weapon was still in his hand, and the body was warm. His neck was broken. Javier had encountered an enemy and quietly disposed of him. There was no communication device, which meant either he wasn't part of a guard detail or Javier had taken the device.

Sighing, Kane rose and stepped to the very edge of the alley where he could scan the buildings across the street. Seeing through a building always took a toll. Javier had to be in position to cover him. He waited, counting the seconds.

Men with guns seemed to be in every doorway, patrolled the rooftops and along the long balcony of the second story. They were out in force, and few people dared to take to the streets. He spotted some teens throwing knives and trying to look tough at the end of the street, closest to the desert. Javier was distinctive. He swaggered with his cool confidence, showing them all how it was done and giving advice. It seemed impossible that he could insert himself into a group on the lookout for strangers, but Javier always managed—and out in the open.

You're a go, bro, Javier's calm voice stated.

Kane didn't hesitate. He'd learned to rely on his team members in any dangerous situation. He allowed his gaze to sweep through the buildings, searching out their package as well as their informant's apartment. X-ray vision was really all about sound. Ultrawide radio waves passed through walls to capture images, allowing Kane to "see" behind the walls of a building. Kane could generate those waves, but it took energy—lots of energy and focus.

He spotted two potential hostages, both female, in the second-story apartment directly across from them. They appeared to be tied to chairs, ten feet into the room, back to back.

The package is on the second floor, third apartment from the left. Two females, just as our informant said. One is slumped over, possibly unconscious. The smaller one is alert.

A guard sat in front of a television set just to their left, and beyond the door, and out in the hallway, a second one sat playing with a handheld game.

He relayed the information to all the team members, drawing a precise map for them in his head. *I can't see the placement of the guards on the roof, Ethan. They're beyond my range of vision.*

No matter. That was Ethan, short and to the point.

Kane swept the small apartment on the ground floor for their informant. They needed to make certain she was legitimate and this was no elaborate trap to capture or kill members of the elusive GhostWalker team. He took a couple of deep breaths and squeezed his eyes closed tight, conscious of the tremors running through his body. Using psychic energy always took a toll, but emitting sound waves and reading them was particularly difficult.

He sent the pressure waves directly toward the small apartment. It had taken months of practice to read the various impressions caused by the distances the sound waves had to travel. Like a ripple effect, the sound traveled in repeating patterns, allowing the sensors Dr. Whitney had built into his body to detect reflected waves.

Kane could see a lone woman in the apartment. Short, wearing jeans and a loose top, she moved with controlled speed, shoving things into a small pack. *She's getting ready to run.* Something about the way the woman moved was familiar to him. His heart began to pound. His pulse thundered in his ears. She didn't look pregnant. She'd suspected she was carrying his child before the escape. It had been imperative to get her out before Whitney realized he'd succeeded in his goal.

He heard the collective gasp from his team as they felt the shock of recognition slam into him. Everyone went completely still. He could taste excitement in his mouth. He could taste—*her.* Once she got into the wind . . . she'd be gone like the ghost she was. But the baby . . .

Mack broke the tension. *Kane? Talk to me.*

It's Rose. My Rose. She's the informer, Mack, and she's getting ready to run. If she gets away from me again, I'll never find her.

Kane didn't take his eyes from the figure moving around the house. Her movements were slow and controlled, with no wasted motion, very efficient. *She knows we're here, Mack. I can't let her get away again.*

We're here to recover the hostages, Mack reminded. *Take a breath, Kane. We won't lose her. Gideon's going in. She won't recognize him as a GhostWalker. She'll know we're out here, but she won't suspect him.*

GhostWalkers recognized one another. Their energy was different, but Gideon was an exception. *He'll go in and get our information and plant a little bug.*

I'm on it, Kane. She won't get away from us, Gideon assured.

I'm telling you, she already knows. Kane couldn't look away from that small apartment. His world had suddenly narrowed to the woman who had eluded him for months. He'd searched everywhere for her, called in every favor, and she'd been impossible to find. And now . . . He was on a mission, and his team counted on him for his full focus.

He swore under his breath as she slid into a harness that fit snugly under her shoulder and strapped a knife to her thigh and shoved another into her boot. She was readying herself for a fight. She stuck something in her hair and added more weapons to her belt. He was particularly impressed with the way she moved, the efficiency. He remembered her as a fragile creature he needed to protect. Rose was built small, like a little pixie. It was strange to see how she handled weapons with such smooth familiarity. He had to be careful of underestimating her. She was a GhostWalker—the same as he was. That meant enhanced psychic ability. She'd grown up with military training. She was probably every bit as lethal as he was or—he conceded—more.

I have to be the one, Mack. She knows me. I helped her

escape Whitney's breeding program. Even thinking about the vile place enraged him. Thinking about what he was forced to do to Rose sickened him. *She's my responsibility, Mack. I have to do this.*

Mack swore under his breath, but each of them, as connected telepathically as they were, heard it. *We're on a fucking mission here, Kane. Don't blow this.*

Ethan moved as if he'd been a racehorse waiting at the starting gate, flowing across the expanse of sand, all fluid muscle, sprinting in silence for the alley. *Give me a minute to get into position to cover you.*

Kane stepped back to give Ethan room to move past him. Ethan flashed him a grin and moved out into the street, a blurring shadow sliding away from the lights. One guard turned his head toward Ethan, and Kane switched his knife to a throwing position, but the guard turned away, obviously not able to track the shadow as it went up the side of the building across from the alley. Ethan was nearly impossible to see without night vision, blending into the side of the building, clinging like a spider as he went up the impossible angle without climbing gear.

Kane held his breath, quartering the area carefully for anyone who might spot Ethan, knowing Javier was doing the same. It seemed a lifetime waiting for confirmation that he'd made it. Kane could hear his own heart beating in his ears. Somewhere a dog barked. Someone coughed, and another man cursed. Laughter broke out. All the while he exercised tremendous discipline to keep from looking at the apartment where the woman he'd been searching for, for months, was getting ready to run.

One man on the roof. He's got a bottle of tequila and an automatic. Great combo. Ethan's disgust was obvious.

More time ticked by. Rose would be packed by now. She would travel light. Just the bare necessities. Kane tasted bitterness in his mouth, but his eyes continued a sweep up and down the buildings and along the street. His first order of business was to protect Ethan.

All clear. Ethan's voice was calm. *Launch "the Eagle."*

Gideon sprinted across the sand to the edge of the building and then into the alley. He clapped Kane on the shoulder, pausing to take stock of the dark streets. Figures moved in doorways, and two men stopped briefly to talk in low voices as they patrolled. A couple of women sat on a porch, silently watching, and down at the end of the street, five teenage boys laughed and prodded one another as they practiced throwing knives.

Gideon put on blurring speed and crossed the empty street to the side of the building. He didn't have Ethan's advantage, climbing easily with only his hands and toes, but Ethan had left behind a stairway made of throwing stars. Gideon moved up fast in the dark, his sniper rifle snug against his back as he raced up the side of the building.

They all could breathe a sigh of relief once Gideon was in place. The man just didn't miss. They all called him the Eagle for a reason. Gideon would cover the streets and windows, as Ethan and Mack would enter the building and bring out the prisoners. Kane would cover them from inside, and Javier would be on the street. They were all fast and lethal when need be, but in a situation such as this one, it was very difficult to distinguish between residents and those cooperating with the enemy, unless they blatantly carried a weapon.

You're a go, Ethan said. *We've got you covered.*

Everything in Kane settled. He turned his attention once more to Rose's apartment, sweeping it carefully, bouncing sound waves through the building to see inside. She stood by the front door, and there was a weapon in her hand.

He took a deep breath to steady himself while his body reacted to the sensors processing the images before retreating from the alley to jog around the buildings to come up on her building from the same side of the street. Mack joined him, easily keeping the fast pace.

We'll need you on this one, Kane.

Kane shot Mack a quick look of impatience. *I've never*

let you down. Give me a few minutes to get her ready to leave with us.

Mack nodded and crouched in the shadow of the building. *Gideon? You in position? Kane is going in. She's armed.*

Don't you shoot her! Mack, you son of a bitch. Nobody better shoot her. There was warning in Kane's voice. He was a dangerous, explosive man, capable of swift retribution. They had grown up with him. They knew him. His tone said it all. He expected them to back off and allow him to handle Rose—even if she tried to kill him, which he figured was entirely probable.

Kane took a deep breath and moved around to the window opening onto a small side yard. He could see why Rose chose this apartment. She had alternative escape routes. He didn't make the mistake of stepping up to the window. Rose was a highly trained GhostWalker. She had survival skills. She was expecting him to come through the front door, a representative of the unit she'd called in to rescue important prisoners the drug cartel was using as hostages against *el presidente.*

It took a few minutes to spot the small shards of glass scattered in the dirt and leaves. He cleared the area meticulously, knowing the sound of breaking glass would alert her instantly. Like most of the GhostWalkers, her hearing was enhanced as well as her vision. Her window wouldn't be nailed shut because she would need a quick escape, but she would have it rigged for visitors. It opened sideways, rather than up, a turn knob on the inside.

Clever girl, he mused silently. He pulled a mini laser cutter from his tool kit and, after attaching the suction cup, carefully cut the glass. The suction cup was silent, drawing out the circle of glass without a sound. He reached in and slowly greased the knob to ensure continued silence. Only then did he twist the knob enough to crack the window. Tiny pieces of glass clung to the edges of the sill as the window slowly opened.

Kane smiled to himself. Yeah. His woman knew how to take care of herself. He reached through the opening, avoiding the glass, and opened it wide enough to allow him entrance. Again he waited until he had found the small strobe trigger before easing his large body through the opening. It was no easy feat, not with the glass sticking out.

As he stepped down silently onto the floor, he projected the sound of slow, deliberate footsteps coming up the sidewalk to the front of her apartment. He muffled his own tread, moving through the sparse room to the open doorway. A small pack was on a chair just to the left of her where she could grab it and run should the wrong person come through the door. Rose had her back to him. She was shorter than he remembered. Her body from the back didn't look pregnant. His heart thudded once at the thought that she might have lost the baby.

She wore jeans and a long tunic top. Her hair was cut short and sassy, a thick cap of shiny, midnight black hair. The memory of the feel of it, soft like silk, bunched in his fist, washed over him, stealing his breath. For a moment, the sight of her shook him.

He inhaled deeply in an effort to drag the fragrance of her deep into his lungs. He could actually feel her soft skin sliding against his, taste her in his mouth. Rose. He would never forget the way she looked up at him with her enormous eyes, so dark brown there was no gold whatsoever in them. Long lashes, black as night, framed those deep chocolate eyes, and she had stared straight into his eyes without flinching away, absolving him of all blame, but damn it all, she'd had no choice. None.

Kane drew another breath as he shoved the memory away ruthlessly. He was a big man, dwarfing her in size, all flowing muscle, his height proportionate with his weight and not an ounce of fat. He loomed over her, nothing more than a shadow, his arms coming around her from behind to take her weapon, and in one smooth motion, he tossed it on the broken-down couch. She tried to whirl around, going for his instep, but his arms became a steel cage, trapping her. His hands settled over her midsection and shockingly, she was round, like a basketball. His heart, after one heavy thump, settled into a satisfied rhythm.

"Shh, Rose," he said gently, trying to breathe calm into her. Her breathing had gone ragged. "There's a gun trained on you. Don't pull another weapon. Just stay still."

Under the palm of his hand, he felt the small rounded belly and a peculiar push as if the baby kicked him, trying to protect his mother. The sheer relief and satisfaction that she carried his child shocked him a little. "No one is going to hurt you." And they wouldn't, not ever again. She carried his baby, and no matter what else, the child would always connect them.

Rose went still. She didn't turn her head but remained tense, her hands gripping his wrists as if to pry them from the slight swell of her belly. "Kane?"

He felt the tension coiling in her, not rigid and tense, but the coil of a snake about to attack. "I'm here, honey. No one wants to hurt you. Just stay still, and we'll sort this out without anyone getting hurt."

"I won't go back. He can't have my baby." The statement was delivered in a quiet voice, but he believed her. Rose might look like a little Asian pixie, but she had a spine of steel. She had thwarted Whitney each time he'd sent a man to impregnate her. She'd fought until they feared they might kill her, and she was a vicious fighter. More than one man had been in the infirmary after a round with her.

"*Our* baby," he corrected, and the rightness of it took some of the knots out of his belly. "You want to tell me why you didn't look pregnant? How did you manage that?"

"I'm not without my own skills. I can camouflage when I need to. I felt all of you the moment you got close. Whitney isn't getting my baby. He doesn't know for certain yet that I'm pregnant, and I'm keeping it that way."

"Whitney didn't send me after you. I don't take orders

from him. We reported his experiments, and he's gone into hiding. I've searched for you ever since you disappeared."

She had begun to relax, but at his words she tensed again.

"To help you, Rose," he explained hastily. "I was the one who helped you escape, remember? I'm not about to hand you over to the enemy."

Kane didn't make the mistake of letting go of her. He knew Gideon had a high-powered rifle on her and was all too aware that Gideon would protect him first. He wanted her away from the window, but that might trigger Mack to send in Javier. It was a very fragile line they were all walking, and one wrong move could result in disaster.

"Then let's just get this over with," Rose said. She kept her gaze trained upward, right out the window, as if daring the marksmen to kill her. "I assume you are part of the team sent in to handle the hostages. For them to warrant a Ghost-Walker extraction, they must be pretty important."

"If I sit you down in the chair, will you stay put? Not do anything stupid?"

She turned her head for the first time to look up at him over her shoulder. His heart jumped when her dark gaze met his. Steady as ever. Cool under fire. That was Rose. But he was shocked at the exhaustion marking her face. He was equally shocked at how not just his body but everything in him responded to her. His every protective instinct, his animalistic side, the alpha male in him—*everything* male.

He forced his voice under control. "You've been sick."

She nodded. "I haven't been able to keep much food down," she admitted, all the while searching his expression, trying to decide whether to trust him. "That's made me fairly weak, and staying below Whitney's radar means moving all the time." She sent him a humorless smile, just a flash of her white teeth, but it was enough to act as a warning. "I will get the baby to safety, and anyone in my way isn't going to live very long."

Kane knew her quiet statement was more than an idle threat. Rose would fight if necessary, and as small as she was, she had psychic abilities and survival skills that made up for her size. He had come to know her in the brief time they'd been forced together. Dr. Whitney, head of the psychic experimental program, had gone rogue, determined to breed supersoldiers. Rose had been forced into his breeding program, but that brief time in his breeding program hadn't stopped any of the women there from training daily. The men tended to forget the women had undergone training almost since birth, while they had joined the military later. The women actually had an edge, although they were smaller in stature.

"I said I'd get you out of here safely, Rose, and I meant it." He tried not to sound aggressive or commanding, when he felt a little of both. He tamped down his take-charge nature. Rose wasn't getting away again, not with danger surrounding her and their child every moment of every day. She needed protection, no matter how independent she was. Kane understood her aversion to him, but her safety took precedence over everything else.

She didn't acknowledge his statement, and with Rose, he had no idea what she was thinking. She appeared fragile, but she had a core of steel and a will of iron. Even Whitney hadn't been able to get what he'd wanted from her. She'd chosen her partner, refusing to accept any of the others Whitney had sent to her, despite the fact that his punishments were horrible.

Kane clamped down hard on those memories. It was difficult to stay cool and disciplined when fury raged through him. Very gently he urged her toward the chair away from the window.

She's out of my line of sight, Gideon warned. *She'll know that, Kane.*

Damn it, don't you fuck with me on this, Kane, Mack snapped. *I'll send Javier in after the both of you.*

Go to hell, Mack, Kane snapped back. *She's pregnant with my baby, and you're damn well not going to shoot her.*

"They're really angry with you, aren't they?" Rose sent him a wry smile. "They're right, you know; you're in danger."

"If you're going to make your try, Rose, do it now, before they send someone else in."

She studied his face, and he couldn't help using the opportunity to do the same with her. Those long, sweeping eyelashes of hers drew his attention. From there his gaze dropped to her high cheekbones, her small, straight nose, and her lush mouth. The women had been taken from orphanages, and Rose had most likely come from China, but how Whitney had managed to get hold of her, Kane couldn't guess.

She touched her tongue to her full lower lip, and his body tightened. "I'm not going to do anything stupid. You're ready for me to try something."

That didn't tell him if she still planned on running, and he was going to have to help Mack and the others get the hostages out. He sighed and changed the subject. "Tell me about the hostages."

"About a week ago, there was a sudden influx of cartel members. It isn't all that difficult to make them; they carry some serious hardware and scare the crap out of the decent people around here. Two murders occurred, heads severed as a warning for everyone and the bodies dumped in the fountain two streets over. The buzz on the street was something big was going down. At first I thought it was a big drug deal, and then I spotted the prisoners. They were brought in at night, dark SUVs with tinted windows. I thought maybe members of a rival gang, but as soon as I saw them—a woman of about thirty-five and a little girl of maybe ten—I knew this had nothing to do with a drug war."

"Actually it does," Kane corrected. "*El presidente* is

waging war with the cartels to get his country back. The cartels have been hitting high-profile members of the government in retaliation. *El presidente* called in a favor from our president and asked for help. His wife's sister and his niece were taken on their way to church. All the bodyguards were killed, as well as the driver. He was told to back off or he would find his sister-in-law's head rolling down the middle of the street. Next would come his niece's head. He believed them."

"And he was afraid to trust his own military or the police," Rose guessed. "He should be. These people are armed to the teeth with the latest weapons, Kane. Something isn't right here. They've all but declared war."

"Corruption here is rampant," Kane agreed. "Someone would tip off the cartel. *El presidente* is a very intelligent man. He knows his administration and his military as well as police departments have been infiltrated by paid informants for the cartel. He asked a personal favor from our president, and we pulled the assignment. None of us had any idea the informant would be you."

"I thought long and hard before I called it in," Rose admitted. She ducked her head, refusing to meet his eyes. "It was selfish of me, that I waited, but I knew there was the possibility that if the hostages were who I thought they were, that a GhostWalker team would be called in. It was a calculated risk, but I couldn't just ignore the fact that those monsters would kill them. I was afraid to try a rescue myself with so many of the enemy guarding them."

His heart slammed hard against the wall of his chest. She'd contemplated the idea, that much was obvious. His Rose, pregnant with their child, would have risked herself for strangers.

"We'll get them out, Rose, but you stay put. I don't want you running again. You need care. I can offer that to you, as well as safety. The last thing I want is for Whitney to get his hands on you or the baby. I don't know why you trusted me to be the father of your baby, but you did. I'm asking for that same faith now. I swear to you, on my life, I will protect both of you."

She lifted her head and looked him straight in the eye, searching his expression. For a moment he had the uncomfortable feeling she was looking into his mind, which was entirely possible with a GhostWalker. There were things buried there best kept hidden. Especially from Rose. He refused to look away, keeping his expression blank. A faint smile curved the bow of her mouth. His breath nearly exploded from his lungs. He dreamt of her, night after night. He thought of her every minute of every day.

Intellectually, he knew Whitney had found a way to "pair" a couple by using pheromones, and he'd certainly made Kane crave Rose physically. He couldn't get near her without his body reacting with a permanent hard-on from hell. But the doctor hadn't paired Rose with him. She'd been forced to choose from three different candidates, and she'd chosen him, but she didn't have the same physical drive to be with him that he had for her, which posed a major problem for him. He had too much respect for her and too much honor to force himself on her. But the thought of never seeing her again, of spending his life without her, drove him insane. He also knew he would never *ever* be able to tolerate another man in her life. And quite frankly—that sucked.

"All right."

That softly spoken assent surprised him. He studied her face in an effort to read whether or not she was telling the truth.

"Then you'll wait here for me to come for you."

She shrugged. "I won't run."

He was missing something; he just couldn't quite figure it out. His mind was already shifting, his radar going off, and instinctively he put himself in front of Rose as he swung around to face the bedroom door, knife in his hand. Rose tried to jerk her gun out of the hidden holster, but the man facing them shook his head, a grin on his face.

"Naughty, naughty, Miss Rose. I can't let you shoot him, even though Mack thinks he's a major pain in the ass. He is my brother, after all."

"Actually," she corrected, "I planned on shooting you."

Javier's grin widened, but his eyes were ice-cold, his stare sending piercing icicles stabbing right through Rose's mind. "Well then, everything's fine. You carrying my nephew there?" He indicated the small basketball shape beneath her loose tunic.

Her eyebrow shot up. She didn't wince, and she didn't take her gaze from his. She kept her voice low and taunting, as if she didn't realize she faced the biggest threat of her life. Kane knew better. He felt the little tremor that ran through her body.

"Maybe a niece."

Javier snorted. "Don't get your hopes up. He's too damn mean to throw a girl. Mack's getting all papa bear on us. You good, Kane?"

Kane noticed Javier's body was angled toward Rose, half in, half out of the shadows, making him a difficult target, and the tiny knife was still concealed in the palm of his hand. He smiled at Rose and joked, but he was ready for any trouble, those cold, cold eyes never leaving his prey. Kane shifted his weight, subtly moving to cut off Javier's angle of attack. Javier glided slightly as well and shook his head.

You know better than that. Mack would skin me alive if anything happened to you.

Rose sighed. "Nothing is going to happen to him. I'm Rose Patterson, by the way."

"Javier Enderman, ma'am. Pleased to meet you. You reading my mind?"

"No," Rose said. "I'm smart. I know what you're both thinking."

"Then you know I've got to get him out of here in one piece, ma'am. And that none of us wants you to hurt him."

Kane huffed out his exasperation. "You're making me sound like a two-year-old you all have to babysit. Tell Mack we're on our way, and let's get it done."

"They're armed to the teeth," Rose said. "And they have trip wires strung around the windows and in the hallways leading to the apartment. You're not going to get in through the ground floor."

Kane made a strangled growl in the back of his throat and crouched down in front of Rose, catching her chin in his hand. "You scouted them out with my baby in your belly?" He bit out each word through clenched teeth.

"Yes," she said very calmly, her dark eyes sober. "Before I made the decision to call in reinforcements. I told you I'd decided I couldn't rescue them alone. Did you think I made that assessment from here?"

"Damn it, woman. You do something like that again, and we're going to have trouble."

She looked at him a long time. *You have the same eyes. A different color, of course, but you both can look very scary.*

It was the first time she'd used the more intimate means of telepathic communication. He knew Javier frightened her, and he wanted to pull her into his arms and hold her close to comfort her. It took a minute to realize *he* frightened her. She wasn't showing it, but he knew.

"Rose, neither of us wants to send you back to Whitney or to harm you in any way. You're close to delivering the baby, and you're going to need help. Stay and wait for us here."

"I said I wouldn't run."

Again she looked him right in the eye. He couldn't detect any evasion, but still . . . Kane sighed and stood up. "I've got work to do. I'll be back to get you."

Rose nodded. She remained seated in the chair as Kane started back to the bedroom. Javier never took his eyes from her, even as he backed toward the bedroom, his body between her and Kane.

Stop trying to intimidate her and let's go, Kane snapped.

You first. And I'm smiling, Javier shot back.

Like a snake, Kane pointed out and went out of the apartment the same way he'd entered. Javier followed him into the night.

CHAPTER 2

The moment that Kane and Javier were gone, Rose covered her face with her hands and allowed herself a brief moment to shake uncontrollably. She had to drag in several deep breaths to keep from crumbling completely, to keep from shedding ridiculous, stupid tears. She'd always been so fearful in comparison to the other women she'd grown up with. They had no problems or qualms with their training—she'd always been tentative, forcing herself not to show fear when at times she'd been terrified— like now.

Kane Cannon. She remembered every moment of their time together in vivid detail. The way he smelled. His incredible strength. The feel of his skin against hers. She had chosen him for the father of her child because she knew she had no choice. Whitney had grown impatient with her, and when he knew she was fertile, he would send *his* choice. Kane Cannon was ruthless and dangerous, capable of swift violence. He was unrelenting and merciless if need be, but one of her psychic gifts was the ability to know when someone lied to her. Kane had been the first man who hadn't lied.

He found Whitney and his experiments distasteful, and when he was drawn into the breeding program and realized the women were virtually prisoners—that they hadn't volunteered but were forced into the program—she knew everything in him rebelled. She had known the moment she spoke to him that he would risk his career—his very life—to reveal Whitney's vile experiments to the authorities. Time had run out on her, and she knew Whitney was determined that no matter what it took, he would get his supersoldier baby from her, so she had chosen Kane.

She'd been so frightened and horribly saddened, wanting her first time to be with someone she loved. She had been terrified of Kane when he'd entered the room. She knew Whitney was watching and listening. If she didn't cooperate, they would tie her down, and she honestly wasn't certain she had the courage to go through with it. The first thing Kane had done was smash the camera and recorder, and then he'd disposed of Whitney's listening device and sat down on the edge of her bed.

He'd looked so big. He towered over her with his height, his wide shoulders, and large hands. Everything about him was intimidating, especially his piercing green eyes. She shivered uncontrollably as if she were still locked up, waiting for the inevitable to happen. Her heart thundered in her ears and pounded in her chest, but she'd been determined to at least have the best man possible for the father of her child. Kane was a good man in spite of the fact that he could be deadly when needed. She'd watched him for weeks before she'd made her decision. If circumstances were different, she knew she would have chosen him anyway, but right then, she was terrified.

And then he touched her. Exquisitely gentle. There was nothing rough about him when he brushed the hair back from her face. "This is bullshit, Rose. I'll find a way to get you out of here. We don't have to do this."

Her world changed instantly with those words. It was so unexpected after the brutes Whitney had sent to her. She still had bruises from the last one making his try. The worst thing—and what Kane didn't know—was that she'd chosen him. She'd watched him from the exercise yard, and she'd seen the differences in him. At that point he didn't even know she—or the breeding program—existed. She'd drawn him in by making him her choice. The shame would last her entire life. She'd brought him into the horror of her world, and now he had no more choice than she did.

Rose covered her face and rocked back and forth. She knew he despised himself for getting her pregnant, for being unable to stop Whitney before he touched her, but he had no idea Whitney would never have considered pairing them if she hadn't chosen him. Kane felt guilty, but *she* was the guilty party.

The baby kicked hard, and she automatically rubbed her palms over her swollen belly in a soothing motion. She could barely face him, barely look him in the eye, after what she'd done. She knew about the pheromones, knew once Whitney paired them, Kane would have no choice but to crave her body day in and day out. She'd seen the effect on the other men. They had been willing to kill to get to her. Willing to force her just to have her. She'd done that to Kane, a man with principles and honor.

She crushed down the memories and forced herself to stand. It had taken so much effort to be able to appear cool and in control, but she didn't have to waste energy keeping up appearances.

"You and me, baby," she whispered. "I'll keep you safe."

She felt very alone and vulnerable, her time too close, and she hadn't established a safe birthing place. She'd made friends with a couple of women, one she'd been certain could help her give birth, but now the cartel had ruined that. She had to run fast and far, and now Kane had complicated everything—but she owed him. He thought it was the other way around, but she hadn't been able to bear the idea of one of Whitney's psycho soldiers touching her. They all made her skin crawl.

She'd watched Kane, the way he moved, the sound of his voice, the way he treated others. And she'd made that fateful decision. The baby kicked again, this time a little harder, breaking into her thoughts, and she found a small smile on her face as she rubbed her tummy again.

"You don't like it when I'm upset, do you?" she asked softly. "I'm upset on your daddy's behalf. I did a very bad thing, and I have no way to make up for it." She moved in silence to the window and peered out.

Her lights had been off for hours, and she knew she'd established that pattern weeks ago. No one would think it odd. She kept to herself and stayed inside after dark, never turning on lights. The neighbors probably thought she tried to save money by not using electricity, but she had excellent night vision, thanks to Whitney's enhancements. She stared at the street for some time. Kane and the others would be setting into action their plan to rescue the hostages. She had to quit feeling guilty and sorry for herself; that did no good, and there were two people who desperately needed help. She had seen the extreme violence the cartel was capable of. They would kill the hostages no matter what *el presidente* did. The GhostWalkers were their only hope.

She was already in dark clothing, and with her ability to camouflage her appearance, she knew she could aid the GhostWalker team should they need it. Her telepathy wasn't particularly strong, but Kane's was, and she tapped into the flow, knowing how to do so from when they were together working against Whitney.

She closed her eyes, allowing her mind to expand, to reach out for the flow of energy, into the current Kane generated with his team.

Working my way into position, Mack, Kane reported.

Let's get this done. Mack was all business, and the familiar voice settled the tight knots in Kane's gut. There was no way to go into a mission with his brain divided. He had to push Rose out of his mind and concentrate on getting the hostages out as quietly as possible. They expected to leave dead enemies behind, but they wanted to be quiet about it. This was a take-no-prisoners mission and needed complete silence. *Moving now.*

Mack was a blur, no more than a shadow as he went up the side of the building, retrieving the tiny star stairs as he went up, gaining the roof. *In position,* he reported.

Kane and Javier managed to gain the sidewalk just outside the two-story apartment building. It was their responsibility to ensure Mack and Ethan had a clear path through the building to the desert. Gideon would protect them from the roof and then make his way along the rooftops to the edge of the desert.

Kane waited, counting his heartbeats while loud voices boomed through the entryway to the apartments and then slowly—too slowly—faded. He bounced pressure waves through the walls. The entryway was empty, but there was a man two stairs up, just leaning against the wall.

On the right, he told Javier.

Javier was smaller, a lean 'killing machine, and his shadow would be less noticeable. The sentry would feel the draft and look up, but he'd be too late. Kane, knife in one hand, ready for the throw, opened the door with the other. Javier somersaulted in, coming to his feet just a scant distance from the stairs, his knife hurtling through the air to bury the blade in the sentry's throat.

Kane slipped into the foyer, right behind Javier, allowing the sentry to catch a brief glimpse of him, just enough to distract him from the real threat. As Javier threw the knife, a second guard emerged from a room just to their left. Kane was on him, one hand muffling sound as the other delivered the killing blow with the blade. He shoved the body back in the room, and Javier added the second one. Neither bothered to do anything about the blood spatter. There was old blood on the floors and walls, some very recent, as if the apartments were used to violence.

We're in, it's a go, Kane said as he and Javier started up the stairs, taking care to feel each individual step for sound before they placed their feet.

Mack signaled Ethan, and Ethan slipped over the side of the building, making his way to the window, leaving behind the stars for Mack to use. There were no ropes, and no one would ever think they could climb up or down the two-story structure.

Guard on the balcony, Mack, Ethan cautioned suddenly. *I can smell his cigarette smoke.*

Rose stepped out of her apartment to get a better look. She could see the guard on the balcony clearly; he was smoking a cigarette and staring down at the street. It took her a long time, even with her night vision, to spot the man clinging like a spider to the side of the building. Her heart leapt.

He's directly in line with you. All he has to do is look up once he turns.

There was a moment of silence as each member of the team realized Rose had tapped into their communication through Kane.

Talk to us, Mack made the decision, trusting Kane's judgment that she was on their side.

Ethan moved with infinite slowness, inch by slow inch, turning upside down right there on the side of the building. He hung with his head down, clinging to the side with his toes and one hand while he, with that same agonizing slowness, took his knife from between his teeth, transferring it to his one free hand. There in the dark he looked like a giant spider, looming over unsuspecting prey.

Mack had already started down the stars Ethan had lodged in the building, retrieving them as he descended. Now he hovered above Ethan, a dark shadow completely motionless, just waiting.

Rose kept her gaze glued on the guard. He used his fingertips to crush the glowing tip and snapped it over the narrow balcony to the street below. *He's turning.*

I've got him now, Ethan reassured, his voice absolutely calm.

Rose watched, one hand protectively over her baby and the other around the hilt of her knife. They wanted silence. She couldn't use a gun, but . . .

The guard turned and took a step, a single fatal step. He never saw Ethan as he dropped down just like a spider, driving the point of his knife deep. He kept his grip on the guard, easing him to the balcony floor in silence. Mack joined him, shoving the throwing stars into the loops on his inside vest. Ethan stepped back, and Mack took the lead.

The balcony door was open. Inside the room, the television blared loudly. Two chairs, back to back, held the woman and a little girl of ten. They were tied, hands and feet. Both had gags in their mouths. The little girl's head swung toward them as they stepped silently into the room. Her eyes went wide with shock when she realized the shadows were large men coming out of the night at her. The mother didn't move, her head hanging as if she wasn't conscious.

Mack put a finger to his lips and shook his head. The little girl froze. There were tears swimming in her eyes. Ethan crossed to the mother, crouching down beside her. Both eyes were swollen closed. She had cuts on her mouth and chin and bruising around her neck. Her dress was torn in several places, and there was evidence of bruising beneath the garment.

Ethan swore under his breath as he cut the ropes. Her hands were nearly purple. She was barefoot, and both feet were cut and bruised as well as swollen.

She's in bad shape. I'm going to have to carry her.

That was bad news. Mack was going to have the child, and with the woman needing a ride as well, that put both men in a more vulnerable position. But they were prepared.

We'll move in ten, Kane announced calmly.

Roger that. Mack cut the child free and lifted her into his arms, soothing her in Spanish. "Your uncle sent us to get you and your mother out of here. We have to be very quiet."

The child frowned and put her mouth next to Mack's ear. "What about my little brother?"

Mack stiffened. No one had said anything about a brother. "Where's your brother, sweetie?"

"They took him away."

We have a complication. There's another child. A boy. "How old is he?"

She muffled her cough against his shirt. "Five."

Kane, the moment we hit the ground running, drop back with Javier and find that boy.

Javier lay at the top of the stairs, his body stretched out on the floor. A low light illuminated the end of the hall and cast shadows down the corridor. A guard sat in front of the door to the third apartment. He had his chair tipped back and his legs sprawled out in front of him. His weapon was in his lap, and he appeared to be sleeping, but neither Javier nor Kane was deceived. Every few seconds he stroked his finger over the trigger as though caressing his gun.

Will do. Hold. The guard's alert.

You want us to draw him inside?

Javier glanced at Kane and nodded just once. He eased his body down the threadbare carpet. Anyone could come out of their apartment and conceivably step on him on their way to the stairs. Both doubted anyone would be showing their face with so many armed men in the building.

Get his attention, Kane said.

Mack whispered to the little girl, and she nodded her head once. He moved her closer to the door. "Be brave, sweetheart."

She swallowed hard, closed her eyes, and pressed herself tight into Mack. "Mommy. Mommy, wake up. Hurry."

Her voice was scared, hushed, perfect for their needs. Mack positioned himself on one side of the door, and Ethan went to the other. Mack pushed the little girl behind his solid body.

The guard's head came up alertly. As he stood, he looked right at Kane, who was pressed against the wall, deep in the shadow. The chair came down with a thud inches from Javier's outstretched fingers. Javier never so much as winced. The guard's boots were old and worn, thin in places, and Javier just barely missed getting stepped on as the man swung around to face the door, his finger still on the trigger as the other hand twisted the doorknob.

Javier rolled out of the way as Kane moved into position behind the man. The guard kicked the door open and took a step. Kane slammed the knife home with one hand and jerked the weapon with the other, preventing him from firing. Mack whirled around and covered the little girl's eyes.

"Keep your head down. Stay tight against me. We're taking you home," he whispered. "You have to stay very quiet." He dragged the protective vest from his pack and quickly dressed her in it before lifting her. He waited for Ethan to put the unconscious woman in a vest as well and shift her into a fireman's carry. They were both vulnerable, packing the hostages out into enemy territory.

Kane lowered the body of the dead guard to the floor well inside the room and went back to the doorway, peering up and down the hall before signaling Javier. The two of them moved like wraiths, Javier disappearing down the stairs while Kane guarded the hall.

You're clear to here, Javier stated.

What's happening on the street, Rose? Kane demanded.

Staying quiet, she announced. *Get moving. We have to find that child before they're on to us, or they'll kill him.*

There was no "we" involved in finding the boy, but Kane didn't have time to argue with Rose. It was imperative to find the boy before the rescue could be discovered. He signaled Mack to start down the stairs with Ethan close on his heels. Kane dropped in behind them, moving silently, his gun in his fist this time. He was using a silencer, but still, they wanted to slip out without alerting the enemy force.

Something is happening at the end of the street. Teens are running in all directions. They look scared, Rose reported. *Get out of there.*

There was no urgency in her voice, but Kane sensed it, as did the others. Javier went through the door first, and after visually clearing the street, waved Mack and Ethan through. They ran flat out, dark shadows moving through the open street for the desert.

Bring in the bird. We'll rendezvous in four minutes, Mack said. *Gideon, you've got eight minutes from my mark.*

Roger that. Gideon was calm. He kept his eyes on the street, sweeping rooftops and windows. Mack and Ethan were past the buildings now and running hard through the desert toward their destination. His job was to back Kane.

Rose, get moving, Kane ordered, even as he began quartering the buildings. They wouldn't have taken the child too far from his mother and sister. They wanted leverage, and a five-year-old was perfect to manipulate a woman. *Get on that helicopter.*

Rose slipped back into her apartment and shrugged into her pack. She traveled light. She hadn't invested in much for the baby, just the bare necessities, and she knew better than to add anything that might slow her down. She wasn't getting on the helicopter without Kane. Kane could give all the orders in the world, but she didn't trust anyone else. She owed him, and she knew he would protect her and the baby, but the others . . .

She'd started this mess by calling in a team. She hadn't done enough research and found out about the boy. That omission was on her. Now Kane and the other man, Javier, were going to be left behind if they didn't find the boy in eight minutes.

Got him. At the end of the block. Corner apartment; he's in the back room.

That's impossible, even for you, Javier protested. He'd

been standing with the teens just outside the apartment. He hadn't gotten that churning in his gut that meant that trouble was close.

Remember something spooked those kids from their little party? One of them was dragged inside, and he's being used as a target. They're forcing the child to stab him repeatedly. Looks like everyone inside is having a good time but the two kids. Kane's voice was grim.

He moved fast, heading down the street toward the corner apartment, staying well into the shadows along the sidewalk. He stumbled once, weakness overtaking him, but he kept going. The sight of the two boys, one five, the other a teenager, caught in the hellish situation turned his stomach. He cared little that using his psychic talent drained his energy. He ran on sheer adrenaline, sprinting down the street, Javier on his heels.

They halted abruptly outside the apartment, one on either side of the door.

If we go in guns blazing, we might hit the kid, Javier pointed out.

Kane swore under his breath. *Five men. One holding the kid. The teen is tied standing to a post of some kind. They're all drinking.*

It was unnecessary to add the last, because the stench of alcohol was permeating the air outside the apartment. They had to get inside without triggering a firefight. Kane felt a prickle of unease down his spine and spun around at the same moment as Javier.

Rose swept past them and knocked on the door before either could stop her. She looked completely different. Her hair was dark and thick and seemed to trail down her back. She looked very young, like a teenager. There was no evidence of her pregnancy; if anything, she looked too slim.

The door was yanked open from inside, and a large man, disheveled and armed to the teeth, lost his angry expression and began to grin like a macabre puppet. He had scars on his face and a gold tooth.

In Spanish, Rose asked for her brother. "His friends said he came in here, and he needs to come home."

The man nodded several times and reached for her nape, curling his fingers around her neck and jerking her to him. His eyes went wide. Shocked. He gurgled, and blood bubbled from his mouth to dribble down his chin. He hunched a little, another sound escaping, this time a gasp.

Kane and Javier fell in behind Rose, using the large man as a shield as they entered the apartment. Kane went left, Javier right. Kane took out the man forcing the five-year-old to stab the teen. The knife sliced through his neck, the tip protruding out the other side. On his knees, the dead man slumped over, falling away from the child. Rose shoved the big man to the ground and, stepping between his legs, threw her knife, still dripping with blood, into the heart of a man sitting in a chair clutching a bottle of tequila. Javier stepped right into the fourth man, hand-to-hand, nearly dwarfed by the size of the guard. His eyes were flat and cold, his smile never changing as he shoved his weapon deep and twisted to ensure the kill.

Kane whirled around to rush the last man. The guard had his finger on the trigger and was bringing his weapon around to center on Kane. Three throwing stars slammed deep into the guard's stomach and chest, climbing toward his throat, but his turn toward Kane caused the aim to be slightly off center. He squeezed the trigger as Kane hit him low, taking his legs out from under him. The bullets spit across the ceiling so that chunks of debris rained down.

The boy screamed loudly over and over, the bloody knife still clutched in his hand. Javier batted the weapon away, snatched up the child, and sprinted out the door, running at top speed toward the safety of the desert. It was up to Gideon to protect them now.

Javier has the package and is coming your way, Gideon reported calmly.

Men poured into the streets, some half dressed but all armed. The sound of the automatic was loud in the silence of the night. For one moment chaos reigned, and that was the only moment they were going to get.

Rose! Go! Get out of here, Kane snapped even as he came together with the falling guard, jerking the automatic from his hands and tossing it aside.

The guard gripped Kane's neck, trying to strangle him, adrenaline giving him extra strength. Rose stepped in close, shoved a knife in the back of the guard's neck as Kane pressed his gun against the man's heart and pulled the trigger. Kane caught Rose by the wrist and jerked her behind him. He didn't bother going out the front door; they'd never make it. He walked fast through the small apartment, clearing the doorways visually and trusting Rose to watch their backs as they moved briskly to the rear of the apartment. There was no way for them to save the teenage boy; they could only hope someone in the apartments rescued him before the cartel members decided to question him—if he was even alive.

Kane peered out the bedroom window. There was no door leading outside, but the window faced out into a narrow corridor. The only scenery was a wall. Using his elbow he smashed through the glass and then cleared it from the frame. There was no point in wasting time reprimanding Rose for not listening and going with Javier. They had to find an exit and get out of the hot zone. The helicopter wouldn't be waiting for them. Gideon had to follow Javier to protect the packages. He and Rose were on their own.

He lifted her and she slipped through, crouching down just to the left of the window, giving him room, her gun in her hand. He was a big man, and he had no choice but to break the wooden frame to get through. He muffled the sound as best he could and hit the ground running, Rose behind him. They made it to the door leading outside. It hung on one hinge, paint peeled, splintered, obviously kicked in on more than one occasion. They could hear pounding footsteps coming toward the door. It sounded like an entire army.

Rose swung around, intending to go in the other direction, but Kane stopped her with a touch to her shoulder, stepping back and throwing the stars at an angle up the wall. He leapt and caught his fingers in a crack, drawing himself up, using the first star, a good six feet above the ground to stand on. He climbed to the next one and reached down for her.

Without hesitation, Rose jumped, her arm outstretched. Kane caught her wrist and drew her up. They climbed fast. Each time she took a step up, she reached behind her and withdrew the star until they were at the top. Kane went over the edge first, rolling onto the rooftop. Rose used a one-hand push. As pregnant as she was, rolling was out of the question unless she had no other choice. Landing, she crouched low beside Kane. He could hear her panting.

You all right?

She was silent a moment, fighting to catch her breath. *A little out of shape.*

Kane studied her face. She avoided his eyes, concentrating on her breathing, but she didn't look like she would freak out on him.

We're away. Mack's voice was grim. *Can you make the alternative site?*

That's negative. Kane's voice was as rock steady and calm as ever. *I'm activating the tracker.*

Mack swore. *You make it out of there, Kane.*

Roger that.

Kane took a long look around the roof. It appeared clear, but he wasn't so certain. The smell of alcohol drifted on the slight breeze coming in from the desert. He signaled to Rose to stay where she was and inched his way, using toes and elbows to propel himself across the rooftop. He skirted the large rusty metal housing the cooling system and spotted a guard scooting across the roof toward the edge. He knelt up and peered down into the street. A broken bottle lay beside an open bag. The man must have dropped it when he heard the shots.

Don't you fucking move, Rose. Kane allowed his anger at her to show. She would have been safe if she'd just gotten on that helicopter. She didn't respond one way or the other, and he didn't look at her, concentrating on the enemy.

If he could kill the guard before anyone realized they were on the roof, they had a chance to escape. It was a slim chance, but they were GhostWalkers—they didn't need a clean walk through the park to make it.

His order was met with silence. Her breathing was back under control, and when he glanced at her, she looked small and alone. Probably frightened. Maybe he shouldn't have sworn at her, but damn it all, why didn't women ever listen? He'd been scared—*terrified*—for her. He couldn't bear to look at her with blood spatter all over her clothes and in her hair. She'd been cool though. He had to hand her that. Insane, but cool.

He didn't hurry. Hurrying could get one killed. The urgency of their situation didn't matter, only crossing the distance between him and the one man who could tell the rest of the world where they were. He inched his way, taking care to move in complete silence. The guard breathed hard, the sound loud in the night. Below them, the sound of shouts and footsteps echoed through the darkness. Lights flashed as men frantically searched the yards and apartments.

Kane patiently inched closer, breathing softly, never taking his eyes from his prey. His heart slammed hard in his chest. He couldn't make a mistake, not with Rose and his child on the roof with him. She couldn't fall into enemy hands. The guard shifted, and Kane froze. The man leaned farther over the wall to search the street below, watching the frantic activity. Kane inched closer. He could touch the guard now, but the automatic weapon was *over* the short wall. If the gun was dropped, the searching cartel members would know their quarry was on the roof. The longer the time went by, the less likely they could get away.

Kane could hear screams as innocent people were pulled

from their apartments to allow their homes to be searched. The door-by-door search was loud and ugly, the men furious at having lost their hostages. By now they would have found the bodies of their slain friends. Gideon was gone like the ghost he was, climbing down from the rooftop to the desert edge, where he raced to meet the helicopter. Kane and Rose were on their own with a street full of very angry enemies.

The guard muttered something and sank back on his heels, fishing for his cigarettes. The automatic rifle lay loosely in his lap as he lit a match. Kane was on him instantly, rising up, locking his arm around the sentry's neck, one hand on the back of his head. He applied pressure, snapping the neck with his enormous strength in one motion. Almost gently, he lowered the guard to the rooftop, crushing out the lit cigarette. He'd had plenty of time while inching his way across the roof to ensure the sentry was alone.

Rose. Kane called her to his side. *Let's get out of here.*

She remained silent, coming to him without hesitation. He caught her wrist. *We're going to have to climb down. Once we're on the ground, stay in the shadows and head for that truck at the end of the street. It isn't the best plan, but it's all we've got. You take lead.* She was less noticeable than he was. They wouldn't be looking for a woman.

There was no doubt in his mind that he was going to be captured—or killed. But he could get Rose to safety if she just did what he said.

Rose stepped past him to peer down into the street. Crowds of people were milling around, some crying, others silent, most clutching one another in fear.

You aren't sacrificing yourself for me.

We aren't going to argue about this, Rose. That's our child you're carrying. Do you have any idea what will happen to you if they capture you? Start down and get to the damn truck. I know you can hotwire a car.

She stepped in front of him, forcing him to look down at

her, to meet her glittering gaze. *I can change our images. It won't last long, but it will be enough to get both of us through the street to the truck.*

Too risky. He dismissed her offer immediately. *Get moving.*

She didn't blink. She continued staring up at him with her wide, dark eyes, her expression the same.

Damn it, Rose. This is no time to start acting like a woman. Get your ass down to the street and do what I say. Obviously, yelling didn't come across as well using telepathy. Intimidation and absolute command just didn't have the same ring, he could tell by her total lack of reasoning.

Sadly for you, you have no authority over me. Get your own ass down to the street. I'm not trading your life for mine when I know we both can make it out of here. Just because you have to turn control over to me for a few minutes, you can't take the chance, and that's just stupid.

Kane scowled at her—his blackest, most fierce scowl. Every man he knew backed up when he gave them that look, but she just stood there, barely coming up to his sternum, looking like a little doll. He swore under his breath. *We don't have time for this.*

No, we don't. I suggest you get moving.

She was going to be the biggest pain in his ass. They really didn't have time to argue, and it was evident by the stubborn look on her face that she would stand there until hell froze over. One of them had to be reasonable.

Cursing, Kane went over the side of the building, keeping to the darkest areas, slamming the stars deep so she could have an easier climb. With every crack he found for his fingers and toes, he swore—and there were a lot of cracks in the old building. There was a reason men didn't go into combat with women. Rose was a prime example. Stubborn as hell. Illogical. *Completely* illogical. This was the last time she was going to refuse to listen to him. And it sure as hell was the last time she was going into a combat situation.

He made it to the ground and turned back to catch her around the waist. At once he realized how pregnant she was. For some reason, she just didn't seem that big until he touched her. Then he had the feeling she had a beach ball under her shirt. He set her down gently and swept her beneath his shoulder, holding her close just for a moment. He didn't know if she needed the comfort or if he did, but she didn't move, her arm slipping around his waist, her head resting on his chest.

We'll make it, Rose, he reassured. *Do your thing, and let's get out of here.*

Rose straightened with a brief nod of her head. *I'll need you to stoop a little. Slump down so you're a little shorter and stay very close to me. Just follow my lead. I'll get us through the crowd.*

Kane swallowed his protest. He'd asked her to put her faith in him more than once. Why was it so damned hard to turn over control to a woman? Hell. He'd gotten her pregnant in a place where she had no choice, knowing Whitney would take her baby from her and use it for his experiments in his quest to make the perfect supersoldier. She'd given him her trust when he didn't deserve it. He owed her. Taking a breath, he nodded and slouched, moving very close to her, one arm around her waist.

They stepped out onto the street, into the mass of people. Rose walked hesitantly, as if each step was difficult. He tried not to notice the stains on her clothes, but even in the dark he could spot the blood spatter. Lighting was poor, but if anyone examined her, they couldn't fail to see the spots. Families clung to one another, fear on their faces as men with guns searched their homes. He and Rose moved with infinite slowness through the throng. His heart pounded, and he avoided eyes.

Halfway to the truck, Rose stopped abruptly, hunched over with both hands on her obviously swollen belly, panting. If he hadn't known she was acting, he would have panicked. An older woman murmured to her in Spanish, asking questions. Rose replied in a gasping voice that she was too early, and the labor was intense.

The older woman marched up to one of the cartel sentries and whispered to him. It was evident she knew him. The man looked annoyed and shook his head twice, but the older woman persisted.

You deliberately stopped in front of her, Kane guessed.

That's her son. She's been providing information to him about the movements of the police and soldiers. I made certain I was extra nice to her, bringing her groceries and helping her out just in case I needed an ally.

He had to hand it to her, she planned for every contingency. She was casting an illusion even he had to believe. She looked Mexican, her hair longer and thicker, and he supposed he did as well. She also looked ragged and very, very pregnant. Each step was labored. She panted. She looked as if she might give birth any moment.

The guard gave in with a dark scowl and motioned them forward. The older woman handed her keys and pointed out a battered sedan, telling her to be careful.

You should get in the car and begin sliding across the seat on the driver's side. The moment we're apart, the illusion will dissolve, and if anyone is looking, they'll know something isn't right. Start the car. I'll drive because I know the back roads and a place we can hole up for a short while. If we get away clean, we can use the car and then ditch it as soon as we're in the clear. If they see us, we'll have to ditch the car sooner, and I'm not in good enough shape to walk far.

Kane nodded and pulled open the driver side door, bending with her as if handing her inside, keeping contact in an effort to preserve the illusion as long as possible. He inserted the key and turned it to start the engine. For a heart-stopping moment the engine stalled, and then it turned over. He jumped into the seat and scooted over as fast as a big man could in the small space.

CHAPTER 3

⸻

"Go!" Kane commanded as he settled into the passenger seat, pulling his gun from beneath his shoulder.

Rose slammed her foot on the gas and took off as fast as possible in the old sedan. The doors and windows rattled as the battered vehicle shuddered its way onto the street. She didn't glance in the rearview mirror to see if they were drawing attention. She wanted to get off the streets as fast as possible and onto the trail leading into the desert. To do that, she had to outrun anyone chasing them.

The sedan belched smoke and shuddered as she whipped around a corner and took a second one sliding. "Are they following?"

"Keep going," he instructed, the grimness in his voice the only answer he was giving her. He crawled over the seat and smashed out the back window.

Rose took another turn and then a fourth. She glanced in the rearview mirror. "Are you certain?"

"They're trying to catch up." And they had better and faster cars. Kane kept that to himself. Their only advantage

was that whoever was pursuing them was uncertain if the
occupants of the sedan were racing to a hospital as had been
reported, or if they'd really seen something suspicious.

"We'll ditch the car if I can get some space," she said.
"I planned an escape when I first moved here. Of course, I
thought I'd have a better vehicle choice."

"If I forget to tell you later on, Rose, you're one hell of
a woman."

She laughed softly. "You might hold that thought until
we actually get away clean." She jerked the wheel again.
"Can you see anyone?"

"Just glimpses. They aren't on us."

"I've been running without lights. I don't think they'll
see us take this trail, but if they backtrack, they'll find the
tire tracks."

Before Kane could ask what she was talking about—he
didn't see any trail—she'd spun the wheel again, throwing
him across the backseat. The car slid in a wide arc, fish-
tailed, and spit sand into the air. She didn't let up on the
gas but drove even faster. Kane cautiously lifted his head
to peer out the back window. The woman was going to lose
him if she kept it up. He'd nearly gone flying.

"Climb back up here. We're going to have to jump."

She stated it so calmly he almost didn't comprehend.
His head snapped around. "Are you out of your fucking
mind, Rose? You're pregnant. You can't jump out of a moving car."

"Well, it's that or go with it into the ravine. I prefer the
sand. Move it, soldier. You've got about fifteen seconds."

She wasn't kidding. The woman was insane, already
opening the driver's door and bailing before he could stop
her. Kane kicked open the backseat passenger door and
dove. He hit hard and rolled, his lungs burning for air. The
sand clogged his mouth and he spit, staring up at the night
sky, wondering what the hell had just happened.

The sedan continued forward, shooting off the cliff to
fall into the deep ravine carved from hundreds of years

of flash floods. He heard the crash as it bounced off rocks and scrub trees, but strangely, the sound was somewhat muffled. He rolled over and came up on his knees, looking frantically around for Rose. She lay thirty feet from him in a fetal position, knees drawn up to her chest, her hands locked around them. His heart jolted hard.

He ran to her and crouched down beside her. "Rose?"

He swore he could hear each separate beat of his heart. She groaned softly, and he let out his breath. She slowly turned onto her back. Blood smeared her face from the sand burning it as she hit the ground. She'd obviously covered her belly instead of her face. Her breathing was loud and ragged as she fought for air.

"Don't move, Rose." His voice sounded strangled. Without the enhancements of her illusions, she looked like a broken doll, smashed on the sand. His first instinct was to gather her in his arms and just cradle her against him where she'd be safe, but it was too late for that.

"Give me a minute," she gasped.

Pain didn't show on her face, but it was there in her eyes. And fear. She was very frightened. He smoothed back her hair. "Don't be afraid, Rose. I'm not going to let anything happen to you or the baby."

She swallowed hard and let out her breath. "I'm counting on that."

He could feel the tension ebbing out of her. Grateful that she was beginning to trust him a little, he swept his arm around her shoulders to help ease her into a sitting position.

She managed a small smile. "I think I should have thought that particular part of the plan through a little better." She looked around her. "We've got to get moving. I'm hoping we can disturb the sand enough to cover our tracks, and they'll think we went into the ravine with the car."

Kane looked around him. Sand stretched out for miles. "This could be bad, Rose. The farther we get away from the city, the more chances are we'll get caught out in the open."

"Not if you know where you're going."

He sighed and reached down to help her to her feet. She swayed unsteadily and clung to him. That small show of fragility shook him. Rose was such a mixture both ultra-feminine and ultrasoldier. She didn't flinch from combat, yet she leaned into him, so soft and vulnerable, his heart ached.

"Enlighten me." He sounded gruff, but she'd twisted his insides up, and he wasn't certain how to react to her. He damn well wasn't going to force himself on her ever again, but just being close to her made him feel different inside.

She moved, a soft, subtle, very feminine retreat. He felt something hard press against his chest, right over his heart, and he stiffened, glancing down at the barrel of the gun and the absolute steadiness in her small hand. His gaze jumped to hers. Her eyes stared without blinking, no hesitation. The woman meant business. So much for soft and feminine. Fury burst through him, but he didn't move, didn't show her anything at all.

"Throw it away, Kane. You're either with me or against me. If you're with me, throw the tracker into the ravine."

There was nothing sweet about her voice. He considered wrapping his long fingers around her neck and strangling her right there.

"If I throw the tracker into the ravine, we have no resources—no backup. They'll come get us in a few days. We just have to lay low."

She still didn't blink. "This child is never going to fall into Whitney's hands. Not *ever.* I need help, Kane, and I'm willing to trust you, but only you. You have to make a decision."

Fury knotted the muscles in his belly. Anyone who knew him would have been alarmed by his calm demeanor and the cool, flat look in his eyes. "What are you going to do, Rose? Shoot me?" His voice dropped lower than ever, softer, even more deceptive. "You're going to shoot the father of your child?"

She blinked. He slapped the gun away, turning sideways

to present a smaller target. His fingers closed in a brutal grip around her wrist and he twisted, dropping her to her knees, extracting the gun from her fist and holding her locked in position. With one hand he engaged the safety and shoved the gun into his belt.

"You ever point a gun at me again, Rose, pull the fucking trigger. Do we understand each other?" He chose not to look at the pain on her face or the tears swimming, turning those dark eyes to soft, melting chocolate. He didn't let up on the pressure on her wrist. If she moved, it would break. They both knew it. "You don't know me, Rose. You just think you do. I'm not the sweet, malleable man you took me for. You aren't going to manipulate me."

She swallowed and blinked rapidly in an effort to dispel the tears. "Let me up."

"Are you going to try to stick a knife in me next?"

"If you don't let go, I'll most likely consider it."

He eased the pressure on her wrist, allowing her to get to her feet, but he was much more careful, not trusting her now. She pulled away from him and put both hands protectively on her swollen belly. She was trembling, but her eyes met his steadily, even defiantly. They stared at one another.

"We don't have all night," he reminded.

"No, we don't. But I'm not moving until you throw away the tracker. I'm more scared of Whitney getting my baby than I am of a drug cartel. I'll go down fighting, Kane."

He clenched his teeth. Damn, she was stubborn. He could tell by the set of her jaw, her raised chin, and the flash of fire in her eyes that she wasn't bluffing. She planned on staying right where she was..

"You are aware these people like to chop off heads." That should make any woman reasonable, let alone a pregnant one.

"I've seen them do it. It's not a pretty sight," she answered, her chin raising a notch.

Okay. Maybe pregnant women weren't reasonable. It wasn't like he'd ever been around a woman about to give birth. It could be they were all nuts. And every good sense he had was flying out the window. He should have put her over his knee and taught her a lesson, especially after she had the audacity to pull a gun on him, but instead, he wanted to kiss that little chin.

"Rose." He used his most logical and sensible tone. "If I toss the tracker, and something goes wrong, we aren't going to have a ride out of here."

"I'm used to relying on myself. Don't worry, if you're afraid, I can take care of both of us. I know you surround yourself with that big, bad team . . ."

She broke off when he took a step toward her, the taunting laughter fading from her eyes. He noted one hand had slipped inside her jacket, fingers curling around the hilt of her knife.

"Don't piss me off any more than you already have," he snapped and ripped the tracker out of the lining of his shirt. He threw his lifeline into the ravine. "Let's get the hell out of here."

"There's none inside your body?"

He gave her his blackest scowl, and this time, he really was on the edge of losing his temper. "You'll just have to trust me."

She had the grace to look ashamed. Rose turned and walked out into the night, head up, body confident. They were walking *away* from any road he could see. He followed without comment until he reached the top of the first rolling dune. Turning back, he raised his hand to the sky. It was incredibly difficult to move air when there was little breeze to "push," but he'd done it a time or two. Rose had remembered from their conversations in her small prison room.

The wind tugged at the grains of sand, filling in their footsteps and the places where they'd both landed and rolled. He took his time, making a thorough job of it. The tire tracks were smudged in places, but it certainly would look to the world as if they'd gone into the ravine with the sedan. If anyone went to recover the bodies—and he was certain they would—their ruse would be discovered, but it would be too late.

He turned his head to look at the woman carrying his baby. She had continued walking, trusting him to get the job done. There was some satisfaction in that. She didn't want him, but she needed him. He stretched his legs a little to catch up, but her shorter strides made it easy. Every now and then he sent the air skimming over their tracks, just to ensure their safety.

Rose walked briskly at first, her spine stiff, but after the first mile, she eased the pace, glancing back at him. "I'm sorry about the gun, Kane. I didn't know what else to do."

His heart twisted. Damn her anyway. She was tying him up in knots, and he was in grave danger of buying into her feminine frailty all over again. He thought it best not to look at her. Instead, he studied their surroundings. She wasn't in the best of shape; he could hear her breathing begin to grow heavier. She stopped on the pretense of looking around as well, but he knew she needed to rest. He didn't make a comment on her lack of physical fitness, after all she was pregnant. But surely even pregnant women could walk a mile without breathing hard.

She shot him a glare he couldn't fail to catch even in the dark without his night vision. She breathed in and out twice as if trying to remain calm when he was annoying her. "You're shouting your thoughts, and rather rudely too."

His eyebrow shot up. "I'm not the one breathing like a racehorse at the end of the race. Aren't women these days supposed to be in great shape even when they're pregnant?"

She dropped her hand to her belt, and he stepped close, his fingers curling around her wrist with a loud slapping sound. She winced and glared at him again. "I might want to shoot you, but the noise might attract the cartel. Actually, I'm getting my GPS out just to make certain we're on the right course."

"Are you going to tell me where we're going?"

"A while back I met an elderly man," she said as she consulted her GPS and then turned slightly to the right to lead them more directly into the desert. "We became friends of sorts. He was ill and there was no one to help him, so I did." She slipped the GPS away and began walking briskly again. "He had no family and was dying of cancer. He had moved to the apartment near mine. We talked all the time, and in the course of the conversation, he told me about the home he and his wife had built in the desert."

Kane shook his head, easily keeping pace with her. A slow smile started somewhere in the pit of his stomach. That was his woman—resourceful.

"You can barely see it from the air, and it looks small, abandoned, and nothing more than an old, broken-down roof lying in the dirt and sand. It's perfect. I've been bringing supplies to it about every three weeks. I haven't gotten a lot, but I didn't want to leave evidence that anyone had been around the place."

He flashed her a quick, appreciative grin when she glanced at him. "I'm going to have to watch out for you. You're smart and always thinking, aren't you?"

"I had to think about the baby, and I didn't know he would have a secluded house in the desert no one knew about. Did I mention the dune buggy?"

She sounded a little smug, but he supposed she had the right. She certainly took care of business. They walked in silence for another couple of miles, and she stopped abruptly, hunched over a little, one hand pressed tight to her side, as if she had a stitch. Her breathing was ragged again. He waited in silence, noting she seemed not to want him to notice. He had to quit making comments on her being out of condition. He stared up at the clear night sky instead, pretending interest in the stars, but the scent of her enveloped him.

Now that they weren't running for their lives, his body insisted on reacting to hers. It was physical, he reminded himself. They'd talked months ago, conversing in low tones or using the more intimate telepathic communication when they feared the guards would overhear them and report back to Whitney. Kane had been impressed with her courage. Mostly he respected that she treated him as if he were a human being and not a monster bent on rape. She could have been crying and screaming, but she had cooperated, trying to relax, even going so far as encouraging him despite the circumstances.

He pressed two fingers to his throbbing temples. Every time he thought about her first time with him, he got a sick feeling in the pit of his stomach. For him, their union had been paradise, her body hot, velvet soft, so tight he thought he was in heaven. But he knew, no matter how slow he'd gone, how careful he'd been, he'd hurt her.

She straightened up, breathing deeply. "I'm sorry. I just need to rest."

He handed her water and watched carefully to see that she drank it. She looked exhausted and the smears of blood along with the sand burn on her face bothered him more than they should have. He used water on the hem of his shirt to gently wipe the smears from her face. She stood without protest, allowing him to clean her face.

"Does it hurt?"

She sent him a small smile. "In the grand scheme of things, no. I've been thinking about the kid. We just left him there for the cartel to slice and dice while they questioned him."

"Javier has the kid," Kane soothed, slipping his arm around her shoulders and bringing her close to his warmth. Maybe everything was just too much for someone so fragile. She was disoriented and couldn't remember things clearly.

She shook her head. "The teenager. The one tied up. I felt his pulse, and he was alive, but he was unconscious, maybe dying. There was a lot of blood on the floor around him. I should have done something. You know they'll kill him."

"Sweetheart," he said softly, "we had no choice. We couldn't have taken him with us. He didn't see us. Hopefully they'll realize that and let him go."

"They were never going to let him go." She turned her face up to the sky.

Rose looked so sad his heart gave a curious shiver, and it took great effort not to pull her into his arms. He had to keep reminding himself, what he felt for her had nothing to do with emotion, and she felt *nothing* for him. He thought of her as his woman. The one woman. The only. She belonged to him, and he wanted to comfort and protect her, to hold her close to him and make her world a wonderful place. She would be appalled if she knew how he felt—not just appalled but frightened. And if he was entirely truthful with himself, she might have cause to be afraid. He planned on courting her.

He hadn't gotten off to a very good start. She'd already tried to shoot him, and she definitely had considered shoving a knife into him. The remark about her being out of condition hadn't helped his cause either. Kane frowned. So far, his scorecard read pretty much zero. A big fat zero, to be exact.

"No, they were drunk and they wanted *el presidente*'s nephew to kill him. I'm sorry we couldn't save him, Rose, but we had no time, and we had to get the five-year-old to safety."

"I know. It's just hard to think of his mother waiting for him to come home, knowing those horrible monsters took him from her for no reason other than their own amusement."

Kane didn't know how to comfort her, so instead, he took her hand and set a much slower pace, catering to her short legs and lack of physical fitness. The terrain changed from pure sand to patches of saw grass. A few hearty flowers tried to grow among the thick stalks. Rocks formed a rough terrace along several of the rolling hills of dirt and sand. This was barren country, without the natural beauty of the desert. The land was so stark, he couldn't imagine why anyone would want to build a home in the middle of such a wasteland—unless they were in hiding.

"Who exactly was this man you befriended? To come out here, he must have a lot of enemies."

She didn't look up at him, but he caught her smile. "He was in his eighties, and let's just say he lived a very full life opposing the government. He lost his children and his siblings to the fight and eventually his wife."

Kane closed his eyes for a brief moment, trying to hold on to his sanity. "You befriended a rebel wanted by the government."

"Well, yes," she confirmed. "He was very adept at hiding his presence. I was on the run, he was on the run, it was sort of natural. And he needed help."

She didn't know it, but she damn well needed Kane. She didn't have any sense in her pretty head. None.

"You do realize even a man in his eighties could kill you, Rose, if he thought you were a threat to him, especially one who spent an entire life killing those he perceived as enemies."

She walked in silence beside him, choosing not to see his logic or answer his charge. He scowled down at the top of her head. She was so headstrong she just blazed a path straight to trouble. He was going to have to put a stop to it, that was all. She definitely needed looking after, whether she thought so or not. Satisfied that he wasn't just being selfish, he walked up the sloping hill, noting the vegetation was thicker in the area than most of the surrounding dirt and sand.

"You're about to walk right up the roof."

He halted abruptly. "You're kidding."

She looked pleased—and a little smug. "Yes, it's right there. Take a look around. The place is amazing. To get here, you have to know the GPS location. He was always careful to come in different ways and leave no tracks. There is a dune buggy, and he dragged a carpet behind it to cover the tire marks in the dirt and sand. That was how he would get his supplies. He has a truck parked in a garage in the village right on the edge of the desert. He drove the buggy across the sand and left it in the garage when he shopped with the truck."

"Clever. And no one ever betrayed him?"

"According to him, everyone who knew about his desert retreat is dead."

"Just who is this saintly man?"

"His name was Diego Jimenez."

Kane felt something inside him go still. "And he just happened to tell you about the place?" Diego Jimenez led a shadowy group of rebels determined to overthrow the previous government. They did so by bombing oil and natural gas lines. They had a reputation for killing locals who didn't agree with their policies. Jimenez had lived by the sword, betraying everything humanity stood for. He had an extensive family, and Kane doubted that they were all dead. He was evil, pure and simple, and Rose couldn't see beyond a dying old man. Leopards didn't change their spots, and snakes were snakes.

He took a careful look around, using night vision. The night seemed still, but what had been a place of refuge suddenly felt hostile.

"I know what you're thinking, but I took care of him until he died. He gave me the location and the keys. He knew I needed a place to lay low until after the baby was born."

She gestured toward the dirt- and grass-covered roofline. He could see the low rectangular stone structure was situated between the two sloping hills. The way the house had been built, it would catch natural light and crosswinds. From the front the structure looked like a half-buried ruin, which, he was certain, was the entire idea. The shrubs on the roof had been planted and carefully cultivated to look part of the natural surroundings. The dirt looked as if the wind had blown it there, again all natural. Kane walked up the slope to inspect the roof. He had to really look to find the portals that allowed light into the subterranean rooms below. The entire structure looked more like an ancient bridge built between the two slopes, now buried in soil and shrubbery and tall grass stalks.

They walked down the sloping ground to the front door. The walls showing were quite thick.

"The glass in the windows is bulletproof," Rose said as she unlocked the door.

He caught her shoulder and shoved her none too gently behind him. She didn't protest, but he heard her sigh overly loud. It didn't matter. He knew she didn't—couldn't—see Jimenez as evil, but he knew better. He didn't trust rebels, not even eighty-year-old dying rebels. It was just too generous a gesture to hand over the keys to the desert retreat. Something was going on here, something he didn't trust or understand, but she wasn't just walking into that house without him clearing every inch of it first.

He handed her back her gun and stepped inside. The interior of the house was cool without being cold. He moved easily in the dark, staying along the wall as he moved through the wide entryway that spilled into a large living room. The furniture was sparse, a couch and two chairs, but they appeared well made and in good condition. A low coffee table was cleared of any magazines or objects. The room held no ashtrays, and the air seemed clean.

He noted two separate arched doorways leading to other rooms and made his way to the nearest one in silence. The floors were hardwood with handwoven, very expensive rugs thrown artistically in front of the couch and chair. The room he entered was a single bedroom. A large double bed with a carved wooden frame came out from the center wall with a large, low chest at the end of it. Bookshelves surrounded the headboard, forming a bridge up around the wall. He could see beneath the bed that no one hid there. A closet drew his attention, and he slipped inside the room and moved to the side of the door. In one move he turned

the knob and pulled it open. The space was empty of everything, even clothes.

Rose wouldn't get the significance of that. Or of the fact
that no paintings hung on the wall, and that there were no
objects on shelves, no books. She had been raised in a military compound, a stark life that didn't encourage owning
art and beautiful things. This had been Diego Jimenez's
hideaway, supposedly his last line of retreat. This would
be where he would keep his most prized possessions, and
yet the entire residence was empty of everything but the
starkest furniture, as if it had been prepared for Rose—or
someone. This situation had all the warning signs of a trap.

He cleared the bathroom, a much more spacious room
than he would have thought the underground living quarters would have, and moved on to the kitchen. Again, the
room was large. A dining table and chairs for six sat beneath an ornate chandelier. That bothered him even more.
If the chandelier was real, and it certainly looked like a
work of art, this "rebel," who should have been poor and
on the run, was incredibly wealthy. This was no hovel, dug
out in the middle of the desert. An architect had designed
the home, taking into consideration light, space, and crosswinds. That took money.

A man on the run would have a secure room, a place
he could go to hide if the law was closing in as well as an
escape route. He went through the kitchen back into the living room and studied the layout. Not in the common room;
it would have to be the bedroom where Jimenez and his
wife slept.

"I'm coming in," Rose declared and stepped inside the
open foyer. "There's a generator. It's very quiet. It will heat
the water, and we both can take a shower."

She sounded so hopeful, it took effort not to sweep her
into his arms. She looked exhausted, dried blood on her
arms and scratches down one side of her face, a badge of
courage, where she'd protected the baby instead of her own
head. That made him mad all over again.

"Who the hell jumps out of a moving vehicle eight months pregnant?" he demanded.

"Someone who doesn't want to get shot." Her eyes flashed the most interesting little sparks there in the darkness. "And if you had taken care of the guard *before* he fired his weapon, we might not have had to jump."

"Which I might have been able to do had you not interfered." As excuses went, it was pretty damn lame and childish. She'd managed to be very helpful, *but* that wasn't the damn point. She had no business going into combat pregnant. "You don't have much sense, do you?"

If the furious sparks in her eyes could have found fuel, he would have been in trouble. As it was, he reached out and took the gun from her hand just to err on the side of caution.

"The *only* stupid thing I've done so far is to pick you as a partner. I'm tired and I want a shower. Get out of my way."

"Not until I clear his safe room and the escape tunnel."

She went still. Her tongue darted out to touch her lower lip, drawing his attention to the full, angel-like bow. "Safe room?" She pushed strands of hair away from her face. Her hand trembled. She put it behind her back.

She'd definitely recognized the significance of what he'd said.

"There isn't a safe room."

"Why? Because he would have told you?" Damn it all, was she going to believe him or some lying old man who had his own agenda? All Kane wanted to do was protect her . . . Well, okay, that was a fucking lie. That wasn't all he wanted from her, but his intentions were noble. Damn it, maybe they weren't all that noble either. She was tying him up in knots. What the hell kind of woman did the things she did?

"Oh, Kane." Her voice shook.

She looked as if she crumbled right in front of him. She

sank into the chair, pressing her hand to her swollen belly, taking long, slow, deep breaths.

"There's no need to hyperventilate," he said as gently as possible. "We'll be fine. I'll check the room. Take your gun, and *don't* shoot me."

She sent him a wan smile as her fingers closed around the butt of the gun. "Tempting thought," she murmured, her expression both rueful and apprehensive, "but I'll restrain myself."

That little smile turned his heart over. He touched her face with gentle fingers before he could stop himself. She didn't jerk away. Her skin was soft, like the petals of a rose. His knuckles brushed the silk of her hair. Immediately the memory of her body beneath him filled his mind. His body reacted, hard and full and aching for her. He ignored the urgent needs as best as he could, brushing the pad of his thumb along her cheekbone and down her jaw, tracing the beautiful bone structure, oddly grateful she remained still beneath his exploration. He *needed* to touch her, and maybe she understood he really had no choice.

"Stay right here, Rose." He gentled his voice. She really did look exhausted, and the walk in the desert had obviously taxed her endurance. *Unless . . .* He frowned. "Did you get hurt when you jumped from the car?"

"Just go clear the room."

"And the tunnel. He would have had an escape out of here. A man like Diego Jimenez would never have allowed himself to become trapped."

She pressed her fingers to her eyes as if her head were pounding. "I should have thought of that. I don't know why I just accepted what he told me."

He crouched down beside her, his fingers curling around the nape of her neck. "You needed to hear you had a safe place to go, Rose. That's human nature."

She looked directly into his eyes, and every cell in his body reacted to the pain he saw there.

"I'm responsible for our child. You trusted me to take care of her. I told you I would."

The naked mixture of stark honesty, guilt, and exhaustion was nearly his undoing. He had to stop himself from pulling her into his arms and kissing her until they both were sated—which would probably be never for him. Instead he grinned at her. "I throw males. I'm damned sure of it. We're having a boy. I'll be right back."

He heard her soft laughter as he swaggered away from her, back to the bedroom. He had to get this done, ensure they were safe for the night, and then they'd have to find somewhere else to hole up until he could get word to the GhostWalkers. He had no doubts that when the political bullshit was gone, Mack and the team would come looking for him. They wouldn't stop until they found him alive or found his body. They wouldn't believe the tracker in the ravine. With no evidence of bodies in the wreckage, they would know he had walked away alive with Rose.

Kane examined the walls carefully for any evidence of difference. With a subterranean structure, it wouldn't be difficult to excavate enough dirt to provide a hidden room. There had to be an entrance, and one that was fairly easy to get to in an emergency. It wouldn't be positioned where anyone bursting through the door could readily see. It wouldn't be on the wall the bed was against. He ran his hands over the remaining two walls. Neither felt different. He couldn't find a crack that might indicate a door. Puzzled, he stood in the center of the room, frowning.

He couldn't be wrong. Diego Jimenez was notorious, and the bounty on him had been astounding, in a country where poverty often overcame good sense. *El presidente* would have sent the entire military at his disposal after the man if he knew his hideout. So there was a back door. He studied the room again, aware of Rose's restless movements in the next room. He had to make certain there was no enemy in the panic room or waiting in the tunnel.

There were no cracks, so what did that mean? The door

had to be there, so . . . He stepped close to the wall he would have chosen. It was situated in the farthest end of the room that, if used, would take them deeper underground and away from the front opening that was aboveground. He ran his fingers along the actual corner seam of the room. It seemed to blend flawlessly, yet when he looked at the ceiling joint, he realized this had to be the door, cleverly blended. There was no heavy furniture to cover anything, just a solid wall.

He ran his fingers along the edges, looking for a way in. It had to be easy. There would be no time for a combination. Jimenez would want fast access. Could it be that easy? A spring-loaded door that fit snugly but was made for a fast exit? The family wouldn't hide there. They would run. They could barricade the door from inside the panic room. There was no need to do so in the bedroom. Gun in his fist, finger on the trigger, he put his palm flat on the edge of the inside seam and pushed.

The door swung inward soundlessly. He crouched low and scanned the interior. Inching inside, he took stock of the room. It was built with thick walls, and one side housed a case filled with guns of every caliber, ammunition, and grenades. Nothing had been touched. He frowned over that. If the old man had removed his valuables, why hadn't he taken the weapons? He could see the metal bars, three of them, that fit across the wall from inside this room. An arched doorway led to the escape tunnel.

Kane followed the passageway all the way to the exit point, grateful he had excellent night vision. It was damned dark, but the tunnel had been formed for a quick escape, and the floor was smooth. Markers, painted in white, gave distance so anyone running could clearly see where they were at any given time. Simple but effective. He was beginning to admire the old man. He didn't waste time and effort on elaborateness.

Kane followed the winding tunnel about a mile and came out on the other side of the sloping hill. He couldn't even see the house from where he was. Just inside the tunnel, hidden from view, was an army Humvee. He knew the engine would be gleaming. This Hummer was an M1165 with frag armor and bulletproof windows. More, it was outfitted with the latest weaponry, the CROWS system. He sighed. This scenario became worse with every passing moment. How the hell did a man like Jimenez manage to get his hands on that?

He spent some time booby-trapping the exit, just in case the old man had set Rose up in some way. He had no answers for the why of it, but that didn't matter so much. Keeping her safe was the main mission. He went back to her, satisfied they could spend the night and get some rest.

"I think we're good, Rose. I found the escape tunnel in the bedroom. I'll start the generator, and you can take a shower and get some rest."

"Thank you," she whispered, her voice almost hoarse. She stood up with a groan and immediately bent over, taking slow, deep breaths and letting each one out carefully.

"Are you hurt? Don't lie to me, Rose. If you hurt yourself when you jumped from the sedan, you need to admit it, not be ashamed. It was a dumb plan, but we got away."

She gritted her teeth, breathing through her mouth. When she could speak, she made a strangling sound deep in her throat. "I'm not hurt."

He glared down at her with a sick feeling in the pit of his stomach. "What the hell is wrong with you?"

"Nothing is wrong with me. This is called having contractions, you big oaf," Rose snapped back, her glare maybe outdoing his by a shade.

CHAPTER 4

Contractions. Kane's stomach dropped right out of his body. He stared down at her, his mind going fuzzy. That was one of those words like menstruation, period, or female products. The list just wasn't uttered in male company. Contractions fit right in there. God. This was *not* happening. He forced his brain under control, ignoring the pounding in his head and the roaring in his ears.

He studied Rose's body carefully. She wasn't due for another four or five weeks, right? He knew when she got pregnant. When he'd first seen her, she had looked slim, but that had been an illusion. On the other hand, she never looked as—*big*—as she did at that moment.

"What?" Rose demanded, glaring up at him.

The warning signal flashed bright red in Kane's head. Telling a woman she was as big as a beach ball wouldn't win any points. How did one describe how she looked? A basketball? Volleyball? He studied her furious little face. Yeah. He was in trouble no matter what he said. Description was out of the question. He needed diplomacy, something that flew out the window when he was near her and she said words like contractions.

He'd jump out of a plane without hesitation in the heart of enemy territory, but damn it all, ask him to kill someone, not deliver babies. She didn't take her eyes off him, and that expression on her scowling face demanded an answer.

He cast about desperately in his mind and then hit on a way out. He shrugged, trying to look casual as well as impressed. "You managed such a great illusion, looking slim earlier, it was hard to remember it was an illusion." There. A compliment. He hadn't stepped into the mud and sunk— yet. She was still looking at him, hands on her hips, waiting for more. He was beginning to sweat. Hell.

"You can't possibly be ready to have the baby."

"Which is why I wasn't already here." She had a little bite in her voice. "I still had several weeks to bring in supplies. Thank God the birthing kit I put together is here."

He squeezed his eyes shut tight and let out a groan of his own. Birthing kit. Just add that to the growing list of banned words. Okay. He took a deep breath and let it out. Someone had to take control of the situation, and obviously she was too exhausted to do so. Someone had to man up and set her straight. There was no one else.

"Then stop. Right now. Just stop."

"*Stop?*" she echoed in a near shriek.

"Look, Rose." He used his most soothing, reasonable tone. "Doing this now would just be illogical. The baby isn't quite ready, and we're too far from help. Just think about something else. You're upset and worried and you need to rest."

Her mouth opened and closed twice. She looked at him as if he'd grown two heads. "Are you kidding me?" she demanded. "Because this isn't the time to be joking around."

She looked as if she was contemplating ripping his belly open with a knife and proving something to him. He took a cautionary step back and held up a hand to placate her. It was clear to him that pregnancy made women insane.

"I'm trying to help you, Rose. These—these . . ." Hell. He wasn't going to use the word *contractions*; that would make it too real. "These pains you're experiencing, maybe they're something else. The fall from the car could have caused them." And that was more than a reasonable assumption.

"They started before the jump from the car."

His stomach tightened into half a dozen hard knots. "Then why the hell didn't you get on that helicopter where we could get you medical help?" he demanded, angry all over again. "Damn it, woman, do you have any sense at all?" Now she was making him just as insane as she obviously was.

"Whitney is *not* getting this baby. I don't know those men you were so willing to send me off with. I have a plan, and it doesn't include getting on the helicopter. And don't yell at me. I'm in a delicate condition."

She looked suspiciously amused now. He wanted to shake her. Instead he took a long-suffering breath and let it out to force himself to be calm and *reasonable*. Reason and logic were the keys to dealing with a woman in her condition. "Is there a possibility that you hurt yourself in the jump? That these pains are something else?"

She shrugged. "I'm hoping they're Braxton Hicks contractions. Sometimes a woman can have false labor weeks before she goes into labor."

Relief exploded through him. Of course. He'd just been thrown for a minute. Braxton Hicks sounded like the real thing. "Okay then. That sounds good. Let's just get you in bed to rest. All this running around can't be good for you. I can hike back tomorrow to the ravine and find the tracker and . . ." He broke off, frowning. "Why are you shaking your head?"

"You are such a chicken. *Bock. Bock. Bock.*"

He refused to allow her very bad chicken impression to ruffle his feathers. He was above petty name-calling. The point was getting her in bed and out of danger. She couldn't fixate on the pain, and it would just go away. He was certain of it. "Come on, Rose," he said, keeping his voice low and gentle. "I'll help you to the bathroom."

She rolled her eyes. "Keep in mind I killed a man a few hours ago for less. I can make it to the bathroom on my own. Just turn on the generator and get me some hot water—please."

He turned away from her before he shook some sense into her. He was trying to help her. Didn't she get that? Kane stalked through the kitchen into the pantry where she had stocked meager supplies. While searching the house he had discovered the generator. He crouched down to study it. It ran on gas. There were four large cylinders feeding it. He started it, shocked at how loud it was. When he closed the door behind him, he realized the room was soundproof. The generator couldn't be heard outside the room where it was housed.

"You hungry?" he called. He was starving.

"Not really," she called back.

She sounded so weary and, if he was not mistaken, close to tears. He needed to find a way to connect with her. For all her bravado, she had to be scared. She'd *chosen* him to be her partner, and she was counting on him. She hadn't tried to run from him. If she'd been serious about shooting him, she would have pulled the trigger without hesitation. She was a GhostWalker, trained practically from birth. She didn't want him dead. She wanted his help.

He stood in the middle of the pantry, head hanging down, dragging in deep breaths. He had little fear when it came to confronting an enemy. But assisting at a birth—he shook his head. No way. Not when it was Rose. He had to get her to a hospital. If he could get to Mack, his team would come rescue them and bring a doctor.

Lights flickered on in the bedroom, and he heard her moving around. He turned them on in the pantry to inventory their supplies. She'd stocked the place mainly with canned foods, but she'd included protein such as ham and tuna and chicken. She had several shelves of vegetables and a variety of soups. He wasn't going to starve. He brought out a can of chicken and rice soup and heated it, hoping to tempt her to eat something.

The shower abruptly went off as he poured two bowls and put them on a tray. The tray was intricate, hand-painted, and expensive. He gave her a few minutes to towel off and slide into bed. "Can I come in, Rose?" He didn't want her to feel threatened in any way, although, if he was being honest with himself, he believed she belonged to him and he had the right to walk into her bedroom. He wanted her to feel the same way.

"I'm decent."

He paused in the doorway. She looked small, a porcelain doll with eyes too big for her face. The shape of almonds, they were dark and mysterious, eyes a man could fall into and never find his way out of. She looked exotic, her hair disheveled and still damp, midnight black, cascading around her face, giving her that little pixie look. He could have sworn tears stained her face, but her eyes were clear.

"I brought soup just in case you changed your mind. Are the pains easing up at all?" He manfully kept the hopeful note out of his tone.

"All the activity must have set them off. They seem to be getting farther apart, and they're shorter in duration. From all the research I've done, that means false labor."

He felt like a man given a reprieve right before a death sentence, but he kept his features expressionless. He wanted her to count on him, and she couldn't do that if she knew he was petrified of delivering a baby.

"Will you try to eat something?" He walked farther into the room and set the tray on the end table. "It might help."

She flashed him a smile that told him he didn't know what he was talking about, but she picked up the bowl of soup and spoon, sank down in the middle of the bed, tailor fashion, her back against the headboard, and regarded him

steadily. "So? You found an escape tunnel. I've been looking around. Everything of value is gone. I didn't pay attention to that when he sent me here the first time. I was just
so happy to find a safe place to give birth."

He nodded his head. "That makes sense." The son of a
bitch would have known she was desperate to find a sanctuary for her child. Jimenez had dangled the house like a
carrot in front of her.

"What do you think it all means?" She patted the bed
beside her in invitation and moved to the far side of the
mattress to give him room.

Sitting with her on a bed might not be the best of ideas.
He wouldn't be making any moves on her, not while she
was so pregnant she looked like she might explode, but his
body didn't have the same sense his brain did. The moment
he saw her or smelled her, every cell in his body went on
alert.

"I'm not going to bite," she said.

He realized he'd hesitated too long. "I didn't want to
make you uncomfortable." Which was partially true.

"It isn't like we haven't shared a bed before," she reminded.

Immediately the image of her writhing beneath him rose
up to haunt him. His cock reacted, hard and full and aching,
desperate for the feel of her tight, hot sheath surrounding
him. Cursing under his breath, he eased his body gingerly
onto the bed, trying not to inhale and draw her scent into
his lungs.

"Are you going to tell me what you think about Diego
Jimenez?" she prompted.

"Tell me how you met him," Kane said. "I need all the
information to make any kind of judgment." The soup
tasted good. He hadn't eaten for hours and realized he was
very hungry. He nudged her with his shoulder. "Just try it,
sweetheart."

She surprised him by eating a few spoonfuls before she
spoke. "I'd been moving, staying in the back country or in

the mountains mostly. There were women willing to help me when they found out I was pregnant, but I knew I had to find a place Whitney wouldn't be able to track me so easily to have the baby. I couldn't take the chance of a doctor or midwife writing anything on paper. Whitney is searching for me; I know because he sent a couple of his goons on two occasions that I know of. I barely escaped both times."

"How the hell did he find you?"

"I don't know. I tried looking for a second tracking device. There was one in my hip, but I removed it myself. I got rid of all my clothes, everything I had previously owned, but he always seems to be breathing down my neck." She looked at him. "I promised you I would take care of the baby and keep her out of Whitney's hands, and I mean to keep that promise."

"Why the hell did you pull a gun on me, Rose? You knew I helped you escape. You knew I turned him in. I risked my career and my life to try to get his ugly program dragged into the light of day."

She took a couple more spoonfuls of soup, her gaze downcast, but he felt her stiffen, as if steadying herself to tell him the truth. "I was afraid. I knew you trusted your team; I could tell by the way you worked with them, that easy camaraderie that only comes when people have relied on one another through dangerous situations. You told me to get on the helicopter, but you weren't getting on with me. You would have sent me away."

"Where you would have been safe and had medical attention," he reminded. He could tell she found it difficult to admit that she was afraid.

She bent her head again, and he couldn't help but look at the vulnerable nape of her neck. He had the sudden urge to lean over and brush his mouth over that soft spot.

"I needed *you*, Kane, not your friends. They aren't my friends. They aren't people I trust. I've lived too long in captivity and I've had a taste of freedom. I won't let our child live like I had to, with Whitney documenting every single moment of my life and dictating what I could and couldn't do."

"I understand." And damn it all, he did. She'd been trained to be a soldier, experimented on, and then shoved into a breeding program. It was a monstrous life she'd led, and had it been him, he would have done anything to get free and stay that way. "Tell me about Jimenez."

She flashed a brief, rather wan smile. "I'm getting there in my own roundabout way. I knew I had to find a safe place to have the baby, and just in case, learn how to deliver it myself."

"You fucking have to be kidding me, Rose," he burst out. "You make me crazy. You really do. Both of you could die, don't you know that?"

"Of course I know it," she said. "I'm not crazy and I'm not stupid. I'm careful, Kane. I studied hard. I was careful to learn about pregnancy and what I needed to make the baby healthy."

"You didn't have a blood test, or any of the tests, did you?"

"How could I?" she defended. She sounded close to tears. "I did the best I could for her. Better both of us dead than back with Whitney."

Kane put the empty soup bowl down and slipped his arm around her shoulder. "I know you did. It's just the thought of you out there alone, trying to figure it all out by yourself, when I should have been there with you, makes me want to shoot somebody."

She leaned into him. "Preferably not me."

He laughed at her choice of words. "Not you, sweetheart. You might make me want to pull out every hair on my head, but I'd never hurt you."

Rose studied Kane's face—that face she dreamt about for eight long months. His beautiful, masculine carved features and his vivid piercing green eyes took her breath away. She couldn't look too long at him, afraid he'd see her reaction. From the window of her cell and the workout yard, she'd watched him just like a stalker might. Looking had turned into longing. He was a strong, confident male, definitely one who was skilled in his chosen profession. She watched other males, all strong as well, step back when he walked through a small crowd, yet he always seemed to treat everyone fairly. She loved everything about him from his wide shoulders to the strong lines in his face and his sudden, heart-stopping smile.

She had dreamt of him long before she betrayed him. Wanting him. Building fantasies and unrealistic dreams until she became almost obsessed with him. When Whitney insisted on bringing in those horrible men with their lecherous smiles, uncaring that she didn't want them, men willing to force her, she'd become a desperate woman who would do anything to escape. A woman who would sell another human being into a living hell to gain her own freedom. She swallowed hard and looked away, ashamed of her need and her cowardice. She sold him out, and even now, she couldn't let him go.

"Rose, what is it?"

His voice was so gentle it turned her heart over. She felt his baby kick inside her, a strong reminder she would always have a part of him. The soup tasted like ashes now, the seeds of guilt and shame stripping her of all appetite. She placed the bowl on the nightstand. He was a man of honor, and she'd taken his pride, forced him into an untenable position with no way out. He loathed himself for getting her pregnant, and no matter how many times she told him it had been her choice, her decision, he refused to allow her to shoulder the blame. He was waiting patiently for her to answer his simple question—"What is it?"—but the answer wasn't nearly as simple as the question.

"I'm sorry I got you into this, Kane, but I'm not sorry you're here with me. I'm afraid."

There. She'd admitted it out loud. If the truth were told, she was *terrified*. She was so tired and she desperately needed to rest, to spend twenty-four hours without fear.

She'd been alone for so long, scared for herself and for the baby. She looked up at him, ashamed, but unable to lie to him. "I need you."

She loved his face, all those hard lines, his strong jaw, those cool, clear eyes. There was no subterfuge in Kane. He didn't have a hidden agenda—not like she had. He didn't lie about how he felt. He didn't hide the fact that his body wanted her and he was uncomfortable with it. She doubted if there were too many men like him in the world. She didn't need just anyone; she needed him.

"I figured that out when I came up behind you in the room and you didn't put up much resistance." He smoothed back the hair falling around her face and ran the pad of his thumb down her skin.

Rose tried not to shiver. Just as he'd entered the room where she waited for the informant, she'd inhaled and drawn his scent deep into her body, down into her lungs. She'd wanted to hold him there forever. She'd been so shocked that Kane had been the one to come for the hostages. Could a woman fall in love with a man just by observing him? By watching him through a window? She was afraid she lived in a dream world, not reality, because she had been alone and frightened far too long. There was no one else but Kane. Who else did she have? The other women in the compound had escaped and scattered to the winds, leaving her to face the birth of her baby alone. She wanted to burrow into him, stay in his arms where she felt safe, where she felt she finally had a sanctuary.

He thought he'd hurt her when he'd had sex with her, that she had chosen him as the lesser of all evils—and maybe that was true to a small extent—but he'd made her feel beautiful and special when no one ever had. He made her feel as if she mattered for the first time in her life. He'd been so gentle. She dreamt of him nearly every night, and now, being so close to him, the image of him rising above her, his body locked deep inside hers, flooded her mind and refused to leave.

"Rose," he prompted. "Talk to me about Jimenez. I think it's important. How did you meet the man?"

"Diego moved into the apartment across the street from mine."

"*After* you, then. You were already established in your apartment?"

Rose nodded, her heart beginning to pound. She knew where this was going now, and she couldn't believe she'd allowed herself to be duped.

"Who lived in that apartment when you first arrived? And why did they leave?"

She was so tired. She just wanted to weep. And go to sleep. She shifted, a subtle movement, sliding closer to him, dropping her head on his chest. He had one of those thick chests that inspired fantasies and made a woman feel perfectly safe. She was very fond of his chest—a little hard though—but she found the perfect spot for her head. His arms closed around her, and her heart jumped. So did the baby. She closed her eyes and took his hand to press his palm to her belly where their child played. Beneath his palm, the baby pushed as if in greeting.

Rose expected him to pull his hand away, but his fingers, beneath hers, spread wide to take in more. She relaxed a little, allowing some of the tension to ease from her body. "There was a multi-generation family in the apartment when I first moved in. It was crowded, so I just figured they'd found a bigger place to live."

"Had they told anyone they were moving?"

She was disgusted with herself. The family had children. The kids would have talked to their friends about leaving, and word would have gone along the street and through the neighborhood like wildfire. That was how it worked, and yet she hadn't even given it a thought that the family had moved in the night and the elderly gentleman had moved in the next day. She sighed out loud, letting him know she was aware of screwing up. "No, they hadn't told anyone. There was no gossip. I heard them leave, of course. I heard everything. A truck came, and men I assumed were friends loaded the furniture onto the truck."

"Had you ever seen the friends before?"

"No. And now that I'm thinking about it, I didn't see any of the family the entire day prior to the move. Not even their son, and he always was in the street with the other boys in the neighborhood. I can't believe I just walked right into their trap."

"Whitney plays games, Rose. He loves to play his games."

"I don't understand." There were tears in her voice, burning her eyes, clogging her throat. She was so damned tired. She didn't want to appear weak to him—he already thought she didn't have a brain in her head and she was out of shape—but the thought of Whitney still orchestrating her life depressed her beyond belief.

His palm brushed caresses over her belly, a soothing motion that not only calmed the restless baby but eased some of the tension out of her. "He has to have some sort of way to track you, Rose, and when you managed to elude his private little army of psycho GhostWalkers, he thought you were worthy enough to play one of his games."

Rose was silent, turning over the idea in her mind. She couldn't remember a time in her life when she had been anywhere but a military compound training for combat. Whitney had watched every move they made. There had been no privacy, everything documented as if he were studying insects under glass. He had often tried to pit them against one another when they were little girls. He had tried hard to make them rivals, and then later, wanted them cohesive, working as a unit. Yes, he liked psychological warfare. Everything was an experiment to him. He liked to create situations, sit back, and see what developed, and found amusement in watching them all figure out what he was doing.

"How is he tracking me, Kane?"

He frowned up at the ceiling. "I don't know yet, sweetheart, but it has to be by satellite, and the feed is intermittent, which explains why he keeps losing you between the times he sends his team after you. And it explains why, once he knew you were in this country, he decided to isolate you in a spot where he could send a team in under the radar and pick you up."

"Before I have the baby?"

"I don't think so. I think he'll wait until you're vulnerable and weak. He wants you both, and he knows you're going to fight him."

She turned her head up to look at him, although she continued to rest against his chest. "Then we have time."

"If I'm right. It makes sense. If you buy Jimenez's story and retreat here to wait for the birth of your baby, all he has to do is wait until he's certain you had the baby and send in his force. You'll be weak and vulnerable. You'll be afraid the child will get hurt, and he'll have all the leverage he'll need to use against you. Cooperate or you won't see your child. That's Whitney's logic, and it's actually sound."

"Except you're here, and he doesn't know that."

"The mission was covert, and he has no idea anyone was sent in, let alone my particular team. But he'll find out eventually. He has sources placed high in the administration."

"I need to rest, Kane. Just a day or two. Hopefully my body will settle down and I can move without risking an early birth."

She was asking permission, and she hated that. It was important to her to make her own decisions, but she needed his protection, and if she was relying on his strength, she'd better use all of it, including his judgment.

Kane nuzzled the top of her head with his chin. Her heart jumped a second time. She held her breath, waiting— needing. "I think resting might be the lesser of two evils. I want you somewhere safe to have the baby, Rose, but the baby has to be safe too. Running without thinking is plain foolish. We'll take precautions and give you a day or two to rest. But I want to find out how he's tracking you."

Relief washed through her. She didn't have to move, hopefully not for at least twenty-four hours. She didn't have to be vigilant or do anything but crawl under the covers and go to sleep. Kane was there, and he'd watch out for their baby.

As if reading her mind, Kane suggested, "You're falling asleep, sweetheart. Slide under the covers and close your eyes."

"I have to brush my teeth first. But don't worry, once I'm under the covers, I'll be asleep," she assured, allowing the first tendril of happiness to sneak in.

Rose knew she was dropping her guard and she was going to get hurt, but did it have to matter right at that moment? She felt brittle—full of tiny holes as if pieces of her were long gone and spiderweb cracks veined the shell of her body. One wrong move and she would shatter. She was drowning, pure and simple. She had no reserve left and was running on empty. If Kane didn't save her, she was going down for the last time, and this time, she wouldn't come up again.

"Rose."

Her heart thudded in her chest. His voice was so incredible, a sexy, low tone that resonated through her entire body. He made her feel different—feminine instead of a soldier with death on her hands. He made her feel as if life could be lived with laughter and happiness a part of it.

"Look at me, sweetheart."

If she did, her heart would be in her eyes. Her lashes fluttered reluctantly. She was *not* going to cry again. What was wrong with her? She hadn't cried once until she laid eyes on him again. She didn't want to look like a tragic drama queen to him. She was just so tired, and, if she was honest, so happy to see him.

He caught her chin and forced her head up. The pounding in her chest was alarming. The baby drummed against her ribs, almost as frantic as she was. She moistened her lips, steeling herself to meet those gorgeous eyes. She was so broken, and Kane was the kind of man who would fix a woman, the rescuer, the hero, a man who could be counted on. She was using a good man, and she hated herself for it. The shame would be there in her eyes for him to see as well as her heart.

The pad of his thumb brushed over her lips, and her womb clenched. The baby shifted. She forced herself to lift her lashes and look into his eyes. Everything in her stilled— settled. Kane, with his tough face and piercing eyes, looked at her and *saw* her. She could tell he wasn't looking past her or at an illusion she created. He saw her weaknesses, and it was all right with him. She didn't have to hide from him. She didn't have to project what he wanted to see. For the first time in her life she could just be herself in front of another human being.

"Are you afraid of me?"

She hadn't expected the question. Her mouth went dry. Was she? Not in the way he meant. Kane, for all of his ferocious soldier abilities, was gentle inside. She'd known that the moment she laid eyes on him. He could shift into battle in a moment, become a fierce protector, a fighter, and she had no doubt he would kill swiftly if need be, but he was gentle inside where it counted.

"No . . ." She had difficulty maintaining eye contact when that wasn't exactly the truth. He deserved truth from her, and she'd promised herself she'd give it to him, no matter the cost, if he stayed with her. "Yes."

He leaned forward and brushed his mouth along hers. Featherlight. The breath of hope. Stealing her soul. Her heart jerked. Her stomach somersaulted. She held herself very still while sensations poured through her veins and rushed to invade her cells. She'd already taken him deep into her lungs, and she knew she'd never be able to get him out again.

"You smell a little like heaven, Rose," he said and

shifted his weight, moving off the bed in one fluid motion that reminded her of flowing water. "I keep my promises. If you believe nothing else, believe that."

She did believe he kept his promises. She believed in him. And that was the entire problem. She was a woman who had been betrayed at birth by her own parents, dumped in an orphanage because she wasn't male. The orphanage betrayed her by selling her to Whitney. Whitney betrayed her by raising her as a soldier instead of a child, and then conducting his experiments. In the end, he'd taken everything from her, including her dignity, forcing her into a breeding program, reducing all those years of work and discipline to nothing at all. He treated her as if it was only her body that mattered, not her psychic talent or all of her training. She was intelligent and able to fight as well as the male GhostWalkers, but Whitney had denied her even that. Believing in anyone was absolutely insane. Yet there was Kane.

Kane left her there on the bed, taking the empty soup bowls with him. It was difficult to leave, but he was scaring her, and that was the last thing he wanted. She was stressed enough and in a delicate condition. He could stitch his own wounds and those of his team. He'd even been known to push a bullet through his skin a time or two, but this baby thing had him rattled. He didn't have a clue what to do in the particular situation.

At the door he paused and looked back at her. She seemed so small and lost and alone. "I'll be back in a few minutes to tuck you in."

That bought him a ghost of a smile. "I'm not three."

"I know. I'm not doing it for you." He turned and walked away from the sight of her.

She was enough to break any man's heart. For one moment he wished he was the hero type, the white knight charging in to save her, but he was a man, awkward in the presence of women, and he'd already made a few blunders. He washed the few dishes and went back into the pantry to look at the birthing kit—just in case.

He was a man who believed in preparing for emergencies. Having babies fell under that category. Beside the kit she'd put together were several books, and because he was reluctant to open the sealed plastic container and look at the contents, he browsed through the books. The titles told him a lot about Rose. She planned well for things.

One book was on natural childbirth, another focused on nutrition for the pregnant woman. Both books had been read many times. The pages were worn and dog-eared. Another book on parenting caught his attention. He flipped through it and found many passages underlined. There were notes in the margin Rose had made to herself, multiple reminders to find other titles on various subjects. Like Kane, Rose could kill a man with her bare hands without blinking, but diapering a baby was out of their realm of expertise.

He closed the book slowly, the revelation hitting him hard. She had to be every bit as scared as he was over the birth of their child. She had no more experience than he did. Just because she was a woman didn't mean that she understood any of this. She'd never had parents to give her a blueprint. Neither of them had the least idea of what they were doing, but at least Rose was trying. She was determined that their child would have the chance in life she never had—to grow up in a loving home.

Kane had grown up on the streets. He didn't know any more about parenting than Rose did, but he had a family. His team were all members of that family, GhostWalkers every one of them, intensely loyal to one another. They would extend that same loyalty to Rose and his child.

His child. He sank into a chair a bit overwhelmed by the idea. He'd searched for Rose for months because he was tied up in knots with wanting her, but he hadn't honestly thought too much about what it would mean if she was truly pregnant. *His* child. *Their* child together. They had created life. Both had DNA that wasn't altogether human, and both had psychic gifts. What would that mean for their child? Rose hadn't had the benefit of doctors for prenatal care. He rubbed his temples.

A child was a huge responsibility. Did he want that? Hell yes. The moment he fit his palm over Rose's belly, swollen with his child, the baby had rocked his world. That little flutter pressing hard against his hand to let him know there was life there, a life they'd created together, had found its way into his heart. He was solidly with Rose—Whitney was not getting their son.

He padded silently back into the bedroom, the birthing book in his hand. Rose looked at him, her expression drowsy—and sexy. He nearly groaned aloud. Was it perverted to find her incredibly sexy in her present physical condition? He should have brought the other book, the one about how her body changed during pregnancy. It had advice for husbands. He liked the way the word fit. Husband. Yeah. He could do that—with Rose.

"I just came in to say good night," he offered, keeping his tone low.

"I'm glad you did. I wanted to say I'm glad you're here. You can sleep here. It isn't as if we haven't shared a bed," she added. "There's plenty of room."

He wasn't getting in a bed with her. What was she thinking? His body was already doing enough raging at him. "I think it's best to keep a lookout." They wouldn't be coming until the following night, he was fairly certain, but he wasn't taking any chances. He wasn't going to sleep and leave her vulnerable. "I think I'll catch up on my reading."

She flashed a small smile. "Good choice there. But I really don't mind about the bed if you change your mind."

"Thanks. If I get too tired, I'll keep that in mind." He turned to leave.

"Don't go. Not until I fall asleep. I feel . . . safer with you in the room."

"The lamp won't bother you?"

She closed her eyes, settling against the pillow. Kane walked silently across the room and pulled the comforter closer to her chin, knowing he was using the gesture as an excuse to touch her again. Her skin was soft beyond his memories, and her hair against the pillow looked like a fall of blue black silk. Her lashes were long and feathery, as midnight black as her hair. He felt at peace when he looked at her, which, considering the state of arousal she put his body in, was strange. His whole being settled in her presence.

Asleep, she looked younger than ever and terribly innocent. She didn't belong in a world of violence. He'd told her to rest, that they would be safe, but he knew better. If Whitney was truly playing one of his games, it wasn't going to be so damned easy. He'd be sending someone to see if Rose had taken the bait and was in residence. That meant they were going to have a visitor soon. With a soft sigh, he ran his thumb down her soft cheek and then settled into a chair and began reading.

CHAPTER 5

"Think cold-blooded snake," Kane whispered aloud to himself as he stretched out in the saw grass up at the high point of the knoll, his ghillie suit covering his body. He could pick up the heat in an enemy's body, and there were many other GhostWalkers capable of the same thing. Rose had slept most of the day, waking only to eat soup or drink water. He loved that she was actually resting. She looked so worn out, and the fact that she could actually sleep meant she trusted him to look after her. That was the best feeling in the world. Lying in plain sight wasn't.

Diego Jimenez had chosen his hideout carefully. Open ground gave him a view of anyone coming at him from any direction. It would take vehicles capable of moving fast through sand to reach him, and he'd see and hear them coming miles before they ever arrived, but he hadn't counted on GhostWalkers. Kane had the elite teams to worry about.

Whitney may have gone underground, but he had billions of dollars at his disposal and connections all the way to the White House. Thousands of men in the military had taken the psychic tests, but only a few qualified psycholog- ically. Whitney had nevertheless experimented on some of those not completely qualified for his own personal army. Those men had disappeared from the service and were now working covertly for Whitney. Those were the men Kane expected.

He took another careful look around. Whitney would send a scout first, someone just to ascertain that Rose was in residence and very pregnant.

You in position, sweetheart? It went against everything male and protective in him to expose her to their enemy, but there was no way Whitney was going to try to kill her. By giving Whitney what he wanted—the satisfaction of being right—it would buy them some time. Rose needed time to rest and build her strength again.

I'm good. Sitting out under the stars, patting the baby, and reading on how to breast-feed.

His entire body clenched. His cock sprang to life right there on the sand, full and hard and aching with need. Erotic images poured into his head. She had full breasts, not too big, as her body frame was small, but they were beautiful. He'd been doing his best not to stare, and now she had to actually put more fantasies in his head. He didn't need her to add any to his long, considerable list.

If you need to practice, just let me know. He tried for humor, but he wasn't laughing. The vision of lying be- side her, turning toward her, and taking her breast into his mouth, pulling her close against him, was almost more than he could stand.

Well, it's not like I've ever done it before.

He groaned. His cock jerked, and blood pounded through his veins. What the hell did that mean? It sounded like she might need help, and if so, he was her man, quite willing to do whatever was necessary to get her ready for their child.

What does the book say? Even using telepathy, his voice sounded hoarse and strangled.

Well, I should have been reading this instead of the birthing book. I should have been preparing my nipples. Apparently I can get sore if I don't.

He took another long, careful look around, just lifting his head enough that his gaze could take in the terrain surrounding the house. *A man ought to take care of his woman,* he said, meaning it. She might not think of herself as belonging to him, but as far as he was concerned, she did. If she needed her breasts taken care of, he was the *only* man who would be doing that. *How's that done? Maybe I'd better be the one reading the book.*

Maybe . . .

That was worse, and he swore this time. She'd just drifted off. Was she reading? Speculating? Imagining? He broke out in a sweat. *What does the book say about pregnant women and sex?* He'd gone so far as to imply he wanted to spend time on her breasts; he may as well go all the way.

There was the smallest of hesitations, telling him she was a little nervous, but she answered in a steady, intellectual tone. *Actually quite a lot. Apparently, if there are no problems with the pregnancy, a woman can have sex without worry.*

He smiled, took a breath, and leaned so he could search the night sky. *That's a good thing to know.*

Well. She paused, taking a breath. *Since we're on the subject, do you think men find pregnant women attractive?*

This man does. At least, he qualified, because he'd never really thought about it before, *I find you attractive. I don't think I've ever really looked at a pregnant woman one way or the other until I saw you that way.*

Far off, he heard a muffled sound, like a distant beat of strong wings. *Incoming.*

Are you sure? You sound so calm. Maybe you're wrong.

I'm not wrong. Can you do this, Rose? He had to know if she was going to panic. *I can kill whoever they send, no problem.*

Of course I can do this. I'm pregnant, not brain-damaged. My condition doesn't change my personality.

Kane rubbed his chin. Being pregnant might not have changed her personality, but it certainly made her a bit testy. There was a definite bite to her voice. He found himself grinning like an idiot. She had a way of making him feel incredibly happy for no reason at all. In the end, it wasn't really Rose who was different, it was Kane. He admitted the truth to himself even as he watched the helicopter appear in the distance, no running lights, settling to the sand about a mile out. They weren't taking any chances that Rose would hear them. *He* was the one who didn't want Rose sitting out in front of the house as bait. He detested that she wasn't safely out of Whitney's reach.

It feels a little like I'm using you to lure them in.

Warmth flooded his mind. Reassurance. *They don't want me dead. Whitney wants our baby. They might try to take me now, but I'm armed and I've got you—my secret weapon.*

The confidence in her voice shook him to the core. She was sitting calmly out in the open, waiting for the enemy to make a move, relying on him to keep her and their child safe. Rose might appear small and fragile, but she was first and foremost a soldier, trained almost from birth. Whitney and his team of killers might have done better to remember that. Whitney didn't have much respect for the women he'd designed and trained over the years, focusing on their weaknesses and flaws rather than seeing them as human and three-dimensional. It was Whitney's flaw, that megalomaniac ego that pushed reality into the background.

Kane's fingers tightened around the rifle. He was actually guilty of the same thing. He persisted in seeing Rose as someone in need of protection. *I'm sorry. I don't mean to underestimate you, Rose. I have great respect for your abilities.* He felt it needed to be said. He was ashamed of his need to protect her, but it wasn't going away. If anything, the need was growing stronger.

Don't apologize, Kane. You've treated me with more respect and better than any other man in my life. Believe me, I appreciate you.

Kane kept his gaze on the desert. *Four men running this way. They're spread out, standard pattern. All armed, but only two are carrying extra gear.*

Do you think those two are going to hang around?

He caught the apprehension in her voice. *You know they will. They're going to wait it out and report to Whitney when you have the baby. I can take them out, and we can get the hell out of here if you're up to it.*

Her hesitation alarmed him. *I don't think it's a good idea right now, Kane. I'm getting the contractions again. They aren't as regular as the ones the other day, but they're harder and lasting longer.*

She was definitely frightened. The word contractions scared the holy hell out of him. He took a breath and fit the rifle to his shoulder, tracking each of the men through his scope. He had taken the rifle from Jimenez's private arsenal, recognizing his favorite sniper rifle. It felt like an old friend. He'd cleaned it, taken it apart and put it back together, test-fired it several times, and repeated the entire operation until the rifle felt like his own.

Once he'd seen the Humvee and the CROWS system, he knew he had to tell her the truth. No way could Jimenez have acquired that system without serious backing—and he feared he knew exactly who that man had been.

Rose, Jimenez left a hell of an arsenal behind. All military issue, all the very latest technology, which meant he was in bed with Whitney.

That doesn't make sense. For all his failings, Whitney is a patriot. He wouldn't put weapons into the hands of a rebel.

Kane could see the enemy now, see their grim, dark-striped faces clearly. Dressed in desert camouflage clothing, they ran at a steady pace, covering the mile quickly.

They're spreading out. Look unaware and sweet and innocent.

It's a little hard to look innocent when I'm as big as a house.

He suppressed his unexpected laughter. She wasn't as big as a house, not by a long shot. *Hell, Rose, from the back I couldn't even tell you were pregnant. Only your tummy is round.* He congratulated himself for being wise not to use the beach ball reference. *You might not think you're innocent, sweetheart, but pregnant or not, you're very innocent.*

What does that mean?

It means, he said, *once you have that baby, I've got a whole hell of a lot to teach you.* Before she could reply and tell him to go to hell, that she didn't plan on sticking around, he gave another report. *Flanking you now. One coming around on your left side.*

I can't see him yet.

The knots in his gut unraveled a bit at the calm in her voice. He admired her, plain and simple. He was lying prone, rifle in hand, watching the enemy. She was a sitting duck. He watched each man reach a position where he was able to see the one side of the house.

Checking you out now, sweetheart. They've gone to ground. Keep reading the book. What else does it say?

Oh dear. This isn't good. You know the part where women can have sex as long as there aren't any complications? Not so much in the last month. Sex can bring on labor. My dreams are shattered.

He loved the laughter in her voice. Her teasing tone told him she was lying her ass off, but he liked that she was comfortable enough to tease him about sex. He was tied to her for life and would never find a woman with quite the same appeal, but she had no ties to him other than the baby—certainly not sex. He wiped his chin on his sleeve and kept his eye to the scope.

Your dreams? he echoed. *I'm suffering here, woman.* He

shifted just enough to ease his body into a more comfortable position in the sand. Teasing back and forth about sex was dangerous when they had enemies coming at them, but he understood it was simply another form of comic banter soldiers often used to relieve the tension. *Now you go and tell me something like that.* He had no problems with camaraderie. He could do camaraderie standing on his head—but not when she was putting images of his body locked with hers in his head.

Sorry, I couldn't resist. The book actually does say that.

She hesitated, and his body reacted, tightening in anticipation. She seemed suddenly uncertain about sharing some piece of information. For a woman forthcoming about things, that didn't bode well. *Tell me.*

She sighed. *I think the baby dropped.*

His heart thudded. He blinked, and the man he'd been watching was gone that quick out of his line of sight. Kane marked where their enemy had gone to ground, but that didn't mean the bastard wasn't on the move. *The baby dropped?* he repeated, feeling like he'd been hit over the head with something really hard. *What the hell does that mean?*

When I took my shower this evening, the pressure was off my ribs. I think the baby moved down into the birthing position.

I haven't read the book, Rose. He searched every inch of the sandbank where the enemy had disappeared, trying not to panic—not because he'd lost sight of the enemy, but because he had a very bad feeling about babies dropping and what that meant.

She hesitated again, and that small hesitation continued to freak him out. He studied the sandbank. Had blades of saw grass moved? There was no wind. Not even a breeze. The night air had cooled, but it was still warm. Stars were everywhere, glittering like diamonds scattered across the sky. It was a beautiful night. He always marveled how something so ugly as murder could take place in such peaceful settings. The night was made for a man and woman to sit quietly and enjoy the constellations and each other.

"I see you," he whispered under his breath. The saw grass bent toward the house, and he caught a glimpse of the outline of the enemy's shoulder. *On your left, Rose. He's moving toward you. Don't look. If he gets too close, he's a dead man.*

He checked the other three before putting the rifle back on the one closest to Rose. The others were holding position.

Don't shoot him. Rose's voice was tight, even shook a little. *They need proof. Whitney wants documentation of everything. They're probably trying to get a clear picture of me. He has to maneuver into position.*

That little wobble in her voice had him stroking the trigger. Ice flowed in his veins normally when he was waiting for a kill shot, but tonight, with Rose sitting out in the open surrounded by the enemy, his mind was a little difficult to discipline.

This is fucking bullshit, Rose. I'm going to kill them all and we'll get the hell out of here. We have the Humvee.

Kane. The soft note in her voice turned his heart over. *I love that you want to protect me, but I'm telling you, I can't travel. I can't do it. If I could, I'd say let's go for it, but it's too soon for the baby to be born, and I think my body is so worn down it just can't hold her anymore.*

Kane wiped the sweat from his face with one hand, watching the enemy closest to Rose. The man was still easing himself forward. Now he was within fifty feet of her.

Kane knew Whitney had "paired" him; hell, he'd even agreed to it, though he hadn't known exactly what it meant at the time. As far as he understood it, it had something to do with pheromones. Didn't that just mean he would forever remain sexually attracted to her? If so, if that was all, what the hell was wrong with him that every cell in his body demanded he get Rose out of the situation?

Now that he'd found her again, his child growing inside her, now that he'd watched her sleep and listened to her soft laughter, admired her courage and respected her fighting capabilities, he feared pairing was far more than sexual. Whether Whitney's program had done that or whether he was just falling like a ton of bricks for the woman, he didn't know, but it was messing him up having her in danger.

What's he doing?

She sounded nervous, yet she tried to cover it. His heart twisted. He wanted to gather her into his arms and hold her. *I hate to admit it, but you were right. And just for the record, that might be the only time I ever say those words to you, so treasure them.* He figured if he teased her a little to lighten the tension, it would help both of them. *He's recording you sitting there looking all content and smug outside your hideaway. Whitney will love that.*

I try to please.

His stomach settled. Her tone was stronger. Something was wrong, though, and he wanted these men gone. *You all right?*

She hesitated, and the knots were back just like that.

Rose? he prompted.

The contractions are pretty hard, Kane.

Kane rubbed his jaw. Once again he'd underestimated. She hadn't been afraid of Whitney's men. She'd probably been sitting there, armed to the teeth, waiting for them to make a wrong move. She was worried the baby was coming too early.

As soon as you can get inside without looking as if there's a problem, go in. Hopefully they'll leave faster. Two of them plan on staying behind, but they can't risk you seeing them, so they'll have to set up camp a distance from here.

How long will you be, Kane?

There was a distinct quaver in her voice. He swore under his breath, the urge to just shoot the bastards and get to her nearly overwhelming common sense. *I won't be long, sweetheart.*

He hoped he was telling the truth. He knew that two of Whitney's men would return to the helicopter, probably as soon as Rose went inside, now that they had their visual confirmation for their boss. The other two might set up camp immediately, believing she was alone, or one might remain watching. If that happened, Kane was going to have to reenter the house using the tunnel, and that meant a long hike through the sand without being seen. Visibility on such a clear night was virtually miles. He'd be crawling, and Rose would be waiting, maybe going into labor.

I should have just shot the bastards. It would have been easier, Rose.

She laughed at the frustration in his voice. *I'm going in while I can. I'll be fine. If the contractions are real, they'll grow stronger still and get longer in length.*

Through his scope he watched her pick up the folding chair and carry it back inside. No light escaped from the house. Once she was inside and the small light she'd used for reading disappeared, so did the house. Kane remained absolutely still. The men were in motion, one moving right up to Jimenez's subterranean hideaway. He examined the sand all around the house. Kane was grateful that he'd always covered his tracks when patrolling outside and familiarizing himself with the terrain.

The one close to the house joined a second man. They conferred, waved at the remaining two, who took off running for the waiting helicopter. Kane turned his full attention to the two left behind. They were up and jogging straight toward him.

"I don't know why he just won't let us grab her," one grumbled. "You know this is a bullshit assignment, Fargo. He was pissed at us because we didn't get the job done. I'd like to get my hands on the little bitch and teach her a lesson. Whitney's been on my case since she rejected me.

And he's been on yours ever since your little bitch tried to disembowel you." The man snickered and then spit.

The spit landed four feet from where Kane lay in the saw grass. He remembered the speaker. Carlson James. Kane had looked up his service record the moment he'd gotten out of Whitney's compound. James was a troublemaker in every unit he was put in. He'd been reported killed in Afghanistan two years earlier, but not before an arrest warrant had been issued for the suspected rape of a female officer. Kane knew exactly why Whitney had chosen the man for his private army. He needed someone ruthless, without morals, who would have no qualms forcing a woman to have sex with him. Carlson James fit that bill.

Why had Whitney chanced sending him? Not only had Carlson's ego been seriously bruised by Rose's rejection, but he was paired with her too. Kane heard the rage smoldering in the man's belly when he spoke of Rose. He had to be eaten alive knowing another man had touched her—that she was carrying another man's baby. Kane didn't trust him at all. Carlson was the type of man who would turn on Whitney if the right circumstances presented themselves. It was a stupid move on Whitney's part.

"We'll have to set up camp a couple of miles from here," Fargo said. "This is one shit assignment. At least my bitch isn't knocked up by some other man." He laughed as he brushed past Carlson.

Kane held his breath as Carlson snarled, exposing his teeth, one hand going to the knife at his belt. Tension stretched out. Fargo glanced over his shoulder and abruptly came to a halt. His eyes glittered, a dangerous excitement. Both men were jacked up on something, and Kane feared it wasn't a drug. Whitney wanted his soldiers aggressive. Both of the men wore aggression close to the surface. They looked like two bulls squaring off.

Fargo shook his head. "We've got a job to do, Carlson. If we don't get it done, Whitney will send his hit squad. He warned you not to touch her."

Carlson's hand dropped from his knife, but Kane didn't get the feeling he was appeased. The man shrugged. "Yeah. I heard him."

"It's my job to see you don't go near her."

Carlson's smirk was a parody of humor. "We'll see how good you are at your job."

"Don't you worry about me. You want to take first watch?"

"She's as big as a cow," Carlson snapped. "Where the hell is she going? I'm heading for bed. I've already got sand in my mouth. I hate this place."

The two set off, griping and complaining, moving toward the south. Kane watched them plow over the rolling sand dunes. He was not going to let Rose outside again if there was any way to prevent it. Seeing her pregnant would only provoke Carlson further. What game was Whitney really playing? Something was off about the entire setup.

Swearing, he rolled over, keeping his weapon clear, staying very close to the ground so if either man looked back they wouldn't be able to see him. He slithered down the slope leading to the house on his belly, much like a lizard.

I'm coming in, Rose. If the lights are on, turn them off.

They aren't on.

There was something not quite right about her voice. He took another careful look around, ensuring the enemy was still heading away from the hideaway before he lifted his hand, moving the air in the gentlest of breezes, pushing the sand over his tracks, paying particular attention to the saw grass where he'd lain hidden. When he was satisfied the ground could stand a close examination, Kane opened the door and went in. He made certain to drop the heavy metal bar across the door, sealing them in and making certain no one could sneak in that way. Tomorrow night he would set a few traps around the house, several feet out in a circle, which would warn him if anyone—like Carlson—got too close. He slipped inside the house and let out his breath, aware of the tension coiled inside him.

He felt a little like a rat caught in a trap. He preferred open places where he could maneuver. He would be more help to Rose outside, where he could pick off the enemy easily, than here inside. Something clicked in his brain. Diego Jimenez would have felt the same way. How did he manage to relax here, knowing he was hunted? Had he relied solely on the fact that his hideout couldn't be seen easily? Kane couldn't believe Jimenez would think that way.

There had to be a warning system. He and Rose had missed it. The system couldn't consist of motion lights; Jimenez wouldn't want anyone who hadn't actually spotted the house to be alerted by a light coming on, nor would that help during daylight hours. Kane moved through the dark house to the bedroom, turning the puzzle over and over in his mind. He stopped abruptly in the doorway, staring at the empty bed. His heart stopped beating—at least it felt that way. The jolt was sickening.

He spun around, eyes wild, feeling frantic. Had he missed something? He drew his weapon and stepped close to the tunnel entrance, looking for signs that someone had used it to come into the house.

Rose! She hadn't contacted him telepathically. If she was in trouble, surely she would have. *Rose, answer me, damn it.* He bit out each word, authoritative. Commanding. The edge of ruthlessness more apparent than he would have liked, but he was trying not to panic.

"In here. I need your help."

His heart began beating again, but the taste of fear remained in his mouth. He found her in the kitchen, waving at him from a nearly invisible ledge built along the windows. A single hard-backed chair was set just under the ledge. She'd obviously climbed onto the chair and inserted herself, baby and all, onto the ledge.

"What the hell are you doing?" he demanded.

She handed him a rifle. "My job." She reached for him, wincing as her belly slid along the ledge.

He took her into his arms, carried her through the house to the bedroom and, resisting the impulse to drop her, sat her gently on the bed. "Your job is to keep from having the baby early, Rose, not play soldier."

Her eyes darkened from rich chocolate to nearly black. "I do not *play* at being a soldier. I *am* a soldier. We're a team, and I do my part, which is to watch your back."

Fury burned in her eyes. He'd touched a sore subject, no doubt about it, but he wasn't going to back down. She was pale. Little beads of sweat dotted her forehead. He could tell by the way she involuntarily rocked that she was in pain. He glared at her. "You were supposed to rest, not put yourself in danger looking out for me."

"Diego made this house defensible. I knew that meant he would have places he could see out but no one could see in. Or he could shoot from, if needed. It didn't take that long to discover he built a shelf in every room along the windows so he could see anything coming at him or shoot anything endangering him. I just climbed up there and watched your back, just like you would have done for me."

There was no apology in her voice, and he knew he wasn't going to get one, no matter that *he* was right. She'd climbed up on a chair to reach the nearly hidden shelf where she had to lie on her stomach, rifle in hand, tracking the enemy. He wasn't a man known for his temper, but she was skating the edge of it more often than anyone he'd known.

"So you stood on a chair and pulled yourself up there." He couldn't look at her without wanting to shake her—or kiss her—so it was just easier to be angry.

"That's exactly what I did." There was defiance in her voice, and that told him she hadn't thought it was such a hot idea either. "Kane." Her voice softened. Dripped over him like warm honey. "Don't be upset with me. I don't want you upset with me."

He made the mistake of turning his head. She sat on the edge of the bed, rocking back and forth, her hands cradling their baby, looking so far from a soldier his treacherous heart turned over. She looked vulnerable and beautiful and *his*. He'd never experienced the sensations taking place in his body—or his head. She'd slipped inside him and had coiled tightly around his heart. That mixture of fragile porcelain doll and fierce fighting soldier was a potent combination, keeping him off balance.

Her eyes, those melting chocolate almonds, blinked back at him all too innocently. She looked close to tears. He shook his head, ran both hands through his hair until it was completely disheveled. "I'm not upset. Well, a little. I don't want you climbing on chairs in your condition. It's not that I don't think you're capable, Rose; I do. It's just that a man feels the need to protect his woman—and his child. The thought of you falling or hurting yourself or the baby is . . ." He searched for a word that was appropriate to say around a woman. "Distressing."

She nodded. "I'll be more careful. Really." Blink. Blink.

He was falling hard. One more little bat of her eyelashes and he was going to be on his knees. This wasn't going the way he wanted it to go. He was totally wrapped around her little finger with just one little blink of her long lashes. For God's sake, he was a tough guy, wasn't he? Why the hell was he turning into jelly just looking at her?

"You'd better be," he said, his voice gruff. "Have the—um—pains eased up?"

She shook her head. There was fear in her eyes.

He stepped closer to her. Her scent surrounded him, making it more difficult to think straight. He put his palm on her belly, spreading his fingers to take in as much territory as possible, willing the baby to stay put. "How early?"

"Too early. Nearly five weeks, Kane." Her voice shook.

Keeping one hand on the baby, he curled the fingers of his other hand around the nape of her neck in a slow massage. "We'll get through this."

"We have to stay," she said. "You know I can't leave like this."

"You just need to rest," Kane replied soothingly, hoping it was true. He had a bad feeling, and he manfully didn't point out that climbing on a chair and lying on her stomach might not have been the best way to stop labor.

"Kane." She looked up at him, her eyes going wide. "Why didn't they know you were close by?"

"What are you talking about?"

"Whitney's men. They didn't know you were here," Rose said.

"That was the point."

She shook her head. "I always know when GhostWalkers are close. I'll bet you do as well. They walked right by you, and they didn't have a clue."

"You're a GhostWalker. They probably thought they were feeling you."

She shook her head. "Not after I went into the house. You were only a few feet from them, Kane. They should have felt the surge of energy around you, but they didn't."

"Or they didn't notice because they weren't paying attention." But he didn't think that likely. Two men left out in the desert alone? They'd been on alert. They may have dropped their guard a little when Rose went into the house, feeling as though she was trapped there and they had the upper hand. But she was right—Whitney's two men should have felt the buildup of energy emanating around them.

"These men," Rose said, nuzzling his hand with her cheek, "they flunked the psychological evaluation but not the psychic testing, right?"

Kane was certain she didn't realize she was rubbing her cheek against him much like a cat. He laid his hand against her face, loving the feel of intimate contact with her. "Not only did they bomb on the psych eval, but their psychic abilities were extremely low."

Her eyebrow shot up. "How did you know that?"

He grinned at her. "We have this really savvy techie who

can hack just about anything. She hooked up with another woman who escaped Whitney, and between the two of them, they manage to snoop into almost anything Whitney has documented."

Her hands covered his over the baby. "Who? What are their names?"

She looked so eager for news, he was sorry he knew he would be disappointing her. "Jaimie is married to Mack, the leader of our unit. I should have shot them both for eloping like that too. She's been with us since she was a little kid. We all grew up together on the streets of Chicago. Jaimie's psychic, and she was enhanced by Whitney, but he never was around her when she was a child."

"And the other woman?"

He could tell she was holding her breath. "Whitney bought her from an orphanage somewhere in Europe. They call her Flame. She's married to a Cajun GhostWalker we all call Gator. Flame wasn't raised in the compound with you, sweetheart. She escaped from a different facility."

Tears filled Rose's eyes and she blinked them away, turning her head, allowing the silky cap of hair to fall around her face. "How many women did he do this to?" Her voice was very low, and it trembled.

He sank down onto the bed beside her and pulled her into his arms. It was awkward trying to hug her, so he simply lifted her onto his lap. Modesty be damned. If she gave him a hard-on all the time and he had to walk around with the damned thing, she could just deal with it.

Holding her against his chest, he rocked her gently. "Jaimie and Flame have been monitoring Whitney's computer as often as they dare. There's been no mention that any of the women who escaped with you have been recaptured. I think he concentrated mainly on you because he suspected you were pregnant. Mari found her sister, Briony. They're both married to GhostWalkers, who just happen to be twin brothers as well. I believe Mari's sister just had twins."

He nuzzled the top of her head with his chin. "When

we're out of this, I'll take you to see her. They're very well protected where they are."

"But they still have to live in a virtual prison to stay that way, don't they?" Rose said. She burrowed closer to him, as if trying to hide from the truth of their lives.

"He made certain it would never be easy to live on the outside for any of you," Kane replied, choosing his words carefully. What she'd said was the truth. The women—and any children they had—would always have to look over their shoulders. There was no entirely safe place, but there was safety in numbers and preparation. "We're banding together, Rose, the four teams, finding places we can protect so our women and children can lead as normal a life as possible."

"We don't even know what normal is," she pointed out, closing her eyes as another wave rolled over her body, tightening her belly and pressing down hard on the baby. She took long, slow breaths like the books told her, trying to get on top of the contraction.

Kane tried not to swear. He held her, automatically breathing with her. He felt the way her belly was gripped with a tight band. There was no ordering her to stop. No logic was going to dictate when the baby was coming. He tried to push down his own mounting fear. There was no doctor and no way to get her to a doctor. He'd thrown their link to his team down into the ravine. He couldn't leave her to go try to find it, which would be like looking for a needle in a haystack. But they would come. His team would come for them. He had absolute faith in them.

When the contraction had let up, he set her on her feet. "Let's get you back in bed."

"Would you get me a glass of water?"

He didn't know if she was getting rid of him so she could cry while she undressed, or if she really wanted the water, but he obediently went into the kitchen to get her a drink. He leaned for a moment against the sink, head down, breathing deeply, trying to steel himself for the possibility of delivering a baby. He'd never really considered that he might have no choice.

Not one for inactivity, he went through to the pantry, grateful she had stored books on actual delivery. He thumbed through a book to see what to do with a baby once it was born. The more he read, the more alarmed he became. He had no business trying to deliver his own baby. His blood roared in his ears, his heart hammered hard. If he could have, he would have just hyperventilated and gotten it over with, but his body refused to panic. His lungs kept breathing and his head kept assessing the information, even when his mind screamed at him that he was insane to try something like delivering a baby.

"Kane, where are you?"

It was a good thing he wasn't panicking, because she sounded like she was. "I'll be right there," he called.

"Well, you might want to hurry. My water just broke."

CHAPTER 6

Kane took a deep breath and went into the room. Rose was dressed in a long shirt she'd found in the closet and was trying to clean up the floor. He could hear her softly weeping, and it nearly broke his heart. "Rose. Come here, sweetheart. This isn't the end of the world. The baby's going to be fine." He injected as much firm belief as possible into his tone as he reached down to lift her to her feet.

Rose leaned into him, trembling, her arms sliding around his waist. "I'm so scared, Kane."

"I know. But we're in this together, and we make a great team. You were smart and provided all the right books for us. You've read them and I've skimmed them. Shouldn't you be in bed?"

Still clinging to him, she lifted her head and met his eyes, a small, wan smile on her face. "According to the books, once my water breaks, I have to deliver, and it should speed up the procedure. Staying on my feet as long as possible should help cut down the time. I don't want to be doing this one moment longer than I have to."

"I'll get the floor and then while you're resting in between—um—you know—I'll make something to keep the baby warm once he's born."

Rose didn't let go of his solid strength. There was something about Kane, something steady and absolute and calming. He wouldn't desert her. Her mouth was dry, her heart pounding, and she'd never been so scared in her life, but she wasn't alone.

At first, she had to admit, she had idiot girl feelings, not wanting to look like an elephant in front of him and certainly not wanting him to see her in such a vulnerable *messy* situation. Okay, maybe she still did have a little of that vanity, but it was only a tiny impractical part of her; the rest of her was so happy he was with her she wanted to weep forever. "I don't want the baby to die, Kane," she admitted in a low voice. "Do you think I aggravated the situation by climbing on the chair?"

His fingers were soothing on the nape of her neck. It seemed every time he touched her, he brought her calm. She could fall in love with him for that alone.

"Of course not. I think you've been having the real thing all along, and we're just getting to the good part. We'll do this, Rose. You have to believe that."

She looked up at him. Looked into his eyes, searching for—yes—there it was. This man would stand with her no matter how bad it got. She let out her breath, relaxing just a little. "I believe in you, Kane."

"All right, let's get this room prepared. We'll need towels and water and especially something to keep the baby warm. Are you always so organized?" He took the old T-shirt she was using to clean the floor and crouched low to finish the job, sending her a little grin over his shoulder.

That grin made her stomach flutter. A slow, answering smile touched her mouth. "I really am glad you're with me," she said and had to turn away from those beautiful eyes. He was far too good-looking to ever really look at a woman like her—if the doctor hadn't paired them.

He wrapped a hand around her bare calf, preventing her from moving away. He rubbed gently over her calf, down to the elegant rose tattoo circling her ankle and back up her calf. "What is it, Rose? Why look so sad? We're about to have a baby."

She closed her eyes briefly, savoring his words, the sound of his voice. What man would react like that? She'd trapped him, taken his honor, and yet he still treated her as if she mattered, as if she was someone special to him when he should despise her. She opened her mouth to tell him, but a swelling pain went from front to back, increasing in strength, holding her in its grip. She dropped one hand to his shoulder to steady herself and breathed through it, trying to imagine surfing a large wave.

Kane's hand on her calf anchored her and kept her centered as she did her slow, even breathing. When the contraction eased, she took a deep breath and let it out and looked down at the man she was counting on to see her through this. He looked calm and steady. Her stomach settled and her heart took up a rhythmic beat.

Kane stood up, leaned down to brush a kiss on top of her head, and went out to collect the things they would need. How the hell had this happened? Rose should be safe in a hospital. He was no medic. He could sew up his own battle wounds, but this? He shook his head. This was one of those do-or-die situations, and he had no real choice. The baby was coming, and it was up to him to see Rose through it.

When she looked at him with her amazing dark eyes and told him she believed in him, he was a total goner. If he hadn't been wrapped around her little finger before, he certainly was now. He had to make this happen, and make it as non-traumatic as possible—for both of them. He prepared the room as quickly as possible, bringing in the birthing kit with sanitized instruments as well as towels and blankets. He boiled water to sterilize it just to be safe, and then set about making a small incubator.

Rose had two more strong contractions while he was

constructing the small, crude incubator, really just a box with a blanket protecting the sides and bottom, and a soft light to keep the temperature constant. Rose walked around the house with him for most of the night, stopping to breathe when the contractions came. They came more frequently and were of longer duration. Kane began to really pay attention to how long each lasted. At first he didn't say much, just wrapped his fingers around her calf and breathed with her, but she was tiring, and the contractions reached a point where she could no longer stand. At times he traced the rose petals on her ankle, until he was familiar with each one of them.

He helped her onto the bed, where they'd laid one of the two plastic-backed sheets from the birthing kit, and arranged her in a semi-sitting position, trying to mimic the drawings in the book. Her breathing changed significantly, and after two contractions nearly on top of each other, obviously very strong, she looked up at him with wide, frightened eyes.

"I don't know if I can do this anymore, Kane."

He knew she was ashamed of the admission. Rose had remained stoic, which he was grateful for, but now she was on the edge of panic.

Kane pushed aside his own attack of nerves and brushed the damp hair from her face. "Remember what the book said, sweetheart. You must be in transition. This is the most difficult phase, but it won't last long. You have to change your breathing to stay on top of the—er . . ."

"*Contractions*," she snapped. "Say it. *Contractions*. It isn't a dirty word."

Definitely transition. The book mentioned a woman in that particular stage might consider doing harm to her man. He should have searched the bed for weapons. He nodded his head and forced the word out. "Contractions. Of course. My mind went blank there for a moment."

"I'm sorry." She let her breath out; her eyes went wide, her gaze clinging to his.

He took the initiative this time, breathing in short "push out" breaths. She matched his breathing, never once looking away from him. The moment the contraction was over, he wiped her face with a cool cloth. "You're doing great, Rose. You're very close now." He hoped he wasn't full of bullshit and that his guesswork was right. He sent up a silent prayer, not that he was a praying man all that often, but certainly enough that it should count for something.

She never once screamed or cursed at him. She breathed with him, staring straight into his eyes until sometimes he thought he might be drowning in the intimacy of the moment. He hadn't realized just how intimate something other than sex with a woman could truly be, but he actually felt closer to her than ever before. He couldn't ever imagine forgetting these shared moments and knew, no matter the outcome, he would always treasure the way they shared faith in each other. He had thought it would be a terrible ordeal, but as bad as it was, there was something raw and beautiful about it.

She closed her eyes and lay back, looking as if she'd fallen asleep. Dawn was creeping into the room, and faint streaks of light illuminated her face. She looked exhausted but peaceful. He frowned and reached to feel her pulse. She was actually asleep. What the hell had happened to the contractions? He scrubbed his hand over his face, trying to clear the cobwebs. He felt drained himself. If he was tired, she had to be ten times more so, but to go to sleep?

He massaged the back of his neck, trying to think. Where the hell had he tossed the book? In the long hours of labor, he couldn't remember where he'd put it. *Be logical, Kane,* he admonished himself. Transition, the book had said, and then what? Pushing came next. They were close. He took another deep breath and washed his hands one more time before pulling on sterile gloves. He very carefully laid out the various items from the kit, hoping when the time came, he'd know what to do.

As far as he was concerned, all that mattered was that

Rose and the baby came through it alive. Damn Whitney and his games. Rose had been frightened to trust his team, and now she was stuck in a hideout, enemies watching them, and about to deliver their child. Her eyes flew open and she gasped.

"Help me to the bathroom, Kane."

He almost did, but then he remembered what he'd read about pushing. "That's the baby, Rose," he said matter-of-factly. He flashed an encouraging smile. "We're about to meet our child. You just have to help him a little more, and then he'll be in your arms."

"There's so much pressure."

"He wants out," Kane said, keeping his voice very calm. Inside he felt every muscle tighten up, but he refused to panic. Rose needed him, and if he never had the chance to do another thing for her, he would do this.

He pulled the two chairs he had brought into the room for her to set her feet on. He wanted as much gravity as possible to help. "I know it's uncomfortable to move, sweetheart, but this will help deliver him faster and make it easier for you to push."

She clutched at his sleeve as he moved her into position, her eyes frightened. "I can feel her coming." Her terrified eyes met his. "Kane."

Just his name. That whisper. Her voice said it all. Complete trust, and how the hell had he earned that from her? Fear. Overwhelming when she'd faced down a monster like Whitney and another like Carlson.

Kane didn't know how either of them got through the next twenty minutes. He would tell her to push, and she would bear down and try to direct her breathing down as the books had told her, but he was a little worried with the amount of blood and fluids. He should have expected it, but it was still frightening to know there was no doctor available if something went wrong.

His heart began to pound in awe as the baby's head appeared, a thick thatch of blue black hair like his mother's.

"I see him, Rose. He's covered in hair." The head disappeared again, and he waited while Rose panted. One quick flick of his eyes and he could tell she was exhausted, but he knew her now, knew she wouldn't stop until their child was safe.

He felt pride in her, enormous respect, but most of all, a growing love he couldn't stop. It didn't matter that she didn't feel the same way about him; this experience together changed his life forever.

"She's coming," Rose said.

"You can do this, sweetheart. Let's get him out."

He felt a little like a catcher at a ball game, reaching to help ease the small head out of the tight opening. "Wait, honey. Let me clean his mouth and nose."

She panted, straining silently until he nodded, and with one more push, the baby slipped into his waiting hands. His heart stood still. Tears burned in his eyes and throat. "We have a son, Rose." Damn, he was small. He practically fit in his hand, but he had all the right parts, and if his lungs were anything to go by, he was healthy. His little fingers curled into fists and he scrunched up his face at the indignity of being brought out into the cool air.

"Is she okay?" Rose asked, her voice portraying her anxiety.

"Look, honey," Kane held the baby up for her to see. "I was right all along. We've got a son." He placed the baby gently on her stomach. "Do you have him?" He hated to let go, but he had to deal with the cord and placenta.

Rose's hands settled around the baby as Kane clamped off the cord and then, taking a quick breath and sending up a silent prayer, cut the lifeline between mother and child. He waited for the next contraction to help Rose push the placenta out. She was bleeding quite a bit, enough to worry him. He didn't know what was normal and what wasn't. She hadn't torn. The baby was small.

He cleaned the baby as best he could and wrapped him tightly in a warm blanket. Rose had brought baby clothes, diapers, and blankets. Once again, he couldn't help but be thankful for the way she had prepared for the birth. Rose was obviously exhausted, but she took the baby readily and held him while he washed her carefully, trying to be as sterile as possible, and replaced the plastic-backed sheet with a clean one. He added one of the large pads that had come with the birthing kit, before pulling up the covers over her shivering body.

"He's so little, Kane." Rose sounded awed.

"Are you crying?" He felt a little like crying himself every time he looked at the two of them. His Rose. His child. The baby looked so right in her arms.

Rose reached out and tracked down his face with gentle fingers, a small, enigmatic smile on her soft mouth. Her fingertips traced the path of tears he hadn't even realized were on his face. He was completely overwhelmed with the sheer wonderment of the moment. Creating an actual life from their bodies seemed too big a miracle to him, now that he actually saw the evidence of their union.

Rose smiled at him, brushing away her own tears. "I'm very happy," she murmured. "I was worried. He's early, and yet he looks so amazing and perfect."

"I've been thinking about that, Rose. I think the only thing we can do right now is to keep him as warm as possible and feed him as often as he'll eat. Is he trying to eat yet?"

"I'm not very good at this," she admitted. "And I don't think he's getting much."

Kane moved around the bed to help her. He took the baby, cradling him protectively, while she tried to get herself into a more comfortable position. The baby felt featherlight to him. He looked down into the little scrunched-up face, and his heart expanded, his breath exploding out of lungs. His son. He'd never thought to hold his child in his arms.

"You're a little miracle," he whispered to the boy. "Look at this, Rose. He has fingernails. They're so tiny you can barely notice them." He inserted one finger into the tiny fist in order to inspect the little hands more closely.

He looked down at Rose, and their eyes met. Time seemed to stand still as they smiled at each other. He felt a little lost in happiness. It wasn't a natural state of mind for him. He'd never thought much about being happy. He just was. He had a family, made on the streets of Chicago, but nevertheless a solid family. He loved each of his brothers and sisters and was fiercely loyal to them as they were to him, but this . . . Rose. The baby. Something like this could bring a man to his knees. He didn't want to lose her once they were back in the real world, but he had no idea how to make her stay with him. His own parents hadn't wanted him.

"He's beautiful, isn't he?" Rose asked, her voice almost shy.

"Because he looks like you," Kane agreed. "Are you strong enough to try to feed him?"

"The book said I should try right away."

She didn't sound too sure. Kane handed her the baby and reached behind her to adjust the pillows for her. He should have been a gentleman and given her a little space, but he couldn't tear his eyes from the sight of her. Was there anything more beautiful? He doubted it. She cradled the baby to her, looking down at him with such love in her expression, Kane felt the welling of intense emotion all over again.

She swallowed hard and looked at him. "I want you to know, Kane, I wanted him. Never once, not one single time, did I ever contemplate an abortion. When I suspected I was pregnant, I was apprehensive because I was afraid for him, but not because I didn't want him."

He stroked tendrils of her hair away from her damp face. "I wanted him too, Rose. I will admit I didn't like the way he was conceived, but I wanted you to have my baby. I know you think my attraction to you is all about Whitney pairing us together, but he can't make me feel admiration and respect for you. He can't control my other emotions through physical chemistry."

"Thank you for that, Kane." She nuzzled the baby's mouth with her nipple.

They both held their breath while he rooted around unsuccessfully for a few minutes. Rose was patient, but he could see she was afraid he wasn't going to take the offering. Without warning he latched on, and both of them let out a loud sigh of relief and then looked at each other and laughed softly.

"I have no idea how to be a mother, but I'm going to try, Kane," she promised him.

"I have no doubts you'll make a great mother, honey," he said sincerely. "I wasn't exactly raised with parents, but I had a few pointers from a couple of people. Between the two of us, we'll figure it out." Everything inside him went still, waiting for her reaction to his declaration.

Rose looked up at him, searching his face. "I don't want you to stay with us because you think you're supposed to, Kane. I might not look it, but I'm tough. And I'm capable of protecting him from Whitney once we get out of here."

"I think you should know, Rose, for future reference, I rarely do anything because I'm supposed to do it. But I don't want you to answer under false pretenses. I'm a soldier. Those in my GhostWalker unit are men and women I grew up with. We're family and we trust one another. I know they're coming for us. If you stand with me, they stand with you. They'll protect you and our son just as I will."

Her gaze shifted from his. "You worked for Whitney."

"I was *assigned* to Whitney before anyone knew about the breeding program. He was already in trouble, hiding out, although he could use any military base in the world, and he was still considered to be of immense value. After the testimony of several of us, an investigation into his activities was launched. They can't ignore what's happening, and it's driven him farther underground. Don't get me wrong, he still has powerful supporters who believe in his work."

Rose kept her eyes on the baby, her expression blank. Kane wanted to make certain she knew what she was getting into either way. He'd forced her once to do something no woman should have to do with a stranger, and he damn well was going to give her every choice he could. He wanted to make certain he disclosed everything to her.

"Sadly, there is another risk to any GhostWalker, both male and female. Now that some of us have children, I think that risk will grow, especially to the children. There's a contingency in the White House, someone who wants us all dead. It's no picnic I'm offering you, but those we can trust have banded together, and we look out for one another. We're also preparing places we can defend with numerous escape routes. We're pooling our resources to become powerful enough to stop both Whitney and the group who would like to see us all dead."

"So you're saying you will stay with the military in your present GhostWalker unit?"

"Yes."

"What happens when they transfer you somewhere else?"

"Because we opted for the experiments, our contracts with the military are a bit different than normal. Without our agreement, they can't break us up or assign us to anyone else. We try to go where we're needed when they ask, but we have options."

The baby appeared to have fallen asleep. She handed him back to Kane. "I don't want him getting cold, and I'm suddenly so tired I can barely keep my arms up to hold him."

Kane cradled his son close. "Rose, you have to know a few things about me. If you stay with me, I want a commitment. I want marriage, your word that you'll stay and we'll work things out. I'm not an easy man to live with, I know that. Jaimie and Rhianna tell me I'm bossy."

She frowned at him. "Jaimie and Rhianna?"

"My sisters—of sorts. I told you about Jaimie. She's married to Mack. *Eloped*." He scowled, furious all over again that Mack and Jaimie had run off behind his back. "Rhianna's off somewhere hush-hush, and none of us has any idea at the moment where, which will earn her a few harsh lectures when she returns home."

A slow smile crept into her eyes. "Kane, you really are silly sometimes. You're the kindest, most gentle man I've ever met. You're not at all like you think you are."

He knew his horror showed on his face. "Rose, you can't think that."

"Why not? It's the truth."

"Nothing could be further from the truth. I kill people, and it doesn't keep me up at night. If another man tried to touch you in front of me, I sure as hell wouldn't stand there smiling at him."

Rose studied his face as he once again looked down at their son. His expression had gone from shock and horror to something very close to tenderness and love. "I wouldn't want you to smile if another man was touching me, Kane. What are we going to call him? I don't exactly have family names I want to give him."

"Any ideas?"

"I thought when he was born I'd think of something, but my mind is a blank. I did put a baby name book in the pantry along with all the what-to-expect books." She turned her head more closely into the pillows. She'd never been so exhausted in her life. She wanted to stay awake and watch him with the baby, but she couldn't seem to keep her eyes open. "I'm tired, Kane."

"I know, sweetheart. Let me put the baby down and check to make certain you're not bleeding too much, and then I'll let you go to sleep."

She loved the sound of his voice, especially when he called her sweetheart. She could almost believe they were a normal couple thrilled to have their first child together, instead of two strangers brought together by a madman. "I'm sorry you have to do all this."

"I wouldn't have missed it for the world."

He sounded so sincere. That was one of the things she loved most about Kane—his honesty. He meant the things he said to people, even when they weren't nice things. He often got the most endearing expression on his face when he looked at her, as if she confused him and he didn't quite know what to make of her.

"You really are an exceptional man, Kane." She couldn't stop the words from slipping out. He was exceptional.

He bent and brushed a kiss down her face to the side of her mouth. "You clearly don't know very many men, Rose." He kissed her again, this time on her temple. "Which is perfectly okay with me. You did a great job, honey. Our son is beautiful. Thank God he looks like you."

Her lashes fluttered while she tried to calm her wildly beating heart. She couldn't let herself fall for him. She'd committed to being with him, but she didn't want her heart involved. Hearts could break, and she was strong on her own. She had to be to survive. She knew nothing at all about relationships or family. She might be able to figure out parenting, but mostly she thought in terms of protecting her child, rather than raising him. Real feelings for Kane would be a complication. She was already infatuated with him. She told herself it was because he was the first good man she'd ever met, but she had a sneaking suspicion it was a lot more complicated than that—and maybe already too late.

"I think he looks like you," she said. "My hair, but the rest is all you."

"I look like a little old man?"

Her heart fluttered again at his gentle teasing. His fingers brushed at the strands of hair falling around her face, and she absorbed his touch as if starved for it—and maybe she was. She had never been cuddled or held in her life. Kane had changed all that when he'd made love to her. He hadn't forced sex. He'd been so gentle, every touch bringing pleasure—more than physical pleasure. The contact had touched more than her body, and now she craved those small touches. She could tell he was hesitant about too much contact with her, but she wished he'd just lie down beside her and hold her in his arms.

"He doesn't look like an old man."

Kane laughed softly at Rose's admonishment as he nuzzled the baby's head. A little reluctantly, he put him in the little cubicle he'd made to keep him warm. Rose hadn't once brought up the fact that Whitney had experimented on both of the boy's parents, and now he carried their DNA. Whitney had altered their DNA, and there was no telling what kinds of gifts or curses the child carried. Sometimes the psychic gifts were so strong that the person needed another person—an anchor—to be able to filter out the distressing disturbances around them.

He touched the child with gentle fingers, feeling almost overwhelmed with love. How could such a little stranger steal his heart in a matter of moments? Did all parents feel this way about their child? Was it because he'd helped to bring the boy into the world right in the midst of danger? He could barely believe that he and Rose had actually created this little human being together.

He slowly undid the blanket to look down at his son's tiny form. He was born early, yet he was fully formed and already showing signs of body strength in his physical form. He knew, without a shadow of a doubt, that his son was one of the supersoldiers Whitney was trying to create. When the child opened his sleepy eyes and looked at him, there was intelligence there. Granted, Kane had no experience with children, let alone new babies, but his gut rarely lied to him, and he had a strong feeling about the boy.

He sighed as he wrapped the boy tightly. "We won't let him get his hands on you, son," he promised softly. He very gently laid his hand on the boy's head. "Your mother and I wanted you. Whatever else happens, know you were wanted by *both* of us."

He felt Rose's gaze fixed on him and turned to look into her dark eyes. Everything inside him stilled. She smiled at him, and his stomach did a slow somersault. "You're supposed to be asleep."

"I know."

It was her tone of voice—soft and dreamy, almost a caress—that got to him. She looked at him as if he were her entire world. He wanted to be, but he knew she just didn't have any experience. A man like him, without a clue of home and family, a man born to fight wars, had no right being with a woman like Rose. He wanted to be the man in her mind, that fantasy, but he wasn't. If she committed to him, if she married him, it was forever. He wouldn't be walking away, and neither would she. She'd had enough of being imprisoned. Was life with him going to be anything else but a prison?

He had no answers, and he turned away, shaking his head. He drew the chair to the end of the bed and slowly lifted the sheets to check her. Small blood clots worried him a bit, but he had no idea what to do. She rubbed her stomach as the book told her to do, massaging to help everything go back in place, but her efforts were weak. He changed the pad again and helped her shift enough to allow him to change the sterile pad beneath her as well. He tried to be impersonal in his touch, but his body refused to listen to his brain.

Right now, he was with her. He could help her, and he could allow himself to believe both Rose and the boy were his. He was a cynical man, a man who felt at home with a gun in his hands, yet looking at her made him dream of other things. He wanted to be the man in her life, her hero, the man who stood for her. The man she always gazed at with that look in her eyes.

He covered her and stood up, stretching. "Rose. I don't want to go behind your back in this, but I have to leave a sign for Mack and my unit to find us. We can't fight everyone. I can take out the two watching us, but that will tip off

Whitney immediately, and we don't know how he's tracking you. Are you certain you removed the tracking chip in your hip?"

She nodded without opening her eyes. Kane sighed and started to turn away, but suddenly the image on her ankle registered. "Rose, you have a tattoo on your ankle. You didn't have that when we were together. When did you get it?" He lifted the covers once more to inspect the artwork on her ankle.

The tattoo was small, a single red rose with the stem winding around her ankle. Small thorns adorned the stem with three leaves. It was a pretty tattoo, but not something he expected of her.

"Before we escaped"—her voice was drowsy—"Whitney sent in a tattoo artist for each of us, and he put a flower on our ankles. Mari was the only one who didn't get one; she hadn't come back yet. Everyone else has one."

Kane closed his eyes briefly, cursing under his breath. All the women who escaped were in danger. Whitney had an alternative method of tracking them. He had, at some point, determined anyone escaping might remove the chip from their hip, so he'd devised a backup. Something about that very detailed rose caught Kane's attention, but it hadn't really registered until now. The rose petals were layers, and in two places the petals were actually raised slightly. He had stroked caresses over those soft petals half the night and knew the feel of them intimately.

Whitney had found a way to weave a signal into the tattoo. It probably used satellite, which explained the hit-or-miss tracking at times, depending on where she was. Eventually, Whitney would always be able to find her. He examined the petals carefully. The two closest to the center, slightly raised, were the most suspect. When he passed his thumb over the petals, he felt tiny protrusions, almost like Braille dots. What exactly had Whitney done?

Rose stirred, suddenly alarmed. "What did he do? I like my rose tattoo. It was the only thing Whitney ever did that didn't turn my stomach. Is something wrong with the tattoo?"

"I think it transmits to a satellite. I just have to figure out how. I wish Jaimie or Javier were here. They're both very good with electronics."

"I should have known." Rose sounded disgusted. "Why did I ever think Whitney would do something special for us?"

"Because you and the others needed to believe you mattered to him as a human being. Whitney was the only parent figure you had. He shaped your lives. You all lived for his approval. He raised you. Every child seeks the approval and love of a parent. Whitney was all you had."

Rose carefully turned over, wincing a little as she did so. "What about you? Did your parents approve of you?"

"Hardly." He didn't go into detail. What was the point? His youth had been spent on the streets, in alleys and creeping into Mack's basement to sleep, his body covered in bruises when his father had managed to catch him, which was rare. He'd grown into a big kid, and a mean one. Eventually his father feared him. His mother simply didn't care. Her only worry had been where her next fix was coming from. Mack was his family, Mack and the others.

"They weren't very smart parents then. How am I going to get the tattoo off?"

She didn't sound sorry for herself, and he could tell she really loved the tattoo and hated giving it up. The symbol represented who she was.

"I doubt we're going to have to actually remove the rose. We have to figure out how to stop it from transmitting." He stroked over the tiny little bumps. "I think the transmitter is here, in these two petals. I don't know if it's planted under your skin or in the actual ink somehow. I just am not savvy enough about this kind of thing."

"Will you have to cut it out?" There was both apprehension and determination in her voice. Rose was no shrinking violet.

"No way. We'll get it out of there."

"If we can't, you'll have to take the baby and go, Kane."

Once again his eyes met hers. She was serious. He could read the absolute resolve in her expression. If it took separation from her to keep the baby out of Whitney's hands, she was prepared to sacrifice that as well.

He shook his head. "We'll stay together and see this through. My understanding of the way Whitney pairs his women with a man is, they have to be able to complement each other in a combat situation. Your skills and mine should fit together and make us nearly invincible."

"But he didn't choose you for me." Rose avoided his eyes, a blush stealing up her neck to her cheeks. "I chose you."

"Did you think your choice would have really mattered to him, Rose?" he said gently. "He *asked* for me to be assigned temporarily to him. I went to the compound believing there was an outside threat to the facility. He dangled me in front of you like a carrot because we fit together. You took the bait. If my gifts weren't compatible with your gifts, he would never have allowed us to be paired. In the end with him, it's all about being a soldier. A pair should be able to be dropped into enemy territory alone, get the mission done, and get out. Our child should make the perfect soldier. If he didn't think that would happen, he would never have paired me with you." He looked at her for a long time. "You have a choice though, sweetheart. You don't have to stay with me."

She swallowed hard. "And you have no choice. That's my fault."

He shook his head. "You don't get me at all, honey. I don't *ever* do anything I don't want to do. It was *my* choice. Once the program was explained to me and Whitney told me you had asked for me, I could have turned the program down." How could he explain he'd seen her dozens of times and couldn't stand the thought of any man forcing her to have sex? "I thought about it a long time before I agreed.

He explained I would always want you physically. I didn't go into the program blind."

She frowned at him. "You knew what it would mean for you? The rest of your life you would always want me? And you still did it?"

"Yes. So stop feeling guilty. I had a choice; you didn't. But you do now, Rose." It had to be said, no matter how painful he found it to remind her.

She rubbed her fingers back and forth nervously along the hem of the blanket. "Actually, no, I don't. Not anymore. I asked Whitney to pair me with you after you left me that night."

Anger flashed through him. "You did what?" He glanced at the baby and lowered his voice. "Damn it, Rose, you didn't."

She lifted her chin at him. "I wasn't going to condemn you to hell and not go with you."

He studied her defiant expression; all the while he was melting inside. Rose had chosen him to father her child, but she refused to leave him out in the cold. She had insisted she share his fate. She had courage, raw courage, to condemn herself to share a life with a man she barely knew. "You're insane, sweetheart, but I can't help admiring you for it."

He turned away from her briefly, hiding his expression before abruptly turning back, taking her face between his hands and thoroughly kissing her. Just as abruptly he let her go and stood straight. "I've got some things to do. You sleep while you can."

He closed the door to the bedroom behind him, feeling as though for the first time in his life, he was complete.

CHAPTER 7

Rose thought she'd condemned him to hell and then deliberately put herself right there with him. Kane contemplated the thought and what it might mean as they developed a routine over the next week together. If he was living in hell, well, maybe that was just the place for him. He liked holding his son and watching Rose feed the boy. He enjoyed their quiet conversations about nothing in particular. He liked brushing her hair for her, and tucking the blankets around her. He didn't even mind cooking, although they didn't have much in the way of real food.

He knew they were living on borrowed time, but every passing day gave the baby a chance to grow stronger, to age one more day. Kane believed the time gave him more of a chance to continue to gain Rose's trust. He knew he would need it in the days to come. They had a reprieve, but it was a very short one.

Rose always curled up in chairs, feet tucked under her, reminding him of a little cat. With their son cradled in her arms and her silky cap of hair disheveled, as though they'd just made love, Kane couldn't help asking her. "I've been thinking a lot about what you said to me the night you delivered the baby, sweetheart."

She glanced up at him, her gaze a little wary, her lips pursed in a little moue that sent his body into overdrive. He couldn't help it, he wanted to kiss her thoroughly until that guarded look disappeared for all time.

"What did I say?"

"Just that you had condemned me to hell and then you decided to go with me."

A blush stole up her neck and flushed her cheeks a soft pink. She shrugged, looking artfully casual. He wasn't buying her act, even as pretty as it was.

"You really had Whitney pair you with me?"

"It's no big deal." She shrugged and nuzzled the baby.

"You decided to make certain you'd never be physically happy with another man? Why in the world would you do that?"

Her blush deepened. "We don't really need to talk about this, do we?"

Now he was really curious. She actually bit her lower lip, one of the few signs of nervousness he'd ever detected in her. He leaned toward her and took the sleeping baby right out of her arms, leaving her without armor. "Yes, I really think we need to talk about it. That was a huge decision, Rose, that affects the entire rest of your life. You knew we might not get you out of Whitney's facility, and I was never going to be stationed there permanently. I'd like to know why you chose to tie yourself to me like that."

She rolled her eyes and heaved a long-suffering sigh. He snuggled the boy closer to him. He was so small it was terrifying to hold him, but Kane was determined to get comfortable with the process. The child—and Rose—certainly brought out his protective instincts. He waited while she wrestled with herself. Rose wouldn't lie. He knew she wouldn't. She would tell him the strict truth, even if it embarrassed her—as it so obviously did.

"We were already tied together if I was pregnant," she pointed out, "so really, it wasn't like a huge risk."

His eyebrow shot up as she ducked her head, turning slightly away from him. Her body language said more than her words did. "Rose, I do believe you are evading the question."

"Give me back the baby, and I'll tell you."

He cuddled his son closer, pressing one fingertip into the little soft palm. Tiny fingers closed around his. He drew in his breath sharply. "Giving him up for even a few minutes is difficult. Your answer had better be good." He carefully placed the baby in her arms.

Rose looked down at the baby and then back up at him and smiled. She wore her smile like beautiful music; it didn't come often, but when it did, his heart sang. He often just sat watching her, the way she moved, so graceful, like a ballerina. She was incredibly beautiful to him. Everything about her appealed to him. He liked to watch her expression when she bent over their son. So loving. So perfect. Soft and intimate when she looked up and shared that same smile with him. He felt complete in a way he never had and never had expected to.

Rose cleared her throat and looked him steadily in the eyes. He could feel his heart accelerate. The bantering was gone, and she was going to impart something of great importance to him. He felt as if everything inside him stilled—waited. He needed something from her and he wasn't even certain what it was, but he knew this moment might be the one moment that meant everything to him, and he didn't want to miss even the smallest nuance.

Rose swallowed again and, not taking her eyes from his, brushed a kiss over the baby's head. "I didn't want to ever accept anyone else in my life," she announced softly. "You're my choice for a life partner, and that isn't going to change because we're not together."

For a moment the roaring in his ears nearly drowned out her declaration. His heart beat so hard he pressed his hand to his chest. What was she saying? She *wanted* to be with him? Even now when she could walk away from him and the entire GhostWalker program?

"I made the choice before you ever came to my room, Kane," she admitted. "I watched you for weeks and maybe became a little obsessed with you. I'd never seen anyone like you before. Maybe our time together wasn't memorable to you, but I remember every single detail. I remember the way you touched me, how your skin felt against mine, how careful you were with me. I hear the sound of your voice at night, and it comforts me. Nothing has ever made me feel the way you did. If I only had that one night with you, it was enough for me."

Kane stood up abruptly and turned his back on her, uncertain whether he could keep emotion from his expression. She humbled him with her courage. She was an extraordinary woman, and he couldn't believe she'd tied herself to him, especially after one night of sex with him. Granted, he had wanted her first time to feel as if a man loved her above all else. He didn't want her to feel forced or afraid, and he'd done everything in his power to prepare her body to accept his, but the bottom line had been, if Rose hadn't allowed him to have sex with her, then Whitney would have sent another man in his place. That man—Carlson—would have used brute force.

"I guess I'll have to spend the rest of my life proving to you that you made the right decision." If his voice was a little too husky, he chose to ignore it. He wasn't a man given to emotion, and being in such close proximity to Rose and the baby made him feel as if he could spend a lifetime right there in that house in the desert, even knowing the threat hanging over their heads.

"Kane."

The way his name was a caress turned his insides to jelly. Damn, women had power, so much more than he'd ever considered. Rose could turn him inside out with just her tone of voice. He turned a little reluctantly to face her.

"I would have gotten on the helicopter if you'd come too."

Trust. There it was. Stark and honest and handed to him when he wasn't altogether that deserving. Why he'd been so lucky he had no idea, but she'd taken a cynical, hard man and created some kind of knight in shining armor out of him.

"We'll keep the baby safe, Rose," he assured.

If there was one thing he knew for certain, it was that Whitney would never get his hands on the boy or Rose. Whitney would have to go through Kane to do it, and Kane had a hell of a team standing behind him. He might not believe in many things, but he believed in his unit.

Each night when he left the house to scout, he scattered signs for Mack and the others to find. They knew him, knew what to look for, and they would know he was alive. They would come for him—for Rose and his child. He buried the evidence of birth deep in the tunnel where no animal would uncover it and possibly give away to the sentries that Rose had already had the baby.

"I feel strong enough now to help more," she assured, shifting a little to ease her sore body into a new position.

He knew she didn't even notice she was still sore. Rose was determined to pull her weight. It mattered little that he'd already made the *big* mistake of pointing out he was the man and it was his place to protect them both. That hadn't gone over very well. He searched for something more diplomatic to say.

She laughed softly. "You look like you might implode, Kane."

"Talking with a woman is like walking through a mine-field," he admitted and immediately realized that statement was probably one of those truths that would be better left unsaid.

Rose's laughter rang out again, that music that haunted his daytime dreams. He had no idea a man could fall so damn hard for a woman. He reached down and circled her bare ankle with his hand, his fingers stroking over the petals of her tattoo, needing some kind of personal contact with her, no matter what it was. He spent a good deal of his time studying the complex tattoo on her ankle. He'd really grown quite fond of it. He knew every petal intimately, stroking and caressing her soft skin while she fed the baby or just sat holding him.

Rose never objected to his touching her, nor did she now. She shook her head at his comment. "Women are easy to talk to, Kane, if a man just uses logic."

He opened his mouth, then thought better of entering into a discussion on the logic of women with her. He bit down hard on his impulsive reply. She laughed again, and he realized she was teasing him. He found himself laughing with her.

He tugged a little on her ankle, his thumb sliding over the petals of the rose. "I think we can safely say this is the source of Whitney's ability to track you. He's using a satellite, but only intermittently, which means he's using it for something else, something more important, and can only spare it occasionally to check on you and the other women who escaped the compound."

"That's if each of the tattoos actually carries the same ability."

Kane shrugged. "Why bother giving the women a tattoo if it wasn't useful to him?"

She winced. "I know we should have been suspicious. We *wanted* to believe we meant something—anything—to him. He was the only constant in our lives, other than each other."

"I wasn't passing judgment, Rose." His heart ached for her when she looked so sad—a child desperate for the love of a parent—and finding out once again that parent had betrayed her.

"It's just that I know better than to ever give him the benefit of the doubt, and yet, there's this part of me, so childish, that keeps hoping we meant something to him.

He raised us. We did everything he wanted, no matter how frightened we were or how difficult or painful it was." She shook her head and then kissed the baby. "I can't let that happen to him."

"We won't, sweetheart. And we'll find a way to disable the tracking device in the tattoo. Javier or Jaimie will know what to do. They are practically hardwired into their electronics."

"Won't I lead them right to your unit?"

"He won't come after us with Mack and the others helping to protect you. And if he did send someone, they'll run into a wall." He spoke with absolute confidence, believing it the truth. His unit would fight to the death to keep Rose and the baby from Whitney. He glanced out the windows at the gathering darkness. "It's almost time for me to go check on our two friends."

Rose sat outside in the evening for an hour, giving the illusion of being heavy with child, just meditating in the night and seemingly oblivious to the two men watching her. Kane figured the act would buy them a little time. He went out before her each night hunting the two, getting close enough to listen to their conversations, gathering intel he hoped would let them know when Whitney planned to make his move. In truth, all they were doing was buying time for their son.

"Let me put the baby down," she said and immediately stood up.

He hadn't stepped back to give her room, and her body brushed against his. Her scent immediately enveloped him. She smelled like warmth and sunlight. Like silk and satin. He couldn't stop himself, although he knew better. His arms swept around her, and he just stood, holding the two of them, drawing a strange sort of peace from their very existence. Rose didn't step away from him or stiffen as he expected her to. She held their son and leaned into Kane, resting her head against his chest.

He curled his fingers around the nape of her neck. "We

have to actually choose a name," Kane murmured above her head. "We can't keep calling him 'baby.' When he's fifteen he might resent it." His fingers began a slow massage. Night was falling, casting muted purple shadows along the wall. Stars were beginning to scatter across the open sky. He would be going outside as soon as it was fully dark, and tonight he was reluctant, wanting to linger with her. "It's been seven days. That's long enough to figure out what you want to call him."

Rose seemed to burrow closer to him, relaxing beneath his touch. "You're the one who won't agree on a name."

"My son is not having some dumb name. I think you come up with the worst things you can possibly think of just to see my reaction."

Rose's soft laughter told him that he'd guessed right. He bent his head and kissed the top of all that silky black hair. "You're impossible." Reluctantly he allowed his hands to drop away.

Rose didn't move immediately. She rubbed her face against his chest before she stepped away. "It's not like I have tons of family to give me ideas, Kane. All my sisters have flower names—which we're not doing to him."

"Sebastian comes to mind. Has to do with soldiers and courage and looking out for us," Kane suggested awkwardly. "Sebastian is considered the patron saint of soldiers."

She frowned as she put the baby into the warmer. "What does that mean?"

He shrugged. "Just a suggestion. You can choose a name. Just not a crazy one," he qualified.

She studied his face. The hard jaw. The etched lines. Very gently she stroked her hand over his tough features. "Sebastian it is. You can tell me what a patron saint is later, since I have no knowledge of such things. Sebastian Kane."

"Sebastian Kane Cannon. You're going to marry me and use my last name, right?"

"Is that supposed to be a proposal?"

He wrapped his arm around her waist and tipped her head up toward his. "I can make you happy, Rose. And I can protect the two of you from Whitney and anyone else who wants to experiment on us or kill us. I'll always be loyal, but you have to know I'm a soldier. That's who I am. I have a family we'll be part of. My first loyalty will always be to you and the boy, but I'll do what it takes to protect my unit as well."

"Are you trying to convince me to stay with you or to run?"

"I don't want you to stay under false pretenses." He framed her face with both hands and let himself fall into her dark, almond eyes. She could take his breath and any good sense he'd ever had and it was perfectly okay with him. He might feel like an idiot, but that was okay as well—as long as he had her. "Fighting Whitney is always going to be a part of my life. Not just for us but for every other GhostWalker and the children they'll have."

She nodded her head. "I can accept that. I figure he'd just keep coming after me."

"I said children," he pointed out.

A slow smile curved her mouth. "I caught that. I'm actually quite intelligent and quick on the uptake, Kane. I knew you said that for a reason. I'm not afraid of having more children."

"I'm going to kiss you."

A dimple appeared beside the corner of her mouth. "Do you think it necessary to tell me first?"

"I was being a gentleman and warning you."

"I think if you're planning on marrying me, you should know a few things about me. Kisses will be an everyday requirement."

Kane didn't need any more encouragement. He'd been afraid Rose would shy away from physical contact, and he was prepared to take his time—get her used to his touch. Kissing had the green light, and he was more than ready to take full advantage of the situation. A man could do a lot with kissing when he was serious about it.

Kane slipped out of the house as he did each night. Rose always made a pretense of opening the door in the evening and looking around, which allowed him to move into the shadows unobserved. He knew if the sentries were watching, they'd have their binoculars on Rose. They had no idea anyone else was even in the general vicinity, let alone in the house with her. He knew the moment he left, she set alarms and crawled into the space along the windows with a sniper rifle to cover him.

This was the only time he ever really worried. He knew the tunnel left them vulnerable. Rose couldn't watch him and both entrances. And she had the baby to look after, which he'd pointed out repeatedly had to be her first priority. As a wife, she was going to be a handful. She definitely didn't take his suggestions—or his orders. She smiled at him, her eyes looking at him with an expression that twisted him up inside, but she didn't allow whatever she felt for him to stop her from doing exactly what she wanted—or what she thought needed to be done.

He made his way to the first slope before turning back to send a small breeze low over the sand to obscure any tracks he might have made. It was always the little things that tripped a soldier up. He had learned to pay attention to the smallest detail. He stayed low, knowing it would be almost impossible to see him moving along the ground, especially as he stayed in the darker dirt patches or near boulders and waves of saw grass.

The camp Whitney's men had set up was only about a mile away, and they were getting careless. They left tracks often. More, he sometimes smelled them smoking or drinking. Twice he smelled meat cooking. Carlson James often prowled close to the house and seemed to be getting surlier with each night passing. If their orders were to wait until they'd confirmed Rose had given birth, Kane was certain they'd never make the distance. Both men were bored, and neither had the disposition for being dropped in a desert and gathering information over time. Kane was certain that was part of the reason they'd failed to be included in the military's GhostWalker program.

They'd even gotten somewhat sloppy about their camp, leaving supplies out where the coyotes would be drawn in. Fargo wanted to hunt the coyotes to give them something to do, but in that, Carlson so far had prevailed, pointing out that Rose would likely hear the shots.

Kane took up position a scant twenty yards from the camp, maneuvering on his belly, pushing with toes and elbows until he was in the midst of a pile of boulders. Grass and weeds grew sparsely in the cracks. A lizard scooted out of his way but didn't scamper off toward the camp, preferring to crawl beneath the smaller of the rocks to hide.

Carlson James whittled at a piece of wood, shaping a point on the end with his knife. A pile of sticks about a foot long each lay in front of him, each with a sharp point on the end. A few feet away, Fargo was doing the same thing, although he wasn't putting much effort into it.

He sighed. "I can't believe we're stuck out here resorting to hunting coyotes with homemade arrows."

Carlson made a sound of disgust deep in his throat. "You won't let me grab the bitch and get out of here, so what else can we do?"

"I've been thinking about that," Fargo said. "How 'bout we go into town and get us some company. A pretty little senorita for us to pass the time with."

Carlson looked up, speculation in his eyes. The two men stared at each other for a long time. Carlson slowly smiled. "Now that's not a bad idea. You've got something there, Fargo." He glanced in the direction of the subterranean hideaway. "Although one of us needs to keep an eye out around here."

Kane's gut tightened. Carlson's tone had been casual—too casual.

Fargo sent his partner a sharp look. "Don't go getting stupid on me. You know I have to document every damn time you say that bitch's name or refer to her. Whitney's expecting you to break. You have to beat him at his own game. As it is, I'm only recording about half the time you're obsessing about her."

"I'm not obsessing. She pisses me off, that's all. She was supposed to be mine. Once I get my hands on her, she'll be begging to stay with me." Carlson threw his knife point down in the sand beside the stack of makeshift arrows.

"Regardless of what you call it, you have to show him you have discipline. That's what this little game is all about, Carlson. You have to play to win."

"You can say that because you know if you keep me from breaking in there and taking her, you'll get the woman you want. *You'll* win."

Fargo shrugged. "I'm not so sure of that, Carlson. Look what he promised you, and did he deliver? No, he gave her to some other bastard and left you hanging. You did everything he asked of you, and he still screwed you."

"Whitney wants the baby, not the woman," Carlson said, his expression going mean. "He thinks she's going to give him his little supersoldier. He thinks my son will be flawed—like me. I don't have any damn flaws. I should have put a bullet in his head when I had the chance."

Kane found it interesting that these soldiers, as corrupt and damaged as they were, recognized that Whitney was playing games with them too, or maybe someone as cunning and evil as Carlson James would understand Whitney. God knew, the doctor made no sense to Kane.

"He pays us," Fargo pointed out. "A hell of a lot more than the Marine Corps ever did."

Carlson reached for his knife, all the while, his gaze on the house he couldn't actually see. "Yeah. There's that. Man. I can't stop thinking about her and when she sits outside and I can smell her, I get so damned hard even the money doesn't matter so much." He pinned Fargo with cold, warning eyes. "And you don't need to report that to the bastard. We're just talking about money."

Fargo looked a little alarmed. Kane figured Carlson was both volatile and unpredictable. Fargo had the very dangerous position of being the watchdog. He was obviously aware that Carlson was deteriorating the longer he was in close proximity to Rose without having access to her. What did that mean? Was this part of Whitney's experiment? To find out how long a man could be paired to a woman without going insane with need? Need had turned to obsession for Carlson and then to depraved sickness.

Kane wiped the beads of sweat from his forehead with his sleeve. Carlson was a sacrifice so Whitney could find the answer. Kane had been obsessed with finding Rose. Had his need turned into obsession as well? Damn Whitney and his appetite for high-stakes games. He loved to use people as human pawns. Having been bullied in his younger years by not only his parents but other children who didn't understand him, he had developed a need to prove to everyone that he was smarter. He needed the games now just as much as he needed the experiments. The games seemed to be his one source of amusement.

"I just thought if we picked up a little senorita and shared her, kept her while we had to wait, that it might be easier for you, Carlson, that's all," Fargo said. "Once your woman has the kid, Whitney will take it, and you won't have to worry about having that bastard's brat running around."

"It's still her kid," Carlson pointed out. "Women don't like their kids taken from them. If I took her now, at least she'd have the kid."

It surprised Kane that Carlson would be compassionate enough to think about Rose's feelings. He might be brutish and selfish, but he'd thought about what it would mean to take Rose's child from her.

Fargo nodded. "Yeah, but think about it, Carlson. If

Whitney can be occupied with his favorite project, making the kid his supersoldier, then you have a chance he'll leave you and Rose alone if you have another child together. Your kid would have more protection."

Carlson threw another arrow onto the growing stack. "I hadn't thought of that. And Whitney isn't going to give up until he has a kid to play the mad doctor with."

Both men laughed harshly.

"Might not be such a bad idea if you went and got us a woman," Carlson said. "One of us has to stay here and make certain she doesn't take off."

"Maybe you should go, give you a little break." Fargo picked up an empty bottle. "And while you're at it, replenish our supplies."

Carlson shook his head. "I can't do it, Fargo. She's going to have that baby any day now. Do you realize she's alone in there? What happens when she goes into labor? She could die. I'm going to stay right here."

Carlson actually sounded like he was worried about Rose. Kane frowned, not wanting to relate to the man at all. It was difficult not to think about what would have happened if Kane had been in his shoes. Would he have managed to walk away from Rose knowing she was with another man? He hoped so. He hoped he was man enough to want her happy and that if she really chose someone else, he would abide by her decision. His heart hammered in his chest at the thought. Worse, everything male in him rose up to fight against the idea. If nothing else, this was a lesson in the havoc and devastation Whitney created. The man ruined lives and never thought twice about it.

Are you all right?

Rose's voice was soft and hesitant. They'd agreed not to use telepathy with the soldiers so close. They might feel the disturbance in the energy waves around them. He must have been projecting distress for her to reach out to him in spite of their edict.

He kept his eyes on both soldiers, assessing their level

of sensitivity. Fargo rubbed his eyes and Carlson frowned, but neither seemed at all suspicious. Kane had noticed before that neither appeared to have much in the way of psychic talent; now it was truly evident. He pressed his head into his palm, swearing to himself.

Whitney had requested Kane because he wanted the level of psychic gifts that Kane had been born with. Yes, Whitney had enhanced his skills, but he had scored quite high on the psychic tests. Neither of these men could have, or they would have sensed that someone other than Rose was in the house. Kane would have known. Whitney had taken the men who had barely managed to make it into the program. Most of them had flunked the psych evals as well.

Whitney didn't want to pair them with his precious women. He simply didn't have that many women who could be bred to produce a supersoldier, but he knew the women inside and out. He'd had them in his laboratory from the time they were infants. He had dangled Kane in front of Rose like a carrot, knowing exactly the kind of man who would appeal to her.

And Kane? Hell. He'd made it so damned easy. He had the knight-in-shining-armor complex—even his friends said so. He was a rescuer. Of course he would have agreed to do anything for Rose, once he'd learned of her plight. He'd never let a brute like Carlson force her to have sex with him. He'd been duped as well. If anyone thought Whitney wasn't a true master of human study, Kane was going to testify to the truth of it all. Whitney had amazing, if not psychic, insight into the nature of people.

Kane. Now Rose's voice trembled. *I'm coming out.*

Stay put, honey. He should have known better than to take so long. Rose would back him up no matter the danger. *Just watching them for reactions. Strange, neither seems to feel the pressure building around them.*

It was difficult to describe the exact feeling when other GhostWalkers were close or using telepathy. The pressure on their minds built rapidly, pressing into them to varying degrees, depending on the sensitivity level, sometimes as strong as a vise. It was odd to him that these men didn't feel his presence. Each night he'd moved a little closer, and still they didn't appear to know he was there. Several times he used his abilities to move air and that should have changed pressure in their minds, and yet neither noticed.

Rose was nothing if not quick. She realized the implications immediately. He felt the impact of the blow as comprehension dawned. She seemed stunned, so shocked for a brief moment her mind was blank, and then guilt washed over her because they were sharing the same conclusion about Whitney.

I'm sorry, Kane. I played right into his hands, didn't I? I brought you into this, and if I hadn't fallen into his trap, you would never . . .

Stop it! Just stop, Rose. I walked into this with my eyes open. I don't have regrets other than that our first time together had to be a nightmare for you. Leave it alone.

He wished he was back inside to hold her. Rose had no preparation for a life outside of the military, yet she had succeeded in hiding herself and staying one step ahead of Whitney during her pregnancy. She had had no one all that time on the run to wrap their arms around her and comfort her, and he had wanted to be with her. He pushed a caress into his voice, the only thing he had to give her, separated as they were by the distance. *I wouldn't trade what we have for anything else. I don't lie, Rose. If you don't know anything else about me, know that.*

Thank you.

She was weeping. Damn Whitney and his pitiful games. Rose deserved to be loved, and if she had nothing else in her life, if he could only provide that and little else, he vowed to himself that her world would be filled with love.

I'll be there in a few minutes, sweetheart. Not that he was all that much comfort to her—yet.

He had grown up on the streets, but he'd had Mack and

Jaimie and the others as a family. They'd banded together, and Mack's mother watched over them all as best she could. He'd learned trust and loyalty growing up that way. Who had taught those things to Rose? Her childhood had been one of discipline and duty. She'd learned to endure, but she was determined to give their baby something she'd never had—a loving parent. He was just as determined that he would be right beside her.

Fargo picked up the empty bottle and stared at it morosely. "Swear to me that if I go into town after our little senorita and some supplies, you won't go near the woman."

Carlson glared at him. "She's *my* woman, not just any woman. But no, I'm not about to screw up. Just bring us someone who can take a lot of heat. I like it rough."

"It's not like we're giving her back," Fargo said. "She'll take it any way we want to give it to her."

Carlson glanced at his watch. "Rose will be sitting outside in another twenty minutes, and after that we'll report to Whitney. You can go when he shuts down for the night. You'll have plenty of time to get what we want and be back here before anyone is the wiser."

Fargo stood up, stretching. He tucked his knife into his belt and kicked at the empty bottle. "A woman sure beats chasing those coyotes with homemade arrows."

Carlson smirked. "True, if she fights some. Coyotes sure do scream if you hit them in the right place. And they can take a long time to die."

"You're such a sick bastard, Carlson. That's what I like about you." Fargo stumbled away from the camp.

The smile faded from Carlson's face, and he looked again toward the hidden house in the desert—and Rose. Kane didn't like the look on his face, a dark promise of retribution.

Very carefully Kane began to backtrack, crawling, belly down, over the contoured slopes, stopping every few feet to erase his tracks with a small push of air. He had to make it back to get in a position to better protect Rose while she sat outside and put on her pregnancy show.

The baby's restless, Rose sent him. *Come inside. I think he has a tummyache. You'll have to walk him while I sit outside.*

Rose. He put a warning in his voice. There was nothing about the situation he liked. If he went inside, she sat outside without his protection. If she didn't go out, they ran the risk of Whitney's men thinking she was giving birth and breaking in. *Parents allow their babies to sleep for twenty minutes all alone in their own rooms.*

He made his nightly circle around the house, careful to search for any signs that the house had been approached. Once the men settled for the night, he usually checked the tunnel, just to be certain. He was nervous about that entrance. Neither of Whitney's men had gone near the hidden entrance, and he doubted they knew of its existence—which meant Whitney didn't know either.

What game had Diego Jimenez been playing with Whitney? Clearly he'd traded information for delivering Rose to Whitney, yet he hadn't said a word about the weapons, the tunnel, or the Humvee to Rose, a logical thing to do if he was really trying to help her. What did that mean exactly? He had to figure it all out soon, because time was running out for them fast.

He isn't asleep, Kane. I can't leave him.

He swore under his breath and then made an effort to calm down. *Damn it, Rose. Do you have any idea what could happen if Carlson decided he wanted to visit with you tonight?*

I'd kill him, she replied calmly. *I'm no longer in a cage, and I'm not tied up. He'd be dead the moment he showed his face.*

She wasn't going to budge on her threat. If he didn't come in and watch the baby, she was staying inside. *Suppose he decides to dart you from a distance and take you while you were out? That's what I'd do.*

He's not as smart as you, and in any case, you'd come after me, kill him, and take me back, so no matter what, you have to come inside and look after our son.

She'd pulled the "our son" card. How did a man react to that one? Women had sneaky little ways about them. He had all the logic in the world on his side, but it didn't seem to matter, not when she knew how to twist everything until there was no way but hers.

Kane sighed and capitulated. *Coming in. Are you going to win every argument?* He was pretty certain he'd asked her that once before. Maybe twice.

Only the important ones.

He should have been angry at the feminine pleasure in her voice, but he loved her laughter, and he'd take it no matter how it came—even if he was the recipient of her amusement.

He slipped and slid down the last slope to the trail leading to the door. As he turned back to cover his tracks, he spotted Carlson and Fargo. They were hunched low, running to get in place before Rose's normal time to sit outside. She'd already established a pattern, and they were counting on it. That gave him pause. Rose was a trained soldier. She knew better than to repeat patterns, yet neither Carlson nor Fargo had questioned her movements. He'd talked to her about varying the time she sat outside, but she'd been adamant that she sit outside at the same time each night. Which again made no sense until she explained.

Whitney expected her to forget her training, to become undisciplined in her actions because she was a woman out in the world without someone giving commands. He'd told them over and over that they would fail out of their environment. They weren't male, and they needed a commander. Rose was giving Whitney what he expected.

She opened the door, and while the two sentries watched her, he slipped inside.

CHAPTER 8

Kane started for the ledge just below the window, intending to crawl up onto it, but his son let out an alarming wail. If his lungs were anything to go by, the boy was getting stronger with each passing day. Kane changed direction and hurried into the back bedroom. Sebastian was in the warmer. He'd kicked off his cover and was squirming, his face red, eyes closed tight, fists punching the air and his feet kicking. Something inside Kane went soft, and he let out his breath slowly.

"What's wrong, little man?" He used his most soothing voice. Very gently he lifted the boy from the warmer and brought him in close to his chest, upright, supporting the little head.

Sebastian was so small he felt incredibly light in his hands, and Kane was still a little worried that he might accidentally hurt the child by holding him too tight. Each time he took the boy into his arms, he felt that curious melting of his heart. Newborn babies had their own weapons, that sweet helpless need and the soft, newborn skin. He cuddled Sebastian close and walked back and forth until the boy settled.

"I'm a little anxious, my man, and I need you to calm down right now. Your mother is out there exposed to the enemy, and we need to have her back on this."

His son abruptly stopped fussing, his eyes snapping open. They stared at each other. For one strange moment, Kane felt as if he were looking into the eyes of an adult, intelligent and aware. Kane smiled down at him. "We're not going to let anything happen to her, are we?" He talked to the boy as he moved quickly back to the living room. He shifted the baby to his shoulder, using one hand to anchor him and caught up his rifle with the other.

"Don't worry, Sebastian. No one is going to take your mother from us. She's a fighter all the way, and could probably handle this on her own, but we're just going to make sure."

Rose would probably give him a lecture about taking a baby into a combat situation, but that was too damned bad. The boy was born into their world, and he would have to grow up knowing every single moment of his life he would have to be vigilant.

"I'll teach you, son, everything you'll need to know to keep yourself alive and free of our enemies. And how to keep your mom safe." He nuzzled the boy's head. "We'll never tell her that part; it will be our secret."

He shoved the rifle up into the niche of the ledge. It was designed with maximum ability to see outside, yet the walls were reinforced to withstand any incoming bullets. "I'm going to put you down for just a moment while I climb up there. It's a tight fit for us, but we don't mind small spaces, not when it comes to safety."

He kept up a running commentary, explaining everything he was doing, convinced it was his voice and not the subject matter that kept his son so alert and enthralled with what they were doing. He put the boy onto the ledge, tucking his body close to the wall so there was no danger of him falling. It took a moment to slide in and get into a position on his belly where he had full view of the surrounding terrain. Only then did he position the baby close to his chest, dragging the bulletproof bumpers that had been installed for extra protection around the boy.

"See, we're good. I need to get you little earmuffs in case we have to fire this thing. That will be my next invention. And we're very grateful the walls are soundproofed, so no one hears when you cry, my man. We can't have them knowing you were born yet." He went on to explain the mechanics of a rifle and scope and how his son likely had excellent night vision, which would help considerably in night combat situations. And did he see that scumbag Carlson inching his way closer to Mommy? Kane stopped talking abruptly. Telling an infant about putting a bullet in the bastard's head was probably one of those things Rose would deem inappropriate. He looked down at the boy, who stared back at him with wide, intelligent eyes.

"Um, maybe we'll wait until you're a bit older before we discuss shooting bad people and when it's okay and when it's not." He stroked the pad of his finger along his son's soft palm in a loving caress. The boy closed his fist around the finger and held on. Kane found himself smiling as he put his eye to the scope and centered on Carlson as the man inched his way closer to Rose.

Rose sat in her chair, feet sprawled out in front of her, looking up at the stars scattered across the night sky. She didn't appear to notice the close proximity of the enemy as he moved within twenty feet of her. Kane studied her. She rubbed her apparently pregnant belly with one hand. The other was at her side, out of sight.

"Sebastian, your mother is one cool customer." There was pride in his voice. He couldn't help it. She looked so small and fragile, with her porcelain skin and her wide, almond eyes, dark as melting chocolate. She looked *helpless*. "She's about as helpless as I am, boy. Don't you ever forget that or disrespect her abilities. Your mother is extraordinary."

The boy tightened his fingers as if understanding every word. Did people talk baby talk to infants, or hold real conversations? Kane was the kind of man who could never manage to summon baby talk. The boy had to learn from the earliest age possible that his life wasn't normal and never would be. "We'll do our best to give you a childhood, Sebastian," he promised. "But you'll have to know things kids shouldn't have to know. I think truth is best, don't you?"

He shifted the scope to find Fargo. Fargo was observing Carlson, not Rose. He held something small in his palm. He was transmitting to Whitney behind Carlson's back, no doubt about it. Carlson was a sacrificial pawn, caught between Whitney and whatever the doctor had promised to Fargo. Fargo might not like Whitney and even understood on some level that he was just as likely to double-cross Fargo as Carlson, but the man just couldn't resist whatever carrot Whitney dangled in front of him.

"There's a huge amount of speculation about whether or not Whitney has his own psychic ability, Sebastian," Kane mused aloud, "and I'm coming down heavily on the side for it. I think he reads people, whether they have gifts and what their weaknesses are. It's why he stays in business. He's a master at manipulation. Never forget that, and never trust anything he says or does."

He rubbed his chin on the butt of the rifle, frowning. "And that leads us to the main question. Why was he in league with Diego Jimenez? What do you think, son? Something stinks about this entire thing." He winked at the child. "And it's not your diapers."

Thank God it wasn't the diapers. Diaper changing ranked right up there with—well—okay he'd pull any other duty gladly. Fortunately, Rose didn't seem to mind and actually, surprisingly, the boy didn't reek like Kane thought he would.

He kept his attention centered on Carlson, the real threat to Rose. Fargo would back his play if it came to it, grabbing her, but he wouldn't initiate violating orders. Carlson pushed his luck again, inching another foot forward.

Rose's head went up alertly. She pushed herself out of the chair. Carlson froze as she slowly and carefully looked around as if spooked.

"Your mommy is so smart," he whispered to the baby. "That's my woman. Scare the crap out of the bastard." He cleared his throat. "Don't use that word, son. Especially never in your mother's presence. She'd probably stick a knife in my gut." He cleared his throat again. "Don't ever repeat our conversations to her either. I'm fairly certain she wouldn't be happy with anything I'm saying to you."

Rose stepped out of the safety box and he switched from praise to cursing. *Don't you even fucking think about taking him out, Rose. You take one more step, and I'm coming out. You ignore me on this and see what happens.*

Already he was shifting his weight, ready to go if she defied him.

Sheesh. You never let me have any fun. I was just messing with him.

He breathed away the tight coiling snake in his belly. She was about as predictable as the wind. *Well, stop. You're giving me a heart attack.*

She didn't make the mistake of disobeying him. She had to have read his intent, but she took her sweet time getting back into the pocket where it would be difficult for either man to make a grab for her without exposing himself for a good thirteen feet of sheer open territory. Rose took one last, suspicious look around, stepped inside the house, and closed and locked the door.

Kane didn't move, watching the two men outside. It took Carlson several minutes before he dared to move, slowly easing this body over sand and dirt as he made his way back to Fargo. Kane let out his breath. If Fargo was really going to make his way into the town, he would do it after he reported to Whitney, and the report was always given at a specific time. Kane spent a great deal of time watching, and it was apparent that Whitney's schedule was tight. He had two hours before Fargo would take off, giving Carlson the opportunity to make a try for Rose—and he was damn sure the man would make his try.

Carlson and Fargo both crouched low, appeared to argue, and then headed toward their camp. Kane continued to watch them for some time, turning over and over in his mind the problem of ethics. If Fargo went after a woman, and he followed and prevented it, he would be leaving Sebastian and Rose open to attack. He rubbed his chin on the back of his hand.

"Is something wrong, Kane?" Rose asked.

What the hell was he supposed to say to that? He had to make a choice, and it was a damned ugly one. Of course, there was no choice, but still, he would have that woman and anything that happened to her on his mind for all time. Unless . . . He could go hunting now, kill both men, and he and Rose could make a run for it on their own without his unit's backing.

"Do you think the baby's strong enough to make a run for it, Rose?"

She remained silent. He turned his head to look at her. "Be honest."

"I don't know. He's way early, and very small. I think the hospital would have him in an incubator. But his lungs work and he's eating. He looks as if he's put a little weight on. I'd prefer to give him a few more days, but if we had to go . . ." She trailed off. "Why?"

He looked away, rubbed his pounding temples, and then handed her the rifle. He'd tell her later, when he had to go out and check to see if Fargo was really going to try to get a woman from town. Maybe the man was all talk. He hoped the man was all talk. Rose took the rifle silently and set it aside, holding out her arms for the baby.

"Don't ever scare me like that again, Rose." He went on

the attack to distract her. "You know damn well what an invitation you were extending to Carlson." In any case, he found he was angry with her. What the hell had she been thinking? The more he thought about it, the angrier it made him.

"Your daddy is such a baby," Rose sniffed, cuddling Sebastian to her. "I don't see why you should have all the fun, Kane. The man wasn't giving me any respect at all. I was trying to give *him* a heart attack, not you."

"Well, don't do it again." Kane scowled his blackest scowl, hoping for sheer intimidation. He'd noticed before that it hadn't worked well on her, but now that all the pregnancy hormones were leaving her body, she might recognize that he was a dangerous man—one not to be trifled with.

She sent him one of her mystifying smiles. It was baffling to him the way she used the secretive smile to answer his orders.

He slid out from the ledge and towered over her. "You would have made one hell of a spy." When her smile widened, he glared at her. "That was *not* a compliment, Rose."

"Really?" She laughed and walked right around him, undeterred by his solid mass. "I thought it was a wonderful compliment." She sank into a chair and deftly brought the child to her breast.

The hard-on was instant and aching. She was beautiful sitting there with her soft skin exposed and their child feeding. He didn't look away anymore, and Rose never tried to hide herself from him. Sebastian's nursing was much stronger than it had been, which made both of them happy. He'd been born early but showed every sign of being healthy.

"In a few days, he should be strong enough to leave," Kane pointed out.

"I agree." She nuzzled the little boy's head. "He's improving every single day."

He couldn't take his eyes off of her. "You're so damn beautiful, Rose. The things you do to my body without even trying are a sin."

She sent him that same mysterious smile. "I was hoping you wouldn't mind teaching me a few things. Although I'm grateful I can do things to your body without trying, I was expecting something a little more concrete and hands-on."

He pressed a hand to his heart. "Okay. That just isn't fair."

She sat there, the baby to her breast, looking up at him with those dark bedroom eyes and delivered her statement in a matter-of-fact, talk-about-the-weather tone. She had a siren's mouth and the longest lashes he'd ever seen on a woman. She had to know she was putting all sorts of erotic images in his head—or maybe she didn't. There was no amusement, no teasing, just her calm statement of facts.

"Why? Am I doing something wrong?" She looked confused.

He bent his head and kissed her, one hand sliding over her breast, feeling her soft skin. "No, sweetheart, you're doing everything right. I'll be more than happy to show you anything you'd like me to."

She nodded her head. "The only way to learn is to gather knowledge."

Kane winced. "What the hell." He frowned at her, slightly offended at her pragmatic approach. "I'm not a science project, Rose."

"Really?" She tilted her head to look up at him, her dark eyes running over his frame, dwelling for one long moment on the hard evidence of his arousal. "I rather thought of you as a very delicious science project."

Maybe the idea of being a science project wasn't so bad after all. He liked the way she was looking at him with such interest. Yeah. He could definitely handle being her project, especially if she thought of him as delicious. He was still cupping her breast in his palm, his thumb sliding back and forth over the firm mound. He felt the shiver of awareness going through her.

Rose deftly switched the baby from her right side to her left. He kept his hand supporting her breast while the baby latched on. "There's something really beautiful about a woman feeding a man's baby," he murmured, grateful she didn't hide her body from him.

"Do you think so? I was afraid that after having a baby you wouldn't find me attractive. It seems that men always lose interest in a woman after she gives birth to a child."

He straightened, shocked. "Why would you think that?"

Little frown lines appeared around her mouth. He had a mad urge to kiss them away. Instead, he waited for her answer, intrigued by her thinking.

"It's not as if I know anything about relationships; none of us do," Rose admitted. "We read newspapers and it seems as if everyone gets a divorce after they have children. Either that," she looked him in the eye, "or men can't be faithful, in which case, there's no reason to bother with getting married."

He would have laughed, but he could see that not only was she serious, but she was worried as well. Trusting him with her future was a difficult thing when Rose had been locked up her entire life. She'd only had a few months of freedom. She needed reassurance. She was being courageous in taking the steps she was taking at giving their son two parents. He was a stranger to her.

Kane crouched down beside the chair, stroking his thumb one last time over her breast, trailing his fingers over the baby's head before framing Rose's face with both hands. "I think any long-term relationship will have rough patches, Rose, but my loyalty to you will be absolute. I can't say what it's like for other men, but I'm wired to be a one-woman man. That woman is you. Everything about you appeals to the man I am. I find you amazing. Having my child only makes you more beautiful to me, not less so. Even your breast-feeding the baby is damned sexy."

She studied his eyes for a long time before he was rewarded with her slow smile. "You're a little bit crazy, but I like you that way."

"I won't always be easy to live with, Rose. I can be a

bit of a dictator, and I suspect that's the last thing you want after being a prisoner for so many years. I've always known what I wanted, and I want you, but I also want you to feel as if you have choices."

Sebastian's eyes had closed. Only occasionally was he actually suckling in his sleep, and she gently removed him and put him upright on her shoulder, patting him. "I think we need to read more in that pregnancy book. I only got as far as the birth of the baby, not when the mother could safely have sex again, because I'm beginning to think that's a very important chapter."

Kane leaned in to kiss her. He loved the taste and scent of her. He loved her response, the way she opened her mouth to him, gave herself to him, the tentative following of his lead, such a mixture of innocent and unknowing temptress. His hand cupped the back of her head, all that silky hair sliding against his palm. Her mouth was warm and sweet and addictive. He could spend the rest of his life kissing her.

Deliberately he let her take her time exploring, her tongue sliding gently along his, until he needed more. He deepened the kiss, a little more aggressive, feeling need rising, enjoying the way it took his mind and body, took his breath and exchanged with hers. Her soft, breathy moan went straight to his groin. There was no stopping, not now when she'd set off a craving that could never quite be sated. He kissed her again and again until they both were gasping for air.

He lifted his mouth inches from hers, staring into her dark, melting eyes. She touched her tongue to her lips, and he glanced down, following the movement. A drop of milk had leaked from her bare nipple, and he leaned down before he could stop himself and licked it off. Her body shuddered.

"That doesn't feel the same," she whispered.

"It isn't supposed to," he said, and with his tongue traced the path the drop had taken down the slope of her breast. "A little anticipation is good for the soul."

Rose laughed softly. "I'm going to remind you of that over the next few weeks."

"Weeks?" he echoed faintly.

"I just gave birth."

"Oh. Yeah. That." Kane pulled himself back and sat on the floor beside the chair. "For a moment I forgot everything but what it felt like with your body surrounding mine."

She smiled down at him, warmth in her eyes. Warmth and something else, something he'd never expected to see in a woman's eyes. He saw the beginnings of hunger in her eyes, but there was more now. Heat mixed with satisfaction washed over him. She was looking at him as if she might be falling in love with him. He couldn't imagine why, but he'd take whatever he could get.

He grinned at her. "I'll just sit here, staying out of trouble, while you put our son to bed."

"That's a good idea. I don't have a lot of willpower when it comes to you," Rose confessed in her direct way. She blushed a little when she made the admission.

No way was he letting that go. He stood up and pulled her out of the chair. "What did you have in mind?" His voice had gone low and husky, and every nerve ending was standing at attention.

She put Sebastian in his arms and dropped her hand low, resting it on the heavy bulge in the front of his jeans. "A lesson, of course. I don't like wasting time."

He nearly dropped the baby. "Rose." He groaned her name. "Sweetheart, this is a little like playing with a stick of dynamite." Ten minutes in her company, and he was ready to explode. "I can't make love to you, although, believe me, I want to."

She smiled that mysterious smile that made his blood go hot. "Go put the baby down, Kane."

He didn't hesitate; after all, he was going out later to kill or be killed, and he might just die a happy man. He gently placed the sleeping boy in the warmer and went back to Rose. His heart nearly stopped beating when he walked into the room and saw her. She had tossed a pillow on the floor and was kneeling there, waiting for him. Her hair was a little wild, her eyes dark and fathomless but excited. She moistened her lips and crooked a finger at him.

"This is every man's dream, honey," he announced as he walked toward her. "Are you certain this is what you want to do?" He kicked off his shoes and dropped his hands to the buttons of his jeans.

"Let me."

The soft command in her voice was nearly his undoing. There was immense pleasure just in the knowledge that a woman would be eager, even find joy, in pleasing her man. Her fingers slipped each button open, brushing over the thick length of him, sending waves of heat rushing through his groin.

"You have to tell me what to do," she whispered as she slipped her hands into the waistband of his jeans and began to slide them down his thighs. "And remember, I'm a per- fectionist. I want to learn to give you the most pleasure pos- sible. That's important to me, Kane. I want to do this right."

His cock sprang free as she pushed his jeans and shorts to the floor. He steadied himself with a hand on her shoul- der to step out of them before kicking them away.

"As much as a man loves to see his woman kneeling at his feet, this might be more comfortable for you if I lie on the bed, Rose. You'll have more control." He held out his hand to pull her up.

She gave him that tiny little frown. "But this is for you."

He shook his head. "No, this is for both of us. If you're not comfortable with it, and you don't enjoy it, then we both lose. Take your time a little exploring my body. I took my time with yours, remember?"

She flashed a small smile as she put her hand in his and allowed him to pull her up. "I doubt I'll ever forget what you did that night. I didn't know I could feel that way. I honestly never expected to feel pleasure. Rockets went off, and it was my first time. Everyone warned me it would hurt, but you . . ."

"It did hurt." Gripping her upper arms, he walked her backward into the dark bedroom.

"For a second. I can't remember anything but the pleasure. I want that again. And I want to give it to you."

Using one hand, he pulled his shirt over his head and tossed it aside. "Don't do anything you aren't comfortable with, Rose."

She put one hand on his chest and pushed. He sank back onto the bed, his heart skidding to a halt as she removed her top and bra, allowing her heavy breasts freedom. She robbed him of all breath as she dropped onto the end of the bed and crawled over his body. The sheer unexpected attack, the erotic image of her moving like a cat, arching her back, her lithe body rolling from side to side as she crawled up and over him, sent his temperature soaring and lust rolling off him in waves. Her breasts trailed invitingly over his legs, leaving her heart-shaped bottom swaying with enticement.

The sensual brush of her hair against the inside of his thighs sent another rush of heat through his veins. Rose did the unexpected. She ran her hands over his thighs and bent her head and kissed the inside of his leg. Again his cock jerked in anticipation. Her hair brushed his sensitive erection, electrifying his nerve endings. He closed his eyes as her fingers sank into the heavy muscle of his thighs, kneading deep. He felt the featherlight touch of her soft lips sliding over his legs. The contrast between the two sensations was extraordinary, or maybe it was simply that she seemed to be totally immersed in her exploration of him.

Rose took care in kissing her way up his legs and over his hips, using hands and mouth to memorize every detail of his body. His hips bucked against her involuntarily, but she didn't speed up, in spite of the evidence of his body's hunger. She'd stated she was a perfectionist, and he believed her. She didn't leave one square inch of his hips, groin, or legs unattended. By the time he felt her breath bathing his cock, he was on fire.

Her tongue seemed a velvet rasp over the mushroom head, a small lick, not tentative, and then . . . He held his breath, fingers bunching the comforter into his fists in an effort to lie still while she played. She needed this, a sense of control and knowledge. He had taken exquisite care to explore her body, to learn every inch of her erogenous zones, and clearly she was repaying him with a bonus.

He watched her through narrowed eyes. She was so damn beautiful. She had a look of intense concentration on her face. He gasped as she nearly swallowed him. Her mouth was hot and tight and silky smooth. There was no way to catch his breath, with the sensations rocking him. And then she was doing that slow licking, moving over the base of his cock, down lower, massaging with gentle fingers, committing his body to her memory, taking in his reaction as she used tongue and fingers.

No one had ever made him feel so important—or so turned on. The explosion was building to gigantic proportions, and she hadn't even really paid all that much attention to his cock. Her hands slipped under him, fingers massaging and kneading his butt. At the same time, she leaned down and engulfed his thick, hard erection again. She did something with her tongue, flicking and teasing along the underside, where his most sensitive spot was, and he couldn't control his reaction.

His hips bucked again, this time a little more wildly. She didn't grab the base of his shaft to stop him; she simply cradled his butt in her hands and urged him into her. She pulled back several times but seemed eager—more than eager—to keep exploring her ability to bring him pleasure. And she was damned good at it for an amateur, mostly, he was certain, because she was so enthusiastic. She *wanted* his pleasure, and to know that she could give it to him.

Where the hell did you learn this? Because if there was a book floating around, he was going to read the thing.

Silly man. I'm just following your example. You're the teacher; you did this to me, our first time together, remember? Her voice was almost as much of a silken caress as her lips.

She was back to licking. Sometimes her lips slid up and down him and then she'd make slow circles designed to drive him insane. He closed his eyes and let the small explosions behind his eyelids carry him on a gathering tide of ecstasy.

Rose wasn't mechanical; she was loving him, just as he had done to her their first time together. She wanted this experience for him, not for herself and, he realized, that was her secret. She was giving herself to him in the same way he had given himself to her. Fully. Without reservation. He had made the commitment to her that night, giving her not only their son but his unswerving loyalty for life. As simple as it sounded, he had tried to show her, without words, that he would love her and stand for her. The act had been physical, but the way he had gone about it had represented so much more.

Rose had understood him. He felt the buildup from his toes, burning up through his legs, the fire spreading downward from his belly until the feeling centered in his groin, like the gathering of a volcano. Her mouth was smooth, hot silk, wet and wild, moving, not just in a steady bob but spiraling up and down, her tongue sometimes flicking, sometimes using flat, broad strokes that sent his pulse rocketing.

"Sweetheart, I'm not going to be able to hold on." Already his hands had shifted from the comforter to her hair, gripping harder than he wanted, but he could barely think, his teeth clenched, breathing hard to try to slow down.

I want you to.

He knew she felt the tightening in his entire body, but did she know what to expect? "Not this time, Rose." He felt like a saint, trying to protect her.

She did that strange little flicker with her tongue and moaned, sending a vibration through his cock. He was lost, fireworks going off. He heard his own harsh groan as the world around him exploded. He should have pulled her head off him, not down onto him, but the pleasure was too intense to do anything but go with it. He realized he was holding her there and instantly tried to release her.

Rose didn't fight him, but she coughed a few times before sitting back, wiping at her mouth and down the front of her. Her hands went to support her breasts, now full and hard. She winced a little as if they were hurting her. She looked satisfied and very pleased with herself.

"I think I managed to do that mostly right, at least up until the end." She surveyed her body, making a face. "This is kind of a messy business, isn't it?"

He wasn't certain he could find his voice. He reached up to touch the hard little bead of her nipple, dripping now. He brought his finger to his mouth and licked at the little droplet. "You taste so sweet, Rose." He rubbed at the remaining evidence of his desire for her, using her shirt to clean off her breasts. "I think things got a little out of hand."

"I'll have to practice a lot more to get that right."

He shook his head, his smile welling up. She made him happy, even when she was still treating him a little like a science project. "You can practice all you like, Rose. I don't mind." His body was still shaking with the shocking pleasure.

"It's actually quite arousing to know I can make you that excited." She reached for her bra. "But all that activity made my milk come in, and I hurt. I'm going to stand in the hot shower and see if that helps."

"I can help," he offered, afraid of offending her. She looked so tempting with the milk leaking from her breasts. All he had to do was latch on and relieve the pressure for her. Everything about her was sexy, even the milk in her breasts. He felt a twinge in his cock all over again when he shouldn't be able to move for hours.

She leaned forward to brush a kiss along his chin. "I think that might make me all the more excited and needy,

Kane. I want you, and my body isn't ready yet. The hot shower is as good as it's going to get for me right now."

He pushed himself up on his elbows, glancing at the clock. He wouldn't mind joining her in the shower, just to watch her. He was seriously in danger of becoming addicted to her—especially after what she'd just done. He knew if he insisted she would allow him to suckle the excess from her. He liked the idea of her wanting him, but he didn't want to leave her needy, and he couldn't finish anything he started.

"Rose." He stopped her from scooting off the bed. "That's the most beautiful thing anyone's ever done for me. Thank you."

"I was telling you how I felt." Her gaze held steady on his.

"I was listening. I think you were very articulate."

Her slow smile rewarded him. "You could use a little cleanup yourself."

He was off the bed immediately, his hand removing the bra from her and tossing it aside. He cupped her breasts, supporting them as he walked her into the bathroom. "You take over the support while I take care of your clothes and get the temperature just right."

Rose nodded and stood, holding her aching, burning breasts in her hands. She'd never felt so hard and unattractive as in that moment. She didn't know whether to laugh or cry. She had loved telling Kane with her mouth what she couldn't say out loud. There was no other man for her. Everything about him was perfect for her. He'd showed her nothing but respect from the very beginning. And as far as she was concerned, he was the hottest man she'd ever seen.

His hands were gentle as he stripped away her jeans. She was a little embarrassed over her soft belly when she was so used to having a tight body. She wanted him to see her at her best, and unfortunately, she was feeling awkward, uncertain, and her breasts hurt like hell. The need pulsing between her legs didn't make her happy either.

She stepped under the hot water and leaned back against him, letting his hands support her breasts and keep her upright while the heat penetrated her skin and allowed her milk to run free. The relief was gradual but felt like heaven. She was conscious of Kane holding her close to him, his body like the trunk of an oak, hard and solid, an anchor in every storm.

She closed her eyes and just absorbed him. There was something about Kane that under any circumstances made her feel safe—and cared for. The way he looked at her made her feel alive, aware at all times of herself as a woman—not just as a soldier.

He glanced at his watch and, although he showed no signs of hurrying or being impatient that she took her time under the hot water, she had the feeling that he was growing anxious. As soon as they turned off the water, he handed her a large bath towel and then dried off. She followed his example at a much more leisurely pace.

He was fully dressed in combat night gear by the time she was dried off.

"What are you doing?" Rose frowned, watching him shove weapons into every conceivable loop and hidden pocket. "You don't look like we're settling in for a cozy evening."

"I'll have to go out and check on the two idiots outside. They're hatching a plan to kidnap some girl from a village. I need to know if they're really going to go through with it. If Fargo leaves, Carlson will make his try for you tonight, no matter what."

Horrified, Rose wrapped the towel around herself tightly. "They're going to do what?"

"That was the plan. It seems the booze isn't keeping them warm enough at night. They're bored and restless, Rose. Neither one of them has the discipline necessary for an assignment like this one. Whitney studies humans, and he enjoys throwing them into the very situations he thinks they should rise above, but he knows their natures work against them."

"Well, you can't allow them to take a woman from the village."

He went silent. She tried to read his expression, but he wasn't giving away his thoughts. Rose put a hand on his chest before he could leave the room. "You can't allow them to take a woman from that village, Kane; promise me."

His hand came up and trapped hers. "Sweetheart, I told you I would never lie to you. I'm not making promises I might not be able to keep."

"But . . ." She began a protest, but he leaned down and captured her mouth.

Tiny sparks electrified her mouth and raced along her insides, rushing through her veins like a drug. Heat spread through her body. Her mind went a little fuzzy, and she kissed him back, wrapping her arms around his neck.

Kane stepped back, gently capturing her wrists. "We'll talk about this when I know more." He kissed both hands and let her go. "Let's just get the information, and we'll discuss it when we have to make decisions."

CHAPTER 9

"You said when you came back with more information we were going to discuss this, Kane. You just told me Fargo was already gone." Rose stood directly in front of Kane, refusing to be intimidated by the sheer size and enormous strength of him.

Kane took a step toward her, towering over her. "I didn't expect him to leave so damned soon. It means Carlson will be getting his courage up to defy Whitney without Fargo as a deterrent. If I kill them both, we'll be forced to leave because no one will be reporting to Whitney. He'll know they're dead, and he'll send a force after us. Mack hasn't contacted us, and you said yourself the baby needs more time."

Rose breathed away her fury. She wasn't really angry at Kane, just the situation. Was she never going to be free of men like Fargo and Carlson? "All right then. You won't go after him. Then you watch the baby and I'll go. Because, Kane, one of us has to do it."

Kane shook his head, no expression on his face. His

eyes had gone flat and cold, something Rose recognized as trouble. "I thought about it. How could I not? Fargo will find some poor woman and drag her back . . ."

"*Rape* her," Rose said. "Just say it, Kane."

"Damn it, yes, but you and I both know Carlson will be coming here tonight. I can't leave you and Sebastian unprotected. It's a hell of a choice, but it's my choice. You and Sebastian come first every time. I've had to make worse choices, and I've lived with them."

He was not going to apologize for choosing her over a stranger. Carlson would come for her, he knew it with every breath in his body, and he damn well wasn't leaving her and the baby to the depraved, diseased mind of Carlson James.

Rose took a breath and let it out. It wasn't quite the easy decision for Kane as he was making it out to be. She could see the distaste in his eyes.

He held up his hand, preventing her from speaking. "I've thought a lot about this before I ever told you, Rose. Carlson will come. I'll take care of him and then—*only then*—I'll go after Fargo."

"I understand why you think it's necessary to protect us from Carlson, but really, it isn't, Kane." How could she convince him? He was a man's man. He believed that it was his duty to protect her, and in truth, she liked that quality in him. Right at this moment, though, it was a bit bothersome, but it didn't make him less appealing to her. "I don't want any woman to spend five minutes in Fargo's hands. I trust you to go out there on your own and stop that man. Do you really have less faith in me?"

Kane opened his mouth and shut it, scowling at her.

Rose shook her head, continuing the attack while she had him. "I have no doubts that I can protect Sebastian. If Carlson makes an appearance, have no worries; this time I won't be tied up and helpless when he comes to visit."

She remembered every single moment of his visits. His foul-smelling breath. The depraved look in his eyes. His

hands roving her body freely as if she were his possession. He had never gotten the chance to actually have sex
with her, but he'd certainly treated her to a taste of what
he would do given the chance. She despised the man. "He
touched me, and I wanted to throw up. I'm not going to
allow some other woman to have that happen to her if I can
prevent it. You can glower at me all you want, but we're
wasting time here."

He shook his head. "You can't go, Rose. You know you
can't."

"Then you have to. It's either you or me. That's the *only*
choice."

He swore. "Then I'll kill Carlson now, go after Fargo,
and we'll leave tonight. We'll be one day ahead of Whitney."

Rose glanced toward the bedroom where the baby slept.
"Whitney can track us because of my tattoo. He'll send his
men after us, Kane. Go after Fargo. You can make him disappear. If Carlson doesn't make his try, we can give your
unit another day to find us. Carlson will have to report to
Whitney that Fargo went into town."

She saw his jaw harden. His eyes went so bleak and
cold she shivered. There were depths to Kane she didn't
know yet. He looked unyielding, but he took a step toward
her, wrapped his hand around the nape of her neck, forcing her to step into him. She smelled him, that faint masculine scent that was all outdoors and predator. The scent
enveloped her. Her heart skidded to a halt and then began
to pound. He lowered his head and took possession of her
mouth.

Her body, of its own accord, melted into his. She felt
every single weapon imprinted on her skin, but most of all,
she felt the explosion of heat from his mouth to hers. Fire
raced down her throat and entered her bloodstream, melting her from the inside out. When he lifted his head, she
stared at him a little dazzled, uncertain what to think or
even how to think.

"Get the baby ready to leave. Follow the tunnel to the

end and check out the Humvee in case we need it. Pack supplies and everything warm you can for Sebastian. Choose weapons we both can handle with as many rounds of ammo you can find for them. Don't forget water."

"What are you doing?"

"Whatever is necessary. You're a soldier. Figure it out." He turned and left her standing there, her heart pounding.

There was no arguing with him. She recognized that now. He'd been malleable and sweet, but only up to a point. Kane had his own brand of honor, and no one—not even her—was going to deter him when he felt he was right. She should have known. She recognized a dangerous man when she saw one, and she had chosen him in part because he was dangerous—she knew if she got away from Whitney, Kane would fight with his last breath to keep her safe. Now that she'd seen what that entailed, she couldn't very well be angry at him.

She ran to the door, stopping him right before he opened it. "Kane."

He turned to look at her with his piercing, implacable eyes.

"Be safe. Come back to us."

"No worries, sweetheart."

Kane flashed Rose a smile and slipped out into the night where he belonged. There was freedom in darkness. He was born to rule the night. He looked up at the night sky. Stars were everywhere, and he could see the thick swirling ribbon that was the Milky Way. The tight knots that had developed when Rose argued with him unraveled, and everything in him settled. This was his world. He was familiar with it, comfortable in it. This was where he belonged.

Now that he'd made up his mind, there was no hesitation. Rose couldn't live with Fargo's actions, and that meant both Carlson and Fargo died tonight. Carlson had to go first, because no matter how good a soldier Rose was, she was first and foremost his woman, and that meant he protected her whether she liked it or not. That was the biggest part of his personality, and she'd better understand it wasn't going away because she was a capable—even brilliant—soldier. He would never knowingly expose her to danger and certainly not a week after she'd given birth.

He shook his head at the peculiarities of women. He would never understand Rose, not if they lived together a million years, and he could see that she was having the same problem understanding him. Was it like that with all men and women? Or just men like him? He could be a first-class bastard if the situation called for it. He didn't have a lot of experience in relationships. He'd avoided entanglements until he'd seen Rose looking at him through her window. She had become his princess in the tower, and he was the white knight to the rescue.

Kane began to run, the easy, steady pace he could keep for hours if need be. He was familiar with the terrain now, having gone over it three times in every twenty-four-hour period for a week. He knew every boulder and shrub. He knew every patch of saw grass and the dark, rich patches that indicated an underground source of water.

He approached the enemy camp from the south, staying downwind. He could see a faint light but couldn't see the source immediately. Dropping lower, so as not to skyline himself, he slowed his pace, moving with stealth as he stalked his prey. The overpowering stench of blood hit him as he reached the top of the slope overlooking the base camp.

Carlson and Fargo had tucked their camp between slopes, enabling them to have a fire when they wanted to, as well as shelter. Unless you came right up on them, the site was impossible to see. Empty bottles were strewn around on the ground. This was no soldier's encampment, rather it looked like a couple of men enjoying a vacation.

Great globs of blood left a trail in the sand, dark, obscene smear marks that led toward the faint flickering light. An agonized scream, animalistic, impossible to identify, sent chills down Kane's spine. He'd seen men tortured and had-been on the receiving end a time or two and knew that sound. Laughter rang out, then the low murmur of a voice.

"Hey, don't die on me. It's going to be a long night before the real entertainment gets here. You're helping me out, suffering for a good cause and all. A little pain is good for the soul. I need something to make me feel good. My little whore of a woman is about to have another man's baby, and I'm pissed."

The terrible squeal came again, more animal than man. The sound made the hairs on Kane's neck stand up. The stench was awful. Carlson was a sadistic bastard. If torturing a man—or an animal—made him feel better, something was seriously off about the man.

A part of Kane had actually felt a little sorry for him. He knew what it was like to crave Rose, to think about her night and day, to dream of her when he managed to close his eyes and nothing—no one else—was going to sate the ever-present hunger for her body. Kane knew he could have sex with hundreds of women, and none of them would ever satisfy him again. He'd accepted that premise when he'd signed on to be paired with her. Had Carlson had a choice as well? It didn't matter now. All that mattered now was stopping the son of a bitch.

He dropped even lower, topping the slope. Rocks surrounded a small fire. A makeshift rack made of two thick sticks with a third suspended between them hung just to the left of the fire. Two coyotes hung there, still alive, panting and shuddering in pain. Blood dripped steadily into a dark, blackened pool beneath each of them. A crude arrow protruded from each body.

Carlson had obviously done this many times. Neither arrow had struck anything vital but had incapacitated the animals. A third coyote lay stretched out in front of Carlson, pinned through his body with a circular wooden stake. The animal continually tried to crawl away, only to be held back by the stake. Every movement had to be causing excruciating pain. Carlson crouched over the animal, poking at it with a knife. Several patches of fur were missing. If the animal bled too much, he cauterized the wound and waited a few minutes to start again. Clearly he was skinning the animal alive.

He poked the coyote again and laughed harshly when the creature snapped at him, the air, and finally his own leg. "I can't have you trying to bite me, now can I?" Carlson murmured. "I wonder what will happen if I just take this one eye right here?" He plunged the tip of his knife into the flames and waited until it was glowing hot.

Sickened, Kane eased himself into a good position and put his rifle to his shoulder, finger on the trigger as he took aim. As Carlson leaned in to take the coyote's eye, Kane shot him through the back of his neck. It was a kill shot, pure and simple, and Kane didn't miss. He shot the coyote, putting him out of his misery, and then shot the other two that were hanging, waiting to be tortured.

He eased his body back and wiped his mouth with the back of his hand. He'd run across a few sadistic men in his time, but this man had all the makings of a killer. He was practically bathing in blood. Did Whitney know? Had he delved into Carlson's background? If he had, he would never have allowed this man to create a child with Rose. Whitney wanted soldiers. Men loyal to their country. Men willing to fight for a cause, not kill indiscriminately.

He had to cover his tracks, leave the body where it lay, so Whitney wouldn't be able to know for certain who had killed his man. Whitney wouldn't hear from either of them late the next evening, and he would send a team to collect Rose.

Kane took care of his rifle first, as always, and then blew sand across his tracks as he made his way back toward town. Once away from the actual camp area, he didn't worry about his tracks. He began to run, using his steady, ground-eating pace. Fargo had a good head start on him and he would be moving fast, wanting to kidnap a woman while it was still dark and get back to camp before anyone was the wiser.

He worried about leaving Rose and the baby alone for so long while he covered the miles to the town. The sand seemed to stretch in front of him forever. He had a good sense of direction, but without a GPS or the stars, he might have had a difficult time locating the town. He expected to overtake Fargo. His entire unit was abnormally fast runners, even in full combat gear. Few could match them. He definitely should have caught up with Fargo.

The fact that he never came up on the man meant either of two things: Fargo had taken a different route, or one of his gifts was his speed. Whitney had enhanced their physical capabilities by playing around with their DNA— something that was never part of the original contract for psychic enhancement. Had he done the same to his soldiers, even knowing they were psychologically flawed?

Kane swore softly, swerving to find a dark patch of richer sand and dirt so he could crouch low and give it some thought. If Fargo had already made it into town, it would be stupid to follow him. There were too many ways the man could slip past him in such a wide-open desert. He swore again as he cast back and forth for signs that someone had followed this route into town. It was the most direct route, and he couldn't imagine that there was any reason for Fargo to take any other.

If Fargo managed to slip past him and make his way back to the base camp, he would find Carlson and the dead coyotes. "Damn it!" he said aloud. If he'd just done what he thought was best and stayed with Rose and the baby, waiting for Carlson to make his move, he would know she was safe. As it was, he had no hope of finding Fargo in the vast desert.

The only thing left to do was to return to the base camp and hope he beat Fargo to it. Why in the hell had he ever allowed Rose to persuade him against his better judgment?

Resolutely he turned back and began to trot across the rolling sand. He'd have to stake out the camp. The unfortunate woman Fargo returned with would have to be dealt with after the fact; it couldn't be helped. He couldn't prevent Fargo from grabbing her, but the man wouldn't have a chance to use her unless he took the time to stop along the way. And was he going to force her to walk across the desert?

Kane stopped abruptly. No way would Fargo do that. He had to have a vehicle somewhere, which meant . . . He groaned and rubbed his hand over his face. What the hell was the matter with him? Of course they had someone in town. Whitney would have sent at least one, possibly two to back them up, to watch over them. He *expected* them to screw up. He was documenting everything in his microworld of experimentation of the human spirit. Who was watching the watchers?

"Stupid, stupid mistake," he hissed between his teeth and set out running back to Rose.

He didn't have to worry about burning himself out with running for miles. His lungs and heart were made for running. He covered the ground fast, not bothering to look for Fargo. They were in trouble, no doubt about it, and the only concern was to get out of the trap they were in.

As he neared the subterranean house, he used telepathy. *Rose! Answer me now. Are you okay? Have you been attacked?*

The lag time before he felt her stirring in his mind seemed forever. His mouth went dry and his heart pounded, not from the run, but from very real fear. Was he too late? Had someone already attacked the house?

Everything's quiet here, Kane. What's wrong?

Inside the kitchen I've been constructing a baby seat for Sebastian. It's as good as we can get for his protection. Did you get the supplies into the Humvee like I told you?

Of course. She was obviously on the move, he could tell by her voice and the distraction.

Rose dragged on her jacket and a belt loaded with weapons and ammunition, put the baby in a front pack, and caught up her gun. *I'm dressed and have the baby. Going into the kitchen now.*

Kane circled the house and continued on toward the back entrance where the tunnel emerged. *I'm clearing the back, so don't shoot me. Get the baby secured, put the weapons where I can easily reach them. You're the driver. We're going to blast out of there and hightail it away from the town back toward the border.*

We're you able to free the woman?

Of course she would be asking him that. She'd been a prisoner, and had he not accepted Whitney's proposal to be paired with her, eventually they would have forced someone on her. She didn't want another woman to suffer at the hands of a brutal man. He couldn't blame her, but right now, he had to think about Rose and Sebastian.

No, Fargo had too big a head start.

He could feel her in his mind, quiet. Thoughtful. *If Fargo reached town and more than likely went to a bar to drink, that's where he'd grab the woman. But how was he planning on getting her back to his camp?*

Oh yeah. That was his woman. Intelligent all the way. Fargo sure wasn't going to be dragging a woman across the rolling hills for miles. He would have a vehicle, one that was more than likely stashed for them when they had to go into town for supplies. Diego Jimenez had done that very thing, keeping his truck in a garage just waiting for him.

Kane answered her the only way he knew how, with the truth. *I think Whitney has at least one man observing Fargo and Carlson. He expected them to fail. He put all their weaknesses right in front of them. Booze. Women. You. That's what Whitney does, Rose—it's what amuses him. He finds a man's weakness, and he exploits it to see if he can put him in situations that force him to either succumb to the weakness or overcome it.*

Rose sucked in her breath. *Kane. Does that include the*

two of us? Is he playing an elaborate game with us? He tracked me all this time. He had to know I was pregnant with the child he wanted. Would he take the chance of losing the baby before he could get his hands on him? Just to see if I could truly escape him?

Kane was coming around to the upper slope. The terrain on either side of the tunnel sloped upward, successfully hiding the fact that there was any kind of opening at all. The Humvee could run down the path between the two hills for several miles and remain unseen as long as there were no eyes in the sky. Someone would have to come to the top of the slope, where they would be skylined. Even lying prone would be difficult to keep from being seen.

Diego Jimenez had thought out his home and his escape route thoroughly. He had shown the house and truck to Rose, but not the weapons, tunnel, or Humvee. Why? The question nagged at him. It had been all along. Why wouldn't Jimenez disclose everything about his home if he meant it as an escape route for Rose? Something wasn't right. Kane knew he'd better figure it out fast.

He went down on his belly and slithered cautiously up to the rise, careful not to push any dirt down the other side of the hill. He lifted his head just enough to peer down onto the narrow trail that led away from the house. He couldn't see the actual entrance to the tunnel from the angle, but it didn't matter. He was looking for company.

I just found a letter from Diego addressed to me, Kane. It was in the locker where I was storing extra weapons. Rose sounded worried. He could feel a tinge of fear pushing its way into his mind.

Tell me. He prompted. *But do it in the driver's seat. As soon as I give you the okay, I want you to drive the hell out of there. I'll be coming down to you on the driver's side.*

He took his time, searching every square inch of land around him. He was vaguely uneasy. Something was wrong; he just couldn't put his finger on what it was. Radar was going off, but he couldn't find any signs of the enemy.

He thanks me for taking care of him while he was dying and then goes on to say that Whitney provided money and guns to help him fight the past government because the former president was heavily involved with one of the drug families. He said Whitney was upset that the U.S. was aiding the country in any way as long as that el presidente held office.

She broke off, and Kane could picture her frowning as she turned the information over in her mind. *He said he owed Whitney for all the aid over the years. When the new president took office and declared war on the cartels, Diego was no longer needed but felt the debt had not been fully repaid. Evidently, Whitney felt the same way.*

Kane sighed, his gaze restless as he quartered the area for enemies. *So you were the last payment to Whitney.*

Something like that, yes.

Kane could tell she was upset, maybe even crying. He wrapped her mentally in his arms, wishing he could spare her more betrayal. Whitney wanted her to break under so much betrayal. He hadn't counted on the cartel kidnapping *el presidente's* sister-in-law and niece and nephew. He hadn't counted on Rose doing the right thing and reporting it to the authorities. He hadn't foreseen *el presidente* asking the U.S. president for help or the U.S. president sending an elite squad of urban fighters into the country to rescue the hostages in secret.

He said if I found the letter, that it meant I found the weapons he left as well as the tunnel and Humvee. He felt, after what I'd done for him, that I deserved a chance at least to get away.

You nursed him through his dying days, Rose. He owed you.

The sorrow in her hadn't let up. There was more, and his heart sank. *Sweetheart, I'm heading down into the open tube. Drive straight ahead about fifty feet. I'll meet you there.*

He slid over the side like a lizard, scooting belly-down,

still not trusting that his gut was giving him false information. *Something* was a threat, he just hadn't identified it yet.

Halfway down the slope, a boulder jutted out of the dirt and sand. Kane scrambled around it, heard an angry buzz, and threw himself into a roll. Splinters of rock rained down, two embedding in his pack as he somersaulted by.

Sniper, Rose. Three o'clock. He continued rolling down the slope, knowing a good marksman could hit him. He'd never felt quite so exposed.

The Humvee tore out of the tunnel into the open, roaring between him and the shooter as he landed hard on the flat trail. He yanked open the passenger door and dove inside. "Go. Go."

She stomped on the gas, and the vehicle grabbed and took off, racing away from their haven. Kane slammed the door closed and checked to make certain the baby was surrounded by the bulletproof vests they'd found in the tunnel. He'd lined the makeshift car seat with one as well. The boy was locked in facing the seat for added protection and appeared sound asleep.

He expected the shooter to fire a few more rounds, but if the man did, nothing hit the Humvee, and Kane couldn't imagine facing anyone but a good marksman, which meant the shooter was on the move.

"Keep straight, sweetheart," he instructed, checking the loads in the various weapons and placing them strategically around the Humvee. "He's out there, and he's going to come after us."

"Is Sebastian all right?" Rose shot one look over her shoulder at the baby.

The Humvee wasn't the most comfortable ride, bouncing them all over the place as she went over rocks and patches of thick shrubs. Just as Kane could see in the darkness, so could she. There was no need for lights. The trail was grown over with shrubbery. Rocks rolled down the slope on either side. She went right over them, gripping the wheel as it jumped in an effort to get away from her.

"Diego gave me up to the cartel." Rose's voice was grim.

"Are you certain?"

"It's in the letter. He told them Whitney would pay a fortune for me." She leaned forward, peering out the window. "Apparently he has two sons who have been on the cartel's wanted list. In return for me and his connection to Whitney, the cartel will leave his family alone. The plan is to ransom me and the baby to Whitney."

Kane swore through clenched teeth. Not only did they have to worry about Whitney and his men, but now they might have the cartel breathing down their necks. That information certainly ruled out going back into town.

"I take it he left the guns and Humvee to clear his conscience before he died."

She nodded. "He said he couldn't live with himself if he didn't at least give me some kind of a chance."

"Why did the cartel wait?"

"I think they were busy trying to find the men who stole their prisoners. I'm a helpless woman, about to give birth, trapped in a house in the desert."

Kane narrowed his eyes. "Get out of here, Rose. Right now, go up the slope. I have no idea where this trail comes out, but if he had some deal with the cartel, then my guess is, the moment you left the tunnel in the Humvee, they knew it and they'll be waiting wherever this trail comes out. We have no idea how long it is."

She had already started up the slope, angling the Humvee to race up the sandy hill as quickly as possible. The heavy vehicle had no trouble going through the shifting terrain, mowing down shrubs and bumping over rocks. They topped the rise and burst out into the open desert.

At once, in the far distance, they could see a line of lights, pinpoint lasers slicing through the darkness, bouncing crazily as several vehicles dashed over the sand. The trucks were a few miles away but coming for them. Rose angled the Humvee away from the caravan, presumably the cartel, and made a run for it across the desert.

"Make a wide circle and head back toward the canyon where we dumped the tracking device," Kane advised. "At least we'll have cover there to hold them off. Sooner or later my boys will come to the party."

Rose nodded and then pointed toward their left. "That's got to be Fargo with the woman."

A single vehicle wove drunkenly across the sand, sliding sideways, circling and careening down slopes to nearly stall out as it powered up the other side.

"He's drunk, Kane."

"Damn it, Rose." His heart sank. She was already swerving to intercept.

He glanced back at the line of lights piercing the darkness. Stopping to rescue a woman wasn't on his agenda, but apparently it was on Rose's. "Damn stubborn woman," he hissed under his breath and tossed his rifle aside.

Fat lot of good a gun was going to do him. He couldn't just shoot the bastard and be done with it. Fargo was driving the vehicle, and he was going at a dangerous rate of speed. If Kane shot him, the car would overturn and possibly kill the kidnap victim. He didn't think Rose would look too kindly on that outcome. He was going to have to actually take control of the truck.

"Come up behind him. Match his speed." What the hell point was there in arguing with her? She had a look of sheer determination on her face. "I just want to remind you that you're taking our son into a combat situation." He couldn't help the righteous tone. He wasn't getting blamed later on. She could take full responsibility.

Rose shot him a quelling look. He felt the Hummer rumbling as she picked up more speed. The woman wasn't afraid of racing. She had to adjust her angle several times as Fargo kept weaving and circling.

Kane kept his eye on the line of vehicles behind them. The heavily armored Humvee topped out around sixty miles an hour. Rose seemed to be pushing that just a little. The heavy vehicle was scrambling his insides as it threw them from side to side and then up and down. The smaller, lighter trucks and Jeeps were definitely gaining on them, but they were still a good distance away. She had to cut Fargo off quickly, or they would be out of time.

The soldier wasn't paying any attention at all to the Hummer bearing down on him. He threw a bottle out the window and spun the truck twice before fishtailing several yards. Only then did he notice the Humvee running without lights coming up behind him.

Kane was already exiting onto the roof. He could see a woman lying in a heap on the seat of the truck. He couldn't tell if she was alive or dead, but with every bounce of the truck, her body shook like a rag doll. Rose brought the Humvee directly into position behind Fargo and his prisoner. Kane timed it, knowing he had the ability to easily cross the distance and land safely.

He launched himself into the air, knife in hand, gaze fixed on the landing. Something hit him hard in his left side, spinning his body around, the sting turning into a blossoming pain, driving his body back and away from his landing. He hit the sand hard and rolled, only then realizing he'd been shot. The marksmen had made an extraordinary shot from some unknown location.

Headlights caught him as Fargo wheeled his truck around, howling with laughter, as if they were playing some fun game after a drunken party. The truck bore down on him, flying at him at a high rate of speed. With the truck spotlighting him, the shooter couldn't fail to hit him, and there was nowhere to run—nowhere to hide. He couldn't even defend himself exposed as he was. He kept rolling, testing his body, leaving a blood trail, drawing his legs and arms up in readiness to push himself to his feet.

Rose spun the Humvee around and drove hard to intercept the truck. Kane managed to gain his feet, facing the oncoming truck. He saw Fargo's head disappear into a raw mass of blood and tissue as the marksmen shot again. The windshield and seat turned bright red. With no one at the wheel, the truck began to veer over the uneven terrain, every bounce taking it on a different path.

Rose once again inserted the armored Humvee between Kane and the shooter. He sprinted for the safety of the vehicle, jerking open the door and diving inside. Rose took off away from the line of advancing headlights, trying to get every ounce of speed she could out of the multipurpose vehicle.

"How bad?" Rose demanded.

Kane inspected his side. A hunk of skin was missing, but little else other than his pride. He slapped a pressure bandage over it. "Maybe he wasn't going for the kill and he knocked me away from Fargo's vehicle on purpose so he could kill the man. Who the hell knows?"

"Who is he?"

"Whitney's cleanup man. Get us the hell out of here, Rose. The cartel is on our ass, and we've got another player in the game." He took a quick look at the baby to make certain the boy was okay.

Sebastian opened his eyes and looked back at him. Kane smiled at him. "You're good, son, just hang in there a little longer."

"I'm going to try to take out the shooter, Rose. In any case, the cartel is going to be on us in another few minutes. We can't outrun them. We're too far away from the ravine to go to ground, so I'll have to give them something to think about."

"I don't like the idea of you exposing yourself to the shooter. We don't even know where he is. How are you going to get a fix on him?"

Their eyes met in the mirror. She shook her head. "No. No way. You are not going to give him another shot at you."

He grinned at her. "We've got the weapons to protect ourselves, Rose, and we're going to need to use them."

"Look at the truck," Rose said, pointing at the pickup that had been careening through the desert out of control.

The driver's-side door flew open, and a body hit the ground, bounced, and then lay still. The truck swerved back and forth before the new driver took control. She spun the truck around and headed back toward the line of lights, now much closer.

Kane opened the hatch above his head. The shooter would no doubt have his eye to the scope, but Rose was pushing the speed of the Humvee past sixty-five and redlining the heavy vehicle.

"Sweetheart, we don't want to kill the engine," Kane cautioned as he took a slow look around. He had an arsenal mounted on the roof, and he could sit inside safe and warm, if he knew where the bastard was.

He reached back and pulled out a helmet, raising it slightly. A bullet tore into the top, knocking it out of his hand.

"Got him. He's at three o'clock. High ground. He's on the slope up there." Rose kept her heading toward the ravine, as though they still had no idea of the sniper's position. "And just so you know, Kane, that bullet could have taken your head off."

"Yeah, I got that." He'd been hoping the sniper's first shot had been a miss on purpose. "I think they have no idea who I am, Rose. It's possible they think I'm Carlson stealing you away. Whitney set his watchdogs on Carlson and Fargo. They've eliminated Fargo, so they're coming after me."

"I agree that it's got to be Whitney's man," Rose called back to him. "So if he's driving us toward the canyon and away from that slope, what does that mean?"

Kane had a sinking feeling he knew what it meant. Whitney had a crew waiting for them. He didn't bother to answer the question. Rose knew what it meant as well. Of course Whitney still had no way of knowing that Rose had given birth to Sebastian. They thought she was still pregnant. With the cartel behind them and the sniper driving them in a direction, Kane was certain Whitney was dropping—or had already dropped—more men into the combat zone.

"The canyon offers the only viable cover, and we can't run in this thing forever. We have enough ammo to give it a good fight, and I can take out a good portion of the cartel's vehicles and men when they close the distance. Forget luring them to open fire again. Drive straight for the ravine."

"We might be driving right into Whitney's men."

Kane shrugged. "Then we make our stand there. I think we'll have more of a chance. Otherwise all they have to do is wait for us to run out of gas and then water. We've got Sebastian to think of, Rose. Head for the canyon."

She nodded and kept to the course, the Humvee bumping over the uneven ground, followed in the distance by a stream of bouncing lights as the cartel followed.

CHAPTER 10

The canyon was several miles away across open ground, but it was their only real cover. The M1165 Humvee with frag armor included two-inch-thick bulletproof glass. The doors alone weighed a good 250 pounds. Along with the state-of-the-art CROWS system mounted on the roof, they had firepower and protection but little speed.

Kane liked the idea of staying inside the Hummer now that they had half the cartel on their asses as well as a sniper and spotter. With the CROWS system, a remote-controlled weapon platform mounted on top of the vehicle, the gunner could sit in the vehicle and use a joystick, watching the action through a "TV" screen. The system had the capability to zoom in, use night vision, infrared, daytime, or heat sensor, with some very heavy-duty weapons. If necessary, and he hoped it wouldn't be, he could disengage and use the system manually.

"They're coming up behind us," he said.

Bullets sprayed across the back of the Humvee. The first of the cartel vehicles had outdistanced the others and had gotten within firing range. In the distance they heard a massive explosion, and the ground shook. The blast seemed to trigger several smaller detonations. Kane saw a large mushroom plume rising out of the desert in the direction of Diego Jimenez's subterranean house.

"What the hell was that?" he demanded.

Rose shot him a fierce look. "That was me being pissed off. If the cartel—or Diego's sons—thought they'd be using his home and tunnel, or any of the weapons he acquired from Whitney, they have another think coming."

"Remind me never to get you angry at me," he said.

"Don't ever betray me."

Kane grinned at her. "You're so damn sexy, *soldada hermosa,* especially when you go all blow-things-up and scary on me."

She pursed her lips and made kissy noises. "Just a gentle reminder."

He laughed out loud. "Just so you know, I'm the jealous type."

Her eyebrow shot up. "Fine time to tell me. I thought I was going to get to take lots of lovers. Guess not."

"Damn right you guess not."

A heavy caliber weapon rocked the Humvee. Rose ducked and then bared her teeth, eyes flashing fire. "Check the baby and then teach that idiot a lesson in manners."

"I do so love it when you go all soldier on me."

"Quit flirting with me and get the job done."

"You started it by blowing up the house," he pointed out righteously. Dutifully he took another look at Sebastian. The bouncing of the Humvee didn't seem to bother him, although he did open his eyes to stare at his father through narrow, sleep slits. "We're fine, son," Kane soothed. "Mommy's a terrible driver, but she's having fun, so we'll overlook it this once."

Sebastian's little bow of a mouth curved in a smile, and his eyes closed.

Kane settled in front of the screen, his hand on the joystick. The lighter, much more mobile truck leapt onto the screen. One man was in the bed of the pickup with a machine gun. Another was strapped to the roof with a rocket launcher. A third man leaned out of the passenger window with what appeared to be a grenade in his hand. The driver, with a look of determination on his face, fought the wheel as the tires bounced over the rough terrain.

"This is a cool system," Kane said. "I've got one sweet weapon for distance and damage." He could hit someone a good one and a half miles away.

"You sound like a kid in a candy store. Shoot them already, or you'll be doing the driving and I'll be the one having fun," she threatened.

"Bloodthirsty little wench," he muttered. "I'm on it."

The M2 .50 caliber, able to tear a vehicle apart, seemed ideal. "Keep it steady. I don't really want to waste a lot of ammo on these morons. Do they not see the weapons?" Even as he asked the question, he fired a series of three rounds, hitting the roof, the back of the truck, and launching one through the windshield.

The truck explosion was spectacular. He grinned at her. "And that's how it's done, sweetheart."

She laughed and shook her head. "My man is crazy."

He felt the shift in his heart. A warm glow in his belly. He liked being her man. He grinned at her and gave her a small salute.

The Humvee was approaching the entrance to the canyon. There was only one real way down, consisting of a narrow slope that ran down over boulders and shrubs. The Humvee would have no problems, and that had to be where Whitney's men would be waiting, if they were there.

"You know you can't take us down there," he cautioned. "They'll have mines."

"Great minds think alike," she said, although she didn't sway from her course.

Kane studied the walls of the canyon, looking for signs of activity. His gut was telling him they were heading straight for a trap. Twice he looked at her grim face, but he said nothing.

"Be ready," she ordered. "We need a direction. Left or right?"

At the same time they both answered the question. "Right."

Their eyes met. "Left."

Two seconds later, just before they would have gone down the slope into the canyon, she cut hard to the left and ran parallel with the canyon. "If we both have the same answer, Whitney may have known that's what we'd do."

"Or he guessed we'd do just what we did," he pointed out, laughing. "We could play this game all night."

"Fire already," she ordered.

Kane sprang into action, understanding her intention, but his mouth went dry. He knew the capabilities of the vehicle, but not of the driver. She planned on him opening up a path for them and taking them in. The Humvee was top-heavy with the mounted weapons in place. He didn't want the whole damn thing to flip over. Nevertheless, he fired several shots to blow the boulders and trees out of their way, clearing a rough trail for them to take.

Instead of trying to go straight down, Rose angled the vehicle to take the incline at a slight slant. The moment he realized what she wanted, he was able to clear her line of travel much more easily.

Three of the cartel vehicles followed the Humvee. One of the trucks chose the easy path and drove right into the minefield Whitney's men had set. The blast, although not designed to destroy, took out the unprotected undercarriage of the truck. The truck popped into the air and came down on its side. One man was flung from the back and landed hard, not moving. The one strapped to the roof hung face-down and made a slight effort to move. The driver and passenger both were still alive, one screaming relentlessly.

Three of Whitney's men popped up with automatic weapons, firing indiscriminately, hosing down all four men. Instantly, Kane zoomed in on their positions. With the distance he had on the weapon, he was able to fire into their nest without difficulty. The third shooter returned fire from the safety of his blind, so Kane swung his attention onto him and sent a couple of presents his way. The explosions rocked the earth and silenced the weapons.

"Kane!"

Rose's voice turned his attention back to their chosen path. He came around immediately to center his weapon ahead of them, blazing a trail down an impossibly steep incline. Boulders and large shrubs gave way to trees and thick undergrowth. She took it slowly, aware that the remaining vehicles chasing them, although four-wheel drive, were much lighter and ill-equipped to traverse such a difficult route. It wouldn't do much good to soften the trail up with heavy weapon fire. They'd committed to the sharp drop, and they had to trust the vehicle to take them down into the depths of the canyon.

Several grenades struck the ground around them, blowing part of the land away just feet from the Humvee. The Hummer shook with the force of the explosions and careened violently, sliding for a heart-stopping moment before the tires gripped solid ground again. A flurry of activity in the narrow valley below revealed a small force of men waiting for them. They'd disrupted Whitney's plans, startling his men. The barricades hastily put in place to stop them had been bypassed by taking the steep route. Whitney's men rushed to regroup and cut them off.

The Humvee hit the bottom, bouncing hard into the nearly dry creek bed, and jolted over the heavy rocks, away from Whitney's soldiers. The sound of machine guns was loud and mini explosions erupted all around them, so that for a time the world was gray and black with the debris and smoke surrounding them.

Behind them, one of the cartel's trucks rolled, smashing everything in its path. Small saplings splintered and cracked. The truck uprooted shrubs and plants, sending them, along with smaller rocks, tumbling down the slope, creating a mini avalanche. The rolling truck landed hard, upside down, wheels spinning nearly on top of the Hummer.

The boom resounded through the narrow gorge. Sebastian woke with a cry, and Kane put a calming hand on the boy.

"Is he all right?" Rose demanded, staring straight ahead, trying to maneuver through the rocks and boulders in the creek bed.

"He's fine, just a little shaken up, aren't you, buddy?" Kane crooned.

"We're jerking him all over the place," she said, worried.

"We've got him tucked in tight. He's barely moving," Kane soothed her. "Do you hear your mommy, Sebastian? She isn't worried about the gunfire, just you."

"We're taking a *lot* of gunfire," Rose said unnecessarily, "but they aren't hitting anything. Just around us."

Which made it damn difficult to drive. Whitney's men were aiming in front of them, blasting away, pitting the creek bed and throwing more debris into the air so that rocks hit the sides and roof of the Humvee.

"They want you alive, honey, so they can't exactly blast the Hummer. They have to stop us, not kill us. Well, not kill you. Apparently I'm disposable."

Rose drove up the side of the shallow creek to avoid a huge crater and then back down into the hellfire. Kane steadied the joystick, swinging the M2 .50-caliber around until he had the two-man team tearing up the creek bed in his sights. He sent off three rounds and swung the weapon back to protect their flank as one of the cartel's lighter jeeps fell in behind him.

He hesitated. The jeep was drawing fire from Whitney's men. The second vehicle, a red jeep, turned tail and was making its way back up the steep slope. For a moment it looked as if the red jeep would make it, putting on a burst of speed, but then it stalled, stopping. The passenger bailed out, diving as far as he could from the jeep and scrambling for cover, still clutching his rifle. In slow motion the jeep flipped, slamming into the ground, rolling, picking up speed and momentum. Halfway down the slope, the driver lay crumpled and broken, his body sprawled out over a pile of rocks. The jeep hit a boulder jutting out and took to the air.

One of Whitney's men hit it with a rocket in midair, turning the vehicle into a fiery ball of orange red. The explosion rained down metal and shrapnel. Behind them, the cartel's jeep inched closer, one of the men half standing, clinging to the roll bar, as if he was considering jumping to the roof of the Humvee.

"He's plain psychotic," Kane said aloud.

"Have you considered shooting them?" Rose demanded.

"No, he's actually providing a little cover for us."

Kane's belly took a dive, suddenly hardening into a series of tight knots. The hair on his arms raised. "Get us out of here, Rose."

"In case you hadn't noticed, that's what I'm trying to do." She glared at him.

"No, I mean out of this creek bed."

"How am I supposed to do that? We don't exactly have a lot of options here, Kane."

He ignored the bite to her voice. The hair on the back of his neck was now tingling, much like the whiskers on a leopard, a kind of radar, and right now, although he couldn't explain it to her, he knew his warning system was shrieking at him.

"Fucking do it, Rose. I don't care how. Get us out of here."

He swiveled around constantly, looking for the threat. Everything inside of him urged him to take Rose and Sebastian and get out of the Humvee.

"Now, damn it!"

Something was just up ahead, just where the creek bed began a long slow, sweeping bend. He strained his eyes trying to see, nearly standing, one hand instinctively reaching out to protect his child, but the sense of urgency was so strong, he covered the child and the makeshift car seat and armor with his own body.

Abruptly the Hummer lurched as Rose fought the wheel, driving them up and over an impossible set of rocks. Kane swung around to look behind them, still protecting Sebastian. Unable to follow, the cartel's jeep continued on a few more feet and suddenly vanished as if it had never been, dropping down into a large crater, a sinkhole a good hundred feet deep.

Rose swore under her breath as the Humvee rocked from side to side, laboring to climb over the dense shrubbery and rocky incline.

"We can't make it straight up," she said. "I'll try inching my way up, but if they start shooting . . ." She broke off abruptly as the hillside above them exploded and rocks and dirt rained down on them. "That's what I was afraid of. We can't get back into that creek bed, Kane. They're going to trap us."

Kane was already back in his seat, hand on the joystick. They were going to have to shoot their way out. "Keep moving forward, even if it's running along the bank."

She complied. "We're awfully close to that sinkhole, Kane, and we weigh a hell of a lot."

"I know, sweetheart." He centered the screen on the mortar gun wreaking havoc above them. "When I say go, move up a few feet and keep running parallel."

He blasted the mortar gun and all around it, firing round after round, providing cover. "Now, Rose." He kept it up, pounding the area to prevent them from pitting the canyon wall and destroying any path they might find to take them out or around the stronghold Whitney's men had established.

Rose was already jolting them forward, the Humvee rolling over the thick foliage and smashing down the displaced dirt.

Where the hell are you, Mack? Because if his team

hadn't gotten the message loud and clear that he'd left for them in the desert, he and Rose and Sebastian were bound to have to dig in and hold off Whitney's little army. They had enough water and ammunition to last for a time, but they needed reinforcements—and soon.

Mack had to have sent out a couple of birds to look for signs, and he'd left an abundance of them each night. The last sign had been unmistakable: *Come now.* They had to have seen his messages, and he'd pointed them back to the ravine. Surely . . .

The ground around them exploded. Rose swore louder this time but kept the Humvee moving forward. One tire dropped into air on the passenger side, so that they tilted ominously. They kept moving forward relentlessly. Trees were thicker now and much larger than the saplings and thin round trunks they'd encountered, presenting an additional problem.

"Kane." Rose's voice shook. "In the air, coming at us. Three o'clock."

Two helicopters were coming toward them fast, just above the tree line, swooping in low, racing right for them. "Are they yours?" she asked.

Her voice was strictly neutral, but he could see hope flare in her eyes. "I'm sorry, sweetheart, they aren't."

She took a breath, her knuckles white as she gripped the wheel hard, guiding the Humvee around a large tree, rolling over two smaller ones. "If this goes bad, Kane, you take the baby and get out of here. He has a better chance with you. They want me alive, and they'll try to be more careful. They don't know he's born yet."

"Not a chance." He was already lining up his shot, the first helicopter in his sights, as it came right toward them. He could see the grim faces, the heavy artillery they carried. They planned on hitting the Hummer, knocking it out of commission and forcing it to halt where they could surround and control it. Most likely, they planned to drop their men on the roof.

"They think I'm Carlson James, Rose. He's disposable. Whitney's pissed at him. They'll try to kill me, believing I'm him. I don't want Sebastian anywhere near me. If it really comes down to it, I'll buy you enough time to get him away."

He took the shot just as the helicopter peeled off. He caught it on the tail, throwing the bird into a spin. Smoke trailed it. The pilot fought hard, but the helicopter began to spin out of control. He took it down as close to the ground as he could, allowing the men inside to bail and run. The helicopter dipped, pitched, rolled to the left, and slammed into trees, sending orange flames and black smoke shooting into the air. The pilot's screams were cut off abruptly as the helicopter came apart, pieces of metal flying in all directions.

"You can't play the hero trying to save me, Kane. This has to be about keeping Sebastian out of Whitney's hands. That's the only thing that matters." She glanced back at him, a warning in her eyes. "You know I'm right."

Kane continued firing now, as Whitney's men advanced, trying to ring them in. The second helicopter showed a little more respect, but they were taking heavy fire. The .50-caliber tore up everything in its path, and Kane used the weapon liberally, pounding the ground to keep the soldiers from advancing.

"It's bullshit to even talk about, Rose. We'll make it. We just have to hold on until Mack gets here."

Damn it, Mack, you're late. Kane sent the distress call, feeling trapped.

He wouldn't leave Rose behind. He couldn't do it. He had to find a way to save both Rose and the baby. He knew he could make a stand and buy her enough time to make a run for it, and if Mack and the others were on the way, she'd have a decent chance. They *had* to be on the way.

The Humvee suddenly ground to a halt, sliding slightly toward the upper edge of the sinkhole. They hadn't covered much ground, and the soldiers were shooting at the tires. If the tires went, they would have the runflats to depend on, but it wouldn't get them very far or very fast.

Mack. What the hell are you doing?

Damn, Kane, try to live without your daddy for a few. I'm just finishing up my dinner here.

The instant relief was overwhelming. "They're coming for us, Rose. Mack and my boys. They're within telepathic range."

"Helicopter coming in ten o'clock," Rose said, her voice grim. "He means business, Kane."

The helicopter filled his screen, and he saw the grenade launcher aimed at them. The first grenade hit just in front of them, and the world seemed to explode. The large tree blocking their escape to their left was blown into the air, splintered, raining branches and leaves all around them. The Hummer lurched as Rose kept it moving straight into the crater the explosion had made. The gunner had inadvertently aided them, clearing the path and at the same time, forcing the soldiers closing in, trying to surround them, to pull back.

Rose bulled their way through the debris and smoke, getting them back on the path, driving straight toward the nearest group of vulnerable soldiers. Kane pounded them with heavy rounds, forcing them to give way.

We're coming in fast from the east, Kane, Mack advised. *ETA, three minutes.*

Be advised there's a bird in the sky.

Roger that.

"They're coming in from the east, three minutes," he repeated aloud to Rose. "We're almost there, sweetheart."

"How the hell are they going to get us out of here?"

"We're going to climb out. Straight up, honey. Whitney's boys aren't going to shoot you or Sebastian."

"Are you out of your mind? We're going to go up a rope into a helicopter with the backwash from the blades, sharpshooters taking potshots, and a *baby*?"

He grinned at her. "Sounds like a fun date, doesn't it?"

She shook her head, a small, answering smile curving her soft mouth. "You really are nuts. You'd better hope Whitney wants us as bad as you think."

"My boys can keep the peace," Kane said with absolute confidence.

The Humvee limped over the pitted terrain heading doggedly toward the east and freedom. The first helicopter had circled and was coming in for another try.

This an exclusive party, or can anyone join?

Mack McKinley's voice filled his mind.

A second helicopter burst out of the night sky, silent and lethal, no running lights. From the open door, a rocket streaked through the darkness, trailing vapor, seeking a target.

The enemy's helicopter tried to maneuver, but it was far too late; the rocket was on top of them. The helicopter burst apart, spilling wreckage and flames in every direction.

"Find us stable ground in an open area," Kane yelled, fending off the soldiers with his heavy caliber weapon.

"I'm doing my best," Rose shouted back. "There aren't a lot of open areas here; that's why we chose it, hoping for cover. There's the creek bed, but I'm not certain we can trust the surface."

Can you spot an open area, Mack? We're a little pushed for time down here.

Creek bed is the only area possible for us to drop down to get you. You're nearly past the sinkhole. We're coming in.

"Get down into the creek, Rose. It's our only option."

She turned her head. Her dark eyes met his, and there was stark fear there, not for herself but for their child. She resolutely turned back and took the Hummer bumping and bouncing back into the creek bed. She drove a few yards to get as clear of the trees as possible and then abruptly leapt up to crawl back to the baby.

Kane fired repeatedly, cutting a wide circle around them. From above, he could hear covering fire as well. Once Rose made up her mind to do it, she was all business, paying no attention to the battle taking place outside. She gathered up the baby, strapping him into a front pack in order to leave her hands free. It took a few minutes to wrap the large bulletproof vest around both of them.

Kane paused just long enough to make certain it was secure. She leaned down and caught his face in her hands. "You'll be right behind us, right? Right behind us. No hero crap. You'll get into that helicopter no matter what."

"I'll be there."

"Promise me. Say it. I promise, Kane. I need to hear that."

He leaned forward and kissed her mouth, uncaring that bullets were flying. She needed reassurance, and he was giving it to her in the only way he knew how so that she could read his honesty. "I promise."

We're in position, but we're sitting ducks. Get moving. Mack's command was a definite order.

Kane put his hand where the baby's head was hidden by the vest. "Go."

He went back to giving covering fire, trusting his men to do the rest. Gideon Carpenter had eyes like an eagle and could shoot the wings off a fly. Javier Enderman—well he just looked where he wanted to shoot, and that was as good as pulling the damned trigger.

Rose pushed open the heavy door to the roof and cautiously put her head out. Once she caught that rope, she would be committed. Kane expected hesitation. She didn't know the men in the helicopter the way he did, but there was no vacillation, and that told him a lot about her. Once she made up her mind, she followed through. She'd pulled on thin gloves, and she caught the rope, one foot looping it.

She went up as fast as possible. She was strong—after all she was a GhostWalker—but she was a sitting duck and expecting someone to shoot her at any moment. The backwash from the helicopter blades was hellacious. The rope spun a bit, and that made it difficult to keep Sebastian facing away from the biggest threat. They were using a pulley system as well, which helped move the rope up even faster.

She was halfway up the rope before she realized the night had gone eerily silent. No one on the ground fired at them. Not a single soldier—as if a cease-fire had been declared and everyone was abiding by it. She climbed faster, afraid the silence was the lull before the storm.

A man caught her around the waist and hauled her into the helicopter, dragging her deeper inside, not letting go until she was steady. Barely glancing at him, she unstrapped the baby as fast as possible, looking around for the safest, most protected place she could find. She used the vest to construct a barrier around him. She was quick, her movements efficient as she turned back, pulling her automatic rifle back around her neck to the front by the strap, and stepping to the entrance to provide cover for Kane.

"Ten o'clock, your side, Gideon," someone barked.

Gideon fired without hesitation, the shot ringing out in the night. "He's down, Top. We're ready."

Her stomach tightened. *Every*one was going to be shooting at Kane. These men and she would have to keep the shooters off him. She put the rifle to her shoulder and looked into the night scope. Only seconds had gone by, but it seemed an eternity.

Climb fast, Kane. She tried not to allow her fear for him to show in her mind. *We're waiting for you.*

Just waiting for Top to give me the okay, sweetheart. I'll be right there.

His voice was steady, but she knew it would be. Very little seemed to shake the man.

Has to be easier than delivering a baby, right? he teased, laughter in his voice.

The knots in her stomach tightened with dread. Her mouth went dry. She was rock steady in combat as a rule, nothing fazed her, but deep inside she felt jittery.

Damn straight.

Coming up now, honey. Top just gave me the word.

She glanced down, although she knew she shouldn't, to see Kane leap up, gripping the rope. She'd never seen a man climb so fast. Hand over hand, he went straight up as the backwash from the helicopter's blade blew the rope into a whirling frenzy, not nearly as bad as with her lighter weight. His strength was beyond her comprehension, and she had to force herself to stare into the scope to protect him.

He was more than halfway to the helicopter when two of them with her began shooting rapidly. She spotted a soldier lifting his rifle, and she took the shot, seeing him go down. A volley of shots rang out, and the helicopter jerked.

She gasped and looked down. Kane was right at the entrance, reaching with one hand to pull himself inside. She never actually heard the bullet tear into him, but she saw his body rock back, away from the helicopter, and she flung herself forward and with both hands caught his wrist.

Don't you let go of that rope! Rose put every ounce of command she had into her voice.

There was blood everywhere, all over him. He was too heavy, much too heavy, and she had no time. One of the men beside her leaned out with her and caught him under his arms.

"Fucking shoot that bastard," came a command behind her.

"On it, Top," two voices said simultaneously.

Kane was unconscious, but when the bullet hit, instinct had him clutching the rope, his only lifeline, with his remaining hand. They had to pry it out of his closed hand. Before the sniper could shoot a second time, at least two men behind her fired over her head.

She didn't have time to identify the man beside her who was keeping Kane from falling to his death. "Get him in. Get him in. We don't have any time. Set up for a transfusion. Move. Move. I need a medical kit. Open one fast, get out the iodine."

She put every ounce of strength she had into helping the

man beside her haul Kane's dead weight into the helicopter. She dragged him inside and laid him out, scrambling to kneel beside him, her knife out. She cut away his clothes, exposing his belly. The bullet had torn into his abdomen and ricocheted through his chest.

"Get a needle into him before his veins collapse," she snapped, not looking at the grim-faced men surrounding her. Her entire being was focused on saving Kane—and she only had minutes. Her palms burned, scorching, unbearably hot.

"Iodine. Hurry, pour it over his belly and my hands and knife." She held them out, and even as they poured, she cut into Kane's flesh.

Someone—again, she didn't know or care who—crowded tight against her back and placed a blade firmly against her neck, a threat one shouldn't ignore, but she did. If the bastard wanted to kill her, so be it, but she wasn't going to take even precious seconds to try to make him understand. There was no way to explain how she had known the moment she laid her hands on Kane that the artery was severed and he was bleeding out fast—too fast.

Everything around her faded until she was in that deep tunnel where there were only her hands answering the needs of a critically injured human being. Already the energy was surging through her. Her fingertips tingled and burned. She plunged her hands into his body, unerringly finding the artery. She grasped it between her fingers, slipped on all the blood, and had to fish again. The artery felt like a noodle, or worse, a squid. She wasn't squeamish unless she allowed herself to think about failing.

"What the hell are you doing?" a voice demanded.

"Don't distract her."

That had to be the master gunnery sergeant. She could tell by his voice. It sounded as if from a great distance, but she was aware of all them on some level.

She could hear sounds. Harsh breathing. The blades of the helicopter. The rustle as one of the men fed plasma through an IV, holding the vein open for life-saving blood, if she could just do this. *If.* There it was. Oh, God, she had it.

Live, Kane. Don't leave us alone.

She felt the ends and pushed them together, closing her eyes, taking a slow, deep breath and breathing down, through her body, sending the healing heat, that scorching-hot heat through her veins and out the fingers of her hands. She had to fuse the ends together, but it was delicate work to keep the blood flowing through while she held the severed ends with heat.

The intense burn took her breath away, but she held on. For a moment everything went dark, and there were only stars and a fading sensation. Her stomach lurched. She became aware of the blood all over her clothes, of her hands inside Kane. The blood was up to her elbows. She couldn't fix the rest of the damage done to his organs, but they had a chance of keeping him alive until the surgeon took over, if she could hold on.

"Hurry. Use me for the transfusion. Whitney always gave pairs compatible blood." Now it was her own voice that came from far away, or maybe from a deep, deep hole. "Have your surgeon meet us. And for God's sake, hurry. He has to be set up for the operation wherever we land. Can you do that?"

"The doc will be there."

She turned her head tiredly, and her eyes met a pair of cold black eyes surrounded by ridiculously long lashes.

"Who has my baby?"

"I've got him, ma'am," another voice said. "Name's Ethan Myers. You must be Rose."

She was too tired to state the obvious or even look. The knife slowly disappeared from her throat. Only then did she feel the slight sting. The threat had been all too real. She did manage to look up at him from over her shoulder, and her heart dropped. She recognized the one called Javier. Death stared back at her. There was no expression on that face.

"Rose," the man with the black eyes spoke her name gently, the man they referred to as Top. "Javier is going to support your back while we make our run. Can you hold on?"

"Yes." Because there was no other choice. None. If she didn't, Kane was dead.

"I'm putting in the needle. You're going to feel it. I'm Mack McKinley, by the way."

"Just do it. Are you certain the baby's all right?"

Ethan answered, "He's fine. He looks very aware. He keeps turning his head toward the sound of your voice."

The smell of the blood made her want to gag. It felt like she was bathing in the stuff. She was going to have nightmares for the rest of her life, but it was Kane's blood, and she wasn't losing him.

Do you hear me? I won't lose you. She heard the small internal sob and hoped she hadn't lost control in front of the others. *Not now, not when we're so close. Hang on, Kane. Just a little longer. Fight for us. Fight for me.*

Her body trembled now as the helicopter dipped and bumped, flying fast over the desert. She could feel the heat draining from her body and flowing into Kane's. She was certain she was sitting upright until she felt Javier's arm suddenly slide around her waist and ease her back against his chest. She thought rather fuzzily that he was far stronger than he looked. In the distance, Mack McKinley, the one they called Top, was barking orders into his radio.

She shivered, cold creeping into her bones. Javier rubbed her shoulders.

"Hold him a little longer. Don't let go."

No, she couldn't let go of him, because her fragile repair would burst, and Kane would bleed out before they could get him to the surgeon.

She was vaguely aware of the helicopter setting down. Of grim-faced men surrounding her, helping to lift Kane onto a gurney, setting her there with him. She never let go, even when they rolled her into the sterile tent hastily erected and the doctors and nurses regarded her bloody hands inside Kane.

She looked around at them with their masks and gowns, afraid to turn him over to them.

"It's all right, Rose," Mack said gently. "We've got him now."

The cold took her then, like it always did when she used this particular talent, sliding inside her, freezing her from the inside out. Her teeth began to chatter, and she couldn't move her stiff body, as if every muscle was completely frozen.

"Let them take over," Mack said again. "She's holding him together, Doc."

A pair of hands came into view, and Javier lifted Rose. "Let him go," he whispered. "He'll be safe." Those black, killer eyes jumped to the doctor. "Won't he, Doc?"

Those softly spoken words penetrated, and she released Kane into the hands of strangers.

CHAPTER 11

———❦———

Kane yawned and stretched, wincing a little when his wound, now almost completely healed, pulled a little. Keeping his eyes closed, he inhaled, just to breathe in Rose's scent. She wasn't in bed beside him, but she was close by. He had woken up to her every morning now for several weeks. He could get up and walk around with a cane, but only for short periods of time. He found convalescence very irritating. His body was weaker than it had ever been, and physical therapy and training seemed slow.

He caught the fragrance that was only Rose's, a combination of fresh spring and wild summer. He could hear the soft pad of her bare feet as she came into the room and crossed to the bed. Her palm banded his forehead as she checked him for a fever. He reached up and covered her hand, preventing her from moving.

He loved her touch. Her warmth. The softness of her skin. The silk of her hair. He loved watching the way she moved, a little ballerina flowing and fluid as she tidied things. Already the first floor of the warehouse where he resided was being transformed into a home. Rose seemed to love the wide-open space of the enormous warehouse. He and Mack and the others of his "family" had added a couple of bathrooms and sectioned off a living area and bedroom, but that was as far as the building of his home had gotten.

The warehouse was three stories high and took up nearly half a block. On the corner, one side ran along the bay side, water lapping at the wharf where they stored a getaway boat. Jaimie Fielding had bought the monstrosity and was in the process of renovating it when the team had caught up with her. She resided on the top floor with her husband, Mack McKinley. The middle floor was their offices, housing the computers and so many other electronics it gave Kane a headache thinking about it. They had a gym equipped with the best training equipment available to them. They could put together a simulation of any building and do practice runs over and over until they were perfect in their execution. Their security system was state-of-the-art, thanks to Jaimie's brilliance.

Kane had taken the bottom floor for his home in the hopes that someday he would find Rose and they could raise their family there. They had managed to acquire the warehouse next to theirs as well as two across the street. Negotiations were already in the works to try to acquire the apartment building directly across from them. They were putting together a fortress, a compound they could easily defend, one with multiple escape routes: water, land, and even air.

Kane opened his eyes slowly, just to drink in the sight of Rose. She wore one of his thin, button-down-the-front shirts. It completely enveloped her small body. Under the white material, he could see the outline of one of the nursing bras Jaimie had bought for her. He didn't see much else. Her legs were slender and shapely, her feet bare. She must have just gotten out of bed and fed the baby. Even her hair was still tousled, just the way he loved it.

It was amazing to him how quickly she had become his world. Rose and Sebastian. He felt at peace every time she brought the boy into the room and sat quietly nursing him, or simply rocked him to sleep while Kane convalesced.

His doctor, Eric Lambert, a surgeon renowned for his work in gene therapy, was usually the first choice when it came to the GhostWalkers. He had saved the life of Jesse Calhoun, a member of Team Two, and had immediately come to their aid when called. Now, it seemed, he had saved Kane as well. The man came nearly every day, barking orders and examining Kane, but so far, Rose had steadfastly refused to allow him near Sebastian. Kane found her stubbornness secretly amusing.

Rose definitely had an aversion to the doctor, never once leaving him alone with Sebastian or Kane. She was very reserved around Mack and Jaimie and the rest of his family, but that was all right with Kane. Everything about Rose was all right with Kane.

"Good morning, sleepyhead," she greeted, leaning down to brush a kiss across his mouth. "How are you feeling this morning?"

His heart fluttered. His belly tightened. His cock was already as hard as a rock. He'd grown used to the feeling she generated in his body—the instant flood of urgent desire. He even found he loved that rush. He felt alive. His fingers tightened around her hand, and he brought it to his mouth, nibbling for a moment on her warm, silky skin.

"More than good. Eric cleared me for training, sweetheart. I didn't just leap into it. I'm a little sore, but it's a good kind of sore."

She gave him her little frown. "Well, I think you bullied him into letting you get back too early. You almost died, Kane."

"But I didn't. I'm tough. Where's Sebastian?"

"I just put him down for his nap. He's gaining weight finally. The doctor said he's in good condition, considering he was born early." She smirked. "Although he had to guess that from a distance. I don't want him holding Sebastian. I've caught him twice with a needle and tube, trying to take his blood."

Kane smiled, all male satisfaction. "Of course he's healthy; he's my son. Isn't it rather usual for a doctor to take a patient's blood?"

Rose rolled her eyes as she pulled her hand away. "I wanted to thank you, Kane."

"For the perfect son?" He sat up, careful not to wince. It wouldn't do for her to think she might be right about the training. She did like to fuss over him, not that he minded, but his family was giving him a hard time behind her back.

"Well, of course for him," she agreed seriously. "But, for the first time in my life that I can remember, I don't wake up afraid. For the last few months I've been looking over my shoulder, knowing Whitney was a step behind me."

"As long as he's alive, honey, he's going to be breathing down our necks. We can never forget that Sebastian is at risk."

She nodded solemnly. "Unless we're alone, secure in our home, I don't leave him alone, even with others."

He paused in the act of swinging his legs over the side of the bed. "Rose. You can trust my boys and Jaimie. They're family. They'd protect you and Sebastian with their lives."

Rose turned away from him, a graceful, flowing movement that always captured his attention. He reached out and caught her wrist, tugging so that she fell against him. In one motion, he spun her under him, his hands stretching her arms out above her head, pinning her to the mattress.

"I saw that look on your face, Rose," he murmured and bent his head to trail kisses from her chin to the corner of her mouth. "All closed off, refusing to accept my family into your world." He brushed more kisses back and forth across her lips. "So resistant to the idea of good people helping with our baby."

Beneath him she stiffened, rejecting the idea. Tension

ran through her, and for a moment she pushed up with her arms. He easily kept her wrists pinned to the mattress, brushing more kisses over her eyelids and down her cheek, back to the corner of her mouth. When she relaxed under him, he lifted his head and looked at her.

"Whatever am I going to do with you?" he whispered as his teeth nipped her stubborn little chin. "You're giving me trouble already, Rose."

"I'm not as trusting as you are," she explained.

"No?" He could feel her body, warm silk, melting beneath his, drawing his attention to the shape and feel of her.

Kane transferred her left wrist to his other hand so he had both pinned in one hand, leaving him free to explore the way he wanted. "I dream of you, Rose." He slipped the buttons open on her blouse. "Every damn night." He pushed the two edges of her blouse apart to expose her soft skin.

Her stomach muscles bunched. His gaze leapt to the exposed bare skin, and he bent his head to press kisses from underneath her breasts down to her belly button. His tongue tasted that smooth expanse of skin. "When I was unconscious I dreamt of you, just like this, lying under me, my hands on your body. I woke up a thousand times, my body so damned hard I could barely move with wanting you."

"You should have told me," she whispered, her voice unsteady. "I would have . . . helped."

His entire body jerked, not just his cock. Her tone, that whispery brush of velvet, slipped inside of him and wreaked havoc with every nerve ending. His heart went wild, and blood rushed hot through his veins. She could turn his world erotic just with the sound of her voice. He nibbled his way around her soft tummy and then took a small bite.

"What did Eric say about making love?"

Her hands came up to find his hair, smoothing her fingers through the strands. "I've stopped bleeding and I feel healed. It's been several weeks, Kane."

"What did Eric say?" he repeated.

She scowled at him. "As if I'd ask his permission for something like that." She blushed when he kept looking at her.

"I don't want to take chances."

"It's my body. I know it better than he does," she said stubbornly and pushed the shirt completely off her arms. "In any case, you're more apt to have a problem than I am."

He took that as a challenge, kissing his way back up to her breasts where he undid her nursing bra. He licked at her nipples until he had her squirming.

"You're going to get my milk flowing," she cautioned.

"That's all right," he murmured, losing himself in the sweet exploration of her body. "What's wrong with that?"

"It will be messy. I'm going to drip all over us."

"Sex is messy, honey. It's supposed to be hot and sweaty and feel so damn good you just don't care." He kissed his way back down her tummy. Her skin was so hot and soft. The memories of her haunted him day and night. He remembered the way she felt, the way her body fit so perfectly to his.

He took his time, his hands and mouth mapping her body leisurely and imprinting it in his mind all over again. He wanted to know every place that sent her squirming, her hips bucking, her mouth gasping. He loved her breathless moans and the way she was so responsive to his touch.

"It's been too long, Rose," he whispered against her soft belly. He could tell that her body, so long fit and strong, was already firming up. He kissed all the way down to the vee at the junction of her legs.

"Kane."

The little gasp was a plea or a protest. He doubted if she knew which. He swirled his tongue, drawing patterns along her sensitive tummy while his hands eased her thighs apart, allowing him to settle more firmly between her legs. Her thighs were firm and so slender it made his heart pound. He was a big man, and she was very small, built like many of the Asian women he'd seen. She seemed fragile, and with his enormous strength and big hands, he was a little afraid he might hurt her.

His body remembered how tight she'd been surrounding him, strangling him, clamping down on him like a hot, velvet vise. He knew his cock leaked in anticipation, desperate to find that paradise again, but he was determined to do the right thing by her. He wanted to make absolute certain that he wouldn't harm her or hurt her if they made love.

He lowered his head, closing his eyes as her feminine scent enveloped him. There was rapture in the fragrance that was uniquely Rose. He caught her small bottom with one hand and lifted her hips as he bent to her. He felt the satisfying shiver going through her body even before he blew warm air across her mound.

He doubted if she would believe that he was already far in love with her, a complete goner—that he had been before he'd allowed Whitney to pair them, but he could show her. With his body raging at him and his mind filled with an all-consuming love for her, he tasted her. Her body shuddered and bucked with just that small attention—and he was damn good at details. He took his time, lavishing attention on her with his mouth and tongue. His fingers stroked deep into her and withdrew.

He couldn't help but watch the helpless pleasure glazing her eyes. He loved that look. He loved that he could make her as mindless as she could him. He had never thought that seeing to a woman's pleasure could give him back so much. He felt every shudder, heard every moan and whimper as music. Her hips bucked in his hand, her body writhed. Hot nectar flowed, and he devoured her intimately, driving her up time after time until she pleaded and demanded and all but pulled his hair out.

He didn't want to stop. She made him hungry for more with her desperate moans and pleas. He hadn't known how powerful and satisfied a man could feel when his woman tossed mindlessly beneath him, gasping and begging for release. He sent her tumbling over the edge when he heard the panic creeping in. Even as her orgasm tore through her body, he couldn't help stroking her gently with his tongue just to share the experience with her.

His body was on fire, and he swore a jackhammer was in the process of drilling through the middle of his skull. His blood thundered in his ears and hammered through his cock. The sensation in his groin had gone from a dull ache to a savage pounding, but strangely, he found himself very satisfied.

Rose lay under Kane, his larger body sprawled over hers. Her body trembled and shuddered, the sensations almost more than she could take. Kane could do that to her, make her think of her body as belonging to him. He seemed to know exactly the places to stroke, or bite, or lave with his tongue for maximum results. She stroked his thick hair and looked into his eyes. She could see adoration there— more even—love. It humbled her, shocked her. She could barely make herself believe that a man like Kane could feel that way about her.

She knew nothing of life outside the military compound where she'd been raised, and she'd never known love. She was afraid to recognize it in Kane's eyes, but it was hard to miss the emotion when he touched her so tenderly. It was difficult to miss it in the way he looked at her. And it was impossible to miss the fact that there was more than lust in the way he made love to her. This moment had been all hers.

Tears burned behind her eyes. She'd sworn she would always tell him the truth, let him see how she felt about him, no matter the cost to her pride, but her emotions were so strong, so overwhelming that she closed her eyes, unwilling to strip herself naked. She was already so vulnerable to him.

He held her as the ripples continued through her body, asking nothing for himself, even though she could feel the need raging through his body. His erection was thick and hard and pulsing against her thigh. He made no move to sate himself, and she knew he wouldn't. He would put her first. Always put her first. She might not know about relationships, but she was coming to know the man she'd chosen to be the father of her child. He was more than the integrity she'd first seen. More even than the honor. He was a man among men. The man who, for her, stood head and shoulders above the rest. She was fast coming to worship him.

Kane looked down at her averted face and saw a tear trembling on her long lashes. His heart skidded in his chest. Had he hurt her even without penetration? Leaning on his elbows he framed her face, holding her still. "What is it, sweetheart? Tell me."

Her eyes opened, and everything in him stilled. There was so much emotion staring back at him. "Make love to me, Kane," Rose whispered, her slender arms creeping around his neck, holding him to her. "Please, I need you to make love to me."

"I just did," he said, trying not to growl with his body hard as a rock and his head pounding with thunder.

"Didn't you hear me?" That soft little whisper stole his heart for all time. She buried her face in his neck, her mouth finding that sensitive spot at the junction of shoulder and neck. "You know what I want. You inside of me."

"Not until we talk to Eric."

"I said I was fine." Her lips slid like silk against his skin, an enticement, a miracle.

Kane shivered. "I know, sweetheart, but I never want to take a chance on hurting you. Not ever again. When we make love, I don't mind hot and sweaty, or rough or gentle, but I mind hurting you. Loving you is all about making you feel nothing but pleasure. I can't get the damn prison out of my head."

Her teeth nipped him and sent his temperature soaring. His entire body shuddered. He bunched all the black silk in his hand and tugged at her hair. "You're killing me, honey."

"Then make love to me properly."

"You're going to give me hell until you get your way, aren't you?"

She lifted her head and looked into his eyes. She made no effort to hide the dark, passionate hunger in her eyes. "Yes."

He laughed softly, happier than he'd ever been. "You like your way, don't you?"

"Yes."

He pulled her head back farther and took possession of that soft, intriguing mouth. That mouth that could be sassy and sexy and so damn tempting that all his good intentions were in danger of going by the wayside.

"When it comes to your health, I'm absolutely unbending."

"Really?" Her laughter was muffled against his mouth. Her hand slid down his chest. When it hit his stomach, every muscle bunched and tightened. "I think it's only fair to allow me the chance to change your mind."

"Don't you dare." He caught her lower lip between his teeth and tugged gently in warning. "You're going to get yourself in trouble."

Had he ever played with a woman before? Had fun even with his body screaming at him? It was a new experience. He'd never had a lazy morning in bed with a woman. Come to think about it, he'd never had a morning with a woman in bed. He didn't do that kind of thing. He didn't pretend love. He hadn't known what loving a woman was until he'd seen Rose day after day.

He held her close to him, savoring the feeling of being part of her. "The first time I ever saw you, Rose, you were standing in the exercise yard laughing. I couldn't believe the sound, so happy and carefree when, by that time, I'd already figured out that all of you were virtual prisoners. I turned around and felt like someone punched me in the gut hard. A full body blow, you know, rocking me."

She rubbed his taut abdomen, her fingers lingering on

his skin. The lightest of touches, but still, after their intimate contact, her touch shook him—or maybe it always would.

"The sun poured down on your hair and turned it this amazing color of blue black that I'd never seen before, and the shine to it was incredible. Then you sprinted, Rose, flowing across the yard, running up the side of a wall, doing a somersault in the air and landing, almost all in one motion. You walked back to the group of women laughing again, as if you'd enjoyed the flight. And when you walked, hell, woman, it was a fucking sin the way you moved—like the sexiest dancer alive. I forgot all about that high fence and what it meant. You were sunshine."

How could he explain to her how he felt? He was a soldier, a man dedicated to his unit, to his duty. He was good at what he did. He liked the rush he got in dangerous situations and the satisfaction of a mission completed. He'd never considered that there was another side to him, a man starving, out in the cold and rain. He hadn't even known that about himself until that moment. She seemed to live in every moment, worshipping the sun, turning her face up to the rain, even opening her mouth to catch the droplets. That had been the sexiest thing in the world to him. He had been obsessed with watching her, taking every opportunity to guard that side of the compound so he could see her.

He had known it was a dangerous game he was playing with himself. The likelihood of meeting her had been small, but he'd developed a need to see her every day, even if from a distance. He thought he'd hidden his growing need very well, but obviously Whitney had known. Rose had once asked Kane what his weakness was, and he'd replied honestly that it was her, Rose. Whitney had known all along.

Kane rolled over and linked his hands behind his head. Rose did the same. They lay staring at their toes. Her foot was nearly half the size of his, and he rubbed his along hers, wiggling his toes. She laughed, and he closed his eyes briefly, savoring the sound. He threaded his fingers with hers and brought her hand to his mouth to nibble some more on her.

"I knew you came out into the yard three times a day, the gym once, and the training buildings twice a day. I traded shifts and pulled doubles so I could be where you were. I felt like a damned stalker, but after a few times, I couldn't help myself."

She turned her head, her dark, almond eyes wide and a little shocked. "*Before* Whitney paired us?"

He bit down on her finger and then sucked the sting away. "*Way* before."

"Are you certain he didn't pair us before you ever saw me? Because I was pretty much—to the best of my ability—doing the same thing to you."

Her voice was a little shy as she admitted it to him, stealing his heart even more. "If the body reaction was anything to go by, I'd say no to that, Rose. Once he did his thing, every time I got close to you, I couldn't control myself, and I'm pretty damned disciplined in that department." He looked down at his heavy erection. "I still can't. Fortunately, I don't want to."

Her gaze caressed his thick shaft hungrily. "Then let me see what I can do to help out."

"I want to be inside you. You're only making me crave you more."

Her face lit up, and he inwardly groaned. That had been the wrong thing to say. She sat up, her hair swinging around her face in all directions, sexy as hell. He groaned, knowing he was lost. The woman had a hold on him and was slowly but surely wrapping him around her little finger. He caught her finger and bit it, just to try to articulate without words what he thought about that particular fate.

She laughed, leaned down, and took him deep into the heat of her mouth, without preamble, shocking him with sheer erotic magic. She engulfed him completely, pushing her head down, holding him tight for a moment, her throat working as if she might be swallowing and then, just as abruptly, she slid her lips lovingly back up his shaft, her tongue fluttering as she drew the sensitive mushroom head free. He saw stars.

Rose sat up, quickly straddling his hips and very slowly, inch by slow inch, began to take him inside her body.

"Rose," his faint protest came out strangled. His hands went to her hips, but he couldn't find the strength to lift her away from him. She'd engulfed the head of his shaft with sheer fire. He opened his mouth again, but nothing came out but a long-drawn-out groan of pleasure.

"Yeah." She smirked at him. "That's what I thought you'd say."

"Easy, then, sweetheart. We have to go easy."

She smiled her mysterious smile. "I promise I'll be easy on you."

She threw back her head, arched her back, reaching behind her with both hands to steady herself as she continued to lower herself on him. Due to breast-feeding, her breasts were large for her frame, emphasizing her narrow rib cage and slender hips. She looked so wild and sexy he could barely catch his breath, let alone protest.

She did a lazy spiral with her hips, as his shaft penetrated deeper. The movement was exquisite on his cock, a slow gripping like a tight fist, closing around him in slow motion, drawing his shaft deeper into her tight, hot, silken sheath. The feeling was unlike anything he'd imagined, that slow, scorching clasp that took his breath and mind all at the same time. He heard his own heartbeat and reached up to press his hand over her heart so that it beat into his palm.

She wiggled again, an aching circle as her body opened for him, accepting his invasion, taking him farther into her haven. She lifted her hips just a little and dropped down, seating herself to the hilt. His breath exploded from his lungs; the friction sent flames rushing out of control throughout his system. He felt as if his very skin sizzled with electricity.

Eyes narrowed to slits, he watched every movement, as she began an unhurried sensual ride. He loved the undulating motion of her body, graceful and sinuous, her muscles flowing beneath her soft skin. Her eyes were slumberous, her lips parted. He stroked her silken skin, unable to keep his hands off her. She didn't like her milk to start flowing, thinking it messy; he loved the idea of her carrying and giving birth to his child. The evidence of it only inflamed him more.

Her breasts jutted toward him, swaying gently, the nipples hard and peaked. She looked so beautiful with her skin flushed and her eyes slightly glazed. His shaft swelled even more with the attention. He was deeper than ever, thrusting up through those soft petal folds, meeting resistance with each stroke, and driving to meet her downward rhythm. Her muscles tightened around him, milking, eliciting a strangled groan from him.

"You're going to make me crazy," he whispered, feeling on fire.

She had an almost dreamy look on her face, concentrating on each rhythmic stroke as her body rose and fell. He gathered the strength in his body, and as she began her descent he drove up. She cried out, her head tossing.

The feel of filling her, stretching her, her silken body reluctantly giving way for the steel of his shaft, bathing the broad, flared head filled with sensitive nerve endings with her scorching-hot feminine lubrication was an incomparable feeling. He knew he was coming far too close to adoration, but what the hell did it matter when he felt like this? When she looked like that?

"That's right, sweetheart," he encouraged. His hands fell to her hips, urging her to keep going. He didn't want her to ever stop. He could feel every nerve ending as her silken body suckled his cock as she rose over him again.

The mixture of such deep love shaking him and the rising lust as his body anticipated the explosion shook him. He actually felt her stomach muscles clench, and his followed suit. She shuddered with the effort to hold back as she lowered her body over his, circling, gripping, squeezing him tight so the sensation was almost excruciating, whether with pain or pleasure he couldn't quite comprehend.

His hands gripped her hips harder, and he drove into her again as she came down. She cried out, as the ripples radiated through her body. He picked up the pace, thrusting deep over and over, taking them both careening over the edge. Little stars burst behind his eyes, and for a moment he swore there were fireworks exploding in his head—and maybe through his entire body as well.

He flooded her body with jet after jet of his hot seed with her orgasm pulsing around him, still gripping hard and milking the last drop from him. He reached up and drew her down over him, her breasts pressing tight against his chest. The action sent powerful ripples through her body, and he shuddered with pleasure as the almost brutal pressure squeezed his cock.

Rose would forever hear her own heart beating wildly. The sound roared in her ears and pounded through her veins. She hadn't had many sensual experiences, but each time he touched her felt incredibly sensual. The erotic orgasm continued to pulse through her body with shocking intensity. She lay with her head on his chest, allowing, just for a moment, true terror to hold her in its grip.

Kane could shatter her with the wrong look. The wrong touch. One word. He owned her. Shared her skin. Her heart. Even her soul. She touched her head to his heaving chest, inhaling him. This man. *Her* man. Her body came apart and flew. Her soul did the same. She'd never considered, all those months ago, that he would become such a part of her that she wouldn't want to have to find a way to live without him.

It all came down to trust. She'd trusted him with her body. And with her son. And now with her heart. She had just *given* herself to him. All of her. Every inch. Was that

what love was supposed to be? Handing the very core of
your being into another's keeping? The doing of it was terrifying. Exhilarating. So unexpected.

Kane's arms were comforting, as was his scent. She
stayed right where she was, straddling his hips, her thighs
hugging his, feeling safe, even as she felt totally exposed.
He stroked her hair, his hands gentle. She always found
his gentleness surprising. He was a big man and looked as
dangerous as hell. She wasn't used to gentleness or caring.
She hadn't known she could feel the way she did about
anyone, let alone a man.

Because of Kane, she had Sebastian. She had a home. A
life. At least the opportunity for those things if she had the
courage to see it through.

"Are you crying, sweetheart?" Kane asked.

His tone, unfailingly understanding, made her want to
weep the tears that remained gathered behind her eyes.
"Not exactly. It's just that you've given me so much, Kane."

His hand stilled in her hair. "It's the other way around,
Rose. I wasn't fully alive until you came into my life. I
wasn't unhappy, but then I didn't know enough to be. You
showed me what life could be like."

Rose's heart took a slow, somersaulting turn. He'd de-
scribed in words exactly how she felt about her life. She
knew the few soldiers she'd met felt sorry for her, but neither she or her "sisters" felt that way about their lives. They
didn't know any other way to live. They had enjoyed many
aspects of their childhood. It had been harsh and even at
times cruel, but they had been close and enjoyed the physical activities they excelled in.

Now, after feeling an alien in a strange world when
she'd been on her own, she realized she hadn't known real
happiness. Kane had shown that to her. He had brought her
so much, and if he ever betrayed her . . .

A small sob escaped, and she clamped down on it immediately, ashamed of her weakness.

"Baby," Kane soothed. "Listen to me. You have to look at me while I tell you this. I know when you look into my eyes, you know when I'm speaking the truth."

Baby. He'd never called her by that specific endearment. She wasn't a baby, but she felt newly born. The caress in his voice shook her almost as much as the tenderness. Rose took a deep, steadying breath and forced herself to lift her head. If he hadn't heard what her body had said to him, he would see it when he looked into her face. She loved him with every breath she took, and she was terrified. She'd put herself into his hands without meaning to do so, and now he had all the power.

Kane's green eyes searched her face for what seemed a long time before meeting her gaze steadily. "I can only guess how scared you are right now, Rose. I am too. Not of Whitney. Not of being a father. I can handle both of those things, but of you—us. I've never felt so vulnerable to another human being. You have my heart, Rose. It sounds stupid and corny and I'm not that kind of man to say pretty words women like to hear, but if I could—if I could find the right way to say you terrify me without sounding like an idiot—I would."

Happiness swept through her. He was right; she could see the naked truth in his eyes. She liked that he deliberately made himself so vulnerable to her, exposing his feelings and trusting that she wouldn't . . . betray him. He was telling her he understood, taking the chance before she could find the courage.

She found his mouth almost blindly, melting into him, uncaring that her milk was beginning to flow, something that embarrassed her and made her feel decidedly not glamorous or sexy. She felt his firm lips heat, and her heart skittered in her chest. Kissing him was rather like tumbling into a beautiful dream. She could kiss him forever, for always. His hand bunched in her hair, sending a thrill down her spine. There was an instant response, his arms turning to steel, caging her, his mouth moving over hers, deepen-

ing the kiss until she thought her heart might explode from
her chest.

She raised her head slightly and looked down at him,
the tip of her tongue sliding along his bottom lip, savoring the taste of him. "I'm scared too, Kane," she admitted. "I thought you were a logical choice for the father of
my baby." A slight smile welled up. "You're very good-
looking, and you have strength of character and integrity.
There's no cruelty in you. No subterfuge. I thought we'd
live together and be happy and comfortable."

She watched the smile soften his beautiful mouth and
creep into the vivid green of his eyes. "Comfortable?" he
repeated and squirmed a little so that she felt him, semi-
hard, moving deep inside her. "That might not be the best
word to describe us together."

The sensation along with that teasing, suggestive grin,
set off tiny explosions throughout her body. "My point
exactly. My body's reaction to you might be more than
I expected, but with Whitney pairing us, I knew we'd be
compatible sexually. I just didn't know how deeply I would
feel about you. I thought it was too soon. Too fast. But I
realize it's been growing in me since the very first day I
saw you."

"We're in this together." His voice was so tender, so
gentle, she almost felt the sound like a caress washing over
her skin. "And it will get rough, Rose. Whitney isn't going
to let up just because we found each other. If something
happens, you know I'll never stop looking for you. I would
find both you and Sebastian. I'd come for you."

She studied his face. He hadn't raised his voice. There
was a quiet strength in Kane. A core of steel. He would
never back down, never swerve from his chosen path. She
shivered, thankful that *she* was his chosen path.

"I know that," she replied, surprised that the conviction
was strong in her.

"You have to trust me, no matter how bad it gets, Rose.
We can do it if we're together. That's the entire point of a

pairing. We should have all the tools to defeat anything or anyone in battle together. He manipulated our DNA and enhanced us both physically and psychically to fit together in every conceivable situation, so together we're strong."

Whitney had always been the all-powerful figure in her life. She'd never conceived of the idea of actually defeating him. She had run, but in the back of her mind, she'd accepted the idea that in the end he would reacquire her. She had wanted to make it as difficult as possible, and if she could, hide the baby where Whitney could never find him. She even accepted that Whitney might kill her for her actions, but always, she knew, he loomed large, a dark threat that would ultimately find her.

She reached down and rubbed at the tattoo she'd grown so fond of. Instantly Kane covered her hand with his. "Did you tell Mack or Javier about the satellite?"

She nodded uneasily. "Javier and Jaimie spent some time looking at it. I didn't mention because . . . well . . ." Her voice drifted off. The truth was, Whitney already knew where she was, and Kane had been unconscious a lot of the time. The tattoo had become the least of her problems.

The doctor, who she distrusted on principle, had performed a three-hour surgery while she paced, nearly inconsolable, outside the door of the makeshift operating room. The last few weeks, she'd immersed herself in caring for Kane and the baby, and for once in her life, she'd allowed herself to think of nothing else, not even the threat of Whitney.

Jaimie McKinley, who owned the building, had been nice to her, shopping for clothes and baby items, but nothing had mattered but Kane's recovery. She'd barely forced herself to get sleep, afraid if she closed her eyes, he would die. She'd kept Sebastian with them every minute, uncaring that the doctor wanted her to rest or that everyone had offered to watch the baby for her. Rather than accept help, she'd kept them all together.

Jaimie brought meals, and men poked their heads in

constantly to check on Kane, but she tried to ignore them, terrified but determined. She didn't want to admit she hadn't been exactly cooperative with his friends.

A strobe went off, flashing in the bedroom, a signal the front door had been opened. Automatically, she slid off Kane and reached for her robe and the gun she kept inches from her fingertips.

"Sweetheart, no one has the code but family," Kane said. "You just can't break Jaimie's codes."

"Nevertheless." She crept silently across the floor and stood to one side of the door, the gun ready.

CHAPTER 12

"Dr. Lambert is here to check the baby, Rose," Jaimie McKinley called out, knocking even as she pushed open the door to the living area. "You decent?"

Rose tightened her hold on the gun and threw Kane an anxious look. "Why does he have to keep checking him?" she hissed, indignant. "He's a normal baby. The man acts like he's going to grow horns and a tail the way he carries on all the time."

"Be right out," Kane called, shifting off the bed. "Sebastian is sleeping peacefully." He winced a little as he made his way toward the bathroom. "Offer them coffee." He stuck his head around the door. "But put some clothes on first. I don't want to have to kill anyone."

"Offer them coffee," Rose muttered under her breath and dragged on her clothes as quickly as she could. She was a mess. Seed running down her thighs and milk dripping from her breasts. She hurried to the doorway of the bathroom. "I can't possibly . . ." She broke off, seeing the laughter in Kane's eyes. He had pulled on a pair of jeans, and he grinned at her, clearly teasing. "You're so horrible."

He bent his head to brush a kiss over her upturned mouth as he passed her. "The shower's all yours."

She cast an anxious look toward the sleeping baby. "I don't want them touching Sebastian without me right there."

His lashes flickered, sweeping down to cover his expression and then up so he was meeting her eyes. "Is trust already going out the window?"

Remorse and guilt nearly crushed her, but she wasn't going to lie. "I don't trust *them*. I know you've known them a long time, but I haven't. Please be patient with me, Kane."

"Jaimie is family—a sister to me. She'd walk into hell for me—for us. I don't know Eric well, but he's always been the doctor to the GhostWalkers," Kane said. "I don't expect instant trust for the others on your part, Rose, but I do expect you to have an open mind when it comes to my family."

She nodded, her fingers clutching the doorjamb until they turned white. She hated that she was disappointing him. "I'll try." It was the best she could do. For now, she couldn't bear Sebastian to be put into the hands of strangers without her present.

She bit down hard on her lip, more agitated than she realized. It hurt to know that she might be letting him down, but she couldn't bring herself to hand her child over to strangers, even with Kane looking on. He didn't view them as threats, so it would be easy to kidnap the baby. He wasn't watching for it.

Kane padded back across the floor, his bare feet making no sound. She watched him come, heart pounding, until he was looming over her. Up close, Kane was intimidating, yet his hands were gentle as he framed her face and bent to brush a kiss across her mouth. "Sebastian is too important to take risks with. If at any time you're afraid for his safety,

I want you to rely on your instincts. I mean that, Rose. Never be upset because you're protecting our child."

She would have thrown her arms around him and hugged him close, but milk was still dripping, and she'd make a mess. "I'll work on getting to know Jaimie," she promised.

"I know you will." The confidence in his voice steadied her. Maybe he really knew her better than she knew herself.

Kane reluctantly allowed his hands to slip from her face, instead of caressing her as he was inclined to do. Visitors could be a major pain, he was finding, when all he wanted to do was worship Rose's body. And kiss her. He loved her mouth, that soft, shy, velvet paradise he could lose himself in for hours.

He bent over the baby's bed. Jaimie had found a small crib, and the boy slept peacefully, unaware that his mother was upset over company. He touched the baby's hand, aware that Rose watched him without moving, waiting to see if he would pick up Sebastian and take him into the other room. She was naked beneath the robe, not the best garb to follow him out of the room, but she made no move, just held herself very still.

"Mommy is a little freaked out, Sebastian. Until she feels comfortable, you behave and don't be too demanding about seeing visitors." The little fingers closed around his, and he brushed his thumb over the child's tiny knuckles. "Isn't it strange to think we created this little miracle?"

"Yes."

He shook his head over the idea that he had anything to do with such perfection. "Take a long shower, sweetheart, and don't worry about anything. I'm closing the door, and no one will disturb either of you."

Kane left her, strangely proud of her for telling the truth to him about her fears. She wanted to please him, but she didn't lie or make up excuses. He closed the bedroom door softly and went to greet the visitors.

He'd grown up with Jaimie tagging along since she was a little girl. A true genius, she'd caught up with both Mack and him, attending the same school and classes. Her face lit up when she looked up and caught sight of him. Jaimie jumped out of the chair where she'd been waiting and rushed him. He braced himself for the collision. She flung her arms around him.

"Should you be walking without a cane? Are you all right?" She looked past him toward the bedroom and lowered her voice. "Rose won't leave your side. I think she thinks one of us might try to do you in. I'm a little worried that she doesn't get any sleep."

"I told her to watch out for Mack. Was he pissed? He hasn't lectured me yet."

"That you got shot? You have no idea. And as soon as you're a hundred percent, you can pretty much count on him yelling at you. But it's so exciting that you found Rose and the baby."

"I delivered the baby." He'd done it. He may as well have bragging rights.

Her riot of curls bounced all over her head. "No way! Really? Wow, Kane. That's so incredible." The smile faded from her sapphire eyes. "You really scared us, you know. Dr. Lambert kept you in a coma for a while."

"I'm sorry I scared you, Jaimie." He wrapped his arm around her and dropped a kiss on top of her head. "I'm fine now. A little weak, but ready to start real training again. Physical therapy is wimpy, and I need some real work."

"Give it another week," Eric Lambert cautioned. "You nearly died, Kane. You should have died." He glanced toward the bedroom, and just like Jaimie, he lowered his voice. "I'd give a lot to know what she did to save your life. You should have bled out internally."

"But I didn't. And Jaimie, you're making a fuss when you've seen me every day for the past couple of weeks."

"Mostly in bed," she defended. "Or with a cane. Nothing that I can remember has ever kept you in bed. It was scary."

That was going to change. Rose could keep him in bed,

but he refrained from saying so. Just the thought of her showering in the next room sent a heated rush through his veins.

Kane forced his mind away from his woman. "I was up."

"Looking like a ghost."

He grinned at her, pretending to sway like a ghost. When she rolled her eyes, he stepped all the way back to allow them inside. "Would either of you care for a cup of coffee?"

"Sure," Lambert said.

Kane glanced at Jaimie. She burst out laughing. "I'll make it, no problem, *and*, while I'm at it, I'll make myself a cup of tea."

Kane grinned at her and waved his hand at the doctor, indicating for him to sit. The floor plan was open other than the bedroom and bathroom, following the floor plan of Jaimie and Mack's home two stories up. The space was nice, but Kane had already decided a second bedroom would be needed for the baby. By the time he had it built, he was certain Sebastian would be ready for it.

"Your son was born early and yet he appears to be thriving," Eric said. "Even without the help of a doctor," he added pointedly. "He must have amazing genes."

Kane didn't react, although his body went on alert. He reminded himself that Eric was a doctor and specialized in gene therapy. Of course he would be interested in Sebastian and his progress. How could he help it? "He was small when he was born, but with Rose feeding him on demand, he began to gain immediately. We put him in a warmer so we could keep his body temperature constant."

Eric sat back, a pleased expression on his face. "Excellent. Good thinking. Were there any complications that you know of with the pregnancy or birth?"

"Not the birth. Everything went according to the book. You'd have to ask Rose about her pregnancy."

Eric frowned as he formed a steeple with his fingers.

"Rose is not very forthcoming about anything at all, Kane. I've asked her several times, but she simply ignores me."

"She isn't quite ready to trust anyone," Kane said. "Nor should she be. Once she feels safe, she'll be more likely to answer questions."

"I'd like to examine Sebastian and do a few blood tests."

"No." Rose stood in front of the closed bedroom door, her dark chocolate eyes smoldering with fire. "Absolutely not. He's not a guinea pig, and he never will be."

"You misunderstand me, Rose," Lambert protested. "I'm just here to make certain he stays healthy. I need to see what immunities you've passed on to him and . . ." He broke off when she resolutely shook her head, appealing to Kane. "It's necessary for his health and safety."

"His blood is not going to any laboratory," Rose decreed.

Kane shrugged. "Sorry, Doc, but Rose has the right to refuse."

"Neither of you understand. Your DNA is not normal human DNA. You both have extraordinary psychic gifts as well as physical talents. In all probability you've passed these traits on to your child. We need to know what we're dealing with."

Before Rose could reply, Kane held up his hand to stop her. "Actually, Eric, that's where you're wrong. Rose and I need to know what we're dealing with. Sebastian is our child. You don't need anything at all. He's a curiosity, no more to you. He's our son. While we both appreciate everything you've done for us, right now, we're opting not to take his blood out of this house."

Eric Lambert frowned, shaking his head. "I don't understand. Suppose something was incompatible. What if Rose had the Rh factor and neither of you realized it. She didn't have prenatal care of any kind. There are tests that need to be run for his safety. For his health."

"Sebastian's healthy, Doc. We thank you for the concern, but we'll take care of him."

Rose leaned against the closed bedroom door, almost sagging in relief. *Thank you.*

Kane kept his gaze on the doctor. *He's our son. If you're not comfortable with Eric, we'll find a doctor you are comfortable with. I know someone I think you'll like.*

"How do you know whether or not I had prenatal care? You didn't even ask me."

Kane was startled by the outright hostility in Rose's voice. Eric was unsettling, he would admit that. He didn't have the best bedside manner; he was a surgeon and researcher, not a family doctor, but time and again he'd saved the lives of many GhostWalkers.

He saved my life, he reminded as gently as he could. He didn't pretend to understand women and their peculiarities.

Did he? Rose remained stubbornly where she was, arms crossed over her chest, guarding the door and eyeing Eric as if he was the enemy.

Kane shot her a warning look and held out his hand to her. She hesitated, but her expression softened and she crossed to his side, taking his hand. His fingers closed around hers, and he pulled her down into the chair beside him. *Did something happen while I was unconscious?*

"I think we started off on the wrong foot," Eric said, leaning toward Rose. "I'm not always the most social person. I've been told many times I should be a little less abrupt in my approach with people. I'm working on that."

He sounded stiff, and Kane felt a little sorry for him. Eric was an intelligent man—an acknowledged genius in his field if the medical journals were anything to go by—but he had a one-track, very focused mind, as most researchers did. It had to be difficult for such a proud man to work with GhostWalkers, men superior physically and psychically, but without his acute, focused brain. Kane also knew it would be extremely mortifying to have to apologize for anything.

I caught him trying to steal Sebastian's blood after I told him no.

Rose lifted her chin. "I have trust issues, so I guess we're both to blame."

There was nothing grudging in her voice. He felt pride in her blossom, spreading warmth through his body. Rose had no problems meeting someone halfway, and she sounded sincere, but after what she'd revealed, he knew she wasn't about to let Eric near their son without constant supervision. He brought her hand to his mouth and nibbled.

Have you suddenly developed an oral fixation?

He glanced at her, startled. She was teasing him with company around. It felt—intimate. He grinned at her and bit down on her finger. *Yes.*

Jaimie returned with the coffee, handing him a cup and then giving Eric one. "I made you tea, Rose. You seemed to prefer that to coffee."

Rose nodded. "Thank you."

Jaimie returned with the two cups of tea. "I added milk because I saw you used milk the last time, but if it isn't enough . . ."

"This is fine."

Rose smiled up at her, and Kane could tell it was genuine. He felt his belly settle. He hadn't even realized he'd been tense until that moment. He wanted Rose happy, and he wanted her to like and accept his family.

Eric took a sip of his coffee as Jaimie settled into a chair. "Where's Mack?"

Jaimie shrugged. "He's off doing Mack things," she replied with a sweet smile.

Kane frowned and glanced between her and Rose. Something had definitely happened while he was recovering. Jaimie had been enigmatic in her answer, something she would never have done had Kane asked the question. Which also raised the question: just what was Mack doing? He felt a little like Rip Van Winkle, waking up and having no clue what was going on.

Eric sighed. "I really don't have a lot of time. Kane,

I have to at least examine the baby before I go, to make certain he's healthy."

Rose shook her head. "I believe you examined him yesterday. Do you think his condition has changed between yesterday and today? He's asleep, and I'm not waking him up to be poked and prodded again."

A flash of anger crossed Eric's face. He threw his hands into the air. "I can see you're not going to be reasonable." Abruptly he stood up, disgust on his face. "I'll come back when you've talked some sense into her, Kane."

He turned and stalked out, slamming the door behind him.

"That went well," Kane said and took another drink of fortifying coffee. He looked from one woman to the other. "You want to tell me what's going on?"

"Not really," Jaimie said and winked at him.

Both women burst out laughing.

Kane glared at them. "I see how it's going to be around here. You two are planning on sticking together."

Jaimie shrugged. "Obviously we're outnumbered. We have no choice."

"Tell me anyway. And where's Mack?"

"Mack is scouting around the neighborhood, looking for anything that might threaten his nephew. He's gone all protective. A freighter came in yesterday, and all sorts of unsavory characters have been frequenting the bars and shops around here. You know Mack. He and Javier are out gathering information."

Kane's warning system went off. Jaimie was being casual for Rose's benefit. Her sapphire eyes met his steadily, conveying her worry. His heart constricted. Things had certainly changed in his life. He would have felt an adrenaline rush at the first sign of danger. Even an eagerness to go meet it, but now he had so much to lose. Rose. Sebastian. He wanted to wrap them up and keep them safe forever.

"You're not going to be ready for action for another couple of weeks, soldier," Rose said.

He had to grin at her. Damn. Nothing got by the woman. "So how bad is the threat, and how credible is it?"

Jaimie threw Rose an apologetic look. "I didn't want you to worry, Rose. You've been through so much."

Rose shrugged. "This is my life, Jaimie. I chose to come here. Kane and I have Sebastian, and we know they're going to keep coming at us to get to him. I'm prepared mentally for that. You don't have to try to protect me."

Jaimie nodded. "Whitney knows Rose is here."

Kane reached down and rubbed the tattoo on Rose's ankle. "We knew he'd track us here. We're hoping you and Javier can do something about his little homing device."

"We've got that covered already," Jaimie said. "But Mack says no matter when we disrupted the satellite transmission, he would have known you would bring her back here. He just can't track her movements anymore."

"He won't be happy about that."

Jaimie shrugged. "It's Whitney. He's strange. He gets all excited when the GhostWalkers are able to outwit him or foil his little attempts to retrieve them. I think he pats himself on the back, and it just reinforces how clever and brilliant he is. We are, after all, his creations."

Kane scowled at her. Jaimie held up her hand. "Hey. That's a quote from one of his reports. I don't hack into his computer often, but Flame found a way in, and she passed it on to me. We're careful, but we monitor him. We just give him a lot of room. We're lucky he doesn't trust anyone, so he does all his own computer work. He's just not as good as he thinks he is with security. He doesn't keep up on the latest and greatest because his entire world has become DNA and psychic research."

"So did your warning come from his computer?"

"He's very anxious to get his hands on the baby. He sent his 'representative' to 'acquire' him. I kid you not. It's right there on his computer. He was furious that Rose and the baby escaped him. He's determined. Apparently he feels we're far more vulnerable here. The stronghold in the

Wyoming mountains has become nearly impenetrable, and he doubts if he will be able to acquire the children kept there. Once again, he seemed pleased that the teams banding together had managed to not only keep themselves but their women and children safe from not only him, but all outside threats. Again, that's pretty much a quote, Kane."

"We're doing the same thing here."

"True, but we're more exposed because we don't have the ability at this time to clean things up as fast should there be an attack on us."

"But we're getting to that point," Kane said hastily. "We've managed to purchase five of the seven buildings we need to secure the entire area. Rose, if you want to take Sebastian and go to the stronghold in Wyoming, I can arrange it. The teams settling there are excellent. This building is secure, but we haven't set up for street surveillance . . ."

Jaimie looked smug. "Bite your tongue, Kane. Javier and I have been working night and day. We've got the street covered down two full blocks, the roof on three of the buildings as well as this one, and the water side."

"I'm fine with you," Rose said. "I'll help out here. I can work."

"Mack's got weapons and ammo stashed everywhere. We could take on an army. We've got a helipad on the roof of this building, and it's got all the necessary permits. That's how we managed to transport you directly here after your surgery," Jaimie added.

"I knew that was in the works, but didn't know it had come through."

"Where is all the money coming from?" Rose demanded.

Jaimie glanced a little apprehensively at Kane. "Lily Whitney-Miller. She inherited billions, and she shares with all the GhostWalkers."

Tell me. It was a demand, nothing less. Rose was naturally suspicious of such generosity.

"She's Dr. Whitney's adopted daughter," Kane explained. "He experimented on her as well. She was raised with quite a few of the girls."

Jaimie leaned forward, staring into Rose's eyes. "Do you remember her? She was with you in the beginning, when Whitney first took you all. You were in a big house, and he kept you in a dormitory. You were never allowed out of the laboratory."

Rose nodded. "It's impossible to forget that time. Lily was always like a mother to the rest of us. He treated her better, and she tried to get privileges for us."

"She put aside money for each of the other women she was raised with as well. You've got that money, Rose," Kane said. There was a hard knot in the pit of his stomach. Money could change things. She might decide to take the money and vanish.

Rose moistened her lips, her little pixie face very sober. "Do you trust her completely?"

"Yes," Kane said. "She's done too much for all of us to be anything but the real deal, Rose. She just had a baby. And Jack Norton and his woman had twins. They have three babies up there in the mountains. Sebastian isn't the only child at risk."

"Do you trust Eric completely?"

Kane almost nodded and then stopped himself. Did he trust the doctor the same way he trusted Lily? Eric was the official GhostWalker surgeon, and he always came through when needed. Why hesitate? What was the difference between Eric and Lily? Was he prejudiced simply because Eric wasn't a GhostWalker and had no real idea of what they went through? Kane didn't like the idea that he might in any way be prejudiced, but the truth was, there was a hesitation for whatever reason.

"I don't know. He's so intense about research. Maybe that creeps me out a little."

"That's all he's really interested in," Rose said. "I didn't leave him alone with Sebastian. The doctor was so insistent about taking his blood, and I knew once it was out of here, at a laboratory, it would be vulnerable. Whitney would pay a fortunate for Sebastian's blood. I told the doctor that, but it was obvious he didn't care. Taking his blood from this house clearly wasn't in Sebastian's best interests, but for the doctor the research came first. I just don't trust that, Kane."

He nuzzled the top of her head. "I can understand, Rose. You've been an experiment your entire life. You don't want that for Sebastian."

"Exactly, but the doctor can't see beyond what he might learn from studying Sebastian's blood." She sighed, her small teeth biting at her lower lip. "I know a doctor should examine him more fully just to make certain he really is as healthy as we believe, but it isn't safe."

"We happen to have just the man that will help you," Jaimie said, glancing at Kane for permission.

Kane nodded in agreement. "I was going to suggest you meet him, sweetheart. His name is Paul. He joined our team recently, so I didn't grow up with him as I did all the others, but he's got an amazing talent when it comes to healing skills. I trust him."

Rose swallowed hard, but she nodded. "If you're certain, Kane. But his blood can't leave our home."

"It won't have to," Kane assured. "Paul doesn't work like other doctors."

"You can't ever talk about him to anyone," Jaimie cautioned. "If Eric comes back, you can't tell him that Paul examined the baby."

"We have to protect one another's abilities. Whitney would take Sebastian apart to study him," Kane said. "He would Paul as well. Do you understand?"

Rose jumped up and paced across the room. "You've had what? Five years, seven years, maybe ten years of experience with Whitney? I've had my entire life. You don't need to tell me what he's like. We all protected one another from him, and we learned very fast to keep our abilities hidden."

"I know, sweetheart," Kane soothed. "It's just that Paul is . . ." He broke off, unable to explain.

"Has a rare talent," Jaimie supplied. "He's sent out into the field a lot. Whitney would find a way. You're part of our family now, Rose. Paul is family; that's all we're saying."

Rose nodded. Kane could feel her agitation, although there was little expression on her face. The idea that anyone would study her son was abhorrent to her, but she was trying to be accepting. She knew Sebastian needed a doctor and that they would need help with him. The only thing he could figure to do to help ease her mind was to introduce his family to her, one member at a time.

"Who have you met so far?" He kept his voice gentle.

"One they call Gideon and, of course, Javier. Jaimie and Mack." A faint smile touched her mouth, but failed to light her eyes. "They hover over you."

"I'll bet Mack did his fair share of swearing."

"You must have heard him," Jaimie said, astonished. "He's been here every day. A few times you were awake."

"I must have been doped up. I don't remember much." Other than Rose's warm body snuggled next to his. He remembered her kisses, along his mouth and throat, her soft murmurs of reassurance. He remembered feeling safe because she was there. At times he'd woken to the sound of Sebastian crying, and he could pry his eyes open just enough to see her moving around the room, changing and then breast-feeding the baby, singing softly to him. He'd felt—complete.

Jaimie grinned at him. "You were doped up, all right. We'd get you to sit up and you'd just slide down again and go to sleep."

Rose regarded him with troubled eyes. "You scared me. You nearly died, Kane."

He was weak, although he didn't want to acknowledge

it. Bits and pieces of the last couple of weeks were coming back to him now. Jaimie crying. Mack gruff as hell, always a bad sign. Javier and Gideon standing over him. Always, Rose watching them all, one hand free, obviously ready to defend him.

"I'm sorry, honey, I won't do it again."

"Damn right you won't," Rose said, flashing him a fierce look.

His body hardened, a brutal punch of need. She was sexy as hell when she went all commando on him with her little pixie face, so fragile and beautiful. Her eyes too big and her hair all tousled as if they'd just spent hours between the sheets. He knew his gaze went all hungry and predatory by the way her face flushed. Her eyes met his steadily. A soft consent in them that shook him. She'd just had a baby and she'd made love with him; she had to be sore, but she was willing to give herself to him again because his body demanded her.

I can behave myself, he assured.

You don't have to. You never have to. I love your hands on me. Your mouth. I love your body inside mine.

If she meant to soothe him, her words had the opposite effect. He wanted her with every single cell in his body. He took a breath, and pain flashed through him, reminding him he was flesh and blood, not a machine.

Well, maybe not a sex machine, she'd caught his last thought. Laugh lines appeared around her eyes, and her dimples flashed at him, taking the ache in his groin up another notch.

He glared at her, one hand pressed to his aching side. *That's not funny.*

"If you two need to be alone," Jaimie said, "I could always leave."

He threw the couch pillow at her. "You don't need to be putting in your two cents. You and Mack are disgusting."

She laughed at him. "So true. He's magic."

Kane groaned. "You're my sister, Jaimie. You can't put those kinds of thoughts in my head."

"I see. You have that double standard going. It's okay for you and the boys, but not me."

"*Exactly*. There are rules, girl. Rules. Follow them." He held out his coffee cup. "I wouldn't mind another."

She took it. "Not a chance, bro. You're on sick leave, which means you eat and drink nutritiously. One cup limit."

He gave a fierce scowl. "You are not going to boss me around, Jaimie."

"No"—she smiled sweetly at him and handed Rose the empty mug—"but Rose is."

Kane studied Rose's fine-boned features. That same determined expression she got, stubborn as hell and so appealing to him he knew he was a lost man, was right there on her face. Whenever she got that look, he knew he wasn't going to win. He kept his mouth shut. There were other ways to get around his woman, and he was going to find every one of them.

"By the way, Rose. I have put all your necessary papers into the system. Social. Birth certificate. Concealed weapons permit. Driver's license. Everything you'll need here on the outside. The baby's birth certificate states he was born in a military hospital. I'm establishing his records there now. Everything should be coming in the mail soon. Mack's talking to Sergeant Major about compensation for being on the team."

"Wait a minute," Kane said. "You're moving a little too fast. What the hell does that mean?"

"I'm a soldier, Kane," Rose pointed out. "That's all I'm trained for. I'm good at it, just as you are. You don't want out. If I'm part of this team, they can't break us up."

He shook his head. "You can wait a little while. We haven't even discussed this."

"Would you discuss this with me?" Rose asked quietly. "If your time was up?"

"It's not the same thing."

She smiled at him, that serene, sweet smile he was coming to know meant really bad things for him. "You know better. And it's added protection for Sebastian. I'm serving our country just as Whitney wanted. I'm more apt to bring up our son as a soldier, another thing he wants. He knows I'll teach Sebastian everything I know, just as you and every member of this team will, and he's more apt to leave us alone to see how Sebastian does under a full team's tutelage."

Kane bared his teeth at her. He hated that it was sound reasoning. His dream of the little woman sitting at home waiting for him was about to shatter. "We'll talk this out before you commit."

She arched an eyebrow at him. "Does that mean you'll talk until I agree with you?"

"At least give me the chance to persuade you. Jaimie doesn't go out on missions, and she contributes." He was grasping at straws and he knew it.

"Jaimie has a very specific set of skills I don't have. My skills are all in the field, Kane. I'll be an asset to you there, not sitting here at home."

Jaimie bent and kissed his jaw. "I think this is my cue to leave. Mack's going to be down later with Paul, and he'll tell you everything he's found out."

Kane watched the two women walk to the door together. He wanted them close but not conspiring against his wishes. He'd seen Rose in combat. She was fearless and didn't hesitate, as good or better than any soldier he'd worked with, but didn't she want to stay home and be a mother? What was wrong with that? His mother hadn't wanted to stay home either. What the hell was wrong with women these days? Didn't they understand someone needed to be in the home with the children, keeping the family together? Having dinners together? Do all the family things he'd envisioned but never had?

Rose closed the heavy door and turned to lean against it, regarding him soberly. They lived in a renovated warehouse, a massive building with large doors, and draped against it that way, she looked smaller than ever. It was difficult to imagine her in combat, yet he'd seen her, and she was too damned competent, with nerves of steel, for him to pretend she wasn't.

"Damn it, Rose." He pressed his fingers to his suddenly aching eyes. He hadn't even noticed that his head was pounding and his gut hurt like hell. Maybe he was just tired. "You should have at least waited to discuss this with me."

He felt the weight of her stare and looked at her. It was impossible to read the expression on her face. Not breaking eye contact, she pushed herself off the door and walked over to him. Her feet were bare, small and delicate, like the rest of her, making no noise on the floor as she came toward him. She was short enough that with him sitting, they were almost staring directly into each other's eyes.

"You're right, Kane, I should have. We're a team, and I should have given you that courtesy."

"I don't want to be a team. I want you to be my wife. *Mine.* Wholly mine. Not part of this big team, a soldier. I want the woman."

She smiled and very gently brushed at the hair tumbling across his forehead, tenderness in her touch. "You have both the woman and the soldier, Kane. They aren't separate."

"Damn it, I know that." He knew that. He did. "It's just that . . ." He trailed off, feeling damned stupid. He wasn't a little boy or even a teenage boy. He'd grown up hard and fast, and maybe that was the problem. He didn't want that for his son. He shook his head and looked away from her. "I'm tired, Rose. I think I'll lie down for a while."

"Look at me, Kane," she ordered softly.

He did, dropping straight down into those large, fathomless, melting chocolate eyes that threw him every time he fell into them.

"Tell me. I *want* to know."

He shoved a hand through his hair, betraying agitation when, with anyone else, he would have remained absolutely stoic. "I just always had this idea—this fantasy—about coming home to my wife, to dinner, to her waiting there for me. To her being a mother to my children. It's stupid, I know, but when I looked at the possibility of a family, that was it—not our son being left to fend for himself."

She framed his face with her hands. "I don't even know what family is, Kane. I had my 'sisters' when I was young, but even then we were often kept apart and used against one another. I'm learning as I go along, and I'm counting on you to help me with that. I'll do my best for Sebastian. I'll love him and I'll protect him, but quite frankly, I've never cooked a meal in my life. You're going to have to give up your dream of the wife having dinner waiting for you."

She leaned forward and brushed her mouth over his. "I don't want to disappoint you, but I can only be who I am."

He wrapped his arms around her and drew her onto his lap, cradling her close with a wry smile. "I suppose I could always be the girl and stay home."

Her eyebrow shot up. "Girls stay home?"

"If I lied, would that count?"

She nuzzled his neck. "No. I'm your woman. All of me, Kane, and that includes the soldier. My advice is to learn how to cook if you don't already know how."

He was happy just holding her. Maybe a stay-at-home mother wasn't as important as he'd first thought. "Fortunately, I'm a damned good cook."

She kissed him.

CHAPTER 13

Rose liked Paul Mangan right away. He looked very young with his freckles and his wide-eyed innocence. It was more than obvious that he was of Irish descent. He looked a bit awkward and blushed every time he snuck a glance at her. He was tall and slender, with fine hands, almost delicate. She couldn't imagine him as a soldier, let alone him going into combat. While Javier Enderman looked young and could easily pass for a teenager, he had a steely strength about him, and if one looked into his eyes, there was no way they wouldn't feel a chill go down their spine. The killer was in those cold, flat, very hard eyes. But Paul . . . He was altogether different. He just didn't look like he belonged in the Marine Corps, let alone have Special Forces training as well as what it took to become a GhostWalker.

Don't underestimate him, Rose, Kane cautioned as he came into the room.

She couldn't imagine that Paul could possibly see to the health of her child. He barely looked her in the eye, but the moment Kane walked into the room, he seemed entirely different. Rose frowned, watching the boy—no—man. He was definitely a man. His face changed very subtly, which told her part of what she saw was an illusion. She knew all about illusions; she could change her looks subtly or even blatantly if need be. Paul obviously had the same ability to a lesser degree, but why would he need to do so there in the safety of Kane's home?

She studied him as he shook Kane's hand and turned toward her for an introduction, nearly bowing, blushing redder than ever.

"It's nice to meet you, ma'am."

Can he even shoot a gun? She carefully avoided looking at Kane, afraid she'd laugh. "Nice to meet you too. I understand you might be able to look Sebastian over and tell us if he's truly healthy without his blood leaving our home."

His father is Sergeant Major Theodore Griffen. He grew up shooting guns. I doubt that the military would have ever been his thing, he's a gentle man, probably more like his mother than father, but he has an amazing and coveted psychic talent. Whitney would probably kill us both gladly to get his hands on Paul. No one knows about Paul outside of our team.

"I can certainly try. Kane, you need to rest more. You aren't completely healed." He frowned, his eyes nearly glowing as he stared at Kane's chest and abdomen, clearly looking *through* skin, deeper into his damaged organs.

Tell me about him.

Rose found Paul fascinating. His gaze was sharp and focused; his entire demeanor changed. There were frown lines around his mouth and brow, and all of a sudden she could see the quick intelligence she'd missed before.

Obviously he's a genius, like Jaimie. He graduated from high school at thirteen and holds multiple doctorates in chemistry, math, and something else I can't remember. He also has a BA in at least three other subjects. His mother is Shiobhan Mangan, an ambassador's daughter and the current ambassador to Ireland. She kept her last name and they gave it to Paul because when they first were married, Sergeant Major had quite a few enemies.

She studied Paul's face. *He doesn't belong in the military. He has too much empathy to kill, Kane. He shouldn't be around violence.*

No. They put him with us to protect him from Whitney. His psychic ability is . . . amazing. But don't shortchange him; Paul gets the job done when it's needed.

"Who did this surgery?" Excitement edged Paul's voice.

Rose tensed. There was no way he could know. No way. Just in case, she eased away from the two men, putting a little distance between them.

"Eric Lambert," Kane replied.

Paul shook his head impatiently, brushing off the quick answer. "No, before the doc. Who was in the field with you? Who worked on you in the field?"

Kane shrugged. "Sorry, Paul, it was one of the team. I was out of it." He looked at Rose. "Do you remember?"

She avoided his eyes. She had promised herself she would never lie to him, and if they were alone . . .

"I do," Javier stirred from the shadows.

Rose jumped. She'd almost forgotten about him. He blended, perfectly still, until he was part of the wall he had draped himself on. His gaze moved over her with open speculation—and something else. If she had done anything at all to harm Kane . . . She shivered at the dark promise there. She was very good at assessing threats, and in spite of all the skills the rest of this team had, Javier was truly the most dangerous—and unpredictable—of them all. His protective and loyalty instincts must have been off the charts when they tested him.

"What's wrong, Paul?" Javier continued.

"Brilliant fieldwork. He would have bled out, but someone repaired the artery; I just can't see how." Paul narrowed his gaze, stepping closer to Kane and actually crouching down to peer upward toward his abdomen and chest.

"There's a definite wound site, the artery spliced together in some way."

The darkness gathering in Javier's eyes disappeared, and he flashed Rose a smile. "You saved your man, didn't you? What exactly did you do?"

Paul pushed Kane's shirt out of the way. "Clean cut. This is where he went in . . ." He broke off as Javier's words penetrated. He blinked rapidly as if coming back from a great distance. Very slowly he stood, regarding Rose with awe. "*You* did this? How? You have to tell me what you did." Excitement made his voice shake. "You know you saved his life. He would have bled out in minutes."

Kane must have sensed her reticence, because he reached out and took her hand, rubbing the pad of his thumb over her knuckles. The small gesture comforted her. She shrugged, trying to look casual. They thought they knew about protecting themselves from Whitney, but she'd been under the scrutiny of cameras and microphones nearly all of her life. She knew what it was like to live under a microscope. It had become obvious, at a very early age, that each of the girls Whitney was experimenting on needed to hide as many of their abilities from him as possible.

She thought she'd have the chance to learn trust slowly—with just Kane. She hadn't counted on his family. His team, with the exception of Paul, had grown up together, and Kane trusted all of them. He expected her to do the same. Panic hovered close. She could barely breathe.

You can do this, sweetheart. You don't have to answer questions. This is your home. There are no expectations.

His voice caressed her. She forced her head up and looked into his eyes. She could live there. The way he looked at her—as if she was his entire world—it was a heady, potent experience, one she didn't entirely trust. But she wanted to trust him. She wanted this to work. When she made up her mind to do something, she committed 100 percent. She wasn't going to wimp out now.

"Rose, please," Paul's voice trembled with excitement.

"This is the coolest thing I've ever seen and—seriously—the closest thing to what I can do. I've never met anyone like me."

She heard the loneliness—the idea that he could be a freak of nature. All of them battled with being "different." They always would. She could see how isolated Paul must have felt growing up. His father was a big man, a man who was disciplined and understood violence. Paul was just the opposite—a natural-born healer with tremendous empathy for those around him. His father probably had tried to understand him, but how could he? The boy was sensitive, and the idea of killing had to be abhorrent to him.

In some ways, even among the GhostWalkers, Paul was still isolated. He wasn't a soldier by choice. He was far too empathetic to kill. He was a healer, a poet, a man whose very soul cried out for gentleness, yet he was surrounded by extremely violent men. She could see both Kane and Javier were protective of him, but they didn't understand him.

"How? You have to tell me how."

While she could do some extraordinary things, she wasn't quite as empathetic. She made a good soldier and she knew she did. Paul seemed a little lost. She looked from him to Javier and Kane. These men had accepted the boy into their world—their family. They offered him their loyalty and complete acceptance, which he obviously needed. He would give the same back to them tenfold.

If it's easier, Rose, I can take Javier into the other room.

She took a breath and shook her head. She suddenly found she wanted to be a part of them as well. She wanted that same acceptance. If she became one of them—like Paul had become one of them—Javier would give her the same loyalty he gave his family members. She wanted his respect and his protection, for her and for Sebastian. It was difficult to let go of her fears—she had so many—but she'd always believed in facing her fears.

"I'm able to visualize in my head what's going on

in someone's body under extreme circumstances." She chewed nervously on her lower lip, trying to find the words to describe how the talent manifested itself. "I feel heat in my fingertips first. And then my palms. Eventually my hands get so hot it feels as if they're burning."

Paul nodded. "The nerves are raw, and the heat starts running up your arms."

Rose's gaze jumped to him. He understood. He actually understood the manifestation. They smiled at each other. "The first time it happened, I was seven, and one of the girls, Thorn, stopped breathing. We all loved her so much. I was panic-stricken. We all were. Whitney had just left the room, and Thorn suddenly dropped to the floor. She'd been defying him, and he'd used electric shock on her. I ran to her, and my hands burned. I knew I had to . . ."

"Touch her. Put your palms on her," Paul interrupted.

Rose forgot everyone else in the room. She nodded, her heart pounding hard. "It was more instinct than anything else. Once I touched her, I could see her heart wasn't pumping. It had stopped. I could see it in my head."

"And in response, you felt the electrical current needed to jump-start her," Paul said, "running through your own body. It's as if our bodies provide what's missing from those hurt or injured in some way. I always refer to it as psychic healing."

"How does it work?"

"I don't know. I've tried studying what happens to me when I run across someone damaged. Each response is different. I see the patient in colors. Is it like that for you?"

She shook her head. "Not really. When I lay my palms on their skin, I see inside their bodies, not through my eyes but in my head, as if skin to skin, I absorb them into me."

Kane's fingers tightened around her, startling her, drawing her attention. She looked at him, almost afraid of what she'd see. Seeing *inside* someone was a strange, freaky experience. Having her own body react to theirs was almost an intimacy, a bonding between the two bodies, hers

providing whatever the other needed. She didn't tell anyone if she could help it and she never elaborated on what
happened—she didn't want to think about what happened.
It was frightening and exhilarating. It was also very, very
painful.

Her eyes met Kane's. There was nothing but awe. Respect. Love. Her heart fluttered in her chest, and she swore
her knees went weak. He had a way of looking at her. Hungry predator. Intense desire. Amazing, absolute devotion.
All the emotions were there for her, and he didn't try to
hide them. It was always a little difficult for her to believe
he could feel those things for her, but she was trying.

"You saved my life." Kane brought her hand up to his
mouth. "Didn't you?"

She shook her head. "I gave you a chance. I'm not adept
at healing. I can only do it in a crisis. I managed to repair the severed artery, but I wasn't certain it would hold,
so I actually held it together until we got to the airfield.
They'd set up for surgery right there. The doctor who did
the surgery fixed everything else as well. The bullet ricocheted around in there and did a lot of damage. You were
in surgery over three hours, and they nearly lost you twice,
Kane."

"He would have died in the helicopter if it wasn't for
you," Javier said. "We're all very grateful to you."

Rose was so startled, she actually took a step back. Javier seemed to disappear and then just emerge from the
wall itself. She put a hand to her throat, shocked at the way
he was looking at her as well. She had gone from potential
enemy to reserved acceptance. She was grateful she was
on his good side.

"I don't know what happens," she admitted. "My body
takes over my brain and just acts. I barely remember what
I did."

"You cut him open and put your hand inside of him,"
Javier said.

She shivered, remembering his reaction. Javier had

placed a knife to her throat. The gesture had seemed casual but was anything but. She'd kept working, knowing she didn't have much time. She'd found the severed artery and repaired it within minutes, shouting for Mack to give Kane her blood *immediately.*

It had all been hazy from the moment she'd pulled Kane into the helicopter, "saw" the severed artery, and cut him open. Mack hadn't hesitated, starting the transfusion immediately, even as Gideon gave him plasma. She'd been so frightened, wanting to grab Sebastian and leap from the helicopter, taking her chances with the unknown rather than with these grim-faced strangers without Kane.

Oddly, it had been Javier who helped her. He held her stable through the flight, using his own body to prop her up. He'd asked one of the others to slip makeshift pillows under her arms to help keep them up and then had her covered with a warm blanket as she crouched over Kane. Her blood flowed into Kane's body in a desperate attempt to keep him from bleeding to death, while her fingers, deep inside his body, had reinforced her repair of the artery. She would never forget that incredible helicopter ride as she tried to breathe for Kane, willing him to live with every ounce of strength she possessed.

"Whitney never found out about you?" Kane asked.

She shook her head. "I told you, even as children we knew we had to hide our gifts from him. He might help us develop them, but had he known about me, he would have put the other girls in jeopardy just to see me use it. He can be very cruel. He doesn't look at it that way. Everything he does, for him, is justified in the advancement of science."

"That's why you have such a difficult time with Eric," Kane guessed.

Rose nodded. "His need to learn can outweigh his moral scruples. Once a man believes that an individual doesn't count for the good of the masses, he crosses a line and is capable, in the name of science, of anything. Whitney

crossed that line a long time ago. He believes himself far
above everyone else in intellect. He has powerful friends
who aid him. That only feeds his ego and belief that he's
above the rest of humanity. Laws don't apply to him."

"Can you see the fantastic job Dr. Lambert did?" Paul
asked, indicating Kane.

She shook her head. "It never happens unless there's a
crisis. That's why I can't be certain Sebastian is completely
healthy. I know he's not in immediate danger, but I can't
examine him."

"Do any of the other women have this talent?" Paul
asked.

"We stopped sharing information fairly early on because he recorded our conversations. Most of us became
very secretive. Whitney believed we each had one strong
talent and maybe another to a far lesser degree. It wasn't
until he began experimenting on adults that he discovered
there could be more than one strong psychic talent in one
individual. He isolated us after that, but we'd learned to be
vigilant by that time."

Kane tugged at her hand, a little disconcerted to have
Paul staring at his insides. "Come take a look at the baby,
Paul."

"I've never really examined an infant," Paul hedged.
"I'm not certain I'm really qualified to do this."

"You're what we have," Kane said. "That makes you
qualified. Take a look at him." He stepped back to allow
Paul into the bedroom where the small crib was.

Rose hovered close as Paul approached the crib. Kane
indicated for Javier to follow him out of the room. He
wanted to know exactly what threats his family faced. Rose
wouldn't leave Sebastian's side while Paul was with him,
giving him the opportunity to assess the risks.

"Where's Mack?" he demanded.

"Didn't Paul just tell you to rest?" Javier asked, one eyebrow raised.

"The hell with that. What's going on, Javier? Half the team is missing, and don't tell me they're out on a mission somewhere."

Javier shrugged and swaggered into the kitchen to pour himself a cup of coffee. "Mack will be here in a few minutes. He wasn't that far behind us. You got yourself a good woman. She admits she learned to be secretive, yet she's obviously disclosing information to us in an effort to show good faith. That takes a great deal of courage."

Kane glanced up at the admiration in Javier's voice. Javier rarely showed inner thoughts or allowed real emotion to surface.

"You should see her in action," Kane said, "No hesitation, Javier. None. She gets the job done."

"I can see that in her. I put a knife to her throat, Kane. When she was cutting you open on the helicopter. One moment we've pulled you aboard, blood all over the place, and the next she's on her knees, slicing into your belly. It scared the holy hell out of me. I thought she was hacking you up, she was that fast. I put my blade against her neck, tight enough to cut the skin, and she never so much as flinched. I swear she didn't even bat an eyelash. She just kept working fast. Your blood was all over her, and she was shouting orders to all of us. In the end we just did what she said. She's one cool customer."

"I should beat you to a bloody pulp for threatening her," Kane said, "but it wouldn't do a bit of good. You'd do the same thing again."

"I've never seen anything like that, Kane," Javier answered seriously, leaning back against the sink, coffee mug in hand. "Seriously, she moved so fast, no wasted effort, cut right into you in front of us, no hesitation, not even when I threatened her. She's a very unusual woman—and dangerous."

Kane's gaze flicked over Javier. "You admire her."

"Damn right. She reminds me a little of Rhianna."

Javier rarely mentioned Rhianna Bonds. She'd grown

up with them on the streets of Chicago, the only other girl in their "family."

"Does she?" Kane wasn't altogether certain he was happy Javier thought that. Although he never admitted it, Javier was obviously crazy about Rhianna in a weird, possessive kind of way. Kane didn't want Javier looking at Rose that way.

Javier nodded. "Rhianna doesn't seem to have a fear factor, other than when it comes to me, where Rose battles fear, but they both are very dangerous."

"And you like dangerous women."

Javier shrugged. "They're intriguing to me. That edge you come up against. She might kiss you or stick a knife in you. You never know what you're waking up to."

Kane burst out laughing. "Well, she did shove a gun in my gut," he admitted. "She was very serious about it too. That's when I ditched my locator."

"Mack was pissed about that, Kane. It was just as well you nearly died, because he would have killed you himself." Javier took a slow sip of coffee, obviously savoring the blend, before scrutinizing Kane over the steaming mug. "You scared us all, bro."

Kane heard the sincerity in Javier's voice. The man rarely showed emotion; although all of them knew he felt it deeply, he just buried it equally as deep.

They both turned as a cursory knock on the door preceded a flashing alarm as Mack shoved the door open before the alarm had time to deactivate. Mack cursed and paused long enough to punch in the code again.

"Damn thing. Jaimie has to speed that up," he groused. "Can't even keep up with me." His gaze ran over Kane, clearly assessing his condition. There was a shadow of worry in his eyes and few more worry lines etched into his face Kane hadn't remembered seeing. "You're finally on your feet. That woman is fucking overprotective of you." His voice was gruff, almost hoarse, both accusing and shaken at the same time.

Kane grinned at him. "I could get used to it."

"Well, don't. You ever scare the shit out of me like that again, and I'll put a bullet in you myself. We clear on that?"

"Yeah, Top, I get it."

"Good. We've got that settled. Is Paul looking after the baby?" Mack pointed to the coffeepot.

Javier obligingly poured him a cup of coffee.

"He's in the other room with Rose, who most likely heard the alarm and covered you with a gun. She's a little edgy like that."

Mack threw himself into a chair and pressed his fingers to his eyes. "She'll need it. Damn cartel is a little pissed off at her, Kane."

Kane took the blow stoically, but for a moment the blood thundered in his ears. He sank down into a chair, feeling a little weak in the knees. "It isn't enough Whitney is after her? Tell me what's going on, Mack."

The infamous Lopez family was notorious for their bloody sieges and brutal retaliation. They'd virtually declared war on their own government, targeting policemen and their families, wiping them out, decapitating them and leaving their bodies in plain sight for all to see. They had begun going after the politicians recently, ambushing the cars carrying them, killing their military escorts, and carrying out their brutal death threats. Bombs were frequent, blowing up police stations and cars on the roadways.

"Diego Jimenez made a deal with Whitney," Kane explained. "Whitney supplied Jimenez with guns and ammunition and probably money in order for him to fight the former president. That made Jimenez very unpopular with all of the cartels, but the Lopez family in particular. Apparently they targeted Jimenez's family, and when he found himself dying of cancer and Whitney was willing to do anything to get Rose back, he found a way, he thought, to get the cartel off his family's back."

Kane raked his fingers through his hair and huffed out his breath, a sure sign for those who knew him that he was angry. "Rose nursed the old man through his dying days, but he sold her out to the cartel, trading her life for his sons'. He told the cartel where she was and what she was worth to Whitney. They know her identity, and they know she was involved in the deaths of the cartel members sent to acquire her. Damn Jimenez. If he wasn't already dead, I'd kill him myself."

The sound of soft, feminine laughter whispered inside his head. He glanced up and met Rose's laughing eyes. His stomach did its famous flip, and his body stirred to attention. It took a moment to realize her laughter was for him alone and the intimacy of the moment shook him.

She pushed herself off the wall. "It was a natural conclusion, Kane. I knew they'd blame me. They had my name and they lost at a lot of their men. They seek vengeance as a rule; it's how they keep everyone afraid of them. They have to blame someone for all those deaths, and I'm all they've got. It was a war zone out there. There's no trace of any of you. Whitney's men probably cleaned up their bodies, so what's left as an explanation? They *have* to find me and get their answers." She shrugged her shoulders. "You would have figured it out if you hadn't been unconscious and recovering for so long."

"You might have told me," Mack pointed out.

She stood still for a moment, her dark eyes searching his face. "Yes. I should have. I'm sorry for that. I knew it wasn't just going to go away, and by being with you all, it would put you in jeopardy as well. I should have said something."

Mack nodded, accepting her apology. "Jaimie is very good at hearing threats in chatter. She monitors everything, and about three weeks ago, we realized the head of the Lopez cartel had reached out to one of the gangs affiliated with them here in the States, and your name came up."

"And yet you didn't mention this to me."

Mack's expression didn't change as he briefly nodded. "That's true. Perhaps I should have said something."

Kane looked from one to the other. "Are we at war?"

Mack flashed him a grin. "Not me." He held up his hands in surrender. "She saved your life, bro. I owe her for that. And she gave me the most amazing nephew in the world. So permanent truce. Although, you know, I expect her to marry your ass. I had Jaimie do the preliminary paperwork."

Rose went a little pale while Mack looked wholly pleased with himself.

Kane grinned at Rose. "Get used to it, sweetheart. He bosses all of us. I guess you'll have to marry my ass. Boss man says so."

"Both of you are crazy."

"You knew that going into it."

"I'm going to ignore both of you."

"You do that," Mack approved. "Just say 'I do' at the appropriate moment, and all will be well."

She frowned, obviously not really understanding or taking him seriously. Kane knew better. He shot Mack a warning glance. "Paul, is Sebastian healthy?" he asked, changing the subject.

Paul hovered just outside the door, looking awkward. His face lit up. "Very healthy, Kane. He's unusually strong. He's also alert and aware of what's going on around him. When I came into the room, he locked onto me right away, without blinking, almost uncomfortably so, like a predatory animal might. I know you have feline DNA and Rose admitted she did as well. He has a few traits that make me think he's developing at a faster rate than most children, but I'm not a baby expert."

Kane frowned. "Are you saying he's part animal? Should we expect claws?"

Paul hastily shook his head. "No, no, of course not. I'm just saying you might want to expect unusual behavior rather quickly from him. His lungs, heart, every organ is in perfect working order. He's extremely healthy. Really. Nothing crazy, no leopard skeletons inside of him, but his intelligence shines through. Looking at him, you get the feeling he understands. When Rose introduced me to him, that alert stare vanished, and he seemed just like a normal baby, checking out a stranger."

The explanation tumbled out. Paul talked fast, stumbling over his words, trying to convey something intangible when it was impossible. Kane understood. He'd noticed Sebastian's strange stare as well as the too intelligent look the boy often gave him. "Thanks for taking a look at him, Paul."

"When I gave him a few strength tests, he pushed back hard, harder than I ever expected a child his age to be able to do." Again the words fell nearly on top of one another. It was apparent Paul was eager to discuss the baby and all the possibilities he presented, or at least to bounce his ideas off them.

"You know you can't mention Sebastian to anyone," Mack said, startling Kane.

Rose threw him a grateful glance.

That pulled Paul up short. He flushed. "Of course not. Never outside this room and never to anyone not a member of our team."

"Our family," Mack corrected. "Some others consider themselves part of us, but they're not. You protect Sebastian in the same way we protect one another."

"I got it, Top," Paul assured.

He looked so awkward, Kane took pity on him. "Coffee's on, Paul. We were just discussing what Mack's found out about the threat hanging over Rose's head."

Paul threw him a grateful look and headed to the coffeepot.

"What exactly is the threat, other than they know my name?" Rose asked. "As far as I know, none of them saw me alive."

"There was an old woman," Mack reminded. "Her name is Olivia Lopez Martinez. Her son was guarding the outskirts of town when the two of you were escaping.

Apparently you pretended to be in labor. Apparently she took your picture."

Rose's dark eyes went wide. "Damn it. Just damn it. She was my neighbor, and she seemed such a nice woman."

"She introduced you to Diego Jimenez." Kane made it a statement.

I'd been so alone, felt so vulnerable, there in a foreign country with no real knowledge of how to live day to day without being in a military complex. I gravitated toward the elderly to tap into their knowledge and because they were far less threatening. I can barely believe that sweet old lady was born into the cartel.

"She did," she acknowledged out loud. She looked at Kane, wanting to apologize, needing him to understand.

I brought another enemy straight to their door. It isn't as if they don't have too many against them already. I'm so sorry, Kane. I was so scared when it came closer to the baby being born.

Kane stood up, not quite with his usual fluid grace, but he managed without a cane, and went to her, wrapping his arm around her waist. She moved into him, nearly melting into his skin, slipping beneath his shoulder as if she just, for one moment, needed his strength.

"I'm sorry," she said aloud to Mack. "It was stupid of me to trust any of them. She seemed so harmless, and I was about to give birth. I can leave . . ."

"Don't be ridiculous. This is your home," Mack snapped, impatience crossing his face. "We don't turn tail and run, and we sure don't throw our family members to the wolves."

"They kill everyone. They'll go after Jaimie."

Javier had slid back into the shadows; now he stirred, drawing her attention, quite frankly startling her. Kane felt her jump. He was used to Javier disappearing on them, fading into whatever was solid behind him, but Rose scowled.

"Stop doing that. I'm going to have a heart attack."

He flashed a small, unrepentant grin. "I need the practice. Don't you worry about Jaimie, Rose. She can handle herself, and she's got all of us. No one's going to get to Jaimie."

Kane felt a shiver run through Rose, and he tightened his arm around her. *Javier is on our side, Rose. He'd die for Jaimie—and for you and Sebastian. More important, he'd kill for you. He's a good man. He lives by a strict code. He's a man of honor.*

I believe that, Kane, but I also believe it would never be a good idea to cross him—or betray him.

She was a good judge of character, no doubt about it. He rubbed her rib cage with gentle fingers, soothing her as he turned his attention back to the matter of the cartel. "Do they know she's with us?"

"Of course not. They have no idea. Whitney sure isn't going to give her up to them. More likely, we'll get an influx of his men hanging around to help protect her—or snatch her if they get the chance. They'll just muddy the waters for us," Mack groused.

"So what are you worried about?"

"They have her picture. It's been circulating, and they've got bounty hunters looking for her. They put a hefty price on her head."

Kane took the body blow without flinching. His hand found hers, threading his fingers through hers in silent reassurance.

"What are we doing about it, Mack?" He knew Mack. There was already a plan in motion.

Mack's smile was anything but pleasant. "We're adept at urban warfare; they're adept at killing unarmed, terrified people. We have as good—or better—weapons than they do. If they're stupid enough to come at us, they're going to get a fight they won't believe."

"I don't understand what that means," Rose said.

"It means," Kane explained, "that if they find you here, if *any* bounty hunter finds you here, we'll take the fight right back to them."

"And shove it up their ass," Javier added. "If you'll excuse my language, ma'am."

"You can't invade a foreign country," Rose said. "It would cause an international incident. Every GhostWalker could be in trouble."

Mack shrugged. "They'd have to catch us first, baby sister, and that just isn't going to happen. We're ghosts, remember?"

"Have you sent them a message, Top?" Kane asked.

"Not yet. We'll deliver it though, personally, if and when it's needed."

Kane frowned and shook his head, his body straightening. "No one is doing my job for me. I'll take the message to them myself."

Rose tightened her fingers around his and stepped in front of him, as if she could physically block his body from harm. "No one is going to deliver any message. They don't have a clue where I am. They don't know about any of you or what you do. If you go throwing down the gauntlet, you'll be stirring up a hornet's nest. Right now they're looking for a pregnant woman worth a lot of money to a crazy billionaire. They don't know about any of you. They know about Whitney, the man who supplied weapons and Humvees to the rebels. They think he killed all of their people trying to acquire me."

There was a small silence. "She's probably right about that, Top," Kane said. "The cartel has to think Whitney's men shot them all to hell."

"In fact, they did," Rose pointed out. "We only were responsible for a couple of them, and remember, they think I was a hostage."

"Is the word on the street to kill her?"

"Dead or alive," Mack's voice was grim. "Preferably alive, but they'll take what they can get. It's more money if she's delivered alive."

"They plan on taunting Whitney with her," Javier said. "Showing him they will retaliate."

"The bottom line for me," Kane said, "is that they said dead or alive. That's unacceptable."

"You can't go to war with the cartel," Rose said.

The three men smiled at one another, and there was nothing at all pleasant about those smiles.

CHAPTER 14

Rose stood on the rooftop and looked around, a little awed by the view. Three stories up, she could see the ocean as well as a good portion of the city. A garden had been started on the roof, mainly, she could see, for defense purposes. She was coming to realize this team did everything with both offense and defense in mind.

"Urban warfare is different than what you've been trained for," Kane said, indicating the buildings around them. "See all those windows? Every one of them can house an innocent family. Women and children, a good man working to provide for his family—or an enemy can be sitting there waiting for you to give him a good target. Sometimes, it can be extremely difficult to tell the difference between that good man trying to protect his family from what he perceives as a threat, and the man waiting to take you out."

Rose felt a small chill steal down her spine. Sebastian lay quietly in the front pack, snuggled against her, his blue green eyes staring around him in a kind of wonder. She suddenly felt exposed there on the roof and wanted to rush back inside and keep him safe.

"The field of vision is always limited in a city," Kane said, moving along the side of the roof that looked out over the street. "You have to really take your time and study our area here. This is a very three-dimensional world, with a lot of areas for a sniper to sit back and pick off one of us. Gideon Carpenter and Ethan Myers—I think you met both of them on the helicopter—are up here daily, familiarizing themselves with every conceivable cover, both for them and for the enemy."

Rose narrowed her eyes and looked down at the busy street. They were near the docks, and everyone seemed to be hustling to get on or off the boats. She took her time, studying each warehouse, the balconies and small alcoves and fire escapes that could hide potential enemies.

"Once we have complete control of the buildings on both sides of the street, we'll be in a much stronger position. Our biggest problem at the moment is that building right there." He indicated a three-story warehouse that had been renovated into apartments. "So far, we've been unable to purchase it. People come and go all the time. It would be easy enough for an enemy to infiltrate and set up shop right there. Any of the front apartments face our home. Gideon is building his home on the top floor of the next building and Paul has the floor beneath him. The training center will be on the first floor."

"You all are keeping Paul on the middle floor, to protect him," she mused aloud.

Kane shrugged. "The truth is, we do look out for him, but make no mistake, Rose, Paul can handle any weapon. He went through all the same training we did, just as Jaimie did. She can work in the field, just as Paul can, but neither are really cut out for it. The thing is, an enemy would underestimate Paul every time. He's got courage and loyalty and would stand. I'd have him at my back any time."

"Yet you still protect him. All of you do."

He flashed a small grin. "Yeah. We do."

Paul was special, and they all recognized it. His intellect, his powers of observation, and his incredible psychic talent earned him a consideration, but it was his heart that had eventually won them all over. "We're lucky to have him on the team."

"So your plan is to have your homes in these buildings, with each man getting his own floor for his house."

"We'd command this entire street. The water on one side would be an asset and escape route, plus we've got an underground escape as well. Once we secure the buildings, we'll connect the tunnels."

"What about the local police? How are you going to have a military compound in San Francisco?"

"Jaimie's adept at getting through paperwork, and of course, we're more than willing to help the local police any way we can. They know we're military, but these are our homes. This is our neighborhood. Since we've been here, crime has gone down significantly, not only here but in a seven-block radius around us. We know every store owner, every bar owner. We make it a point to keep goodwill. We've already built up a network, and we're friends with most of the fishermen and dockworkers. They'll leave us alone."

"So no tanks driving through the streets."

Kane laughed and swept his arm around her. "Don't sound so disappointed. We'll have plenty of excitement."

"Speaking of which, I thought I'd go shopping with Jaimie this afternoon. Sebastian will be safe with you."

Kane felt every muscle in his body lock down. He stared down at her little pixie face. So innocent looking. So very devious. She'd dropped the bombshell on him without so much as blinking. And what the hell was he supposed to say to that? She wasn't a prisoner. She didn't need his permission. But he envisioned her first foray into their neighborhood with him as her armed guard. And maybe six or seven of the other team members.

Babysit? She wanted him to stay home and watch the baby sleep while she walked among the enemy. There was probably an entire battalion of Whitney's men waiting to kidnap her. And surely some spy had contacted every bounty hunter both in America and overseas, giving her exact location. Along with that, the cartel probably had assassins blanketing the area.

"You look a little pale, Kane. Are you certain you should be walking around so much just yet? We should go in." She took his arm.

There was nothing wrong with his physical strength. If he was pale it was because she terrified him sometimes. "Do you think that's really wise?"

She blinked up at him, giving him that little frown he found sexy. "Yes, absolutely. I think you need to go back inside and rest. Wisest course of action for you, Kane. You're working out too much. Even that rude surgeon says so. I hate to agree with anything the man says, but unfortunately, he's making sense."

He pulled her close to him, bending his head until their mouths were inches apart. "I'm not above putting you over my knee."

She went up on her toes to cover the scant couple of inches needed to find his mouth with hers. "Sounds intriguing," she murmured against his lips. She brushed kisses back and forth across his mouth. "But you'd better really enjoy it, because once you let me up, I'll have to retaliate, just for the sake of all women across the world."

He choked, laughter welling up. The day was foggy and a little windy, but right then, the sun seemed to burst over him. There was something about her that made him feel good. Her small stature, a little Asian porcelain doll with her dark chocolate eyes and her wild, shiny hair spilling around her face, was at odds with her tough core. She made him want to be her hero, the man who she depended on when everything around her fell apart, yet more than likely, it was going to be the other way around.

He framed her face with his hands—hands that were so big in comparison to her. He was twice her size, twice her weight easily, and yet in her small hands he was lost, completely lost. And he wanted to be. Somewhere in between running from the cartel and fighting Whitney, delivering their baby and lying next to her soft body in the middle of the night, he'd given himself, heart and soul, to her.

"I'm in love with you, Rose," he said, looking into those beautiful, dark eyes. He felt as if he was tumbling into a dark, warm, bottomless well.

The laughter faded from her eyes, and she blinked as if her eyes were burning. "You don't have to say that to me, Kane."

"I don't say what I don't mean, Rose."

She took a deep breath and blinked. This time he could see tears glistening on the tips of her lashes.

"Sweetheart." He bent to kiss the tears from her eyes. "That's a good thing, not a bad thing. We've committed our lives to one another. Loving you is good."

"Is it real?" Her voice shook. A whisper of sound. Maybe a plea. Or denial.

"Are you asking me if it's something you can count on? Because if that's what you're worried about, Rose, the way I feel about you isn't going to go away. I'm in love with you. I've never thought it, let alone said it, to another woman. Pairing is about physical lust, not love. Whitney can't manipulate emotion, only our bodies. What I feel for you is real, Rose. It's about you and the person you are."

She searched his face, a long, slow study. He stood very still, letting her see the truth in his eyes. She shook him to his very core. Her strength and courage. Her determination. She'd come to him, committed to him, to a life with him to protect their child. She'd asked Whitney to pair her with him, knowing there was the possibility that they wouldn't find one another—and that she'd never be physically satisfied with anyone else, but she'd done it because she took responsibility for her choice.

How could a man like him, one devoted to duty and honor, not respect and admire her? Everything about her personality appealed to the man in him.

"You might have to say it several times a day for me to believe it," she warned. "I've never been good with fairy tales."

A slow grin teased his mouth. He could feel the warmth spreading through his body—her sun—slowly heating his blood. "So I'm the prince. I always wanted to be a prince."

Rose continued to look into his eyes. Her slender arms circled his neck, and she brought his head down to hers. He watched her eyes go dark and dreamy as his mouth took hers.

Sebastian kicked him hard, squirming as their bodies came together. They broke apart, laughing.

"Sorry about that, son," Kane said, taking him gently from the front pack to cradle him in his arms. "I can't resist your mother. You have to admit she's pretty darn sexy."

Rose rolled her eyes, blushing. "Don't tell him that. You don't know what he understands yet. I'm still reading all those baby books. I have to tell you, Kane, there are so many contradictions with all these so-called experts."

"Well, do we want to start off by lying to him? You are darned sexy. And what's wrong with him knowing his daddy finds his mommy very attractive?"

"I don't know. I don't know the first thing about raising a child." Rose shoved her hand through her hair in agitation. "I'll probably mess up his little psyche."

"By the time we have our fifth or sixth you'll be a pro," Kane teased. He nuzzled Sebastian's head. "Do you hear that, son? You're our experiment, so you'll have all sorts of excuses to do very naughty things."

Rose threw back her head and laughed, the sound music that seemed to penetrate through the fog and float right over the city.

"Listen, Sebastian," he whispered. "That beautiful sound belongs to us for the rest of our lives. That's your mother.

She's sunshine. No matter what happens in our lives, we have that."

Rose swallowed convulsively and tucked her hand into the crook of his elbow. "Enough lessons for the day. I know you're getting stronger, Kane, but we don't want to overdo it. Let's go back inside."

He could barely look into her eyes. She might not think she knew what love was, but he could see it shining in her gaze. There was happiness—and he'd managed—somehow—to put it there inside her.

They made their way down to the door on the roof, leading to the stairwell. They'd been climbing the three stories every day to the roof for the last week to help strengthen Kane and to allow Rose to get acquainted with the neighborhood and give her as much information as possible about urban warfare. She soaked up information at a rapid rate, and when they went to the soundproof firing range on the second floor, she always put her bullets exactly where she was aiming. Kane had no doubt she'd be an asset to their team.

In a way, it would be added protection from Whitney. If Rose was serving on the GhostWalker Team Three, the man, as fanatical as he was about his country, would feel as if she was utilizing her training and might be more inclined to leave her alone.

"Do you want me to take the baby?" Rose asked as they passed the third floor where Jaimie and Mack lived.

He glanced down at her upturned, anxious face and gave her a ferocious scowl. Any other member of his team would have backed off instantly. She just kept giving him that worried look women seemed to wear around men when they were about to fuss. "I am perfectly fine. Our son doesn't weigh much, and I'm not sick, Rose."

Rose studied his furious face. She didn't point out that he was breathing a little hard and small beads of sweat coated his brow. He was overdoing it, pushing himself to get back in shape. Kane wasn't the type of man to want a lot of sympathy. He had already begun working out again, and just this morning she'd woken up and he was already leaving the bed to go run.

"You're not perfectly fine. You're stubborn beyond all hope," she corrected.

He winked at her and continued down the next flight of stairs. Her stomach fluttered, and she pressed her hand tight over it. From the moment she'd laid eyes on him, she'd been attracted, and watching him with others, the unusual respect, the competent way he carried himself, she'd become interested, but that was nothing compared to what she felt now that she'd spent time with him.

She glanced at him, at the way he held their son, and along with the silly fluttering in her stomach, her heart sort of melted and left her feeling foolish. She didn't know what normal was, so she had nothing to compare her strange emotions to. Of course, growing up, all of the women in the compound had discussed the men they'd encountered, but there was always such a separation between them: guards who kept them prisoners and the instructors who trained them.

She dropped back a couple more steps. She'd never felt as if she needed rescuing. She hadn't considered herself the princess in the tower, not once, not *ever.* There was something in Kane, a tough, cynical man, a soldier who carried death in his eyes, yet he could handle a baby as gently as she could. He made her feel fragile and beautiful and so feminine. She wanted to be the princess he carried off.

They passed the second floor, the one housing computers on one side and the training center on the other. There was such freedom in just walking down the steps without seeking permission first. Maybe that was the reason she had to go out shopping. The money Lily Whitney-Miller had set aside in her name was an enormous amount and growing all the time. Jaimie had put through all the necessary paperwork, and for the first time, she had the ability to walk into a store and purchase something. She didn't have to sneak in and steal. She didn't have to hide, and most of all, she didn't need permission.

She glanced surreptitiously at Kane from under her lashes. She wasn't testing him, exactly, but then again, maybe that was *exactly* what she was doing. She didn't want to live with guards, even if the cage was gilded. Kane was so good to her, and she was beginning to believe, one tiny moment at a time, that the life she was living was real—not one of Whitney's ruthless games. A part of her, as guilty and ashamed as it made her feel, had to push to see the truth.

She'd seen Kane's face when she told him she was going shopping. He'd never really answered her about the shopping. She'd allowed the subject to drop, choosing instead to tease him a little because she'd been afraid of the answer, afraid that everything she was living was just an illusion. Whitney was adept at creating illusion.

They'd made it to the first floor, and Kane held the heavy door for her, stepping back to allow her to enter first. A courtesy. So Kane. He was always courteous. Always the gentleman with her. She looked around the huge warehouse. They had begun to make it a home. To her it was an incredible gift, a garden paradise. Was there really an underlying evil? Had Whitney manufactured this as well?

She blinked rapidly, aware of the sudden burning in her eyes, and walked to the window, staring out into the street. Most of the windows had slowly been refitted. Tinted and bulletproof, they didn't have bars on them. She was happy, truly happy, and yet she couldn't stop being afraid that none of it was real. Whitney had deceived them all so many times, she didn't dare believe.

"What is it, Rose?" Kane asked.

She should have known he would notice her sudden withdrawal. He noticed the smallest details about everything.

"Sometimes I feel like I'm holding my breath." She waited, willing him to understand, terrified that he would and he'd be angry with her for not believing.

Kane was silent. She felt him behind her. Just standing there, not saying or doing anything. Had she hurt him?
Probably. How could she not when she was still afraid
Whitney had found another way to torment her? It would
be the ultimate betrayal, and Whitney was capable of such
an elaborate setup.

She turned and looked up at him. Tall, broad-shouldered,
strong jaw, thick chest, yet he cradled their son so gently,
and his eyes were looking at him with compassion.

"If you hold your breath too long, sweetheart, you're
bound to turn blue. Go with Jaimie. None of us has ever just
let Jaimie go anywhere without a few of the boys shadowing
her . . ." He shook his head before she could protest. "We go
out in pairs or with a shadow. We all have enemies, and none
of us has a clue what Whitney might do next. Aside from
that, there's a faction that wants every GhostWalker dead.
They have powerful friends. If you have to prove to yourself
that you're not a prisoner, then we'll handle it."

"You'd let me just walk out of here by myself?" Her
eyes met his. She'd know if he was lying to her.

"No. Taking a chance with your life is beyond my ability to give you what you want. I'd shadow you. Rose, none
of us are completely free in this life. We're dangerous to
others and our own government; while they utilize our ser-
vices, they keep close tabs on us. They fear us. Our only
chance is to live as if we're in enemy territory and we have
to watch each other's backs. It's that or live on the run."

She searched his face for reassurance. She wanted this
life—wanted him. She wanted to believe the fairy tale.
When he called her beautiful, she wanted to believe he
meant it. When he said he loved her, he'd stolen her heart
and soul. She had always faced her life with courage. She
was a soldier, and a soldier endured, but this was different.
This involved emotions. Soldiers weren't supposed to have
emotions, and now she couldn't separate what she felt.

Kane had the power to destroy her. She'd given him
that. She hadn't expected her emotions to be so strong, so

overwhelming. Every single day she was drawn more into his world, into his life—into loving him.

"Tell me what you need, Rose."

Kane just stood there in front of her. Stripped. Vulnerable. Allowing her to see him that way. Showing courage she lacked. Her heart contracted. She moistened her suddenly dry lips with the tip of her tongue. How had she fallen so far, so fast? From the time she'd been a child, it had been drilled into her to know her enemy, to seek knowledge, to have a plan. She'd had a plan until she first saw Kane—in Whitney's camp.

"Tell me what you need," Kane repeated.

She watched his hands, stroking the baby's head. So gentle. She knew the feel of his hands on her skin, the way he touched her so possessively but with extraordinary tenderness. Could a man fake that kind of thing? He reached out and ran his thumb down the side of her face, just a wisp of movement, but she felt it all the way to her toes. It was only then that she realized she was holding her breath for real, and she let it out, forcing air in and out of her lungs.

"I don't need rescuing."

His smile twisted her heart into knots. "Don't ruin my fantasy, honey. I'm the knight in shining armor and you're my beautiful princess. I'm not a man of words. I'm just not. I want to say them to you, but I guess I just feel like an idiot trying to be all poetic." His smile was crooked, almost wistful. "I want to be the man who saves you when you're drowning, Rose, when life overwhelms you. And I want you to be the woman who does the same for me. I can't make you believe me. I can only tell you that I'm standing in front of you, very much in love. It's up to you whether you want to let Whitney take our lives from us."

"He's so cruel, Kane. So cruel. You have no idea what he's capable of."

"I was there. I saw what he was doing. I risked my career, my life, to expose him to the Senate. I can't make you believe in me, Rose. I can only tell you that you're free. If you want to walk out that door, I won't stop you, but if you choose to stay with me, then that gives me every right to protect you in any way that I deem appropriate."

She raised her chin. "Do I have those same rights?"

He cupped her face in his palm, his thumb sliding gently back and forth over her lips. His other palm cradled Sebastian to his chest. "Of course you do. You can't be less than who you are any more than I could be."

She found herself leaning into his hand, her knees a little weak. "He's such a monster, always looming over us, playing us like puppets."

"I wish you could have a normal life, Rose. I want you to be able to walk with confidence down to the grocery store or go shopping with Jaimie or even take our son to a park, but we're different. We're always going to be different. We have enemies, and we can't pretend them away. This, what we create here together, has to be enough."

She had always known, from the time she escaped Whitney's compound, that she would be hunted. It made sense that Kane didn't want her to go off alone without protection, that they always went in pairs or with shadows. If it made so much sense, then why was she panicking? And she was in full-blown panic. Even her usually calm mind felt chaotic. What was wrong with her? She had everything in the world standing in front of her that she could possibly want. He'd even told her that he loved her . . .

She gasped, realizing what was wrong. She didn't believe she could be worth what she saw in Kane's eyes. She'd been taught she wasn't worth anything as a woman or as a human being. She was a soldier, service to her country, easily sacrificed. And she was good for breeding, to provide the next generation soldier who would be so much better than she was.

Her face flamed. Did she really have such low self-esteem that she couldn't believe a man might actually love her? She knew from the start that Kane was physically attracted to her—Whitney had paired them. She knew they would have a great sex life, and she'd believed that he would stay with her for that reason. She'd fallen hard for him, something very unexpected and terrifying. But she hadn't believed it was possible for him to feel the same emotions.

"Baby," his voice was gentle, compelling. "You have to talk to me. If we stop talking, we're through."

"I just realized that I've allowed Whitney to undermine my confidence in myself as a woman—as a lovable woman. When it was physical attraction between us, I was comfortable with that, because it was all part of Whitney's experiment, part of his great plan to produce the perfect supersoldier. But I fell in love with you, and that made me so vulnerable to one of his games. He knew it. He had to have known it. After you left my room, I begged him to pair us together, and I could see how pleased he was. I knew I'd given him another weapon to use against me, but I didn't care. I didn't want you suffering without me suffering. At the time I felt I was being fair and taking responsibility." Her eyes met his. "He knew it before me."

"Knew what?"

"That I'd already fallen in love with you."

"Rose." His voice sent a million birds to flight in her stomach. "Fuck Whitney and what he thinks he knows. You trusted me to make a baby with you. You trusted me to deliver our child and to get you both out of trouble. You can trust me with your heart. God knows, I gave you mine completely. You walk away, and you take it with you."

She stared up at his beloved face, all those tough lines etched deep, those beautiful green eyes that could pierce like an arrow. He could shatter her so easily, it was true, but if she was going to shatter, better it be with him. In the end, he was offering her refuge, love, a home. He was all she needed if she had the courage to accept that he could love her.

Kane was giving her everything, openly and honestly. She could see truth in his eyes. Was she really so stupid that she'd believe what Whitney had taught her over Kane? Rose shook her head. "I'm sorry, I lost my mind for a minute."

He bent forward to brush a gentle kiss over her mouth. "You're allowed."

Sebastian protested, squirming, giving a small cry of annoyance at the change in position.

Kane laughed softly. "Don't blame me, son, your mother is the one who is all mixed up. She's beautiful and intelligent, all right, but I'm beginning to think perhaps she has little lapses occasionally while brain cells regenerate."

"You did not just tell our son that," Rose said, desperate to suppress the laughter welling up. The relief at Kane's reaction to her idiocy was overwhelming. She wanted to weep and laugh at the same time. Instead she was practical, taking Sebastian from his arms. "Clearly, the boy needs to eat. I'm going to be having a little talk with him while I feed him too."

Kane swept his arm around her waist and pulled her beneath the protection of his shoulder. She loved it when he did that. She didn't need protection, but it was thrilling all the same.

"Eric is bringing the physical therapist with him again today," he reminded when she would have sunk into a chair right in the living room.

Rose rolled her eyes. "It's natural to breast-feed, Kane."

"Absolutely, and I love you to breast-feed him. The thing is, I must be some kind of a perv, because whenever you feed him, I want you so damn bad I think I'm going to have to throw you up against the wall and take you right there. It takes a lot of discipline and control to behave myself. I sure don't want any other man getting the same reaction."

She felt the blush start somewhere in her toes and steal all the way up her body. She wouldn't mind him slamming her up against the wall and taking her right then. "I wouldn't say no," she informed him in her best siren's voice.

He groaned. "That was just wrong. Now every time you

feed our son, I'm going to have the hard-on from hell and think about your reaction to my throwing you up against the wall. You just can't put images like that in my head."

She sat demurely in the chair across from their bed and settled herself comfortably. "I believe you put the image in my head, Kane. Which, given that the odious doctor and what I am very certain is most likely a clone of him are arriving any minute, wasn't a very nice thing for you to do." Deliberately she took her time unbuttoning her blouse. Ordinarily she would have covered herself a bit with a blanket, but instead, just to tease him, she unclipped her nursing bra, exposing her firm, round breast.

"I'll just have to sit here, fantasizing about taking a long, wild ride on your very enormous hard-on." She stared hungrily at the front of his jeans, her gaze devouring the thick bulge there. Deliberately she moistened her lips with the tip of her tongue and then ran it around her lips in anticipation.

He groaned and adjusted his jeans. "That's just not right. You're torturing me."

"You deserve it for being right about going out with shadows tailing us. I hate not being right. And anytime you best me, just think of this moment." He was standing close enough to her so she gave in to temptation and reached out to stroke the front of his jeans in long caresses.

He didn't move but pushed into her hands, allowing the friction to deepen. "I did do that, didn't I?" He grinned at her. "*Bested* you, babe. I was *right.*"

She rolled her eyes. "Rub it in, soldier." She increased the pressure on the front of his jeans, drawing another groan from him.

The strobe in the bedroom went off at the same time the intercom buzzed at the front door. Kane sagged. "This just sucks."

Rose smiled serenely and cradled Sebastian to her. She'd done a darn good job of turning the tables on him. Playing together was important. Just like trust. There were so many things she had to learn about relationships. The camaraderie between Kane and Mack and Jaimie was the same she'd shared with the women she'd been raised with. They shared trust, an unbreakable bond, along with the other members of the team. She wanted to be part of that. When she walked out onto the street to do her shopping or go to a movie—something she'd always dreamt of doing— she would feel safe knowing they were watching over her.

She rubbed Sebastian's head, noting his hair was grow- ing fast and thick. He seemed stronger than ever. She'd read in the baby book of the progress he was supposed to make from week to week, and he seemed far ahead both physically and mentally of where he should be. He obvi- ously recognized both of his parents and even the team, although he was much more withdrawn around them. He rarely made a sound around the others. Rose had to watch him closely for cues when he might by hungry or need his diaper changed.

He was always eerily silent around strangers. The doctor and physical therapist as well as any deliveryman prompted him to go completely still, and he stared unblink- ingly at them until they left his line of sight. He had easily held up his head far before the book told her he would, and he was pushing himself up by his arms as well as using his hands with coordination.

"Because you're so smart, Sebastian," she whispered. Inside, she was just a little afraid. If Whitney ever got an inkling that Sebastian was weeks ahead of where he should be in his development, she was certain he would send an army after the boy.

She tried to keep her son away from everyone and often cautioned Kane not to brag about him, even to his team members. If Sergeant Major learned about Sebastian, would he say something to his superiors? Would it be put in a report somewhere for Whitney to find? She knew the man had spies everywhere. Money talked, and Whitney had plenty of it. He also was very adept at blackmailing people into getting what he wanted. Or threatening them.

Whitney had a variety of ways to succeed at his plans, and he was ruthless enough to always come out on top.

She brushed kisses on top of Sebastian's head before switching him to the other breast. "You don't have to worry, son," she whispered, rocking him a little. He always seemed to sense her agitation and reacted, snuggling closer as if to comfort her. "You've got not only your daddy and me but Mack and Javier and all the rest of the team. I know some of them are scary, but they'll look after you always."

Saying the words aloud comforted her. Maybe no one was completely free. She wasn't a prisoner unless one counted love caging her in. It was her choice to stay with Kane and the others. "We can have a life here, Sebastian. It won't be perfect. You'll have to learn about self-defense and guns and hand-to-hand combat, but we'll have fun. I promise you that. We'll definitely have fun."

"Hey, sweetheart," Kane stuck his head into the bedroom, keeping the door closed just in case anyone might catch a glimpse of her. "I'm heading up to the training floor. Eric gave the okay, and they're going to work me a little harder."

She laughed. "Does he know you've been training for the last couple of weeks?"

He frowned at her and gave a quick shake of the head.

"I knew you were lying to me when you said he gave the thumbs-up."

"I *never* told you Eric gave me the thumbs-up. When you asked me if it was okay for me to train, I put my thumb up, that's all. I can't help how you interpret gestures."

"I can give you a couple of other gestures you might want to interpret," she threatened, trying not to laugh. He was impossible to keep down.

"We can discuss that when I get back. Or you could call Jaimie and ask her if she wants to go shopping with you."

She could see the effort it took for him to make that concession. He was determined to give her whatever freedom she needed. "I might put off the shopping until tomorrow, and you can arrange for our shadow escort ahead of time. That way, no one has to scramble or interrupt any plans they might have already made." She leered suggestively. "I think a discussion is definitely in order when you get back. I'll have Sebastian asleep by then. I'm going to play with him now. He likes to be on the floor."

"He rolled over the other day."

She didn't have the heart to tell him she'd seen Sebastian doing that particular trick a few times. He was abnormally strong. She planned on mentioning it to Paul the next time she saw him. There was no question that Sebastian had inherited special DNA from both parents.

"He's great, isn't he?" she answered. "Don't overdo, Kane. Really, just do what the physical therapist says is safe."

He blew her a kiss and shut the door behind him. She could hear his laughter fading away as she snapped her bra back into place and buttoned her shirt before lifting Sebastian to her shoulder to rub his back until he burped.

She loved the way he smelled, all clean and fresh with a hint of his father on him. "Do you feel like playing today, son?" She crooned as she spread the thick rug Kane had brought her just for this purpose. He had more baby toys than any one child should ever have because the team was constantly bringing him gifts.

She stretched out on the floor, lying on her stomach next to him. Sebastian immediately pushed himself up as if doing a push-up from the knees up. He held his head up and looked around the room before looking at her, almost for approval.

"That's a boy. Stretch out. Doesn't that feel good? Your arms are getting very strong, Sebastian. Now push with your legs." She turned him over and took his legs, singing softly as she mimicked kicking and walking in the air.

Sebastian laughed and cooed at her. She loved his bright eyes and the instant response. He rarely cried, watching her and Kane with his intelligent eyes. She leaned down to kiss his foot. "You're such a happy baby," she told him.

Sebastian's gaze shifted from her face to look just over her left shoulder. His eyes went wide and staring, and his mouth opened in a silent scream. Rose rolled away from the baby, trying to get her feet under her. A dark shadow loomed over her, caught her by her hair, and threw her forward so that she landed hard a few feet away, sprawling facedown again. The moment she hit the floor, she rolled under the bed and out the other side, leaping to her feet and grabbing for the knife she kept on the nightstand.

A second man appeared in the doorway, scooping up Sebastian, who stiffened and began to wail at the top of his lungs, kicking and squirming, fighting the large hands of his kidnapper.

As Rose rushed around the bed, the first man caught her by her ankle and yanked. As she went down, he slammed into her back with the force of a linebacker, knocking the wind from her body. She felt a sharp sting in the side of her neck, and the man caught her body up and tossed her over his shoulder.

She hit his back with her head, unable to move. The knife dropped from her hand, the tip sinking into the floor. It wobbled back and forth for a long, strange, slow-motion moment, and then everything went black.

CHAPTER 15

"Keep going," John Baily snapped, his face a stern mask.

Kane wiped the sweat from his forehead where it was dripping down to sting his eyes. He glanced at Eric. The doctor leaned against the wall staring into space, paying no attention to the therapist torturing him. Everything hurt. He could barely breathe, and he wasn't altogether certain he could keep going. Was that the point? Were they trying to drive home to him that he was still weak?

He ignored Baily and stalked across the room to snatch up a towel. Gideon leaned against the wall regarding him with worried eyes.

"Tell him to go to hell," he suggested. "He's a sadist."

"I haven't even been working ten minutes," Kane said, slightly ashamed. "He's got me going up the ropes over and over, and my gut just can't take it yet."

"This is a bullshit workout, and you know it," Gideon said. "I think Eric went to sleep, or he'd be all over this guy."

Lights began flashing throughout the workout room.

Gideon turned and ran for the door, Kane following on his heels. The silent alarm had to have been triggered by one of the team; no one else knew about it.

Two Ghosts coming out of Kane's house. They both carry a precious package. Javier's voice filled their minds. Steady. Cool. Lethal.

Gideon broke off and went up the stairs two at a time. He could serve them better from the roof. He would be their eyes and wouldn't miss if he got a shot.

Kane could hear his blood roaring in his ears. He didn't have to be told what those precious packages were. How the hell had they gotten in without triggering the alarm? Mack met him on the stairs and threw him a gun. He knew the other team members would be pouring into the street, onto the roof, and would be ready to go mobile if their prey somehow managed to get through the gauntlet of team members.

Whitney's two men burst out of the warehouse, running for the waiting SUV. It was dark with tinted windows and should have been running. Instead, all four tires were slashed and the engine was off. The man with the baby tore open the passenger door, looked inside to see the driver slumped over the wheel, his throat a mass of blood. Swearing, he slammed the door, and the two men took off running for the docks.

I've got eyes on them, Ethan reported. He was on the roof of the second building, already making his sweep for enemies. *Heading for the docks.* He caught sight of Gideon running across the warehouse roof toward the ocean side. A movement on the roof of the building across the street sent a chill through him. *Gideon, drop! Drop!*

Gideon threw himself flat as a bullet spit into vent housing, missing his head by a scant inch.

Damn it, Gideon. Are you hit? I don't have a shot. I can't take the shot. Lucas? Again it was Ethan. *Fucking fog.*

He hadn't heard the shot, but there was no doubt one of

Whitney's sharpshooters had gained the roof of the apartment building, where they were most vulnerable. It wasn't a long shot by any means and easily a silencer could be used without fear of losing accuracy.

Shoot that bastard, Ethan, Gideon snapped, keeping down. He couldn't help, pinned down as he was.

I've got him, Lucas Atherton announced calmly. The sound of the shot cut through the drifting fog. *He's down.*

The three men on the roof of the buildings scrambled to become the eyes for the team spreading out like wolves hunting on the ground. People walked along the street, moved through the fish market at the far end of the docks, and workers unloaded cargo along the docks. Traffic moved slowly, and the world seemed oblivious to the drama taking place on the street.

Javier, on a skateboard, dropped into position just a few yards from the fleeing men. He looked like any other teenager out for fun, sliding in and out of pedestrians with ease. He had spotted the SUV waiting in front of the warehouse and had taken a closer look before disposing of the driver.

Kane and Mack burst from the warehouse and ran together, weaving in and out of the pedestrians, sprinting fast. A bullet shattered the glass of a small bookstore, sending shards flying into the air and raining down onto the sidewalk and street. Several people screamed and began running.

Take a left, Top, through the alley. You'll get around in front of them. Javier is closer to them, and Brian's flanking them on their left. Gideon was as calm as ever.

Jacob's closing in from the right, Lucas reported.

Get the shooter, Mack snapped.

Already done, Top, Ethan said as he took his shot. The shooter was in an apartment on the third floor, fifth window over. Ethan fired through the window, watching his bullet hit the target. *He's down. Sweeping now.*

Paul and Marc are right behind you, Top, Gideon added. Paul Mangan and Marc Lands were the best medics they had on their team. If Rose or the child were injured, it would be up to them to save them quickly.

They were surrounding the enemy, closing in fast.

Javier, take the one with the baby, and get him out of there.

On it, Top. Javier's voice never changed.

He pushed hard with his foot, increasing the speed of his skateboard. He had let Whitney's men see him when they came running out, dismissing him as a kid hanging out with his friends, trying new tricks. He'd studied them carefully, knew they were skilled and dangerous. The one he targeted held Sebastian in some kind of pack, leaving both arms free to carry his semiautomatic. The trick was not to try to outshoot them but to make certain his enemy never saw death coming.

He knew they could hear the skateboard coming up behind them, but he sounded like any other teenager, and they'd already assessed and dismissed him as a threat. *Rose is unconscious. I can't tell what they've done to her,* he warned Paul.

The baby? Kane sounded dispassionate, completely disengaged and remote, but there was the sound of death in his voice.

He's got lungs, Javier reported, a brief hint of amusement in his voice.

In another few seconds the two men would be on the docks in the midst of a crowd. Smoothly, Javier shoved again, crouching low, surfing over the pitted alley, coming up behind the enemy holding Sebastian. He swept past, his knife flashing, cutting the throat with one hand as he ripped the pack holding the child away with the other.

The man gurgled, both hands flying to his throat. Javier turned sharply as he shot out of the alley into the throng of people, heading for the market where the rows of booths and tables gave him cover. He flashed past Kane and Mack straight toward Paul and Marc. He shoved the bundle into Paul's hands and swerved away from them, making a show

of weaving in and out of the booths to better give Whitney's man a target.

Javier made the handoff before the enemy went down,
a slow-motion fall, first to his knees, clutching his throat,
blood spraying through his hands, and then facedown, his
head hitting the wooden slats of the wharf.

I've got the package, Paul announced as he did an abrupt
about-face and began to hurry back toward the warehouse,
using the thickening fog for cover from sharpshooters on
the rooftops.

I've got you covered, Gideon assured. The other two
members of their team on the surrounding roofs, Ethan and
Lucas, would provide cover for the converging members of
their team on the ground.

Double-time it, Mack commanded. *We don't know how
many more they sent.*

The baby ceased crying the moment he was in Paul's
hands, as if he knew silence was paramount for safety now
that his team was taking him through enemy lines back
home.

The man with Rose slung over his shoulder halted, staring in horror at his companion. Whirling around in a slight
circle, he changed direction, running toward the end of the
dock. The fingers of fog had gathered together, turning
gray and thick. The sound of his boots on the wooden dock
was loud and eerie coming out of the murkiness.

If you have a shot, take it, Mack said. *Jacob, are you
on him?*

*Roger that, Top. He's got company. A fast boat running
hot.*

Keep them away from the dock, Mack ordered.

At once a barrage of fire from the rooftops prevented
the boat from coming in close to the dock. It veered away
and raced back out to sea. Once again, the man with Rose
switched directions, this time running down the dock toward the pier. The boat circled back in the distance, apparently in communication with the man holding Rose.

Kane paid no attention to anything but Rose. He concentrated on the path to her mind. It had always been easy to communicate with her, but perhaps she had been reaching for him as he reached for her. Now he groped blindly, trusting his instincts as he ran. He refused to allow fear to enter. Emotion wouldn't do her any good. He had to keep a clear mind and trust his team. All of them were in on the action. Javier had spotted the SUV and correctly read the situation, alerting the team, and they operated together smoothly, as they had for years.

Come to me, sweetheart. Open your eyes, but don't move. Just open your mind to mine.

He kept the running command up, over and over, pushing deeper into her mind, trying to find her subconscious, trying to reach her. Rose was a force to contend with. The man running with her just didn't know it.

"You've got nowhere to go," Jacob's voice came out of the fog, disembodied, slightly distorted. "You're cut off from your men. Put her down and walk away."

I've got no shot, Lucas said. *I'm firing blind at the boat. Fog's too thick.*

I've got an angle on the boat, but can't see Rose, Ethan reported. He sent two rounds at the zigzagging boat. The two occupants had good cover with the small cabin.

Kane stopped running as he neared the enemy and went "ghost," sliding into the dense fog, barely taking a breath, his feet making no sound on the heavy wooden planks.

Keep his attention centered on you, Mack instructed Jacob. *We're approaching from behind and slightly left and right.*

They didn't want Jacob to shoot them by accident as they split off from each other, moving in complete silence. Kane had sight of the enemy now, standing near the railing overlooking the pounding waves as they broke over the pier pillars. Rose hung limp, either hurt or drugged. Not once had his efforts to rouse her met with a conscious mind. He didn't stop moving or even hesitate, coming out of the fog, the vapor swirling around him as he approached, striding right up to Whitney's man, eyes locked on his prey, his gun up and ready.

He recognized the man as one of the guards he worked with, David something. Their eyes met. David's eyes went wide. He turned and heaved Rose's body over the railing into the rolling ocean. Kane shot him in the back of his neck, picking up speed as he did, running toward the rail. He tossed the gun to Mack, leapt onto the rail, and dove, following Rose into the sea.

The water was ice cold, closing over his head, taking him down into darkness. He refused to feel the cold or the pounding, rolling force of nature. He didn't fight, rather went with it, waiting to surface until the sucking sensation left and he could kick upward. He took a breath and looked around, knowing the next wave would drive him against the pillars if he wasn't careful.

He spotted her body up against one of the whitened columns, the waves battering her delicate form. He swam, using his enormous strength to pull him through the water, using the wave to push him closer to her.

Rose! Rose, baby, wake up for me.

He refused to allow panic into his world. There was only the distance between them, and he was closing it with every long, strong stroke. He got his arm around her and rolled her over. Her body was completely limp, and for a moment he thought she might be dead. He managed to ride out the next wave with his arm firmly under her.

In the water! Bogey in the water. Ethan's voice filled his mind.

A bullet spit just past Kane as a diver in a green and black wet suit emerged from behind the pillar, speargun in hand. Lucas had taken a shot at the diver but missed. The diver shot at Kane, reaching for Rose in an attempt to get her away from Kane. The spear slid fast through the water, but as the wave came crashing in, it veered slightly off course and just missed his leg.

Go, Jacob, Mack directed. Jacob had been enhanced through DNA just for this purpose. He was the best in the water, and Mack sent him to back up Kane.

Jacob Princeton sliced through the water, moving fast, his body built for swimming, his enhancement allowing him to stay under for long periods of time. He dove under Kane, straight at the diver's legs, yanking him down and away from Kane, who retained possession of Rose.

The fog was dense over the water, like a living gray cloud, muffling sound and making it more difficult than ever to see, but Kane heard the sound of the boat returning to aid the diver. A large body burst out of the water, knife in hand, coming at him like some monster of the deep. A second diver had waited his chance. They had to have been waiting to transport Rose or the baby into the boat should the land operation fail. David had been quick to throw Rose over the railing because he'd known they had men waiting to fish her out before she drowned.

Second bogey, Kane informed Mack even as he caught the second diver's wrist as it came down at him from above, the knife pointed straight at his throat.

The diver was in a yellow and black wet suit, and Kane, in his civilian clothes, was subject to the cold water. He had to let go of Rose in order to keep from being stabbed. He caught the diver's wrist with both hands and kicked the man hard in the gut. The wave took Rose and rolled her underwater.

Mack! Rose. It was a measure of Kane's distress that he addressed Mack, his friend, and not Top, the team leader. *I can't get to her.*

Brian's on it.

The complete confidence in Mack's voice steadied Kane as he struggled against his attacker, fending off the knife, kicking strongly with his legs to keep them both up. The diver would have the advantage underwater. He used his strength to bend the blade of the knife back toward the diver's body, leveraging against his arm. He had to trust

Brian Hutton—and Mack—with the love of his life. He
pushed Rose, the boat, and the struggle between Jacob and
the other diver out of his brain and put mind and body into
staying alive.

The diver gave a little, and with the enormous pressure
he was using, the sudden withdrawal of resistance sent him
forward. The diver somersaulted backward, and they both
went underwater, Kane behind him. He latched onto the
diver's back, his arm around his neck, locking down in a
death grip. It was extremely difficult to wrench the neck
underwater with enough force to break it, but he applied
enough pressure fast and hard that the diver began to lose
consciousness. Without the struggling resistance, he was
able to get leverage and snap the neck.

The knife fell from the diver's hand, and Kane dove after
it. As he surfaced into the thick fog, looking for Rose and
Brian, he heard the sound of a boat bearing down on him.

*We don't have all night, Jacob. The boat's closing in on
you, and the boys don't have a decent shot to keep them off
of you,* Mack informed the team member they'd dubbed
"Shark."

Give me a couple of minutes, Top. Jacob cut the air hose,
dragging the first diver under the water. *I'm a little occupied at the moment.*

The wave rolled them, pushing them toward the pillars. The diver struggled, trying to throw Jacob off him,
but Jacob held him. They rolled together, over and over,
scraping along the floor of the ocean, Jacob holding the
diver ruthlessly. No matter how the diver twisted or turned,
Jacob was tenacious, like a pit bull, refusing to let him go.

They struggled, stirring up layers of fine sand and marine sediment on the floor, adding to the murkiness in the
water. The diver began to panic, fighting in earnest now,
trying to pull his knife from where it was strapped to his
leg. Jacob never allowed him to move from his grip of iron.
He took them down to the floor itself, calmly wrapping his
legs around him like an octopus, his thighs strong enough

to hold him. It was simply a matter of who could hold their breath the longest, and Jacob had been physically enhanced to stay underwater for long periods of time.

The diver's struggles took on new urgency and then began to grow weaker. Eventually his body stiffened as he gasped for air, drawing water into his lungs. Jacob waited a minute longer until he was certain the other man had drowned. Above his head he saw a propeller as a boat skimmed across the surface.

Brian Hutton dove deep repeatedly in the spot where Rose had rolled under with the waves. *Where is she, Top? I can't find her.*

To your right, Brian. Three feet. You can reach out and touch her. Get her face out of the water.

Mack sounded a little tense but steady as a rock. If Top said she was there, then it didn't matter that the fog was so thick and the pounding waves drove him against the pillars—she was within reach. He threw both arms out blindly and then searched just beneath the ever-changing surface, ignoring the sound of the boat approaching. He was vulnerable, aware at any moment a shot could take him. He hoped that if he couldn't see the occupants of the boat, they couldn't see him.

His fingers brushed an arm, and he gripped it, dragging Rose to him, rolling her over to make certain she was still alive. She coughed, and spit water, but she didn't open her eyes, tossing her head from side to side and fighting him weakly.

"I've got you, Rose," he reassured her. She seemed drugged, unable to fight her way out of the drug's hold on her.

He leaned over her to try to make eye contact, and a bullet coming from an unknown direction hit him hard, high up along his shoulder. At first he didn't feel anything but the sharp sting, and then a burning numbness spread through his arm and chest until he could barely breathe, as if ice encased his upper body, freezing it.

Coming at you. On your right.

Mack and Marc had rigged a pulley and harness on the pier. They tossed the rope as close to him as they could. Brian fought the strength of the crashing waves as the power of the ocean tried to tear Rose from his arms. His boots were weighing him down, adding to the difficulty. In the cold water his body began shivering, a bad sign, but worse if it stopped. He couldn't afford to go numb, not before he got her out of the water. He tried not to think about Kane or Jacob and how long they'd been in the water. He couldn't figure out why his left arm refused to obey his commands.

The harness was just feet from him, but seemed a mile. He timed the next wave, kicked strongly, and managed to snag it with his fingertips, draw it to him, and secure it around Rose. Twice water washed over both of them, and he came up choking and coughing. His lungs felt ice-cold, and his movements were slowing. He had no idea of time passing or how long he'd been in the water with the powerful waves battering him.

Rose looked almost blue, but she was breathing, although her heart felt slow to him. Maybe it was just his own heart slowing down. The water was pounding both of them, and it was impossible to see in the fog. The gray vapor wrapped around them, enfolding them in wet mist.

Brian! Stay with Rose, Mack commanded. *She is your responsibility, and you cannot fail in your mission. Hold on to that rope and keep her face out of the water.*

Brian shook his head to clear the cobwebs from his brain. He couldn't quite remember how to hold on to the rope. His fingers weren't cooperating with his brain.

Jaimie, Mack knew his wife was tuned to the telepathic path used for missions. She would be anxious for any news. *Tell Eric to set up for surgery. He'll need to be ready fast. Have Javier bring up a vehicle now.*

Roger that. Her voice shook, but she didn't break protocol.

Brian! Mack put every ounce of command a master gunnery sergeant possessed after years of leading an elite unit of soldiers. *Fucking hold on to that rope, soldier.*

Brian's mind felt sluggish. He heard Mack's command, and he always obeyed Mack out in the field, especially when Mack swore, which was on very rare occasions. Top meant business, and there was no disregarding an order, no matter how difficult. He took hold of the rope, steadying Rose as the next wave took them under. He felt the tug on his arms as Mack and Marc began to pull them steadily through the water toward the pier.

His left arm flopped into the water. He tightened his fingers on the rope, unable to do more than keep Rose's head from going under, but he didn't let go, refused, even though he barely knew what was going on, to let Top down. She moved now, obviously semiconscious, knowing something was terribly wrong but unable to focus.

Don't fight, Brian soothed. *Mack's got us. He'll get us out of this. Just relax and let him pull us up.*

There was a feeble, weak stirring. *Kane?*

Kane heard Rose's voice. She sounded weak and very vulnerable. Most of all, she sounded far away, as if she was calling to him from a great distance.

We've got her, Kane. Mack's voice was as steady as ever. He would never lie—Rose had to be all right.

Kane waited until the boat slipped into place at the north end of the pier, just feet away from where the divers had emerged, before surfacing. He realized that the enemy had prepared at least three different exits. Whitney wanted Sebastian and Rose and had gone to great lengths to acquire them.

He emerged beside the boat in complete silence. The engine idled while they waited, peering through the fog to try to find their divers and Rose. The dense fog was perfect for hiding them from the shooters on the roof but made it nearly impossible for them to see what was happening in the water.

Kane could hear two men whispering, the words somewhat muffled by the sound of the water beating against the
pillars.

"Do you see anything, Randy?"

Kane listened carefully, mapping the exact location of
the speaker in the boat. He adjusted his own position so
that he was lined up with the man.

"They were just here," Randy responded, almost hissing.

From his voice, Kane knew Randy was toward the back
of the boat and in a sitting position. He took a breath and
went into motion, catching the side of the boat with both
hands and powering his body into a back somersault, knees
to chest until he cleared the side of the boat. As the enemy
stood and staggered toward him, Kane exploded his legs
straight out, catching his opponent in his gut. Kane was a
big man, very muscular, and his strength was enormous.
Adrenaline running added to the impact. His enemy went
tumbling over the side of the boat, falling backward into
the water.

Kane landed hard and rolled toward Randy. The boat
rocked crazily, tilting sharply, throwing Randy off balance
as he fired his automatic, drilling holes in the side of the
boat. Kane hit him hard under the chin as he drove upward, putting his considerable weight behind the blow, and
then spinning around to deliver an elbow to the jaw. Randy
clung grimly to the weapon, his finger glued to the trigger.

The sound of the gun spitting bullets was deafening inside the blanket of fog. Kane trapped Randy's wrist, stepping in close to keep the man from turning the weapon
toward him. He slammed the wrist back over Randy's
shoulder, forcing his body backward and his feet out from
under him. Randy went down, and as he did, Kane ripped
the gun from him, turning the weapon back toward his
enemy. The bullets created a bloodred zipper up the man's
chest and into his throat.

The fight had taken seconds, but exhaustion was hitting along with the shivering that signaled his body was

too cold. They had to finish this soon. He peered down into the water, looking for the man he'd knocked overboard. He could just make out the outline of two men struggling just beneath the surface. He recognized Jacob and put the gun down, looking around him for anything that might give him clues to where the men had been directed to take Rose and Sebastian.

Jacob surfaced beside the boat, dragging the body of the man he'd drowned with him. Kane reached down and helped pull the dead man into the boat. Jacob swam to the pier where the diver in the red and black suit was stuck against a pillar. It took a bit longer to get the body into the boat.

"You okay?" Kane asked. Jacob was shivering nearly uncontrollably, and the force of the waves had battered him so that his movements were sluggish.

"Good enough to get the job done. I'll run them out to sea and get rid of them. Javier has a body or two to add to our collection."

Top, we're cleaning up. Is Rose okay? Sebastian?

Paul says Sebastian is as happy as a lark. He thought the entire thing was a great adventure. Rose is still out of it. We're taking her to Paul, hoping he can counteract whatever they gave her.

They drugged her then. Kane and Jacob pulled the last diver into the boat and sank back, shivering from the cold water, arms and legs growing heavier by the moment.

Yes. Mack's voice was grim. *Bring the boat around to the southern pier. Hurry, the wind's picking up, and we've got to dump the bodies before the fog lifts. Javier will take them out. The two of you come in.*

Top, Jacob protested, *I've got this.*

That's an order; come in. Mack's voice was implacable. *Brian took a hit. We're prepping him for surgery.*

Kane and Jacob exchanged a long look and redoubled their efforts at speed.

What the hell happened today, Top? Kane asked as they

slipped across the water toward the southern end of the pier. *Does Jaimie know?*

She's reviewing the security tapes now. We'll go over everything that went right and everything that went wrong when you come in.

And Brian? How bad?

We don't know yet. Eric and Marc are going to do the surgery. Paul's staying with Sebastian.

Of course they would keep Paul away from Eric. Eric wasn't a GhostWalker, nor was he part of their team, and no one, *no one* outside of their team could ever have a clue about Paul's capabilities—and now Rose's. Both had talents that Whitney would want to spread throughout his soldiers, and to do that, he'd try to understand how the talent worked. He had no qualms about taking apart a person for "the greater good of mankind."

Jacob threw the rope to Javier, who tied them off so they could step from the boat. He handed them both a warm blanket, greeting them with a cocky grin, although Kane could see the worry in his eyes. "You two look like hell."

"Popsicles," Jacob said. "Damn cold water."

"That's why you don't see me in it." Javier shoved the body of the man who had taken Sebastian onto the deck and watched it roll over, his expression impassive.

"Thanks for the warning, Javier," Kane said. "I owe you one."

Javier shrugged. "My nephew, my sister. Fuck the bastards. Lucas and I will take care of this mess."

Lucas emerged from the fog with the body of the driver rolled in a tarp. "Walked him right through the market crowd; no one asked a single question." He tossed the body on top of the one Javier had rolled onto the deck. "Looks like a damn garbage dump."

"Whitney needs to realize if he's going to come at us, he'd better send men who can handle the heat," Jacob said as he wrapped a blanket around his shivering form.

Kane frowned as Javier rolled the last body into the boat. "What about the men on the rooftops?"

"Gideon and Ethan are disposing of them. We can't risk dragging more dead bodies through the streets. Someone had to have reported shots fired. And there's blood in the SUV sitting right in front of the warehouse. No body, but plenty of blood," Javier answered.

Javier stepped aboard the boat. Kane and Jacob watched as he disappeared into the fog. Lucas lifted a hand and headed for the slip where their boat was. He would follow Javier and bring him back after they sank the boat and bodies.

Kane and Jacob entered the first story of the warehouse from the bay side. The door was layers of steel. Kane punched in the code, and they entered the first secure room where full body scanners sent information to Jaimie's monitors on the second floor. The door had a retinal scanner, and Kane leaned in.

Jacob laughed. "Our little sister loves these gadgets."

Kane flashed him a grin. "By the time you start working on your building, she'll have security so tight, none of us will be able to get inside any of our homes."

The three-story warehouse was nearly thirteen thousand feet of space and had been sold to Jaimie without any interior walls. They stepped inside the first-story space Kane had converted into his home. It was a good four thousand square feet with a high ceiling and wide-open spaces.

"Take a shower, Jacob," Kane suggested. "I need to check on Rose and the baby."

Jacob didn't object. The shivering made his teeth chatter. Kane pointed him in the right direction and rushed on through to the bedroom, kicking off wet shoes and pulling off soaked socks. He stripped off his shirt and left it in a sodden heap on the floor.

Where the hell is my woman?

Rose was nowhere to be found, and neither was Sebastian. For a moment his heart hammered a protest before he realized Mack and the others would never leave her. Eric had set up surgery on the second floor, and the team would be guarding all the fallen team members. He took the stairs two at a time, rushing up, needing to see with his own eyes that his family was alive and well.

He felt the hushed tension the moment he opened the door. Jaimie sat at her desk, viewing the security tapes over and over. Mack stood behind her, watching with her and occasionally leaning down to whisper in her ear. They'd freeze a frame and study it. Neither Rose nor the baby was on the second floor. He skirted around the makeshift surgery, nothing more than a sterile tent erected to the left of Jaimie's work space. He noted Marc was frantically working on Brian and there was no sign of Eric.

Mack looked up as he approached, fingers still curled around the nape of Jaimie's neck. His eyes were troubled as his gaze swept over Kane, taking in his wet body and dripping jeans.

"You smell like fish," he greeted. "Paul's with Sebastian and Rose. He said Rose is coming out of it slowly. He's helping to push the drug through her system faster."

"What the hell happened?" Kane demanded.

Jaimie swung around in her chair. "I'm looking at all the surveillance tapes both outside and inside. We've got cameras installed on most of the buildings along this street. The SUV was down the block for thirteen minutes. Javier spotted it while he was outside practicing his moves with his boys. He patrols the streets and gets the locals used to him hanging out. He spotted the SUV moving into position just outside your main front door and sent out the alarm."

"We were lucky he was out there," Mack said. "We're going to have to set up regular patrols. We're getting too complacent, using just one spotter on the roof. It's too busy an area to just have only one pair of eyes."

"How did they get into my house?" Kane asked.

"You do know you're leaving a puddle of water in the middle of my office," Jaimie pointed out.

Kane scowled at her. "Cough it up, Jaimie. They tried to take my son and Rose."

"Definitely the physical therapist. He slipped something into the locking mechanism when you opened the door for them. I can't quite figure out what it was, but it's thin and fit right over the lock, so the door appeared to engage, but in reality, the lock wasn't fully engaged."·

"Why didn't the alarm sound? Shouldn't it have?" Kane rubbed at his wet hair with the edge of the blanket.

"Yes." Jaimie sounded affronted. "Whatever they used simulated the lock enough that the monitor accepted it as real. I've never seen anything like it. The way it should work is, if anything, even a thin piece of paper is slipped in, the electronics don't engage and the alarm goes off. They have some tool that fools the electronics into believing the circuit has been engaged."

"So they planned this carefully. They knew about the lock and how it worked," Kane stated the obvious. "They were prepared."

"How?" Mack asked. "We don't have that many visitors. A few construction workers, but we checked them out thoroughly. Deliverymen." He looked at Jaimie. "Who else?"

"We've had the cops here a few times," she said. "Something about the surveillance tape really bothers me, but I can't put my finger on it." She swung back to study the footage. "Go up to our home, Kane, and take a warm shower. Mack's jeans will be short, but you can fit into them. In fact, I think there are a couple of pairs of your jeans left from when you were staying with us while your house was being built. Look in the clothes closet. This is going to take a while to figure out."

Marc stuck his head out of the tent, bloody glove-covered hands in the air. "Where the hell is Eric? He went to get another set of instruments. I need help in here. I can't monitor him and do the operation."

He disappeared back inside the tent.

Get down here, now, Paul. Mack sent the command

instantly. "Get upstairs, Kane. Guard Rose and Sebastian. Don't trust anyone." He glanced at his watch. "Eric ran out of here a few minutes ago to get another surgery kit from his car. I thought it odd that he didn't ask one of us to get it for him but just figured he could find it faster."

Kane turned and ran up the stairs as Paul came running down.

"That's what's bothering me," Jaimie said. "Look, Mack. Look at the tape. Eric goes through the door first, and the therapist follows him. Look at what Eric does." She froze the tape. "Look at his eyes. He stops right there, and his gaze shifts down and toward the lock just as the therapist slips in his tool. Eric knew. Eric has to be working with Whitney."

CHAPTER 16

"Son of a bitch." Mack leaned down to study the tape. The entire time, they'd been watching the lock and the therapist, not really paying attention to the surgeon who had worked at one time or another on many of the GhostWalkers, even saving lives. How Jaimie had noticed the slight turn Eric made and the shift of his eyes as he glanced down at the lock, he couldn't imagine. Especially in the midst of Brian having surgery just a few yards away.

"He knows, Mack," Jaimie reiterated and pulled up the footage inside the second floor and then of the street.

They could see Eric rush out of the surgical tent, call out to Mack, and then run behind the tent out of their sight. He put a foot on the stairs leading up to where Paul watched over Rose and Sebastian, shook his head, and turned quickly to take the stairs leading down to the first story. Clearly he had considered making another try for the baby. He dashed down the stairs and out the door, never entering Kane's home. The street cameras showed him leaping into his car, cell phone out, and talking fast as he sped away.

"Get the word out to the other teams," Mack ordered Jaimie. "There's no telling what damage he's done to us. Everyone he's come in contact with may be compromised. Advise sweeping for bugs and reworking security wherever he's had access. Let Jack and Ken know their home probably has multiple problems. Has he had access to our computer equipment?"

Jaimie shook her head. "No one touches my computers other than Javier. And he's worse than I am about security. Well . . . okay . . . maybe not."

Mack swore under his breath as he paced back and forth. "We've had a snake among us from the very first."

"What if he didn't work for Whitney? What if he's working for the faction that wants all of us dead?"

"I doubt he would have saved so many of us. The death toll would have been much higher. I'm certain he's Whitney's plant." He looked carefully around the room. "Check everything, Jaimie. Thank God Rose was so paranoid about Sebastian. She never left Eric alone with him. They didn't manage to get a sample of his blood. They weren't able to microchip him either."

"Kane did," Jaimie said. "He said it was the only argument he and Rose have had over the baby. He insisted, for Sebastian's safety."

"Top!" Paul called out. "We need you."

Mack reacted instantly. "Tell Kane, Jaimie. The two of you need to go through that house and be thorough about it."

Jaimie watched him disappear into the surgical tent and then made her way up to the third story. As she leaned in for a retinal scan, she stopped suddenly, frowning. She made her way back down to the bottom of the staircase where Eric had hesitated. She pulled out a small penlight and meticulously began going over the railing and walls, paying particular attention to where Eric had stopped.

The staircase was interior, running just on the inside of the building so that there was an escape from the first story and one leading to the roof. The second story was completely enclosed with only a door leading to a fire escape. She ran her fingers along the door. Eric must have known they would be suspicious of him, and he'd run. He wouldn't have considered going upstairs to confront a GhostWalker. He wasn't armed. She knew that because each time he stepped inside the entrance, she had a full-body scanner making certain. No, he'd stopped on the stairs for another reason.

She stepped back and studied the door and then turned around in a circle, inspecting the stairway again. She knew she was right; she just couldn't figure out what he'd done. Reluctantly, Jaimie gave up her quest and went up to the top story. She used a retinal scan to open the door to her home.

Rose lay on her couch, a blanket over her, holding her head and moaning softly. Kane obviously had rinsed off and was now crouching beside Rose, sweeping back her hair with one hand, murmuring soft reassurances to her. Jaimie looked around for the baby.

Kane saw her question and nodded toward the safety of the bedroom. "Paul put him down when he fell asleep. I'm hoping he stays that way until we know Rose can safely feed him. We don't want whatever drug this is to get into his system."

Kane straightened slowly, stretching out sore muscles. He'd managed to find a pair of jeans and had ripped off one of Mack's tees. "I take it they're having a problem with Brian?" He managed to keep his voice even, but every muscle had tightened up all over again. He'd just managed to reassure himself that Rose and Sebastian were going to be fine, and now he was worried all over again.

Brian Hutton had grown up with him. Mack and Kane had protected the younger boy all through school. His parents had moved and left him behind. He'd stayed in a condemned building, foraging on the streets for food and running from bigger bullies until Mack and Kane had come across him. He'd been a wide-eyed kid with a mop of hair and a quick, inventive mind. He also had very quick hands. He was a first-class pickpocket. It had taken a lot to convince him to stay in school and get an education, but he wanted Mack's and Kane's protection, so he'd gone along with their rules. They'd made up a lot of paperwork for him to keep him out of the system and make the schools think he had parents.

"Marc and Paul will pull him through," Jaimie said. "They're good."

"What the hell happened to Eric?"

"He's a plant, Kane. He's working for Whitney. He knew the physical therapist was going to make a grab for Sebastian and Rose. I think he got nervous when I kept looking at the surveillance tapes, and he ran," Jaimie explained.

"That means everything he came into contact with has been compromised," Kane said.

"Exactly. Mack wants a sweep of the entire building. I think he planted something at the bottom of the stairs on the second floor. He was running, but he stopped there. At first I thought he might be trying to come up here and changed his mind, but that didn't make sense. I couldn't find anything."

Kane studied her face. Jaimie knew things. All of them, the entire team, had learned never to ignore Jaimie's gut feelings.

Rose moaned and struggled to sit up. Kane held her down with a hand to her shoulder. "Paul said not to move around yet, Rose. He said once you could sit up, then he wants you drinking water. Lots of water, but he said you'd be unsteady for a while."

"I've got to get this out of my system. I feel horrible."

"I know, honey, you're going to be disoriented for a while."

She frowned at him, clutching the blanket around her. "Kane, I don't have any clothes on. None." She looked very puzzled, her gaze jumping from him to Jaimie.

"I had to undress you," Jaimie explained gently. "You were soaked and freezing. We wrapped you in a blanket and put hot water bottles around you to bring up your body temperature."

Rose snapped her head around and sat up, dragging the blanket with her. "Sebastian? Where's Sebastian?"

Kane's gut tightened. He'd told her three times. She seemed to forget things over and over. He framed her face and looked into her eyes. "Sweetheart, I wouldn't be standing here chatting if someone took our son. He's sleeping peacefully in the bedroom. I'd bring him out to show you, but I don't want him to wake up and need to eat. The drug they gave you isn't out of your system yet."

She frowned and touched her neck. "I couldn't stop them from taking Sebastian."

"Javier spotted them, and the team went into action. We'll be having a meeting soon to discuss what went wrong and what went right so we can improve response time and damage control."

Jaimie sat on the arm of the couch. "No civilians got hurt and, aside from keeping Whitney's men from taking you and Sebastian, that's always the main thing in urban situations."

Kane brushed his mouth across Rose's lips. "We're going to be all right, honey. The team came through. We had one casualty. Brian's in surgery now, but both Paul and Marc are with him, and you know how bossy Mack is. He won't let Brian slip away on us."

"I want to take a shower." Rose shuddered as she rubbed her arms up and down. "I'm itching all over."

"I can put a chair in the shower," Jaimie offered. "You shouldn't try to stand by yourself, Rose."

"I'll go in with her," Kane said.

Fear exploded through Rose's body. For a moment she could barely breathe. "No!" Rose caught Kane's wrist and held on hard. "You stay with Sebastian." She would never forget those minutes, fighting off the kidnappers, knowing

she wasn't going to stop them from taking her son. She'd
failed to protect him. All of her training, all of her resolve,
none of it mattered. She touched her neck again. "I'm
sorry, Kane. I'm so sorry."

She'd been so certain she could do it all herself. She
hadn't trusted anyone else, other than Kane, not really. She
knew Whitney better than any of them; she'd known he'd
make a try for Sebastian. Sebastian was everything he'd
worked for—all the years of experimenting came down to
a child. She knew if Whitney saw him or even got hold of a
sample of his blood, he would know he'd been successful.

She covered her face with her hands, her lungs burning.
She'd almost lost their child. She couldn't ever face Kane
again. Everything was coming flooding back. Sebastian's
eyes widening as he lay on the floor playing with her. He'd
known that she couldn't protect him. She would never forget that moment when both of them had known she wasn't
going to be able to stop the men from taking him. A sob
escaped, and she clamped down hard on it. She wouldn't
cry. Wouldn't make Kane think she wanted sympathy.

"Rose." Kane's gentle voice was her undoing.

He should be railing at her. Yelling. Telling her what a
screwup she was. She hadn't protected her own child from
the worst monster alive. She shook her head, unable to look
at him. She might never be able to look at him again. She'd
failed in the most important mission of her life.

"Rose, look at me."

She shook her head again, even more adamant this
time. Whitney's taunting voice flooded her mind. *Women
aren't of any use; they just don't have the strength or intelligence men do. Their weakness compromises missions and
jeopardizes teams. Men are wounded—killed—because
of the weaknesses displayed by women. Even when using
their psychic talents they have seizures and can't function
properly.*

*Baby, do you really believe that nonsense? Any psychic,
male or female, without an anchor close by will experience*

all of those things and more. Some have had strokes. Some meltdowns. It makes no difference whether you're male or female.

Kane pushed Whitney's voice out of her mind, filling her with warmth. His tone caressed her, gave her the courage to look up at him. His green eyes had gone nearly emerald, a heated promise that made her breath catch in her throat—made her want to believe the impossible. The moment their eyes met, hers filled with tears of guilt, and she looked away again.

"I've put some clothes out for you, Rose," Jaimie said. "I'm going back downstairs to contact Flame and have her start spreading the word that Eric has compromised all of us so the other teams can take precautions as well. He was inside the compound up in Montana as well as being in Wyoming with a couple of the GhostWalkers there. No one will bother you here for a while, so go ahead and use the shower, and if you want to eat, there's plenty of food."

Rose shifted her gaze to Jaimie, alarmed. Had Mack sent for her telepathically because Brian had taken a turn for the worse? She studied her face. No. She was being polite, giving her time to be alone with Kane. She silently shook her head in protest, but Jaimie just patted her shoulder and walked away, leaving her to face her son's father alone.

She swallowed hard. Guilt and shame were ugly things. She hadn't even had time to be terrified. She pressed her lips together and shook her head, knowing Kane was willing her to meet his incredible green gaze again. "I can't, Kane," she whispered once she'd heard the door close behind Jaimie. "I don't think I can ever look at you again."

"Because Whitney fed you bullshit to justify his experiment?"

The small edge to his voice made her glance up at his face. The lines were carved deep, making him look tougher than ever. His jaw was set in a stubborn line she'd come to know. He didn't understand. Her shame wasn't about

Whitney—maybe he added to the voices in her own head telling her what a screwup she was—but her shame was all about the way she'd acted toward his family members. As if they weren't trustworthy enough to be alone with her child. In her mind *she* had been the only one who could adequately protect Sebastian. Okay, there was Kane. She had trusted him—maybe.

Her face flamed. Not completely, not with Sebastian. She was so determined Whitney wouldn't get his hands on their son, and she didn't think Kane adequately understood the danger Whitney presented. She'd been so foolish. Without his family, without the very men she'd snubbed, her son would be in Dr. Whitney's laboratory.

"I'm so sorry," she whispered again, shaking her head. How could there be forgiveness? Kane had brought her into his home and offered her a life with him. She wanted him—but she hadn't really wanted the rest of them. She didn't know how to act with them, what to think or do. She felt such an outsider, and yet they had risked their lives for her son.

"Tell me what happened. All of it. What each person had to do to get Sebastian . . ."

"And you," Kane said quietly.

She shivered continually, unable to stop her body's reaction from the aftermath of the drug, or perhaps the time spent in the cold seawater. She could smell fish on her hair and skin. Dragging the blanket closer, she nodded. "And to get me back. Tell me."

She listened in silence to the quiet sound of his voice as he detailed the rescue and what each team member had contributed.

"If Javier hadn't spotted the SUV, they might have gotten away with it."

"It may have taken longer, but we would have found you and Sebastian, Rose," Kane said. "We had the microchip in Sebastian, and Whitney isn't the only one who can track with a satellite."

She felt a wave of raw fear. "My tattoo. Javier and Jaimie got rid of it."

"They deactivated it. There's a difference."

Now her teeth were chattering, but she didn't care. She was horrified. "If they know a way to activate it, so will Whitney."

He shook his head. "I'll put Jaimie and Javier up against anyone Whitney has in electronics. Jaimie's figuring out how they managed the lock on the door, but my guess is, the doc had something to do with it."

She felt color flooding her face. Once again she'd not trusted the members of his team.

Our team, he corrected. "Our family. We're a unit, Rose. You. Me. Sebastian. And our family. We have to think that way, believe that way. It has to be absolute. No individual is going to be able to fight Whitney. As a team, a family, we're stronger than he can possibly imagine."

He was right. When she'd been in the compounds, if Whitney separated all of the girls, it was much more difficult to fight him, but together, they had too much strength and too many psychic talents for him to control.

"I grew up with every single man and woman in this team other than Paul. You've met Paul. He's no plant. His talent is incredible, and we all watch over him, especially Javier."

Her breath caught in her throat. She knew Paul was no threat. He was too honest—he felt too good—not that he wouldn't fight if he was forced to do so. But Javier . . . He scared her, and yet it had been Javier who had ultimately been Sebastian's guardian. She'd seen the look on his face when he dropped in to see the boy. He always referred to himself as Uncle Javier, and she had secretly cringed.

Rose shook her head. "I'm sorry," she repeated. "I didn't trust them. I didn't want to like them or give them a chance."

"Rose." His voice was a velvet caress, stroking over her skin. "What did you expect? You've never been around a man who wasn't keeping you prisoner or torturing you. Did you think it would be easy? All of us knew we'd have to earn your respect and trust. It's never automatic, not when our lives depend on one another."

"But you trusted them. I should have . . ."

He drew her up, blanket and all, pulling her shivering body against his, and she let him, wanted to melt into him, to draw from all that male heat and strength. She let herself be fragile and vulnerable, she already was—to him. She let herself open to him. He was so deep inside her that she'd never get him out, nor did she want to.

"Why should you trust anyone you don't know? Especially with our child? Every member of my family would be shocked and horrified if you'd easily accepted them. They want you, just as I do, to be leery of strangers." He massaged her shoulders, and then slid his hands down her back, pulling her closer. "Look at Eric. He's been our chosen doctor for all the teams, and yet not one of us realized he was an enemy."

She leaned into him, wanting shelter in his arms, in the strength of his body. He was like an enormous oak tree, solid and unyielding, a sentinel she could always count on. "You were uneasy around him," Rose said. "That's one of the reasons I had trouble with him. I didn't like that he was so interested in DNA. He was always so obsessive about taking Sebastian's blood, even after I explained my worries. But had you trusted him implicitly, I might have acted differently."

When he framed her face with his large hands and her eyes met his, her heart nearly exploded with love for him. There was no censure there, only respect and admiration. She swallowed the lump in her throat. "I don't deserve you to feel like that about me, Kane. Not now. I can't forgive myself for nearly losing Sebastian. If I'd been better with everyone . . ."

He stopped her with his mouth, that sinful, tempting mouth that she often fantasized about. The moment his lips, so cool and firm, settled over hers, her heart shifted, and her stomach did a long, slow somersault. Her heart stuttered. His body heat warmed her. The steely strength of his arms caging her made her feel safe—as if she had truly found a home. The taste of him drove her wild.

Her eyes burned and her throat clogged with tears, even as her body went into familiar meltdown. She nearly dropped the blanket as she kissed him back, sliding her arms around his neck, clinging tightly to him. She gave herself to him, to the white-hot heat rushing through her veins in a fever of need, allowing the sensation to drive away guilt and fear and replace it with—*him*—with Kane.

She fed on him, on the rising tide of feeling, so she didn't have to think, didn't have to relive those terrible moments when she knew she'd failed to protect their child, and Whitney had succeeded in taking him. It took a few moments before her head cleared enough to realize he was swaying a little. Abruptly she pulled away from him to look up at his face. So strong—even powerful. She could see what had always attracted her to him, that intense integrity, the loyalty and honor that was stamped so plainly into that strong man's face. He was no boy; maybe he'd never been one. He was like her little Sebastian, thrown into a world of violence, scrounging on the streets to survive. Right now, he looked a little gray.

"Kane. Sit."

He gave her a crooked smile that nearly took her heart right from her body. "You're so cute when you give me orders."

She frowned at him. "No one's ever called me cute before." She tugged at his hand. "I'm feeling better. A shower will put me right, but you're exhausted."

Of course he was. He hadn't been able to stand up properly only a week earlier. He couldn't do a full workout, yet he'd run through the streets, dove into the ocean, and fought the enemy underwater in cold water while the waves pounded him—to save her.

Rose put one hand on his chest and pushed hard. Kane felt the steady pressure and was surprised, as always, that such a small frame could be so strong. Still, she wouldn't have rocked him, even though he was exhausted, but she looked so beautiful and so determined he couldn't stop himself from giving in to her. That look of sheer grit replaced the guilt in her eyes, and he'd take that any day over her feeling guilty over something she had no control over.

"Stay right there and rest. When I get out of the shower I'll make tea."

His heart tripped, and without thinking his hand snaked out to snag her wrist as she turned away from him. He tugged. The blanket slipped before she could stop it, and she nearly lost her balance. He caught her around the waist with both hands and lifted her onto his lap, facing him, so that she settled over his hips, straddling him. He could feel her heat burning through the material of his jeans, pressed tight right over his eager cock.

She wiggled, and his entire body seemed to burst into flames. He ran his hands possessively down her back. No matter how many times he held her, she seemed so fragile to him, such a miracle. Her skin, even now, smelling of the sea, was soft over all those exquisitely firm muscles.

"Let me take a shower, Kane," she whispered, nuzzling into his neck, her arms creeping around his neck, her body settling into his.

The blood pounded through his veins, thundered through his heart, and roared in his ears, all in reaction to the realization that there was no resistance in Rose. The moment he touched her, her body fit into his, made for him. She *gave* herself to him wholly, surrendering everything to him. His heart contracted. He'd never thought to have a woman for his own and certainly not a woman like Rose who wanted him with the same encompassing fever that he had for her.

"I'm salty and fishy."

He laughed. This could have been the worst day of his

life, but here he was, his son sleeping peacefully in the other room, his woman naked and compliant in his arms. He bit that sweet spot between her neck and shoulder and felt her shudder in need.

"I don't give a damn how you smell, baby," he assured her. "I just need to get these jeans open. Shift just a little." He dropped his hands to the buttons, lifting his hips just enough to slip the offensive material down his hips.

The relief was tremendous. The moment he sprang free, his eager cock encountered her scorching, damp heat. "You're heaven for me, Rose. My sanctuary."

Hands on her waist, he lifted her, positioning her body over him, until just the broad, flared head was pushing inside the heat of her body. The fact that she was already damp, already just as eager for him, was amazing to him. Very slowly he lowered her body over his. Heat gripped him, surrounding him, all that pulsing energy. He drove through the soft, hot folds, sweet fire engulfing him. She threw back her head, arching her back, her throat working convulsively as her breasts pushed against his chest. Her nipples felt like two pinpoints of flames, sending a streak of fire straight to his groin.

He loved the look on her face as she slowly impaled herself on his cock. There were so many ways he was eager to explore taking her, but he wanted this—that sexy, needy look that no woman could ever fake, her eyes half closed, her lips parted, the rush of air and the flush of color. He especially loved the way her chocolate eyes melted into a glittering glaze.

His cock embedded deep, all the way to the hilt. He inhaled, feeling the air rush from her lungs into his as he inhaled. He couldn't close his eyes to savor the sensations pouring over him, not and watch her face too, and he craved the sight of her, so sexy, so feminine, enjoying his body with the same desperate hunger he had for her. He *needed* the sight of her, alive and well. She had somehow become his world in a very short space of time, the need for *her*—not just her body but Rose herself—had become paramount to his happiness.

He mapped her feminine shape with his hands, worshipping her, stroking his fingers over her rib cage, upward to cup her breasts while she rode him with a leisurely rhythm designed to drive him slowly out of his mind. He loved this woman in a way he never thought possible. She'd stolen her way inside him that first time he'd shared her bed. The courage in her had been beyond comprehension to him. He had fallen hard, and he had known then that no other woman would get to him in the same way she did. His respect and admiration for her had only grown from that first meeting. He'd handed his heart into her keeping when he hadn't even fully known what he was doing, and now he was more than happy that he'd done so.

He let her set the pace. Let her use him to drive away the terror of their near loss. He wanted to drive away every demon, every fear—for her. To put the shine back in her eyes, to give her back her faith in herself. She was killing him with the slow spirals she liked to use, a dance of fire, with her silky cap of hair spilling around her face and those dark eyes showing him how lost in pleasure she was.

He could watch the emotions chase across her face forever. His hands slid over her body, memorizing every inch until they settled on her hips. He flexed his fingers, enjoying the tight, hot friction gripping him, the buildup of need until it surged through him, until he couldn't take the slow, lazy pace another second.

"Hold on, baby," he whispered softly.

She reached out and touched his face, looking at him with her almond eyes. "You're mine," she whispered.

That one sultry look, the brush of her fingers against his face, and the possession in her voice was his undoing. "Son of a bitch, Rose, you kill me sometimes," he bit out between clenched teeth. It was either swear or cry when she turned him inside out like she did.

He gripped her hips hard and began to thrust into her,

driving deeper and deeper, filling her, stretching her, taking her up hard and fast. He felt the silken walls surrounding him clasp and spasm, convulse and contract as powerful waves took her like a tsunami. Her orgasm tore through her, pulsing around his cock with white-hot heat, until he couldn't hold back and he went over the edge with her.

She collapsed against him, gasping for air. Kane caught the back of her head in his palm and urged her to bury her face against his neck as they both struggled to regain control of their breathing.

"I love you, Rose," he told her, the words wrenched from somewhere deep inside him. "I think we need a bed. I can't ever make love to you properly if we don't find us a good bed."

She smiled against his shoulder. "Um, Kane? We have a perfectly good bed. You just can't wait long enough to use it."

"You're always getting up to feed the baby and I have to go find you and then . . . well . . . things naturally happen." He brushed a kiss into her wild hair. "Are you feeling better?"

Her laughter was contagious and somewhat muffled against his shoulder. She trailed kisses over the heavy muscles of his chest. "You're so insane. Is this what we're going to do every time I'm upset?"

"Of course. I'm kissing you better."

"Kissing?"

"And other things." He nuzzled her neck and then nipped at her. She squirmed, causing her muscles to clamp down on him all over again, a sensation he found extremely pleasurable. He bit down again just to feel the effect a second time.

"You sound so smug."

"I deserve to be smug." He was certain he did. She glowed. He'd driven the guilt and fear away for a space of time, replacing the negative emotions with sheer pleasure, and that was what mattered. "I'm good." He wanted to give her everything she'd never had. He wanted to be her damn superhero, which was laughable when he could never quite find the right words to tell her what she meant to him.

Her soft laughter teased his nerve endings back to full alert. "You're more than good, and you know it." She turned her face toward his, her lips slightly parting as if to speak.

Kane leaned forward and fastened his mouth to hers, welding them together. Her body shivered in response, and the little aftershocks rippling through her sheath sent shock waves through his cock. He deepened the kiss, unable to ever just kiss her once. Not when she was so responsive and he loved the taste of her more than anything else he'd ever had.

When he finally allowed her to catch her breath, she clung to him, sweeping back his hair, looking into his eyes. "You're not supposed to exert yourself, Kane, and you just ran, dove into the ocean, fought with divers, and made love to me. Your doctor . . ."

He took her mouth again, cutting off her words, taking his time with a slow, lazy kiss. When he lifted his head, she was flushed and her eyes sparkled. He grinned at her. "My doctor is a fucking traitor, sweetheart, and I damn well am not following his orders."

She narrowed her gaze, those chocolate eyes darkening ominously. Her fantasy lips pressed together in a straight, disapproving line. Her tough look. The one she used when she blew shit up or shoved a gun in his belly. Okay, he was a sick, sick man, because instead of being intimidated like any sane man who knew her would be, he just found her so damned sexy. His cock, still deep inside her, thickened and hardened, his one and only weapon—and a very promising one at that.

"Don't you dare start," she cautioned.

Rose put her feet firmly on the floor and pushed up, her sheath gripping him hard, causing nearly unbearable friction on his hypersensitive shaft. His breath caught in his lungs. His cock jerked. She was supposed to sound tough, he knew that, but to him, she was a breathy little sex kitten giving him the come-on.

Even as she turned away purposefully, intending to stalk her way to the shower, he followed her silently. She got five steps until she was beside an overstuffed chair. He caught her around the waist, pushed her over the arm of the chair, holding her down with one hand on the nape of her neck. With one bare foot, he kicked her legs apart, slipping his hand between her legs to find her damp entrance.

"The first time was for you, Rose," he said, or tried to say it. His voice had gone hoarse, almost strangled. This was for him. Her body was his. He wanted to fill her up with him. Brand her with him. Leave his scent all over her. Love her until she couldn't walk or think. Until she knew she would never leave him, never want to leave him alone again.

He slammed home, a hard surge that took him deep, pushing through her sweet, silken folds, until he was completely buried in her, surrounded by all that living, breathing fire. Flames sizzled through his bloodstream, rushing hot to center in his groin. Her soft, breathy moan drove his temperature up another notch, and he lost himself in her. For a few minutes there was only the sound of their bodies coming together, the gasping for air and her sweet, sweet haven, a cauldron of fire burning bright and beautiful surrounding him as her tight muscles clasped him.

He'd had sex, but it had never been like this. He let the sheer pleasure take his mind and he let go, no longer as gentle, pulling her hips back into him as he surged forward, feeling her response, the way she pushed back with him. The fire was already threatening to engulf him, but he held it off as he thrust into her over and over. She seemed to flow like hot silk around him, created for him, the taste, smell, and feel of her wiping out anyone who had ever come before.

Her face was turned partially away from him, flushed with heat, with arousal, her dark hair spilling around her in that disheveled, sexy way he loved. He savored her soft moans and breathy little pleas as he pounded into her scorching embrace.

"I dream about us, Rose," he whispered, unable to stop himself from telling her the truth. He retreated from that perfect heat and slammed deep and hard again, feeling her body shudder in reaction. "I want you like this, so hot, all liquid heat for me—only me—knowing you belong only to me. Knowing you never want me to leave your body."

She moaned, that pleading gasp mixed with the sheer music of her need that he craved. She was close—he knew her now, knew all the signs of her body—and he increased his speed, using more force. Power and heat coiled in his body, a bright, hot energy that gathered like pooling lava. Her body locked down on his like a vise as she came, crying out, a sexy sound that was purely erotic. She vibrated, sending ripples of pleasure banding around his cock. He thrust deep again and again, while she pulsed hotly around him, and then his own body bucked and shuddered with absolute ecstasy. He emptied himself into her, pouring out his heart and soul along with his seed.

He staggered, his legs turning to rubber. For a moment the room spun. His fingers bit into her hips to steady himself, and the world went hazy.

"Kane."

The anxiety in her voice forced him to take air into his lungs and allow his body to leave hers, but for the life of him, he couldn't move, couldn't take a single step. He would have fallen into a heap on the floor. Better for his dignity to hang on to the chair and just sway back and forth until his leg muscles weren't spaghetti anymore.

Well. No. The chair wasn't going to hold him up, and neither were his legs. He was going down into a very ungraceful heap, no doubt about it. And he'd never live it down. She'd hold it over him the rest of his life, and so would the team—but there was nothing for it. The room spun, his hand slipped from the chair, and his legs just refused to hold him up.

Rose straightened quickly, catching him around the waist, surprising him with her strength again. Her appearance was so deceptive, making him always want to be the white knight, rescuing her. He always allowed the fact that she was physically and psychically enhanced to slip his mind, but when he was reminded, like now, he felt such a rush of heat.

"*Don't* even think about it, soldier," she hissed, as she half walked, half carried him the two steps around to the front of the chair. "You just fell on your ass, Kane."

"No, I didn't. I never actually hit the floor," he said proudly, subsiding into the chair. He thought about pounding his chest, but she was glaring at him, hands on hips. "Hell, baby, I just made love to you not once but twice. *And* I totally rescued you from the sea," he reminded her. "I'm your superhero."

She sniffed. "You fell on your ass," she repeated. "My big, strong, white knight fell on his ass. You couldn't keep up."

He grinned at her. Happy. "I can keep it up. Just come over here and kneel down right there." He opened his legs for her in invitation. "You look sexy as hell."

She rolled her eyes, but her mouth curved into a smile. "I'm sure I do, all sweaty with milk running down my breasts. You're insane, Kane, but I think I'm crazy about you." She turned abruptly and left him.

He let himself slide down the chair until his head rested on the back of it, totally spent, drifting between awake and dreaming.

CHAPTER 17

Rose tightened her arms around Sebastian as she followed Kane down the stairs to the second floor. The entire team had assembled in hushed silence. Javier and Ethan crouched beside the stairway and door leading to the outside fire escape, examining walls and railings in an effort to find whatever Eric had left behind. Ethan looked up as they came down the stairs and signaled them to silence.

Is Brian alive? Kane asked.

Paul and Marc saved him, Mack answered the question.

Rose was astonished that she was able to hear the master gunnery sergeant's voice in her mind. She and Kane had a strong connection, something she believed stemmed from Whitney pairing them together. She could initiate telepathy, but it had never been strong, and unlike Mack or Kane, she could never have held a bridge for an entire team.

He'll be down for a while. Jaimie's going to take care of him until we can get a nurse we can trust. We could use Rhianna right about now.

Javier straightened to allow them to get past him.

Sebastian stared solemnly at the man and then suddenly smiled, leaning toward him. The move was unexpected and strong enough that Rose had to catch him with a little gasp. Her heart jumped. There was no doubt her son wanted Javier to hold him. She had to console herself with the fact that Sebastian had already shown he could sense and recognize an enemy.

She swallowed hard and made her first attempt at accepting Kane's family as her own. *Sebastian wants you to hold him.*

Javier's smile flickered for a moment in his eyes and then faded away. He held out his arms for the child. *Top, have Gideon give it a try. I can't spot anything, and I want to hold my nephew. It's time we got acquainted.*

As if testing her, Javier cuddled the baby close and, moving in his silent, fluid way, turned his back and strode out of Rose's sight behind the tent. Rose's pulse thundered in her ears, and she literally had to twist her hands together to hold herself in place beside Kane.

Kane dropped his arm around her shoulders and moved her closer beneath his broad shoulder. He bent his head, turning his body partially, shielding her from the stairs. He brushed a kiss along her hair. "Javier's taking Sebastian away from what we believe is Whitney's camera or some sort of monitoring device." The words were barely audible.

She let her breath out and turned her face toward his, needing to kiss him, uncaring if any of them saw her. She was grateful he was the kind of man who read and cared about her feelings. He nearly lifted her off her feet, his larger frame completely shielding her, reminding her of when he had gotten her pregnant. He had not only destroyed Whitney's cameras and recorders, but he had kept his much larger body positioned over hers to protect her from the guard's prying eyes.

It was silly, really, to think that she needed a white knight, but he made her feel protected, cherished even. There was something to be said for a man who was so willing to offer a woman his own body to use as her armor and shield. She slipped her arms around his neck and clung, unashamed, allowing herself a moment of weakness. It was difficult to trust her son to anyone out of her sight, let alone the most dangerous of all the team members.

He keeps smiling at me.

The moment Javier spoke inside her mind, she felt herself settle, the wild churning in her stomach subsiding. There was awe, maybe even a hint of joy in the tone.

He's so little I thought I might crush him, but he's strong, isn't he?

She recognized an uncle's pride, and something hard inside her broke open. Javier was a man dedicated to his team and his country—but everyone else was an enemy. She could hear in his voice that Sebastian was family and always would be.

Rose blinked rapidly and tightened her arms around Kane's neck for courage. She made herself laugh softly in her mind. *He's very strong. He pushes up off the floor already. Sometimes when he's kicking, I have to duck very fast, because he's got quite the kick.*

Javier's laughter slipped into her mind. Kane urged her forward, and she moved toward the hospital tent. She knew it was impossible for someone like her—someone with her background—to trust the people around her, but they were soldiers, and they knew their jobs. They worked well together, knew one another. They were offering her the opportunity to have everything she'd ever wanted—a family—and to be able to serve her country as part of an elite unit. She spent nearly every waking minute of her life training to be what these people were—a GhostWalker—and she wanted the chance to use her skills again.

She smelled bleach and blood as she skirted the makeshift hospital. *Is Brian going to be able to recover fully?*

Kane had to have been holding a bridge to allow the others to communicate telepathically with her, because once again, it was Mack who answered.

Yes. It will take some time. We were fortunate that we'd already arranged to have surgical equipment here. The "hospital" was going to be set up in the second building up the block, but we haven't fully renovated it yet. We've only set up security.

Gideon winked at her as he slipped by, taking Javier's place at the stairs. *If something is here, Top, I'll find it,* he said with confidence.

Gideon's eyesight is enhanced, Kane explained. *He can see things we can't, and if Javier didn't find anything, then Gideon's our last hope.*

You swept for bugs? Rose asked.

Mack nodded. They had moved around the tent now, out of sight of the stairwell. "Found several in your living quarters and two up here where Eric planted them while his physical therapist was doing his best to kill Kane by overdoing it. Jaimie's checked their every movement with all the surveillance tapes frame by frame. We're confident we were able to find them all."

Rose was listening, but her gaze had jumped to Javier, sitting in a rocking chair, Sebastian in his arms. The man had a big grin on his face.

"Thank you, all of you, for getting Sebastian back," she said simply. Emotion was nearly overwhelming, welling up so fast it was impossible to hold it in check. "You all risked your lives for us . . ."

"You're family," Javier dismissed her stammering thanks with a wave of his hand. "You'd do the same."

The confidence in his voice warmed her. "Nevertheless, I wouldn't have survived if Whitney had managed to get his hands on Sebastian."

Kane threaded his fingers through hers and brought her hand to the warmth of his mouth. "Yes, you would have, Rose. We would have gone after him."

"And we'd never stop until we had him," Mack confirmed.

"The thing I don't understand," Javier said, inhaling the baby's scent, "is why Whitney thinks we would stop. He knows us, or he should know us."

"He can't know our bond," Mack said.

"Javier has a point, Mack," Kane agreed, "He knows us as individuals."

"Which is why he had you assigned to the compound, Kane," Rose said. "He read all about you, what you were like, and he knew you would appeal to me."

"Then he has to know if he took you from me, I would never stop looking for you unless I was dead."

"And then we'd continue," Mack added. "I think there's a part of him that likes to see if we'll win. Like playing a game, only with human beings for game pieces. He sets up a battlefield and throws the players onto the board and amuses himself watching what will happen."

"That's pretty sick," Javier said. He smiled at the baby, his tone softening. "And Whitney thinks I'm a psychopath." The baby wrapped his fingers around Javier's index finger as if in response. "For future reference, a psychopath is considered very bad."

Rose glanced at him. Javier had sounded hurt, yet when she looked at him, he was bending his head to kiss the baby's fingers.

"Actually," she said, "that's exactly the type of grand experiment Whitney would enjoy. It probably doesn't even matter all that much which side wins as long as he can observe and document . . ." She trailed off. "He had to have been here in San Francisco when they tried to take Sebastian. He would have been close enough to observe. He would never plan something so elaborate with so many different ways for his team to escape with us without watching it all play out."

Mack and Kane exchanged a long look. "Why the hell didn't we figure that out ourselves?" Kane lowered his voice.

Javier beckoned Rose. His face had lost all expression, his eyes once more going flat and cold. Sebastian stared up at his face, immediately ceased gurgling happily, and looked carefully around the room with so much awareness in his eyes that Rose shivered as she took him. She glanced at Kane, worried. The baby was only a couple of months old, and already he was picking up his cues from the adults around him, recognizing danger far before he should.

What kind of a childhood is he going to have? There was despair in her voice and fear creeping under her skin. *There's no way for our son to have any kind of normal life, is there?*

Kane stroked a single caress over her hair and then reached out to take the baby. *He'll be safe, happy, and prepared, Rose. It's up to us to make a new normal for him.*

He recognized the difference in Javier and is already alert to the changes in all of us. She wanted to cry for them all. She didn't want that for her son. She wanted her little boy free to play and laugh with others, not living the kind of life she had—already training for a life of warfare by the time she was able to walk.

"This is our life," Kane said aloud. "This is his life. He'll have a playground, and he'll have a happy childhood. He'll just know from early on that, like us, like his family, he's different, and he has to live differently. That doesn't mean worse, Rose, it means different."

Nodding, she swallowed the terrible choking lump in her throat, blinking fast to get rid of the shine of tears in front of the other team members.

Javier touched Sebastian's head with a gentle hand. "He'll be safe, Rose—and very loved. We'll see to his needs, all of us. We'll help provide everything he needs. You tell us, and it's yours."

She looked around her at the circle of faces. They all nodded. Some of the tension eased. She couldn't help smiling. Even as they reassured her, they were sliding weapons into clothing, readying for battle. There seemed to be an armory on every floor, hidden of course, but well stocked with just about any weapon they might need. She knew they went armed everywhere outside the house, probably in it as well.

"You good?" Kane asked.

They were all looking at her, waiting for her answer. Not, she realized, to get it over with, but because they genuinely cared and were ready to do whatever it took to make her comfortable with their future. She took a deep breath, not wanting to disrespect them with an easy answer. Was she? Probably not yet, but she was beginning to believe. She could see the genuine affection they all gave to one another. More than that, she could see that the same intense loyalty that had drawn her to Kane was in each of them.

"I will be," she said honestly. "I need to start training and feel as if I'm part of the entire unit. More than anything, that will make me feel part of everything."

Top! I found it. I'm still searching around looking, because it's a tiny camera and I'm betting someone's watching, Gideon said triumphantly.

Long or short range? Javier asked.

Rose's heart began to pound. "It has to be Whitney watching. He wants to see the baby. What if Eric put a camera that small on our floor? He's visited several times. He could have easily done so."

Kane took the baby and cuddled him close. "There's nothing for him to see right now, Rose. Sebastian's stronger than most babies at this age, but there is no way the camera can capture the intelligence and awareness we're seeing. Gideon can search our home. Eric wasn't allowed in our bedroom . . ."

"Of course he was. He examined you daily while you were recovering," Rose pointed out. "He didn't get to examine Sebastian, but he was there."

Gideon, I'm sending Javier. He's going to check the camera as subtly as possible for range, and then we're

going to look for Whitney. You'll have to check Kane's en-
tire home for possible cameras.

Gideon groaned. *This was a bitch to find.*

Now you know what you're looking for. Ethan, I'll need
you on the roof, Mack instructed. *Lucas, use the tunnel and*
come out on the other side of the street. Blend in. And Ja-
vier, whatever you do, don't kill anyone. We've already got
a bloodstained SUV parked outside our warehouse. The
last thing we need is more bodies to try to dispose of.

Rose lifted her eyebrow at Kane. "Does he have to tell
Javier not to kill anyone?"

"Every damn time," Kane said. "It's just a precaution.
Javier tends to take the easiest path, and if someone's in the
way . . ." He shrugged.

"I can't imagine that he's a hothead," Rose said. "He
seems like he'd be cool under fire no matter what."

"Ice water runs in his veins. He's not quite like everyone
else, baby. But he stands. And he obeys Mack. Javier's a
good man, just a little misunderstood at times." Kane shot
a quick grin at Mack.

Mack scowled at him. "Misunderstood my ass. I need to
sit on that boy." He looked toward the stairwell, and even
though the tent was in the way, he lowered his voice. "Jaimie heard Rhianna was back in the States. She sent word to
come home, that Brian was down, and that you have a son."

Kane's breath hissed out. "She what?"

"She needs to come home, Kane," Mack said. "It's time.
She's part of us, and Javier and Rhianna have just got to
come to terms with whatever the hell is wrong."

"He's still not talking?" Kane asked.

Mack shook his head. "Not one word, but I'm not surprised. Javier has always been one to play things close to
his chest, especially when it comes to Rhianna."

Rose made a noise in her throat to remind them she was
still there.

"Sorry, sweetheart," Kane apologized right away. "We

all grew up together. We formed a family and sort of had each other's back. There were only two girls, Rhianna and Jaimie. They were both quite a bit younger, and we were overprotective any way you looked at it. Rhee was different, her background far worse than the rest of us, with the exception of Javier. She didn't always feel comfortable, although she always stayed with us."

"Javier put a lot of pressure on her, and eventually she rebelled. He sort of rode her all the time, little digs, you know," Mack said. "Very unlike him. He's the strong silent type, but he didn't like her around other men, and he got pretty ugly with a couple of guys. They had a fight a few months back, and she asked to be reassigned without telling any of us first. He's been a bear ever since."

"So he doesn't think of her as his sister? Or he's an over-protective brother?" Rose asked.

Mack shrugged. "He doesn't act like a brother, but who knows with Javier. Rhianna is the only person in the world who can shake Javier up. He's arctic cool until she comes around, and then we can cut the tension with a knife."

Top, he's across the street in the apartment building. I'm guessing second floor, but it could be the third floor. I can't pinpoint the room.

Best guess, Javier, Mack said.

Middle windows either floor. If I was Whitney, and I knew what Gideon and Ethan are capable of, I'd choose second story and my escape route would be the far fire escape away from this warehouse where neither has a shot.

Jaimie, Marc will take over in there. I need you at the computer. Check the recent rentals on the building across the street, Mack ordered. *Paul, go too, just in case I need Marc in the field.*

Immediately there was a flurry of activity as if Jaimie had called both Marc and Paul because Brian had taken a turn for the worse. Whitney would recognize the two of them as healers and believe something had gone wrong.

Jaimie, the consummate actress, backed out of the tent in full view of the camera and then went around the corner, behind the tent, to her bank of computers.

"I keep an alert on the real estate agency that handles that rental property. It flags all new tenants." She was all business, settling in front of her bank of computers, fingers flying over the keyboard.

Rose was fascinated—actually a little awestruck—at the amount of information pouring over the various screens in front of Jaimie. There were ten large computer screens, and data flowed over each of them, coming in from various sources and agencies around the world. She was certain much of what she was looking at was data that was all at a security level far beyond hers. Her existence might be top security, but she obviously didn't have the kind of clearance Jaimie and the others had—not yet. More than ever she wanted to be an official member of the team.

Jaimie glanced over her shoulder. "You are official, or you wouldn't be looking at this data. The word came through a little while ago. With everything going on, there was no opportunity to tell you." She flashed a mysterious grin. "Mack is officially your boss, poor girl."

"Isn't he yours?"

Jaimie tossed her head. "Not hardly. I'm an analyst, not a soldier." She winked. "He's really mean. Ask any of the men."

"Jaimie," Mack made a growling noise in the back of his throat. "I really need that information."

"It's coming up now, Mr. Impatience. You have three on the second floor and two on the third. The Williams family moved into apartment 224, one of the windows facing directly toward us. A couple with two children. A Donald Martin is in apartment 225 right next to the family, and the third one is on the other side of the building, so I doubt he's your man. On the third floor, both apartments recently rented face our building. A Charles Laudry and Tisha Phillips in 334 and Seely Thompson . . ." She broke off, looking up at Mack.

"What is it?"

Jaimie shook her head. "An alias, definitely not Whitney. Rhianna uses that when she sends me personal email. It's always encrypted, a program I wrote especially for the two of us to use. No computer is going to break it easily."

"So Rhee is already back," Kane said.

Rose caught the relief on Kane's face and the affection in his voice, but she didn't ask questions. Mack was already relaying the information Jaimie had given him about the other tenants to his team.

"We can't destroy the camera or take out the ones in your home, Rose," Mack said, "until we go after Whitney. This might be our best chance at him. Stay here with Sebastian, out of sight behind the tent."

Rose nodded and looked up at Kane. She wanted to go, but she hadn't trained with them yet. She knew she'd only get in their way. "Good hunting."

Use alternative ways to leave the building. If Whitney spots us leaving en masse, it will tip him off that we're on to him. Right now he's feeling very superior that we didn't find his camera. I'm heading into the tent as if to check on Brian. From there I'll leave out of his sight and meet you all outside. Stay to cover. Kane and Javier, take the second-floor rooms, and I'll take the third floor with Lucas. Gideon, can you see into the windows?

Doing my best, Top. There's someone moving around in three of the apartments facing us from the third and second floors.

Kane caught Rose's face between his hands and kissed her thoroughly right there in front of everyone. Her eyes went wide and shocked, and he grinned at her before brushing a kiss on top of Sebastian's head. "They may as well know I'm crazy about you," he whispered overly loud in her ear, watching her blush with rising satisfaction.

He loved that slightly bemused, flustered look she got when he was publicly affectionate.

I have no idea what to do when you put on public displays.

Manly *displays,* he corrected. *That's me beating my chest and claiming you.*

She frowned at him, and he was tempted all over again to kiss her fantasy mouth. *Just how long are you going to keep that up?*

"Forever, sweetheart. For always. And that's the damned truth, Rose," he said and turned abruptly to uncover the escape door situated close to the bank of computers where Jaimie always had a fast exit, should one become necessary. The opening revealed a very narrow entrance with a built-in slide that took him straight down to the wharf side of the warehouse. He pushed open the door to exit into the alley in front of the wharf itself.

The wind blew in from the ocean, and fingers of fog stretched greedily toward the buildings. Sheets of mist blew in rapidly, a thick veil difficult to penetrate. The cover would help the team members as they spread out and went into the building across the street by several different entrances. Ethan and Gideon, the spotters on the rooftops, however, would have a much more difficult time.

Kane, Gideon spotted movement in three of the apartments. Are you in a position to see into the apartments?

Give me three, Top. I'm coming to the corner now. Javier, we'll need your boys.

Roger that. They're already on their way. Someone just told them about the SUV parked on the street with the keys still in it.

Kane stayed close to the wall, his clothes blending into the walls of the warehouse as he rounded the corner. It was three steps to the shadowed alcove. They'd taken advantage whenever an apartment had been vacant to study the vulnerabilities of their own warehouses, finding each blind spot from the windows and marking them for future use.

Negotiations so far had proved to be nearly impossible in acquiring the apartment house. The corporation owning the building steadfastly refused to sell. Jaimie was peeling away the layers in an effort to find who actually owned the corporation. The fact that the building had recently been sold quietly, without advertisement, along with the property managers being deliberately evasive had raised suspicions that either Whitney or another enemy had bought up the building.

Kane waited in the alcove, hearing the crowd of boys coming up the walkway, trash-talking loudly. They shoved one another, leapt over a fire hydrant, and threw several rocks at a stop sign. The sound, much like a series of gunshots, was loud despite the blanket of fog.

Movement at the window on second floor, Gideon reported.

One of the boys kicked the SUV as they surrounded it. The others laughed. Swaggering up to the passenger windows, the boys peered in. More fog poured into the street, swirling around the buildings, a moving, living veil.

Kane stepped into the darkened doorway that was one of the best blind spots available. Set back from the street, the deeper recesses allowed someone able to blend into shadows to disappear. Kane did so, steeling himself to use his particular talent. It was wrenching to use his vision, seeing through the walls inside the actual rooms.

The buildup of energy radiated heat in the small confines of the doorway. The building across from him shimmered, the thick walls undulating as if not real, the solid matter no longer solid. He felt the wrenching in his gut, the lurching of his stomach, and fought down the bile. Pain sliced into his head. He ruthlessly pushed the side effects down. Each time was different, but he had noticed some time ago that the salt air and fog seemed to make the initial penetration a little more difficult.

He took a breath and swung his gaze up toward the second floor. The walls fell away, giving him a dizzying moment, but he rode it out, setting his teeth, ignoring the commotion in the streets as the boys tried to enter the bloodstained SUV to steal it. They'd found the pool of blood and had exited fast, yelling. The world dropped away until there was nothing left between Kane and the occupants of Room 224.

Someone sitting in a chair facing the window. He isn't moving, just staring out. No woman. No children. He's in a perfect position to be observing a camera. Gideon?

I have him, Gideon acknowledged. *I have a shot.*

Check Room 225, Mack ordered.

On it, Top. Kane shifted his gaze to the next apartment. Jaimie had said a single male had moved in. A man moved through the apartment fast, away from the window. *The male in Room 225 is armed. There's a second male standing by the door, armed as well.*

I have the first male, Ethan said, *second is out of my sight.*

It's a drug deal. Man with briefcase just walked in. Kane moved on to the next floor.

Checking the third floor. Room 334. Kane looked up to the top floor. The walls dropped away, leaving the occupants exposed. A woman lay on a bed motionless, her head tilted at an odd angle. The man was at the side of the windows in the front room, staring at the street below and the chaos the boys were causing as they ran from the SUV. The male glanced toward the bedroom, seemed to say something, and then walked into the kitchen to open the fridge and pull out a bottle. *Can't rule out. One male moving around. Female in bedroom, lying on the bed.*

Check the roof again, Gideon.

Roger that, Top. Gideon complied.

Moving position, Kane said.

It always took a few moments to recover from using his gift. His body felt weak and shaky, his stomach churning. He dropped his head down to suck in as much air as he could to counteract the dizziness. It only took seconds, but he was running out of time.

While he still had the cover of the boys, he had to quickly get across the street. He slipped from the doorway and, hugging the shadows as best as possible, pulled a hat low, drooped his shoulders, and changed his gait. He appeared shorter and thinner than he was just by changing his posture and the way he walked. Hurrying, he crossed at the crosswalk, sending nervous, furtive glances at the boys, never once looking up.

Roof is clear, Top, Gideon reported.

Javier was already inside, and the two of them went up the stairs toward the second floor. Mack and Lucas had come in from the back and were already on the third-floor landing. Kane signaled to Javier, and they went into the hallway, guns out and ready, senses flaring out to find an enemy. They moved in silence, approaching apartment 224 first.

Gideon, do you have eyes on our man? Kane asked.

He hasn't moved. Not so much as a change in position.

Kane nodded to Javier. Javier knelt and quickly worked the lock. He eased the door open. There was no chain in place, and icy fingers slid down Kane's spine.

Going in. He knew Gideon would take the shot if necessary, but there was something else, some awareness that kept the adrenaline pumping through his system. He could almost smell Whitney's presence.

He signaled again, and Javier dropped low to cover him as Kane went through the door and stepped to the left, clearing the room. The man in the chair didn't move, didn't turn his head. It was possible he hadn't heard their entrance, but even when Javier moved to visibly clear the other small rooms, the occupant of the apartment was unnaturally still.

Kane glided up behind him, finger on the trigger, but still the man didn't move. Kane could see why when he approached from the side. Eric Lambert sat grotesquely sprawled out in the chair, drink near his hand, throat cut open, shirt soaked in blood.

Man down, Top. Whitney was here.

Kane could smell the pipe tobacco, Whitney's special blend. Bile reached his throat and he choked it back. He remembered that appalling scent as he came up from loving Rose. The man had made certain Kane and Rose had mated. Kane had ruined his cameras, so he'd come to see for himself. Kane had never detested a human being more than he did that poor excuse for a man. He would have killed him right there had he not been locked in a cage. The only thing he could do was cover Rose's body with his own, shielding her from a monster's smug, satisfied gaze. They'd looked at each other through the bars. Whitney had seen the resolve there, knew Kane wanted him dead. He'd simply, arrogantly, removed the pipe from his teeth and nodded before walking away. *As if they had been in some hellish pact together.*

"He left you a note."

Kane had seen it. That blood-spattered paper placed carefully and conspicuously beside the dead doctor. Cursing beneath his breath, Kane edged the envelope with his name on it out from the dead man's hand.

Top, Whitney was here. Eric Lambert is dead. He couldn't have left too long ago. The scent of the tobacco made him sick. Kane reluctantly opened the envelope.

So you have finally won our little game, Kane. Your reward is this apartment building. I have signed the deed over to you. You are indeed worthy of keeping the boy. Eric Lambert betrayed you as he betrayed me. Had he gotten your son's blood, he would have given it to your enemy, a group dedicated to wiping every GhostWalker from the planet and undoing years of my work. You prevented him from doing so by your vigilance. I commend you. They will pursue you, all of you, but you have the intellect and the training to keep them from succeeding in destroying you. Congratulations on your win. I would like to get Rose back. She did a superb job of producing a child. You must keep me informed of his progress. Rose can be tiresome in her rebellion, but her genetics are priceless. If you tire of her, get word to me, and I will make you a further trade.

Kane almost crushed the note in his hand. *Tire* of her? As if Rose had little worth beyond giving birth to a child. Did Whitney despise and loathe women so much? He certainly enjoyed seeing them suffer. He had enjoyed Rose being forced to accept a man.

"Damn you, Whitney," he muttered aloud. He looked down at the last paragraph.

I warned McKinley about Javier Enderman, but he refused to listen. Enderman is a psychopath. If you all continue to trust him, he will be your downfall. Kill him now before he destroys you all. I should never have enhanced him, but his loyalty and protective instincts fooled me into believing he could be useful. He is not. I am not infallible, it seems. I have chosen the best, the absolute best of the genetic pool I could find for my mission. Weed him out so that he doesn't poison it. He has one weakness that will bring you all down. He can be bought . . .

Javier was looking over Kane's shoulder, reading the letter. He looked at Kane with flat, cold eyes and shrugged. "He's right, you know. I do have a weakness."

Kane shook his head. "Don't let him throw you."

"It isn't the first time I've been called a psychopath."

"*Don't* let him throw you," Kane repeated. "You don't break. I've known you since you were a child, Javier, and you're no psychopath." He knew Javier had been called that on more than one occasion. It had hurt, whether Javier admitted it did or not. He was very careful not to appear sympathetic. "We all have a weakness. Mine is Rose and now the boy. Whitney profiled each of us, and what he perceives as our weaknesses are actually our strengths. He's never understood loyalty. He tries to separate us, because he thinks we make one another weak. He's alone, and he thinks he's greater and stronger than all of us. He doesn't understand, and he never will, that together we're unbreakable."

"Fuck him. I could care less what that monster calls me."

"Rhianna is back, Javier." If Javier had one weakness, one thing that could make him lose the ice water running in his veins, it was Rhianna.

Something dangerous moved behind those dark eyes. "When?"

"I just heard. She has an apartment in this building."

Javier shook his head and turned away. "We'll need a cleaner up here."

"What the hell am I supposed to do with this deed?"

"Is it legal?"

"Looks like. Jaimie can find out for us," Kane replied.

"We've wanted the building. Jaimie said she was pretty certain Whitney was responsible for the quick sale of the building out from under us."

Kane flashed a small grin. "We've got it now, don't we?" But he didn't want any part of Whitney's gift. It made him feel he was being rewarded for taking Rose's choices from her. He glanced at Javier's set face. "I'm signing the damn thing over to you. You can figure it out."

"What?" Javier stepped back. "You can't give me the building."

"I own the warehouse with Jaimie and Mack. I don't want this from him, but we need it to secure the entire two blocks. We'll have the bay on two sides of us, and we'll only be vulnerable to the city side. We can set up security."

"I'll think about it." A slow smile took some of the shadows from his eyes. "I could kick Rhianna's little ass out onto the street."

"Don't start a war with her again," Kane cautioned. Before Javier could answer, he indicated a sweep of the room. "Look for anything else the bastard might have left behind. He's gone and we're not going to find him tonight, but we've gained more than we lost. He just doesn't know it yet."

CHAPTER 18

Rhianna Bonds was nothing at all like Rose expected her to be. She was incredibly beautiful, not at all the tough chick everyone implied that she was. Average height maybe, but there was nothing else average about her. She was stunning with her large, impossibly blue eyes and thick, curly black hair. There was so much hair that her braid was as thick as her shapely arms. She was not conventionally thin but had a figure one couldn't ignore, with curving hips, rounded breasts, and an extremely small waist.

She was hugged and kissed and greeted as a long-lost sister. Rose noticed Javier was conspicuously missing. Rhianna didn't ask where he was. She took Sebastian in her arms and looked at him with such love in her eyes, Rose wanted to cry. This was a woman who felt deeply. Again, Rose expected her to be like Javier, a cold, female version of the man. She radiated warmth. She was the kind of woman who would walk into a room and be noticed instantly. She wasn't spy material; she was too striking.

Rose found out the hard way that Rhianna was not all

looks. Training began almost right away, and Rhianna was a big part of that. It was grueling and unrelenting. Rose found out quickly that there was no reasonable way to nurse Sebastian and train with the hours she was putting in. Instead of quitting altogether, wanting the best start for him, she opted for pumping her breasts. It was a nightmare, but better that than the alternative of not training. She needed to become part of the team, needed them to know what she could do and that she was good at it. And she was. Soldiering was something she'd done since she was a child, and there was nothing too rough, too dangerous, or too difficult for her. She had discipline and a sense of duty. She discovered Rhianna did as well.

Jaimie sat and watched sometimes, feeding Sebastian his bottle as they ran through the urban techniques, the one thing Rose hadn't trained in. Each man took his turn working with her. They often broke into smaller teams and pitted themselves against each other. The work was satisfying, and at night, she had Kane.

Kane's body was always wrapped around her, protective, loving, and he woke her often, sometimes twice a night, as if he could never quite get enough of her. She loved lying in bed just listening to him sleep. Sometimes he fed the baby a bottle, watching as she climbed the sides of buildings and ran along the rooftops. Other times she fed the baby while he massaged her neck and gave her pointers.

She soaked up the training like a thirsty sponge. It felt so good to be active again, to feel like she belonged somewhere. This had been her world since she was a child, and she savored every minute she could be active. She found herself laughing more, talking animatedly with the team members, listening to them, and occasionally sharing some of her own knowledge.

Eventually, after nearly a month of nonstop training, it didn't matter that she loved every second of her life; she still felt the need to walk down the street and breathe in the air. From the rooftops she found herself watching people going about their lives, envying them their freedom. It was Jaimie who suggested the three women go out shopping. Such a simple idea, yet Rose had to brace herself to ask—no tell—Kane that she was going to go out that afternoon.

"What is it, sweetheart?" he asked her, as if he already knew there was something wrong just by her silence.

Rose forced a smile. "Jamie, Rhianna, and I are going shopping. Just the three of us." She stole a look at his face, those hard angles and planes, and her nerve nearly broke, but she persisted, trying to sound casual. He looked like she'd dropped a bomb. "I need to really get acquainted with the neighborhood, so it will be both fun as well as educational."

"Fun?" He sounded like he'd never heard of the word. "Rose. There's a price on your head."

She dismissed that with a wave of her hand. "I need to do this, Kane."

She'd forgotten that several of the team members as well as the two women had just finished working out. They appeared quite curious. Paul winked at her. Rose looked around the room. Every member of the team had arrived, as if Kane had put out some kind of SOS call—which he probably had. The men were looking at the three women—at her in particular—as if she'd lost her mind.

"You want to go where?" Kane asked through clenched teeth.

No, he definitely wasn't happy. Rose sighed. He'd heard her, he wasn't deaf, but she obligingly repeated herself, knowing he was asking for the benefit of the team members who might not have heard. "The three of us want to go shopping. Maybe to the market and a couple of the boutiques. Not far, Kane, it's only a few blocks down."

"If you're really insisting on going, then we have to go with you." He glared at Jaimie and Rhianna, as if they were to blame for her wanting to leave. "Jaimie knows she doesn't go out without an escort."

Rose refrained from rolling her eyes. "I'm not a two-year-old, Kane. I want to go shopping. It isn't like Whitney's going to have a team out there again. He's been quiet. I believe him when he said to you that you 'won' the game. He's not going to come after me, especially after losing so many of his men."

"Fine, we'll go."

"You have to stay here and watch Sebastian so I don't worry about him," Rose objected.

Something dangerous flickered in the depths of his eyes. "Paul can watch him. Right, Paul?" His tone suggested Paul give the right answer.

"No problem," Paul said instantly, ignoring the way the three women glared at him.

"That's not the point," Jaimie said. "We want to do the woman thing. We've been cooped up with men long enough. We need some woman time."

"I don't like this one bit," Kane groused. "Why the sudden need to bond?"

Jaimie laughed. "You're becoming one of those very annoying males, like Mack. You don't want to be like Mack, do you?"

"Hey!" Mack objected. "I think he's showing good sense. The three of you ought to be locked up somewhere."

"A padded cell," Gideon suggested under his breath.

Jaimie glared at him. "You're not helping the cause."

Rose noticed that Rhianna didn't say a single word. She kept her eyes on Javier's face. He was in the shadows as usual, barely able to be seen. His face was a carved mask, inscrutable. He said nothing at all, but his fingers tapped his thigh, and the movement was mesmerizing, as if all his pent-up emotion was controlled only by those rhythmic taps.

Rose could feel the burning heat from Kane's piercing eyes. She sighed and held up her hand. "I realize that all of you are just trying to protect us, but we have to be able to live our lives. I haven't been out of here in six weeks. That's a long time. Yes, I've been active, but while I enjoy the company, I'd like to experience freedom. I've been a prisoner my entire life, and walking through a marketplace is an amazing treat for me."

She kept her gaze locked with Kane's. In the end, his opinion was all that mattered to her. He shook his head, and she could see fear there—and determination.

"Damn it, Rose. If something happens to you . . ." He trailed off and turned away from her, but not before she saw the burst of emotion cross his face.

"Nothing will happen." Javier stood up abruptly.

"Damn it," Kane said again without looking at her. "Gideon, you and Ethan have the rooftops. Stay inside the marketplace. We can cover them easily there."

"I wanted to go into the little boutique and look at clothes. It's two blocks down," Rose insisted. "Kane, I have to feel like I can breathe."

Kane closed his eyes briefly and swept his arm around her, dragging her close to him. "I know, Rose. I don't want you to feel as if you're a prisoner here. I didn't know you were feeling that way. Jaimie goes out, yes, but she doesn't have a price on her head."

"It's been quiet for weeks; Jaimie said so," Rose pointed out. "She's got all the information pouring in. They stopped talking about me."

She hated the tension between them. Kane's easy smile was gone, and his fingers dug into her hip as though he could tie them together through sheer physical contact. She didn't try to pull away from him, afraid he would think she wasn't happy. She was. She loved her life with him, everything about it, but she had to take the next step and go out into the world. If she couldn't, then how could Sebastian?

Kane shook his head again. Rose laid her palm over his chest, right over his thundering heart. She looked up at him, willing him to look down at her, into her eyes, and see that she loved him beyond all else. This wasn't about their life together, but about needs. The need to walk through a crowd of people or go into a store and shop for her own clothes—things she'd never been able to do. She wanted those things for herself. Maybe she was being greedy, but it mattered that he understood.

"You know the team has to go with you."

"Around us. Not with us," Rose corrected. "We're trained soldiers, Kane. Civilians aren't going to hurt us."

"They're the worst because you don't expect it," Kane corrected. "I should be with you, Rose, close, the first time."

She sighed. "If that's what you need to do, Kane."

"For God's sake, Kane," Javier hissed. "She's got Rhianna with her. What the hell is going to happen to her with Rhee beside her the entire time?"

Rhianna looked more shocked than anyone else. Her gaze jumped to Javier's face, but it was impossible to read his expression. He never so much as glanced at her.

"I didn't think of that," Kane admitted. He looked rueful, raking his hand through his hair. "Sorry, Rhee. I know you can look after her."

Rose suppressed the urge to stomp her foot. Rhianna had obviously earned their respect out in the field; she hadn't. "We'll be fine, Kane. The three of us can kick some serious butt if we have to, and with Gideon and Ethan on the rooftops, nothing can happen."

"I'll be in the street. Lucas too," Javier pointed out, some of the tension easing from his voice. "Lucas can blend. He's a freaking ghost out there."

"This is the way we have to live, isn't it?" Rose said.

"We're used to it," Jaimie said. "This has been our lives since we were little, Rose. We practically lived on the streets most of the time, and we had to look out for one another. It just feels normal after a while."

"And right," Rhianna said. Again she glanced at Javier and then looked away. "Being alone is no fun when you know no one has your back. Looking out for one another is what family does, and we're a tight family."

Rose looked around the room at all the faces. They

weren't her sisters, the women she'd grown up with, but they were offering her a home. A real home. She found herself smiling. "I think I can live with knowing I'm always surrounded by people willing to help me. I hope you know I would do the same for you."

She looked Kane right in the eye when she said it. He persisted in thinking she was a fragile little flower that needed protection.

I know better, baby. It's just that you've become my world. When a man's had nothing, and he finds that one woman who owns his heart, it's damned hard not to lock her away from any danger.

But you know better.

Logic doesn't enter into this, he denied. "Go then, Rose. But Rhianna, you don't leave her side. Not for one damned minute."

Javier stirred, drawing attention, but he subsided when Rose shook her head. "That's not fair, Kane, and you know it. Rhianna is not less than I am. We'll all look out for each other."

Rhianna burst out laughing. "We're going to the market, Kane, not to a war zone. We're highly trained professionals. They're freakin' drug dealers. Sheesh. Have you all lost your minds? Come on, Rose. Let's get out of here."

Gideon and Ethan rushed up the stairs toward the rooftops. Lucas left the room. Rose put Sebastian in Kane's arms.

"You can do this, Kane. I'll sometimes have to watch him while you go out without me. You have to be comfortable knowing the team will look after me, just as they look after you."

"Damn it, Rose."

She laughed. "You seem to be stuck on that little theme."

He caught her chin and kissed her hard, kissed her until her heart was pounding and her knees were weak.

"Just come back to us," he demanded. "And for your information, it's bullshit for me to be relegated to babysitter when you're putting yourself on the line."

She raised an eyebrow. "For *your* information, it isn't called babysitting when it's your own child. Sebastian is far more at risk than I am."

"I don't think so, Rose, not anymore. I think Whitney believes I won his game by stopping him from taking both of you. But he wants you back."

"If you really can't stand this, Kane, then we'll do it your way," Rose capitulated.

Kane was far too distressed for her to try to prove a point. Sebastian would be safe with Paul. She trusted him. If it meant that much to Kane to guard her back, then she needed to concede to him this one thing. Over time, when nothing happened, he'd mellow out—she hoped.

"I really can't stand it." Kane jumped on that, knowing she expected him to reassure her that he would be fine staying at home. "I need to be out on the street watching over you." No way in hell was that going to happen. She could think it all she liked, but if she walked out that door, he was going to be shadowing her every step of the way. If she really knew him, she would have known that.

Rose made a face at him and turned away without arguing, which, in his opinion, she should have done in the first place. It would have saved a hell of a lot of time. What kind of man did she think he was? He protected his own. She was his woman, and when she put her life at risk, he was going to be guarding her precious little ass whether she liked it or not.

Mack leaned close. "You have steam coming up out your ears."

"Why the hell do they have to be so fucking unreasonable?" Kane demanded.

Mack shrugged. "You're asking the wrong man, Kane. I haven't figured out anything yet, and I doubt if I ever will. None of them make sense to me, but I have to give you kudos for trying to discuss it with her. There were a couple of times I thought you might explode, but you didn't show it."

Lucas, you in place? Javier's voice filled their minds even as he walked beside them, trailing behind the three women at a more leisurely pace. "Personally," he told them aloud, "I think the only answer is to lock them up. It's a matter of sanity."

"Then what was that bullshit about Rhianna?" Kane snapped. "It wasn't helpful."

"Hell. What difference did it make? It got the argument over, and everyone knew, with the exception of Rose, that she wasn't getting out the door without you." Javier shrugged. "It saved time. And it's the truth, not bullshit. Rhianna can get the job done."

Kane knew it was the stark truth. Rhianna had grown up on the street, a hard, brutal life, and she was a survivor. She grew up clawing and fighting her way through the worst kinds of criminals as a child. Her body was a killing machine and her mind cool and brilliant. Everyone underestimated her in the same way they did Javier. She looked a certain way, and they took her at face value. No one would ever think she could be lethal. It was generally the last thought they had before they died.

Kane kept Rose in his sight, strolling down the street after her. She paused, and he saw her face light up. She threw her head back and took a deep breath. Had he been keeping her prisoner? It probably felt that way to her. He hadn't deliberately locked her away from the world. The sun was out, and her hair shone almost blue black under the blaze. He loved the way she moved, flowing silk over concrete.

Fan out a little. Mack's voice brought him up short. He was getting lost in Rose's wonder, in the way she absorbed the outdoors and her freedom. She actually threw her arms out once, as if to embrace the world around her.

I should have seen how much she needed this, he confided to Mack.

Laughter floated back to him, turning heads around them. His body tightened. The three women were attracting a lot of attention. His eyes narrowed and his stomach settled. He loved watching her have fun, but that wasn't his job. Keeping her safe was all that mattered. His attention had to be on the crowd, on their surroundings, not on Rose, as much as he would have liked to see her experience the freedom of having fun with friends.

Rose nudged Jaimie. "When do you get to the point of not being hyperaware of the team surrounding us?"

"Honestly," Jaimie said, "it's usually only a couple of them in the crowd and one on the roof. They've been at this since we were kids. Mack and Kane never wanted us to walk through a park without an escort. We lived in a pretty rough neighborhood."

Rhianna nodded. "It was nice back then to know someone cared enough to look out for us. Jaimie had a mother, but she worked all the time. We spent a great deal of time alone."

"What is it like having a mother?" Rose asked. "I never had one."

Rhianna shrugged. "Jaimie would have to answer that. I never had one either." She shifted her gaze to the crowd, her eyes seeking out a familiar face.

"My mother was awesome," Jaimie said. "A best friend when I was young. I grew up too fast for her. Sometimes I felt as if I was a terrible disappointment, although I know in my heart I wasn't. It was just that I never did the things most moms think about."

Rose laughed. "I don't know what moms think about. Me, I think about how fast I can take apart a weapon and put it back together again. Nice legacy to pass on to my child."

"Your child will need it," Rhianna pointed out. "Teaching him survival is the best thing you can ever do for him, Rose. Don't let the rest of the world tell you any different."

Rose smiled at her. "Thanks, Rhianna, that's a nice

thing to say. I'm totally winging it as far as the mother thing goes."

"He's beautiful," Rhianna said. "I've never held a baby before. It was very different than I thought it would be." She sent the other two women a wry smile. "I never even held a doll. Did you?"

Rose burst out laughing again. "Can you imagine Whitney giving us dolls? *Hell* no. You met him. He wouldn't understand why a girl might want a doll. We were learning hand-to-hand combat, not playing with toys."

"Not much preparation for his breeding program," Jaimie said. "What did he think you were going to do once you had babies?"

"I think he planned to take them away from us and give them to professionals who would raise the ultimate soldier under his guidance," Rose said.

"Someone needs to put a bullet in that man's head," Rhianna commented.

Rose loved the feeling of life pulsing around them in the marketplace. She identified half a dozen languages as they moved through the crowd. The place was alive with laughter. Two vendors argued politics. A husband and wife examined wares holding hands. Children raced down the rows, and parents chased after them.

"Isn't this amazing?" Rose asked.

Rhianna grinned at her. "You really love this, don't you?"

"Yes. It's wonderful. Real people."

"They're real, all right. You see that man over there? The one lounging around looking hot with sunglasses and tight jeans?"

"Very hot," Rose agreed.

"He's looking for girls. Young girls with nowhere to go, starving for attention, hungry and scared. He's a hawk, Rose, and he can spot one a mile out. The one over there, just in front of the row with all the flashy cool jewelry to draw kids is a drug dealer. That man over there beats the hell out of his wife, and those two kids are shoplifting, even though they're wearing shoes that cost several hundred bucks a pair."

"Rhianna!" Jaimie frowned at her.

"That's what I see. I'm sorry, Rose. I shouldn't have pointed them out to you. Just because it's how I view the world, I shouldn't put those images into your head."

"Yes you should. How will I teach Sebastian if I can't tell him what dangers to look for?" Rose objected. "How in the world did you learn to spot those kinds of things?"

"Hard experience," Rhianna's voice was strictly neutral. Rose heard the warning. Rhianna didn't want to talk about her past. She glanced at the set face and remained silent.

Jaimie put her hand gently on Rhianna's arm. "Rose was in a breeding program, Rhee. She's been forced to do things and see things neither of us has ever had to face."

Rhianna flashed Rose a small smile. "Sometimes I have a chip on my shoulder. You know, the woe-is-me-I'm-such-a-martyr complex. Ignore me."

"Nice to know you're human. When we train, I swear you're a machine."

Rhianna's smile widened. "If any one of us is a machine, Rose, it's you. You just had a baby, and you run circles around us."

It was the first time any of them had complimented her that way. Kane endlessly told her how beautiful she was, but no one had mentioned her abilities in the field. No matter how hard she'd tried, how much she embraced the things they taught her, how fast she learned, or how many times she hit the target without a miss, no one had commented. She tried not to let the glow she felt show on her face. These women—and Kane's team members—viewed their lives matter-of-factly. They didn't give compliments; they took it for granted that if you trained and worked with them, that you were elite.

She found herself smiling. They'd accepted her not

only into their family but as a member of their squad. She should have known. She had never been told she'd done a good job, she'd never been praised. If she succeeded or excelled at something, she moved on to the next task. Sometimes she felt being a soldier was bred in her bones, the very legacy Whitney wanted for her son. It was who she was, what she was, and she would never know anything different . . . But Sebastian was going to have a choice, if she could possibly give it to him.

"Hey!" Jaimie threw her arm around Rose's neck. "Stop thinking so much. We're out here having fun. I want to go to that wicked cool boutique just down the street. I can't believe I live next to it. It has the hottest boots of all time."

"Of all time?" Rhianna's eyebrows shot up. "I've got to see that. I've been around the world and visited every shoe shop I could find along the way. This shop has a lot of competition."

"I *love* the boots you sent me from Milan." Jaimie dropped her arm and walked in front of Rose, turning to walk backward so she could face her as she talked. "Rhianna and I both adore boots."

"She has boot emergencies," Rhianna explained. "Every now and then I get a frantic SOS from her, and wherever I am, I go out and find her a pair of supercute boots."

Rose laughed. "I wear combat boots."

Jaimie rolled her eyes and dropped back to her side. Rhianna closed in on the other side. "We noticed," Jaimie said. "Hence the boot boutique. Seriously, Rose, you need us. We're going to show you the true code all women should live by."

"A pair of boots?" Rose asked skeptically.

Rhianna and Jaimie looked at each other and then burst out laughing, shaking their heads. "Not *just* a pair of boots," Jaimie corrected. "*The* boots. *Hot* boots."

Rose frowned. "I don't understand."

"Just say it," Rhianna advised. She leaned close to Rose and whispered in her ear. "*Fuck*-me boots."

Rose's mouth fell open in a gasp. "You two are terrible."

"Try walking up to Kane in the boots we find you and nothing else," Rhianna advised. "See what happens."

"I think the same thing would happen if I walked up to him naked," Rose pointed out.

Jaimie and Rhianna laughed again. "I think you're right," Jaimie said, "but it's so fun to see that look in his eyes when you come striding in and sit on his lap. He's so very appreciative."

Rose bowed. "I'm willing to take direction."

"Every woman should have a sexy red dress in her closet," Rhianna added solemnly. "And a black one. It's not only necessary to your soul but to your arsenal. And so are very hot boots."

Rose laughed. "However did I survive without knowing this?"

"I have no idea," Jaimie conceded. "But thankfully, you're with us now, and we can show you the way."

Rose looked down at her combat boots. "I can see I have a lot to learn."

Jaimie touched Rose's arm, and they moved into the shadows just outside the store, Jaimie positioning herself just in front of Rose, partially hiding her from the crowds of people on the street.

Rhianna didn't break stride. *Entering store now. Dove is outside. Eagle, it's on you.*

Roger that. Gideon's voice was calm. *She's covered.*

Rose choked back a protest at the ghastly name they'd given her. That had to be Kane's idea of her. She was no dove, no matter that he persisted in underestimating her abilities—until they were in actual combat.

Mama Bear is much more appropriate!

Jaimie's muffled laughter followed by Rhianna's snort as she pulled open the door to the boutique and disappeared inside changed her mind. They were teasing her, offering her the tight camaraderie that only came when you relied on another to watch your back in a life-and-death situation.

It was only a minute before Rhianna spoke again. *All clear.*

Jaimie stepped forward and pulled open the door. Rose went through, and they were inside. Immediately they were just women again, having fun shopping for shoes. Rose found it comforting that the other two women slipped easily in and out of their roles. It meant she had a chance, someday, to be able to walk through a crowd and feel normal. If she could achieve that, maybe Sebastian had a chance after all.

The shoes were amazing. She'd never paid any attention at all to shoes, and now Rhianna and Jaimie were pointing out everything from elegant heels to really beautiful boots.

"You've got the money," Jaimie pointed out. "Lily put money in a trust for each of the girls she grew up with. That includes you, Rose. It's just sitting there. Granted, we're using big bucks to buy up all the buildings around us and renovate them, but you have plenty to purchase a few special items for yourself. Like these awesome, never-to-be-found-again boots right here." She held up a pair of butter-soft leather boots in a swirling olive green with a square cut toe and a bit of a heel. "What do you think?"

"Or these?" Rhianna held up a pair of bloodred boots that snaked up to the knee. "Short skirt or a pair of skinny jeans. Really dramatic."

"You'd look dramatic in anything," Jaimie pointed out, blowing her a kiss. "Try these on, Rose, they'll go with a sexy outfit."

"Sexy outfit?" Rose echoed faintly. "I don't have a sexy outfit."

"Lingerie," Rhianna said. "You know, thong, corset, a see-through camisole."

Rose shook her head. "I don't have any of that."

"Oh, girlfriend, you need help *desperately*," Jaimie said, putting the boots down. "We're in the wrong shop. We need to go somewhere else."

You've got company. Two women. Both young. Look harmless enough, Gideon warned.

Look alive, Javier warned. *One had a tattoo on her wrist. I just barely caught a glimpse of it, but it could be the Lopez cartel. They've spread through Arizona, Texas, and especially California.*

"It would be a coincidence," Rose said aloud.

Javier warned us some time ago that they had a hold close to here. It makes sense their women might shop here, Jaimie answered as the bell tinkled, signaling they weren't alone.

Rose kept her back to them, while Rhianna and Jaimie turned slightly, observing the newcomers. Both girls were young, no more than early twenties, with dark, curly hair and sunglasses pushed over their faces. They talked low to each other, but all three women were enhanced and could hear the whispered exchange. Evidently one was certain her boyfriend was sleeping with another woman and wanted her friend, Imelda, to ask around. They ignored Rose, Rhianna, and Jaimie completely.

I think they're more interested in what their boyfriends are doing than us, Jaimie said.

We could go to the lingerie store, Rose suggested, sticking with telepathy. *How far away is it?*

A few blocks, three more, I think, Jaimie said.

Over my dead body, Kane snapped. *We're not prepared yet. Buy your boots and get out of there.*

Rhianna sighed. *Have you ever noticed certain people are killjoys?*

Rose laughed out loud. She couldn't help it. Kane was always going to be Kane. His idea of safe was anywhere close to him. She reached for the olive green boots, loving the feel of them. One of the newcomers reached for them at the same time. Rose smiled at her and let go.

"Go ahead. They're beautiful."

The girl's smile was brief, but she took them to the

attendant to ask for her size. Rhianna was already trying on the red boots, and Jaimie had chosen a pair of chocolate brown ones. Rose wandered around the store, looking at everything, a little shocked at the prices and how high the various heels were. "Can anyone really walk in these things?" She turned, lifting them up in the air.

Jaimie laughed. "Rhianna can," she said.

"Really?" Rose asked, whirling around. Rhianna just grinned at her as she pulled off the red boots. "Without stumbling?"

"Piece of cake."

"Look Irma," Imelda said as she walked around the room, showing off the green boots.

Irma barely glanced at her friend; her attention on her cell phone, texting like crazy. Rose felt sorry for the girl. "They really are hot on you," she commented. Even as she said it, she spotted the boots for her. She *loved* the look of them. Soft gray, a leather braid around the ankle and the top of the boot, knee high, with just enough of a heel to be called dress boots, but not so high she'd break her neck, she *had* to try them on.

"I love these," Rose said with a sigh.

Rhianna broke into an approving smile. "So do I. Try them on."

Rose didn't need any other encouragement. She had the clerk get her size and sank down into the plush chair to replace her combat boots with the soft leather ones. Never in her life had she had such a luxury. The boots were ridiculous for someone like her to own. Where in the world would she wear them? She ran her hand over the soft leather. But she really, really loved them. They felt wonderful, caressing her feet, surrounding them with sheer elegance.

She looked in the mirror, while Jaimie and Rhianna made approving noises. "I have nowhere to wear them, and nothing to wear them with, but I absolutely love them."

Jaimie and Rhianna grinned at each other. "Major shopping time, Rose. Get the boots, and the next time we go

out, we'll find the perfect dress. Kane can take you out to
dinner, and we'll babysit."

"And dancing," Rhianna added.

"I don't know how to dance," Rose said.

"We'll teach you," Jaimie offered as Rose sat down to
reluctantly remove the boots.

Get them, Kane said. *If you want them, Rose, we'll find
somewhere nice to go.*

She took a breath and looked at them. She had a child
to care for, a home to keep safe. Did she need the boots?
No, but she really wanted them. The temptation was extraordinary. Whitney would have been disgusted with her.
That thought tipped her right over the edge. She *had* to get
them, if just to prove to herself that she rejected fully his
brainwashing.

*You've got two gang members sitting on the curb di-
rectly across from the shop, and one trying to look incon-
spicuous lounging against the front of the building. He's
got on a coat and his hand is inside of it. A fourth is crossing the street and heading right into the store.*

Gideon's cool voice delivered the message. Without
hesitation Rhianna crossed the store and jerked the cell
phone from the persistently silent Irma standing beside the
door.

"That was damn stupid of you," she hissed. "You should
have walked out of here while you had the chance."

Irma tried to pull a razor blade from her hair. Rhianna's
elbow connected hard with her face. The crack was loud,
and Irma dropped to the floor at her feet. "Get out of here,"
she called to the clerk. "Use the back door. These women
are gang members, and their men are just outside." As
she gave the order, she pulled out her wallet and flashed a
badge of some sort.

Rose couldn't see what it said, but the clerk turned and
hurried out of the store. Rose caught Imelda's wrist as she
tried to run toward the door, calling out to the man moving
swiftly toward them from across the street. Rose delivered

a hard chop to the side of her neck, and the girl went down hard.

I've got the shot, Gideon said.

Let him come in, Rhianna protested. *Too many civilians. His buddies probably have itchy trigger fingers.* Rhianna stepped to the side of the door.

Rose noticed no one protested. Jaimie moved behind the counter, pulling her weapon from her boot. Rose took the opposite side of the door from Rhianna. She preferred her knife. She could throw fast and accurately. And knives were silent.

That's Jose Cortina, a real badass. He's the real deal, Rhianna. Favors a knife. Thinks he's a ladies' man. Has a taste for hurting women and torturing anyone who thinks about crossing him. Javier informed them. *He'll smile at you, half turn away, and then turn and throw a knife. He's a lefty.*

The door burst open, and Jose strode in. Rhianna kicked the door closed and stepped in behind him. "Your girl sent you the wrong picture."

Jose toed Irma's limp body, spit on her, and then looked straight at Rose. "I don't think so. You're worth a cool million."

He looked over his shoulder at Rhianna, his eyes widening in surprise as he took in her face and body. "My lucky day."

"You think so? Your boys outside are having a bad one. Take a look." Rhianna moved slightly to give Jose a better view of the street.

Jose shifted his gaze to peer over her shoulder. The two men who had casually been sitting on the curb were now slumped over, looking drunk. Blood dripped steadily into the gutter. The third man, the one armed with the semiautomatic, stumbled out into the street directly in front of a car. The car had no time to throw on its brakes, and the body flew up and over the hood, smashing the windshield. The gun clattered to the street.

"What the hell?" Jose turned back to Rose with a small smile. He turned as if to leave, his hand a blur.

Rhianna caught his wrist with surprising strength, stepping in close. Jose frowned down at the hilt of the knife sticking out of his chest. "What the hell?" he repeated and coughed blood. It bubbled up around his lips and dribbled down his chin. His knees buckled. Rhianna stepped back and let him fall.

CHAPTER 19

The helicopter swooped in low over the desert, running without lights. There was little sound, only a muffled thump of the blades as it moved in fast, staying below radar to hover just at the edge of the remote village. The town sprawled out in front of them, a collection of adobe homes spreading to the outlying farms at the edge of a hill. Sitting atop the hill, a large estate, the home elaborate, two stories surrounded by towers and fences, looked down on the residents of the village. A shimmering blue pool looked inviting from the air.

The setup reminded Kane of a feudal lord looking down on his subjects. He glanced around at the men—and Rhianna—who were putting their lives on the line for his woman. For him. For his son. He'd lived his life with these men at his back. He could always count on them. What did the man in the mansion have? Money. Power. Just like Whitney, they bought loyalty. They ruled through fear.

Mack signaled the pilot, and the helicopter banked and came to an abrupt halt. The team moved into place as the ropes dropped. They fast-roped down, hit the ground running, in full combat gear. The team was in full force. Jaimie had stayed behind with Sebastian, Marc, and Brian, the warehouse locked up tight under full security. The other nine members of his team ran in formation toward the safe house where their three contacts—members of the elite Air Force Pararescue GhostWalker Team Four waited. That gave Mack an even dozen, more than enough to get the job done. This was a personal mission, and it would require them being the ghosts they were. The night truly belonged to them, and Cesar Lopez was about to find that out.

Mack held up his closed fist, and the nine members of his team went still, sinking low, disappearing into the shadows of the buildings. A low whistle came from the left. Mack pointed two fingers, and Javier slipped into the alleyway, his body disappearing into the darker shadows along the wall. He moved in complete silence, a part of the night, his job to get a feel for their contacts. Kane slipped in behind him, positioning himself on the other wall in order to cover Javier. Gideon was already climbing up the building, going high, his night vision enabling him to see without glasses, covering Javier from his vantage point.

Large panel truck. Beat-up. Paint peeling. Driver behind the wheel. One man standing by the back doors. One approaching you, Javier. Two Rovers two blocks down, both armed. Look military, Gideon reported.

Lopez owns the military stationed anywhere near his stronghold. Also the police, Mack reminded. *Consider them the enemy.*

Roger that, Gideon acknowledged.

Mack wanted them in and out of the village without being seen—or heard. The two military men presented far more of a challenge than those by the panel truck. If the men meeting them were enemies, there was no doubt they'd wind up dead in the street.

Javier gave the exact same low whistle and when the man turned toward him; a little light from the tiny crescent moon spilled over him. *Joe Spagnola.* Javier breathed the identity to the others.

Kane felt the coils in this stomach ease. Joe Spagnola was a GhostWalker familiar to their team. He'd guarded Jaimie for months before the team had returned to San Francisco. He stayed without moving, covering the man by the back of the truck. He was a stranger, but the odds were looking better than ever.

There was a whispered conversation between Javier and Joe before Joe walked Javier around the panel truck to introduce him to the man guarding the back. Javier kept his body away from both men, leaving a clear shot for Kane. Kane wasn't all that worried. Joe and his friend needed to be careful around Javier. He could kill both in a split second, erupting into violence without warning. Still, he never took his gaze from the two men. Another brief conversation ensued, and the second man stepped up to the truck to open the large door.

Malichai Fortunes, Mack. He's got a hard-ass rep, but he's the real deal, Javier reported. *He's a member of Team Four.*

Kane eased his body closer. *Look alive, Gideon.*

I'm on the driver.

This was the most dangerous moment of all. Javier had to step up to the back of the truck and inspect the interior to be certain it wasn't a trap. They would ride in that truck to a safe house as close as possible to the villa. Most of those in town were employed directly by Lopez or their livelihood depended on his goodwill. His team wouldn't find many allies, and most people would gladly turn them over to the head of the cartel and reap a generous reward.

Damn it, two Rovers suddenly got interested, Gideon informed them.

Rhianna, Rose, take care of them, Mack instructed.

Both women hastily peeled off their jackets to reveal clingy tops. Rhianna's generous breasts were framed beautifully. Rose looked like a sexy little pixie as she threw her semiautomatic to Jacob Princeton, the GhostWalker closest to her. Rhianna shook out her hair, pulled out a bottle of tequila from her pack, and tossed her gear to Jacob as well. She sauntered out from behind the building, her hips swaying, Rose beside her. The two women laughed, their voices melodic, seductive, so that the two military men turned their attention toward the sound. Almost at once the two women paused, as if just spotting the two military men.

Instantly they changed direction to intercept the two men, whispering and laughing. Rose allowed Rhianna to take the lead. She wasn't used to using feminine wiles as a weapon, although they'd certainly covered that in her training—but not like Rhianna. She beckoned the men to her with a crook of her finger, looking so tempting Rose was stunned. She was the consummate actress. If Rose didn't know better, she would have thought Rhianna was either an experienced prostitute or she was madly in love with one of the two men and determined to entice him to have sex right there out in the open.

Rhianna put her hand on the nearest one's shoulder and slowly, sensually, circled the two men. Her lips were parted, her eyes devouring them. She whispered something softly in Spanish. Rose barely caught the words, nearly as mesmerized as the two men. "Finally. Two real men. We want to party. Come with us. Please. I need a real man between my legs for once." Her voice dripped with sensuality. With hunger. There was no real way for a man to resist that smoky, needy voice.

They followed Rhianna right into the small spaces between two buildings. She turned, offering her mouth to the first one, while Rose crowded close to his partner. They struck at the exact same moment, shoving the syringes against the exposed necks and slowly lowering the bodies to the ground. Rhianna was all business, breaking open the tequila bottle and pouring it liberally on their clothes. She crouched beside them and opened shirts, and unzipped pants, jerking one pair down around the man's knees. The guns were laid next to them as if forgotten in the dirt, the empty tequila bottle inches from the one with his pants up.

Rhianna was thorough. There was no doubt that both men would believe they'd partied heavily. The drug in their systems would give them a blazing headache, simulating a hangover.

Lucas, we're good, Rhianna confirmed as she straightened.

Rose was shocked that Lucas had managed to enter the alley behind them and was part of the shadows. She hadn't seen or heard him.

Rhianna grinned at her. "I didn't see him either. He's a ghost. We all are."

Rose smiled at Lucas. "You're good."

He looked a little embarrassed by the compliment. *All clear, Mack.*

The three of them drifted back up the street, keeping out of sight, aware of Javier standing in harm's way. He stepped up to the truck and peered inside, a sweeping visual, leaving himself exposed as he did so. When he turned giving the okay signal, his gaze sought and found Rhianna in the darkness. Her chin tilted, but she didn't break stride.

Javier continued around to the front of the truck, approaching the driver from behind. The man stepped carefully out of the truck, hands in plain sight. There was a small exchange. *We're good, Top. Wyatt Fontenot. I know his brother, Gator.*

Didn't know he was a GhostWalker.

He's got the mark, and Joe vouches for both of them.

The mark, Rose had come to find out, pushing down the urge to scratch the itch of her new tattoos, was simply the symbols used by the GhostWalkers. A triangle with three distinct symbols inside, signifying: shadow knights protect against evil forces, using psychic power, courage, and honor. She also had, like every member of the special teams, the GhostWalker crest with the Latin words, *The night is ours.* The ink was a special one that could only be seen by those with night vision—something every true GhostWalker had.

We're a go. Gideon, stay sharp.

I've got you covered, Top.

Javier took a step farther out into the street, a seemingly casual move, but he put himself in a better position to cover the driver and Malichai. Mack signaled his team forward, and they swept into the street, a rush of dark shadows, climbing into the back of the truck.

Kane held position in the alley watching the street, another pair of eyes to keep his team safe. Rose, Rhianna, and Lucas joined the others, easily jumping into the back. Javier went up and over the hood to the roof, lying flat. Kane followed, leaping onto the roof and settling down, facing the back, his semiautomatic ready.

Come on in, Gideon, Kane said.

"Hurry," Wyatt Fontenot hissed.

In truth only a few minutes had passed, but most of the town belonged to Cesar Lopez, and those who didn't were terrified. The last thing they needed was for someone to tip off the cartel czar with the news that a small army had invaded his territory. The pararescue team didn't want their hard-won covers blown, and Kane couldn't blame them. It was a dicey prospect living in the middle of a kill zone.

Gideon leapt from rooftop to rooftop until he could jump to the top of the truck. Javier and Kane made room for him. Malichai slapped the back of the truck and raced around to jerk open the passenger door to hop inside, and then the truck was racing away. Kane watched the buildings flash by. Most of the residents were huddled indoors, knowing from experience that it was dangerous taking to the streets after dark. Even the teenagers were secure for the night.

The safe house was located on the rise of a slope across from the Lopez estate. It wasn't above the Lopez property but rather just a few feet below with an expanse of undeveloped acreage between them. From the windows and balconies they had a good view of the luxurious dwelling. Joe was all business, recognizing the time crunch. He spread out the blueprint of the massive, sprawling home as well as maps and diagrams. A tall fence surrounded the residence complete with eight towers housing guards.

"He's serious about security and has massive firepower," Joe informed them as they crowded around the long table to study the prints.

"I assume there is a command room in the house?" Mack asked.

Joe went back to the first blueprint. "Right here. Everything is controlled from this room. This is your biggest obstacle. Before you move in that house, you'll have to take out the two guards in there. From there they control firepower; the guards and can see everything. Cameras are scattered all over the estate."

Mack turned to look at his team. "So we take that control room first. We shut it down, and everything else will go smoothly. Javier and Lucas, that's your job. You go in through the tunnel and get inside the house. You can't trip any of the sensors in the house. Get into that room and take them down without them seeing you if possible. I don't want anyone killed, Javier."

Javier grinned at him. "You're spoiling my fun, Top, but you want sleeping babes, you've got it."

Mack eyed him sternly another heartbeat or two before turning back to the blueprints spread out in front of him.

"He's got regular patrols along the fence," Joe continued with the briefing. "Dogs. Seven of them, very vicious. He keeps them on the hungry side, and they don't like strangers. When his grandchildren are in residence, they're locked up except at night, and then they roam the grounds without their handlers. The patrols stay safe inside the double fence. The dogs have been trained to leave them alone."

"You control the dogs, Kane," Mack ordered. "You'll have to do that even while you're taking out your assigned guard."

Urban fighting meant endless contact with canines. It was a must that one of their members be able to control animals, and Kane felt fortunate that he had the gift. He nodded. "No problem. I can control animals and multitask." He'd done it enough times to be certain.

"How many guards?" Mack asked.

"At any given time he's got twenty rotating patrols with one guard manning each tower."

"Ethan, you take the towers," Mack said. "You have eight of them to cover, so you'll have to be fast."

Ethan, who could go straight up the side of any building like a spider, nodded, confident he could take out the eight guards quickly without detection. There was a long distance between each tower, but they could run like the wind when needed. As long as Kane controlled the reaction of the dogs, he was certain he would have no problem.

"He keeps ten guards patrolling the fence line with ten off in the barracks," Malichai added. "The number is always the same."

"We'll each take a guard inside the fence as soon as Ethan gives us the signal that the tower guards are down," Mack said. "I'll send each of you to a position, and we'll go at the same time. No shot can be fired. I don't want any weapons used. Put them to sleep with the darts."

"There are ten guards," Malichai pointed out. "We can't go in with you. We can't take any chances of ruining our covers."

Mack nodded. "We understand, but we're down three."

"Two, Top; once I'm finished I'll be able to take a guard out," Ethan reminded.

Mack flashed a humorless grin. "Sorry, Ethan. I didn't mean to leave you out of the fun. Thought maybe you'd need a rest."

"Don't insult me, Top."

Mack laughed and then sobered, resuming their meticulous planning. "Rhianna, you and I both can use teleportation if necessary. Hurts like a son of a bitch, but we don't have any other choice. We'll both take a second guard. You up for it?"

Rhianna nodded curtly.

Rose raised an eyebrow. "Teleportation? Is that for real? I've heard of some extraordinary gifts, but none of the women I grew up with could do that. Levitate, maybe, but teleportation?"

Rhianna shrugged. "It's spotty. Sometimes it works, sometimes it doesn't, and it's always wrenching and pain . . ."

"Dangerous." Javier was looking at Mack.

Rose caught a glimpse of those flat, cold eyes and shivered. Javier had a way of looking without a single hint of emotion, as if he'd gone to another place and he was capable of anything. Kane dropped a hand on Rose's shoulder, spreading warmth through her.

"Everything we do is dangerous," Mack said evenly, ignoring the overt threat. "Teleportation is not exact, but it will get the job done. Rhee, if you prefer another method, we'll work it out."

Rhianna tilted her chin, not looking at Mack but keeping her large, liquid eyes on Javier. "I have no problem with it, Top."

Javier didn't so much as glance at her. "You'd better not have a problem with it."

Mack turned his attention back to blueprints, ignoring the little byplay. Rose looked around at the circle of faces. None of Javier's team seemed concerned. The same thing couldn't be said of the pararescue men. They appeared uneasy. She shrugged off the goose bumps and leaned forward to study the plans.

"His remaining soldiers are housed here in this building." Joe shoved the first blueprint aside and pulled a second one up. "Two stories and they have an escape tunnel that connects with the tunnel from the main house leading to this exit here." Again he pushed aside the blueprint to pull out a meticulously hand-drawn map.

"So those guards have to be disposed of as well before we enter the house."

Joe nodded. "The tunnels aren't guarded. We've gone all the way to both the main house as well as the barracks. The doors leading into the structures aren't locked or guarded either. Lopez has gotten a little sloppy with his security. He's used to everyone fearing his reprisal—even the government. The tunnel in the main house exits into the control room. The control room is bulletproof. When you go through that door into the room, you'll be vulnerable. Both men inside are armed to the teeth, and they won't be sleeping."

Javier shrugged as if men armed to the teeth were of no consequence.

"No killing, Javier, you have to get in and put them out without them seeing you or knowing anything is wrong," Mack said. "That's essential to the plan."

"No worries, Top," Javier said and winked at Lucas. Lucas grinned back at him.

They reminded Rose of two mischievous boys about to play a game they both knew was off-limits but they wanted to play anyhow.

"This is a hell of a time for you to choose to go after Lopez," Joe said. "This weekend was the big family reunion . . ."

Kane grinned at him. "We know. Thought this was a perfect time to pay them a visit."

Malichai shook his head. "You're all a little nuts. He has an enormous family. Right now, in the house, his two brothers and their spouses along with children and bodyguards are present. A grandfather. Cesar's two daughters, their husbands and children, and his son with his wife and daughter. All of them have personal bodyguards. They're all involved in the family business. Don't discount his wife, who looks sweet but would blow you away as fast as he would to keep her position."

"That's what we were counting on," Kane said. "A clean sweep."

"You were waiting for this." Joe made it a statement.

"We have ears in the cartel, and we knew the family reunion was taking place," Mack admitted.

Malichai swung around. "You have someone on the inside?"

"Working their way up, just for information. Nothing big." Mack dismissed it.

"We've tried for three years to penetrate the inner circle," Joe explained. "They're getting more violent. At first the wars were against each other with few civilians caught in the cross fire, but since *el presidente* declared war on them, Lopez has gone after the police, the military, and recently political figures. Decapitated bodies thrown in the streets, killings at the police stations, kidnappings, and now car bombs. It's war," he declared. "We could use a little help."

Mack frowned at him. "I thought your unit dealt with terrorist activity."

Joe didn't respond, and Mack grinned at him. "I see. Running weapons to our little bomb-happy friends."

"As I said, we could use help."

"One thing at a time. We get through this, and then we'll talk," Mack decreed.

Malichai and Joe exchanged a long, frustrated look. "If you make it through."

Mack grinned at him. "We'll make it. I have every confidence in my team."

Rose looked from the papers strewn out on the table to Rhianna and the men surrounding her. There were a lot of variables, and in her experience, the more variables, the less the chance of success, yet they all appeared confident. They were a tight team and relied heavily on one another. Whitney would have said that was their weakness. She thought he was wrong. She thought their reliance and belief in one another was their true strength.

"We'll do this in six phases," Mack said. "Phase one, Kane gains control of the dogs. Phase two, Javier and

Lucas take the control room. Phase three, Ethan takes out the guards in the towers. Phase four, we take out the ten guards in the fence. Phase five is the guards in the barracks. We have to complete each phase to gain the main house. Any fail, and we abort and go home. I want you all coming home."

His team gave him brief, humorless grins in acknowledgment of the order.

"Javier and Lucas," Mack said, glancing at his watch, "you're up. We do this by the numbers. Stay safe. I'll be royally pissed if anything happens to either of you. Wait until you get the go-ahead from Kane and then get in there."

Javier and Lucas grinned at each other. "Got the message, Top," Javier said with a small salute. He and Lucas left the room without further discussion.

"Kane, make your way to the fence and keep those dogs calm."

"On it, Top."

Kane's hand brushed across Rose's face briefly as he stepped away from her. She felt the impact all the way to her toes. For a moment their eyes met. Her heart shuddered in her chest. She loved him with everything in her. Every cell. Every breath. *Be safe.*

You too, sweetheart. You know I won't make it without you.

He jogged away from her. She felt Rhianna's gaze on her, but she didn't look up, needing to compose herself. It was important to set aside all emotion and just get the job done. She couldn't think about Kane going into a dangerous situation, or that if anything happened to either of them, Sebastian would be without a parent. At least she knew Jaimie would take care of him and the team would protect him. She shoved all that aside and took her place outside, waiting for the go-ahead from Kane.

Kane was impossible to detect in the dark. Like Javier and Lucas, he disappeared, a mere ghost in the night, sliding easily and silently from one shadow to the next. A dog rushed the fence, and a guard turned toward it and then looked outward. The dog calmed, whining a little and turning in a circle before lying down and panting. The guard frowned at the animal and resumed walking his route. He was in between two high chain-link fences, away from the dogs, but able to see inside the estate as well as outside. On the flip side, he had little or no cover for most of his route.

Kane inched closer to the fence, reaching out to all the dogs in the compound. There were two on the far side, a great distance from him, and much more difficult to control. When they began scenting strangers, it would set them off if he wasn't able to command them. It was essential to gain domination over them. He had to stretch his range to include them. Both dogs were resistant to the manipulation. He fought for supremacy, ruthless now, aware of time slipping away. They had to be in and out before dawn.

Phase one complete. Javier. Lucas. You have a go. Good luck.

Both men slipped into the tunnel and began moving fast, nearly running in an almost crouch. The tunnel was narrow with a low ceiling and no lighting. It was very dark, almost black, but both men had excellent night vision. There was no hesitation where the tunnel branched off, connecting to the barracks. They continued along the main passageway until they came to the entrance.

Using hand signals, they stood to either side of the door listening for movement inside. A chair creaked. There was a rustle of papers. Lucas pointed to his left. Javier nodded. He laid his hand gently on the door to keep it from making a sound as Lucas pushed the nozzle of a hose just under the door, not enough to go through all the way, but about halfway through the thickness of the door itself. It was enough to fill the room with gas. Both donned masks. The idea was to allow the gas into the room slowly so neither man realized there was a problem. The formula used was one of Jacob's inventions. They'd long ago dubbed him the "mad scientist" with his laboratory and chemicals. He provided all sorts of fun stuff for them to use when blowing things up or, like this, an odorless gas needed to put the two men to sleep. The gas couldn't be fast-acting but had to be gradual, so they yawned and grew sleepy, not suspicious. Gradual took precious time.

Javier counted off the minutes. Time slowed down to a crawl. This kind of combat took nerves of steel. He waited quietly. Lucas didn't so much as move a muscle. They were both used to living in the shadows of the night, and stillness was a big part of that. Something heavy hit the ground. There was a grunt, and then silence. Another minute, and the chair creaked and rolled, hitting the wall with a thump.

Javier gave the thumbs-up sign but waited another three minutes before cutting the gas to the room. They opened the door with caution. A body lay on the floor only a few feet from dozens of screens. An armory decorated one wall, every kind of weapon that might be needed to defend the Lopez stronghold. A second man was slumped down in his chair, wedged against the wall. They didn't touch either man as they leaned over the desk to peer into the screens.

Phase two complete. We're in control, Javier reported.

Mack looked at Ethan. *You're up. Those guards are on the lookout. They can't see you or the tower guards going down.*

I'm on it, Top.

Ethan crawled on his belly through the grass. This would be the longest wait. He had to scale all eight towers and one by one, take out the tower guard without detection. The towers were straight up and down with no real finger- or toeholds so even Gideon couldn't help, and he was the second most adept at climbing.

Ethan slipped out from cover and began the slow journey to the nearest tower. He crawled across the dirt and grass, out in the open, blending—as did all GhostWalkers—with the terrain. The tower was straight up, and he flexed his fingers, slipped out of his special shoes in order to use his toes as well. Top needed fast, so he'd use both. He had microscopic hairs on his hands and feet, and each of those individual hairs had smaller hairs, or setules, each with a triangular tip. Because of the hundreds of contact points, the setules allowed him to climb nearly any surface without fear of falling. He could support 170 times his own weight.

He went up fast and silent, climbing inside the tower and hovering above until the guard bent toward his coffee mug. He dropped down, inserting the dart quickly and retrieving it nearly in one motion. True to his word, he was fast and efficient, changing attack as needed, but eventually working his way from tower to tower without detection. The last guard was lifting a pair of binoculars to look at the tower across from him, aware that he couldn't see any of the other guards. He was reaching for his radio when Ethan darted him, hanging off the edge by only one hand.

Phase three complete.

Mack looked around at his team. "Let's do it. You all know where to go. Get in position and let me know. We can't mess this one up. We have to make this work."

His team flashed him looks that told him they were up for the job, and they melted away into the night, working their way up the slope to lie just outside the fence in the space their assigned guard patrolled. Rhianna and Mack positioned themselves between the two roving guards each of them was supposed to take down.

Mack waited patiently for those the greatest distance away to give the word they were in position. Phase four was extremely dangerous. One miss, and they might as well go home. Everything depended on complete secrecy, a simultaneous attack. To orchestrate such a feat was nearly impossible—unless you had the men and women in your unit he did. He had faith in them. He glanced to his left where Rhianna waited. Teleportation was difficult under the best of circumstances. She would have to shoot her dart and send herself to the next station, ready to fire again. There could be no warning raised.

In position, Top. One by one, his team reported in until he was certain they were ready.

Mack glanced at his watch. *On my mark. Three, two, one . . .*

He exploded into action, shooting his guard in the back of the neck, and instantly teleporting to the second station. The wrenching of his bones was incredible, almost like the g-force in a jet. There was a split second of disorientation, as if his body wasn't quite all there, but his finger on the trigger was steady, and he'd fired the shot before the first body hit the ground. Guards crumpled around the entire estate. He crawled forward to retrieve the dart, all the while fighting the blackness that threatened to engulf him and the bile rising in his throat, protesting the disorienting feat.

Rhianna's first dart went in smoothly. She immediately set herself for the twisting anguish of her body, as if it was being torn apart, as she teleported to the next section of fence. Struggling to breathe when the air had left her lungs in a rush, she shot the dart even while the soldier was still blurry. He went to his knees, his eyes wide, one hand coming up as if to slap at a stinging bee. She felt her own body crumple and she went down, the taste of blood in her mouth.

Breathe. You're holding your breath.

Rhianna cursed silently. It would have to be Javier in the control room, able to see her thrashing like a fish out of water on the ground, gasping for breath. She should have known he'd be watching her. She dug her hands into the dirt and propelled herself forward to retrieve the dart. She still had to go back to the first guard and remove that evidence as well. She tried to push herself to her feet, but there was no way to get air. She fell again.

Rose. Get to Rhianna, Javier commanded.

Rose retrieved the dart and glanced to her right. Rhianna was a force to be reckoned with. She couldn't imagine that the woman would need help with anything, but she sprinted across open ground without questioning the order. Rhianna had already retrieved the dart from the second guard. Blood trickled from the corner of her mouth. She pointed toward the fallen guard in the section of fence just down from her. Rose saw that the man had fallen in the center between the two fences.

She didn't hesitate, leaping straight up to grasp the chain-link just below the barbed wire. Twisting her body upside down, she pushed off with her hands. Clearing the barbed wire, she jumped in between the two fences, landing on her feet beside the body. Retrieving the dart, she reached down to take the man's ID, as all the rest of them had done. Souvenirs to give to Cesar Lopez. She sent word that she and Rhianna had both completed their tasks. When everyone had checked in, Mack gave the signal to proceed.

Phase four complete. We have a go.

Rose had to repeat the process she'd used entering the fences, leaping straight up and gripping the top of the fence just below the barbed wire, and once again turning upside down to thrust herself in the air like a rocket to clear the pointed barbs and land on the other side. One by one the other members of her team cleared the fence, descending on the barracks for the next phase. Rose waited for Rhianna. The other woman stumbled to her feet, swayed for a moment, and then her body went ramrod straight.

Sheer guts, Rose knew. Psychic talent could take a tremendous toll on all of them. Teleportation was a nasty business. In combat, a soldier dug deep and never—*ever*—let his team down. Rhianna was up and over the fence, wiping the blood from her mouth with her arm. She flashed a grin at Rose. The two of them sprinted for the barracks, joining the rest of the team already converging on the building.

Javier and Lucas in the control room were their eyes and ears, using the security cameras set up in the barracks against the guards.

Two up playing cards in the first room on your left. You've got three in the pool room straight ahead of you, the hallway dead-ends to the pool room. One in the kitchen just to the right of the pool room. Four in their bunks.

All of them had studied the layout of the barracks, but with Javier's voice whispering in their minds, the maps were even clearer. They had to enter unseen into each room and either gas or dart the occupants. If darts were used, they had to be retrieved. Each guard would have to give up his ID, in order for Cesar Lopez to return them. This was a psychological assault rather than a physical one. They planned on completely destroying Cesar Lopez. The plan was risky and called for precise timing, something that Lopez—that anyone—would believe impossible. They were ghosts entering his personal stronghold, slipping past every guard, into his very home. He would never feel safe again. Over time he would question himself, and he would lose confidence in those guarding his family. They would strike at his mind—and instill sheer terror in his heart. Cesar Lopez would understand that he was vulnerable—that his entire family was vulnerable.

Rose was particularly grateful that Kane didn't treat her any differently than he did his other team members. He didn't hover, didn't guard her as she feared he might. If anything, they all took extra care to stay close to Paul. He pulled his weight, handling each phase of the assignment as everyone else did, but she noticed the team members seemed to watch out for him a little more than anyone else. She found herself doing the same thing. She noticed Rhianna did as well. If anyone had asked her why, she wouldn't have been able to articulate why exactly, but he seemed out of place in the environment—far too sensitive for this kind of work.

Rose and Jacob released the gas into the room where four guards were sleeping in bunks. Kane, Gideon, and Rhianna took the three playing pool. Mack and Paul darted the two men playing cards, and Ethan did the same with the one in the kitchen.

Phase five complete, Mack reported. *Entering house for final phase.*

Javier studied each room. Most of the occupants were asleep. Bodyguards sat outside the rooms of Cesar and his son. There was no camera in Cesar's bedroom, but every other bedroom had surveillance. His two daughters were still visiting together in the conservatory while their husbands slept in the bedrooms. Two of the teens had gone to the kitchen and were getting snacks, while a third sat in Cesar's den and watched porn. A guard stood outside the conservatory, but no one had followed the teens. Javier relayed the information to his team.

Rose had one job. Kane shadowed her through the labyrinth of halls, up the stairs to the master bedroom. The other team members were each assigned to specific rooms and families. She had to believe they would do their jobs, one by one, putting every household member to sleep and collecting some kind of evidence to show Lopez. Kane held up his hand, and she halted at the top of the wide staircase. The house was dark but for a few dim lights. It enabled them to use the shadows, sliding from one to the other in complete silence.

The whispers in her head began coming fast. *Done. Done. Done.* Still she waited, breathing in and out, amazed at the capabilities and unity of such a large team working together. Whitney's idea had been two-man teams. He had stressed that the larger the number, the more room for error, and yet this unit of men—*her* unit—had penetrated the head of one of the largest and most dangerous cartels with an intricate and daring plan.

You have a go, Mack said.

At the soft order, Kane, lying prone on the floor just feet from the guard, shot the arrow into his neck. The guard tried to slap at what he thought was a stinging bug, but the needle had entered his bloodstream, and the fast-acting concoction had him slumping over, his semiautomatic slipping from his hands. Rose caught the gun and lowered it to his lap. Kane removed his ID. This was going to be the most dangerous moment. There were no cameras. They had to enter the bedroom without detection, put the wife to sleep, and have a talk with Cesar.

The door was bolted, and it took Kane a few precious minutes to pick the lock. They were on a time line. The guards had to wake up before sunrise, and all of them had to be gone and out of Mexico before that happened. Kane inched the door open and went in on the floor, rolling to the right of the bed—the woman's side—staying in the darker shadows. Rose came in after him, softly closing the door behind her. The bed creaked, and she froze, lying in plain sight if Cesar happened to look down.

She counted to sixty and then began a slow crawl to Cesar's side of the bed. He would be armed and wouldn't hesitate to shoot. He was sleeping facing her, and she smiled as she slipped her hand under the pillow to remove his gun. A knife lay on the bedside table, the hilt pointed toward him where he could easily grab it. She waited until Kane had darted the wife and slid into the darkness. She knew his knife was out and ready to throw.

She crouched down, presenting a smaller target, lifted Cesar's knife, and placed it ever-so-gently against the artery pumping in his neck. "I think you should wake up, now, Senor Lopez," she announced softly.

The eyes snapped open, instant awareness there.

"I wouldn't move if I were you, but take a good look at my face. I want you to remember me, to know who I am."

No one wanted Cesar Lopez to remember them. The eyes burned with arrogance, with fury, with the promise of reprisal. Rose smiled at him. "I think, before you go all macho on me, you might consider that you haven't looked at the condition of your wife."

His gaze flicked toward his wife of forty years. He couldn't turn his head, but he could see the outline of her beside him.

"She's sleeping soundly. I want you to really think about this situation you've found yourself in, Senor Lopez, because if you don't, some very bad things are going to happen to you and every single person you love."

The door opened, and dark shadows flitted in and out of the room, dropping IDs on the bed between his legs. The IDs raining down on him were from his guards, his son, his daughters, their spouses, and eventually something taken from each child supposedly safe in his home.

Rose leaned in close. "As you can see, we could have killed every man, woman, and child on your estate and in this house. *Everyone.* You don't know us, Lopez, but we know you, and we know where all of them live. No one else knows we're here but you. They'll all believe they fell asleep. You can tell them whatever you want when you give them back their IDs and whatever else we've confiscated from them as proof that we could have killed them. Call off the contract on me. Walk away and pretend I don't exist. You and I won't have any more trouble. If you don't, my friends and I will be back, and believe me when I tell you, you don't want any part of us. Not now. Not ever."

She allowed the knife to slide against his skin. His breath caught in his throat and he stiffened, fear creeping into his eyes, his body turning to a shuddering mass of jelly. He could see the shadows of men, moving in his room, but he could never identify them. They'd invaded his inner sanctuary, and they'd proven they could kill everyone. He swallowed hard and nodded his head.

"Don't disappoint me, Lopez. Don't ever get stupid. Even if your people found and killed me, my people would take everything and everyone you care about. And then they'll kill you. They're ghosts. You'll never see them coming, and then it will be too late. Do we have an understanding?" She kept her voice very even, very soft. Almost gentle.

His eyes were nearly all white now, his terror mounting. His body had broken out in a sweat. All the arrogance had faded as he faced his own mortality. There was no refuting anything she said. The proof was strewn all over his bed.

He nodded again, this time vigorously enough to have the knife cutting into his skin had Rose not been cautious.

"You realize we'll have to put you to sleep like the others," she said, almost as if she was talking to a child. "Just in case you try to convince yourself that you were having a nightmare, I'm cutting your dose in half. You'll wake up first and see all the proof lying on your bed. You can walk around your house and see the guards, your children, and your grandchildren sleeping peacefully. And you can thank me, Lopez. I'll only have compassion for them this one time. Look into my eyes so you know I'm telling you the truth. Anything—*anything* happens to me, and they're all dead."

He believed her; she could see it on his face. She pressed the needle into his neck and watched him watching her as the drug took him.

Phase six complete. Let's go home, she informed Mack.

CHAPTER 20

⟋

The scent of flowers permeated the air. Rose inhaled deeply and turned her face up to Kane's. His piercing gaze met hers, and her heart nearly stopped and then began to pound. Would it always be like this? Such an extraordinary, overwhelming love that shook her every time she looked at him?

"Do all brides feel like this on their wedding day?" she murmured, waiting for him to bend his head to hers. She couldn't look at him without wanting to be kissed, and Kane always knew what she needed—or wanted. Even the boots she'd left behind in the store were now safely in her closet—a gift from him. He seemed to like giving her gifts. No one had ever done that before, and sometimes she didn't quite know what to say or do when he presented her with another package or left something on their bed.

He didn't disappoint her, his arm sliding around her waist, drawing her close to him, so she could take him deep into her lungs before his mouth touched hers. The familiar butterflies fluttered in her stomach. She would always—

always—love kissing him. The world dropped away in spite of the noise of so many voices, so many conversations swirling around them. Three GhostWalker teams had come to help celebrate their day and to catch up with one another.

Kane had given this to her—this incredible wedding and a memory she never considered she would ever have. It wasn't the white wedding dress right out of the magazine that Jaimie and Rhianna had found for her or the tuxedo on Kane that made him look like her very own handsome prince that meant so much. It was these people—*her* people—surrounding them, celebrating with them. They'd come from all over, filling the warehouse, the one Gideon and Paul and been renovating.

The warehouse had been transformed into a sparkling world filled with elegant chandeliers and ice sculptures, dazzling things seen only between the pages of a book but never experienced. The men were incredibly handsome, just like in the fairy tales, while the women, dressed in beautiful gowns, were breathtaking.

Kane pulled her into his arms as the music slowed into a sweet, dreamy rhythm so that she rested her cheek against his chest and let herself melt into him. They danced past the playpens where Jack and Briony Norton had placed their twin sons. The two boys, Jeremiah Ken and Noah Jack, followed the action with interested eyes, occasionally turning their heads toward each other as if in silent communication.

That was the strange thing, Rose decided, about the babies, the way they seemed so completely intent with each other, as if they were silently communicating. Daniel Ryland Miller, Ryland and Lily's son, was there as well, a strong boy with his mother's eyes and his father's commanding features. Sebastian lay on his stomach watching the other babies soberly, and they all seemed to be very interested in one another.

"You don't think, at their age, Kane, that the babies could already be telepathic and communicating with one another, do you?" Rose murmured speculatively against his chest.

At once, all four boys turned their heads toward her, as if they'd heard her, their eyes bright and interested. Her breath caught in her throat. "Kane, I think they can hear and understand me."

He turned his head to study the expressions on each of the babies' faces. Each of the boys was watching them intently. There was no doubt that they looked more intelligent than blank, but he didn't know yet the developmental process with babies. He glanced at the mothers of each of the boys. Briony was whispering to her husband, Jack Norton, as Kane swept Rose past them. Both parents turned to look with that same speculation they were feeling at their twins and then at the other two boys. Ken and Mari Norton immediately followed their lead when they'd been cuddling together in a corner, which meant Jack or Briony had alerted them to the difference in the babies.

"It stands to reason that all of them would be strong telepaths, Rose," Kane said gently, turning her hand against his heart.

His steps directed her easily around the dance floor, so that she felt as if she was floating. She felt like she could do anything when she was with him. The intricate steps were easy with his strong direction.

"Jack and Ken, as well as Ryland and I, are all natural telepaths. Briony and Mari probably are as well. Lily is. And you have talent as well."

"Not strong," she denied. "I can tap into your talent."

"Nevertheless, it follows that our children are going to be very adept and strong in that area. Don't be afraid for them, Rose. Everyone in this room will stand for those children. We'll love them and guide them and provide everything they need to grow strong and healthy. They'll know they're loved. If anything, the very child Whitney was looking to create might be his downfall. They're bound to inherit strong loyalty genes, to us and to one another.

The way our teams work will only reinforce that. All of us scored high in the protection area, so my guess is, so will they. This is going to work, Rose."

Rose snuggled closer, nuzzling his throat, her heart contracting. The room was filled with so many GhostWalkers, it made her feel as if she wasn't so different from normal. Her child would grow up with them, with all these men and woman who would understand if he—and the other children born—were strong telepaths.

"I'm so happy," she murmured as they danced past Ryland and Lily.

Lily caught her whispered confession, and she nodded her head, flashing a beaming smile.

"You look so incredibly beautiful, Rose," Kane said, pulling her closer. "I'll never forget the way you looked walking toward me. I never thought that I'd have a woman like you in my life. It's all there etched in my brain. And now, the way the light pours over your hair, the way all that silk shines, so black it's nearly blue. The world disappears when I'm holding you." He brushed a kiss over the top of her head.

"You make me feel like a princess, Kane," she admitted. "In my wildest dreams, I could never have imagined this moment."

He stopped her in the shadows and found her mouth almost blindly, pouring his love into her. A tremor ran through her body. Love was such an overwhelming emotion. She could barely think straight when she was kissing Kane, so she gave it up, wrapping her arms around his neck and dragging him closer, giving herself to him.

He'd given her everything she could possibly want for her wedding day. The room was transformed into an amazing glittering world of laughter and camaraderie. There was definitely magic permeating the air, surrounding her. Each time he kissed her or smiled at her, her heart fluttered and her body reacted. Time slowed while they talked to the members of the various GhostWalker teams, as she renewed her acquaintances with the women she'd shared the first few years of her childhood with.

Tears of happiness and of memories turned to laughter, and all the while, Kane was there. His arm steadied her. His smile made her feel as if her entire world was right. His strength steadied her. She looked up at his face, so familiar now. So loved. Every line. Every expression. Those vivid green eyes. She could look at him forever and never tire of it.

"Javier said word filtered down that Lopez was canceling the contract on you, that it was a mistake, but we're still alert for any news," Kane informed her.

"That's what Jaimie said. No chatter on me, which is a good thing."

The good thing was really standing in front of her. How different her life was now. Why had she ever thought she might be exchanging one prison for another? She reached for him, suddenly aching inside. His arms tightened, and once more, they were circling the dance floor, only this time, the heat of his body encompassed her until she could hear his heart hammering beneath her ear. She felt his hands glide down her back to her hips, pulling her closer so that his heavy erection ground into her telling need.

It didn't take much contact between them to ignite a fire. He bent his head, nuzzling her neck and then teasing with small licks that turned almost abruptly into desperate nips. Each stinging bite sent an electrical current rushing through her veins. Her womb contracted as she shivered beneath the assault of his tongue and teeth. Hidden in the shadows, she suddenly wished they were alone. She needed her husband desperately.

The fairy-tale world dropped away. The music. The dancing. The murmur of conversations. All the good-looking men and women who had come from great distances to celebrate with them. Everything disappeared until she was alone with Kane—her Kane. Solid. Real. A man—a soldier—the one person in the world she wanted to

spend the rest of her life with. The man who set her blood
on fire and could bring her more pleasure than anything she
could have imagined.

"Do you think we could slip away? I could change my
clothes," she suggested.

His eyes blazed down at her, going dark. Going hungry.
So Kane. For an answer, he practically dragged her over to
Jaimie. "Rose is going to change," he informed her. "Can
you keep an eye on Sebastian until we get back?"

Mack snorted. "Change? You haven't even cut the cake."

"We cut the cake when you and Jaimie had a sudden
need to visit the stairwell," Kane retorted.

Rose and Jaimie burst out laughing. Mack shrugged.
"Well then, go change."

Kane didn't waste time, his gaze hot as he caught Rose's
wrist and nearly ran with her in a most undignified manner
for the princess and prince, exiting their own wedding.

They barely made it inside the doorway of their home
before Kane's mouth took hers, his body pressing hers
against the wall. He devoured her, a starving man bent on
survival, his tongue stroking, demanding, caressing until
she was breathless and so needy the dress she was wearing
hurt her skin.

"Get it off," she pleaded. "Take it off me."

Kane's hands were sure on the small pearl buttons in
spite of his labored breathing. He would have been a lot
faster, but Rose couldn't help that she kept reaching behind
her to stroke over the heavy bulge in his very elegant tuxedo trousers. She was nearly sobbing with need when he
dropped the dress to the floor and she stepped out of it. She
wore only a lace bra with low-cut cups, so that her nipples
were readily available. A lace thong and garters and high
heels had him groaning, falling to his knees, and stripping
her panties away.

She cried out, her hands going to his shoulders to steady
herself as he pulled her thighs apart and plunged his tongue
deep. Her entire body shuddered, went up in flames, and

she nearly orgasmed right there. He ate her like candy, his desperate, greedy sounds only arousing her more. She was nearly sobbing, nails digging into him, trying to get through the immaculate shirt to his skin below.

The sounds he was making, hot, needy, groaning with pleasure as he savored her feminine cream, all that spicy honey spilling into his mouth, had her knees going weak. She had to clutch him tightly as his tongue and teeth teased her clit and his fingers thrust inside her, stretching, invading, *demanding*. She couldn't stop thrusting against his mouth, holding his head to her spread thighs, the white lace silk sliding over his face as he licked and stroked until her stomach muscles bunched and her nipples hardened into impossible peaks.

"Kane, please." She felt desperate, so hungry for his body she would have done anything.

He bit down gently on her most sensitive bud, thrusting deep with his fingers, his tongue circling, and she felt herself flying apart, rocketing. She screamed, and she couldn't remember ever doing such a thing, but she couldn't stop the sound. His arms slipped up her hips, around her waist, holding her to keep her from falling, lowering her to the unyielding floor.

He rose above her, stripping fast, nearly ripping the buttons off his shirt, not nearly as gentle with himself as he'd been with her, answering her long-ago worry that a husband might not find his wife who had recently given birth wildly attractive.

Kane managed to rip off his clothes in record time, feeling almost desperate to be inside her. He felt like he'd waited a lifetime for this moment—much like he did every single time he took her, which was as often as he could. He dragged her very sexy, silk-clad legs around him, lifting them over his arms so that he could use leverage, and drove deep into her pulsing center.

The feeling was exquisite. Hot, living silk grasping him, clasping tightly, stroking and caressing him. Each time he entered her, he was shocked at the need building so fast in him. He wanted hours inside that tight haven. Dark lust crossed his face, made his fingers flex once right before he began plunging into her over and over, hard and fast, a desperate man. Her breathy cries incited him, her dazed, sexy look, the spill of her breasts over the demi-cups excited him all the more. No one was more sexy to him—no one ever would be.

Sensations tore through him with each hard stroke. He tried to keep her still, pinning her hips, feeling her muscles tighten around him, sending streaks of fire rushing from his groin throughout his body. He groaned, trying to tell her, trying to stop her. He needed more time with her. Always more time. Her keening cries only fed his arousal, sending him careening out of control.

Rose dug her nails into Kane's back. His cock felt like steel driving through her scalding velvet folds. She could barely catch her breath, barely hang on as the room around her spun away and there was only his body pounding into hers, sending fire racing through her, into her veins, into her belly, streaking down her legs so that she locked her ankles, high heels and all, behind his back, rocking with him, thrusting up to meet each surge.

She had no warning, no tightening of her body, only the sudden ripping through of a wild rogue wave, high and long, taking her tumbling over the edge of a cliff, her body spiraling out of control. She couldn't scream, couldn't find breath, could only hang on while she shattered beneath him.

Kane felt her body clamp down like a vise on his, milking and grasping, the friction sending him plummeting, free-falling, while his body burned and his heart raced. She consumed him. Burned him clean. Took him somewhere he couldn't reach on his own or with any other woman. He collapsed over the top of her. Rose. His miracle.

"I love you, sweetheart," he whispered. An admission. A confession. The raw truth.

She put her arms around him, holding him to her. "I love you more than you could possibly know."

He smiled, satisfied, not moving, his body locked with hers, his weight holding her there on the floor, his arms keeping her spread open, their hearts pounding in rhythm. When he managed to bring his ragged breathing under some semblance of control, he pushed her bra away from her breasts, bending his head to suckle there. He teased her nipple, laving and drawing that hard peak into the hot depths of his mouth. She gasped, her body writhing under his assault, her sheath clamping down hard as more ripples spread through her.

He lifted his head and grinned at her. "We don't really have to go back to the party, do we? Because I'd love to just feast on your body all night."

Rose stared up at his face with stars in her eyes. Her arms went around his neck, drawing his head back down to her flushed breasts. "Feast away, Kane. I'll never have enough of you, and after all, this is our night."

One thing about Kane—he never did anything by halves.

Keep reading for a special preview of
the next book in the Leopard People series
by Christine Feehan

Savage Nature

Available in May 2011

The sun dropped from the sky, a molten, fiery ball, pouring red and orange flames into the darkened waters of the Mississippi River. The air was heavy, nearly oppressive with humidity, just the way he liked it. Drake Donovan stepped from the barge with a casual grace, lifted a hand to the men on board and stopped for a moment, there on the wooden walkway, to admire the rolling river. With night falling, shadows delved sweetly into the ripples, giving the water a mysterious, beckoning feel. The pull of the river's secret places was strong.

Groves of trees, tupelo and cypress, graced the water's edge enticingly. He had seen many inlets and isles as they approached the banks. Great blue herons walked in the shallower waters of the bayous, canals, and marshlands, graceful figures drawing one's eye to the beauty of the surroundings.

He listened to the night sounds creeping in as he watched the first of the bats, dipping and wheeling in the air overhead, catching the insects drawn to the massive body of water. Not too far from the river's edge, a small fox darted toward a mouse scurrying into the leaves. An owl sat very still in the dusk, waiting for the sun to sink into the river, leaving the night to blanket the swamps and bayous.

The wildness in him reacted, rising with a great leap, demanding freedom. It had been so long. Too long. His thick five-o'clock shadow, composed of tangible hairs embedded deep into the tissue, supplied nerve endings with tactile information. Always, that guidance system would plug him into the air currents and enable him to read objects. And this time, unexpectedly, when he gathered information, his cat reacted aggressively, raking at him, snarling with his demands.

Drake lifted his nose to the airways, drawing the night deep into his lungs, drawing in—*her*. His heart skipped a beat and then began to pound. Every nerve ending in his body came to life. Need punched low and mean, a wicked, unexpected blow that staggered him. Her scent was alluring, captivating, unleashing a deep, primal command impossible to ignore.

The animal in him leapt hard, challenging the man. Fur rose beneath his skin in a wave of demand, leaving behind a terrible itch. His jaw ached and he felt the slide of canines pushing into his mouth. He tried to breathe, tried to calm the lethal beast pushing so close to the surface. His muscles rippled, contorting before he could get himself under control. He'd experienced his cat's edgy need before, but not like this, not this dangerous, the temperamental leopard pushing so close he couldn't distinguish between man and beast.

His mind became a haze of red, primal instincts drowning out civilized man. Drake had always had enormous strength, holding back his animal side with more discipline than most of his kind, but this time the struggle for supremacy was more like mortal combat. Bones ached and his left leg pulsed with wrenching pain. Strangely it was the pain that allowed him to hold on. He was out in the open, a danger to any male—human or leopard—near him. He kept his face in the shadows and simply breathed in and out, relying on the simple mechanics of an automatic reflex to keep the wild animal caged.

"Just for now," he whispered—a promise he intended to keep no matter the cost. His leopard had been caged long enough. "Wait a little longer."

The beast subsided, snarling his reluctant obedience, more, Drake was certain, because the alluring scent had drifted away on the night breeze than because the man was stronger. He wanted to follow that scent—he needed to follow it, but it was as elusive as the females of his kind always were. The sexy fragrance was gone and he was left with a clawing need and an aching groin as the scent gave way to the normal smells of the river's edge.

"Mr. Donovan? Drake Donovan?"

He closed his eyes briefly, savoring the melodic sound of a woman's tone. She had the sultry lilt of Cajun country in her voice. He turned his head slowly, not believing any woman could match that voice. He didn't know what he expected, but he sure as hell hadn't expected his reaction to her. That same low, mean, wicked punch to his groin, the same assault on his raw senses he'd experienced earlier repeated itself even harder.

She stood several feet from him but he was instantly aware of everything about her. His senses were heightened by his leopard, he had no doubt about that, but this time his reaction was all man. She wore faded and ripped blue jeans and a short tee that clung to her curvy form lovingly. Her face was young, but her eyes were old. Her hair was thick, a dark blond, but heavily streaked with silver, gold, and platinum strands. Beautiful dark chocolate eyes spiced with golden flecks seemed at odds with the sun-kissed hair that was worn in a ragged, jagged cut that would never have suited anyone else, but somehow only enhanced her appearance.

Drake could barely breathe, knew he was staring, but

couldn't stop himself. She stood there, just looking at him with a curious expression on her face, waiting for an answer. Her lashes were long, and she had a tiny scar on her chin and melting dimples. Her mouth was a thing of fantasy, full lips like a fascinating bow, her teeth small and white, although her canines were sharper than normal. He had a strange urge to drag her into his arms and taste her.

She regarded him with a mixture of reticence and wariness. "I'm Saria Boudreaux, your guide. You are Drake Donovan aren't you?" She tilted her head to one side, studying him with concern. "If you don' feel good from the trip, it's all right. We can wait before we get you back on the water. Maybe get you somethin' to eat?"

Her accent curled in his stomach. He could feel the reaction pulse through his groin. "I'm fine, Miss Boudreaux. I'll be staying at the Dubois Inn, as you recommended. You said it was close to the canals and marshes I'll be visiting?" He'd made certain the bed-and-breakfast she'd recommended was rarely visited and near the bayou, where there were groves of trees, marsh, and swamp. He'd rented the entire B&B on the chance he'd need his team, as well as to ensure his privacy.

She nodded. "Call me Saria. It will be easier since we'll be spendin' a week together. Is that your bag?" She indicated his small war bag with a nod of her head.

He'd be damned if she carried it for him. He reached down and lifted it himself, sending up a silent prayer that his very full groin would allow him to walk. "Just Drake then. Thanks for meeting me so late." He *never* had such a reaction to a woman. It had to be the fierce need of his cat.

She shrugged and turned away from him, walking down the wooden sidewalk toward the grove of cypress trees dipping long, shimmery beards of moss into the water. She made no sound as she walked, a graceful, silent sway of her hips so enticing, his breath caught in his throat. He was not a man given to shocking, erotic images at the sight of a woman walking, but every cell in his body went on alert and he had the mad desire to leap on her, pin her under him, and devour her. He shook his head to try to clear the madness from his brain.

It was his leopard; that was the only sane answer. He'd been injured too long ago and his cat had been unable to emerge. Recently the man he chose to work for—well, okay, Drake had to admit it, his *friend*—Jake Bannaconni, had arranged an operation for him, grafting the bones of his kind to his bad leg in the hopes that he could someday shift. He wasn't quite healed, and when he was tired he still occasionally walked with a limp, but his cat was growing more restless as each day passed, eager to test out the new material in his leg.

More and more the leopard fought to surface. He had purposely asked his guide to find a bed-and-breakfast in a remote area with the idea that he might try to allow the animal side of him freedom—it was that or go insane. He pushed down the voice of his surgeon to take it slow. He'd taken it so damn slow he really was losing his mind and his poor, unknowing guide was in danger of being savaged.

He was a man who automatically noticed everything, and there was no way not to watch Saria walk. He felt so damned old and she looked fresh and innocent and so far out of his league it wasn't funny. But still, she wasn't wearing a wedding ring. He breathed normally now, years of discipline taking over. The wildness receded even more. The small breeze caressed the wispy ends of her sun-kissed hair and his heart stuttered.

Saria turned her head and looked at him over her shoulder, a slight frown on her face, her eyes assessing him. She slowed her pace. "Are you all right?"

He gave her a direct stare, the kind that usually scared the hell out of people. "Why wouldn't I be?" He was gruffer than he intended, but she looked so damn young and innocent, and he wasn't having a great deal of success controlling the images of her naked body, writhing under his—and that made him feel like a lecherous old man.

"You're limpin'."

There it was again, that little accent that seeped into his skin and made his cock jerk hard. And he wasn't limping. No way. He kept his stare steady, regarding her without expression. "I don't limp." He walked with ease now, fluid and strong and damn it all, he'd gone from a lecherous old man to a decrepit one in her eyes. Faced with the sexiest woman alive, he had obviously forgotten suave and power.

Her eyebrow raised slightly. A dimple melted into that full, tempting mouth. She gave him a small, half-smile. "I'm glad we got that straight because the dock is a distance away. We can cut through town and a sort of Christmas tree forest, and then maneuver the edge of a cypress grove. That will save a few steps."

He gave her a faint grin, not admitting a thing. "The quicker we get started, the better."

The setting sun dropped a fiery shower of light just before it sank fully into the river, bathing her in red and orange flames. The silken fall of her hair beckoned him, impossible to resist. He reached out and tucked a stray strand behind her ear, his heart pounding. He felt a rush of heat pour through his bloodstream. Blood roared in his ears, thundered in his head.

She was potent, no doubt about it. She went completely still when he touched her, but she didn't bat his hand away, as she had every right to do. Her eyes went liquid and she blinked, locking her gaze with his. She looked untamed, unattainable, and everything male in him responded to that challenge. He felt the ripple of response run through his heavily roped muscles, felt the strength and power of his body. *She* made him wholly aware of his power.

He had the ability to leap huge distances with absolute agility. He could land gracefully in either form—cat or man. He could slink like fluid water over the ground, so silent, not even the leaves dared move. Like his cat, the sheer power of his muscles enabled him to move fast to control prey. Those same muscles allowed him the stealth of freeze-frame motion, holding completely still until he disappeared into his surroundings.

He was power and in that moment, he knew she was wholly aware of it as well. The gold flecks in her eyes grew until they ringed the darker chocolate. She didn't look away. Didn't blink. His body went into overdrive, hard and full and suddenly aggressive. The woman triggered the same exact reaction in the man as the elusive female of his kind had done to his leopard. He would have to revise his opinion of her. Saria Boudreaux was more than the young woman he'd first thought her—much more—and he intended to uncover every secret she had.

Saria shivered as she stared into Drake Donovan's unusual eyes. Piercing. His steady, direct stare was disturbing. She had the feeling he could see right through her, into her deepest thoughts. She blushed at the idea, thankful darkness was falling fast. Drake Donovan was an unusual man. He had stood so still that, although outlined by the river, she had barely managed to see him—and she had unusually good night vision. He seemed to have a trick of disappearing into the background around him.

It didn't make sense that he could fade into his surroundings so easily. He was a formidable if not striking man. His shoulders were wide, his chest thick and muscular. He had the strongest, most impressive arms of any man she'd met. Ropes of muscle rippled enticingly every time he took a step. He had a wealth of thick blond hair and a face that was carved in strong lines. The moment she laid eyes on him, her heart beat too fast and a million butterflies took wing in her stomach. Even now she felt jittery.

She was used to being around men—even being alone with them. She worked the bar, sometimes alone, but she'd never felt so aware of herself as a woman. She could barely breathe. The heat of the evening seemed just a little worse. She could feel sweat trickling down the valley between her breasts and it was a struggle to keep her breathing even. Every breath she took just brought his wild, unusual scent deeper into her body. She had never been so utterly, acutely aware of a man in her life.

He was so silent when he walked, she couldn't stop herself from glancing over her shoulder every now and then to reassure herself that he was following her. He was the type of man she normally would avoid at all costs. She had seen other women around her succumb to physical attraction, or even genuine love, and all had ended the same way: doormats for demanding, needy husbands. That was *so* not going to be her.

She was not even close to his league and she wasn't stupid enough to pretend she was. He had a hard-won sophistication about him, and he carried authority as easily as he breathed. Physical attraction died fairly quickly when everyday life set in and then where would she be? Donovan was the kind of man who ruled everything and everyone in his domain with an iron hand.

He wore his blue jeans low on his hips and his thighs were twin, strong columns. She couldn't help darting a couple of furtive glances at the impressive package in the front. Drake Donovan was perfect as eye candy, but she needed to pull herself together fast. He would eat a woman alive.

She searched a little desperately for something to say to him, feeling awkward. "Have you been here before?" She was a professional guide, for heaven's sake, yet she couldn't even make small talk.

"No."

She swore under her breath. A week with him. An entire week. The money was good, but she couldn't control her reaction to him and it was very clear he didn't want to even engage in polite conversation. She bit down hard on her lip and picked up the pace. Another quick glance over her shoulder told her he'd kept up with her easily.

"You seem a little young to be a guide in the swamps," Drake said.

Saria bit back her first retort. Great. Her first real hottie and he thought she was young. She kept her back to him, trying not to stiffen her shoulders. Who cared what he thought? Just because he was the hottest guy on the planet didn't mean a thing. She didn't want anything to do with him, but he could at least see her as a woman, not some little kid.

"I grew up here. If you aren't familiar with the swamp it can be very dangerous." She couldn't help the little bite to her voice. "There aren't any landmarks out there. If you prefer another guide, there are others available. You won't have any trouble gettin' anyone with the kind of money you're payin'." Like she could afford the loss of income. Pride was a terrible thing, she reminded herself, but she wasn't going to beg for the job.

"When we asked for someone who knew the swamp, plants, and wildlife throughout this area, you came highly recommended by several people," Drake said. "And you did say it was possible we could extend the time if needed."

She couldn't help risking another small glimpse of him. *Mon dieu*, he was beautiful. She could spend a lot of time with him—he was that easy on the eyes. And at least he was talking to her now. "Yes, if you let me know a few days in advance, I can arrange it." Maybe not. Every time she looked at him she lost her mind. There was something compelling about his eyes, those deep gold green eyes framed with impossibly long lashes. He had a five-o'clock shadow that made him look even more rugged.

She made her way through the small town, avoiding getting too near the church, afraid of running into the priest. She hadn't been back to confession since she'd given him the letter and now she didn't want to chance contact. The long streaks on her back and the bite mark on her shoulder were healing a bit, but left enough of an ache that they, along with the nightmares, convinced her to mind her own business. She didn't want Father Gallagher asking her any questions. She'd managed to avoid her brothers, and now, by taking this job, she'd be out in the swamp for at least another week.

"You married?" Drake's voice was very casual.

Her heart jumped. "No."

"I didn't think so. No man in his right mind would let someone like you take strangers out alone into the swamp."

She touched the knife at her belt. "I can take care of myself." *Why had he asked?* She'd seen the way his gaze drifted over her, taking in *everything*. He couldn't have failed to note her lack of a wedding ring. Still, maybe some women didn't wear their ring. She let her breath out. Maybe under that expressionless face he was a little more interested in her than he let on. "Are you?" She couldn't imagine it. She couldn't imagine any woman holding his interest for long.

Silence stretched between them until she stopped again and looked at him. He gave her a small smile that didn't quite reach his eyes. "I doubt I could find a woman who would put up with me."

Her eyebrows shot up. "Are you that difficult?"

"I imagine I might be, yes," he admitted. His voice dropped an octave—became soft, seductive, an intimacy she was totally unfamiliar with. "You'll be living with me for the next week. You'll have to tell me."

Her mouth went dry. Her heart jumped and damp heat collected. His gaze locked with hers and she immediately experienced the sensation of falling into him. It was bizarre, but she couldn't look away, as if he'd managed to take her captive in some primitive manner. His stare was both charismatic and alarming. Her heart began drumming a very real warning. Everything feminine in her responded to him, yet at the same time urged her to run.

She was lost in his gaze, so she witnessed the abrupt change. The green with golden flecks suddenly went antique gold. The round pupils dilated three times wider. He moved, or did he? She didn't think she'd blinked, but his body was suddenly close to her, almost protective, shielding her from something he'd seen without so much as turning his head. Icy fingers crept down her spine. Her warning radar ex-

ploded, and this time the threat wasn't emanating from the
man in front of her. Maybe it never had been and his predatory magnetism had confused her. Whatever the reasons, she
hadn't recognized her alarms for what they were.

"A man is back in the shadows just at the entrance to the
trees. He's watching you." His voice was pitched very low,
nearly inaudible. Had she not had such good hearing, she
would have missed the whisper. "Do you know him? Look
over my left shoulder." He took another step closer, bending his head toward hers as if he might kiss her.

Her breath caught in her throat. Everything in her stilled.
She placed the palm of her hand on his chest, right over his
soundly beating heart, but whether to push him away or to
steady herself as she raised her head, she wasn't certain.

She flicked a quick glance to the tree line and her throat
nearly closed. Red eyes glowed back at her. Something was
there all right—*someone*. She couldn't tell who it was, only
that human eyes didn't reflect back light in that manner.

"We don' need to cut through the grove to get to the
dock. This road curves around and then goes back toward
the canals. It's a little longer but . . ."

"I think a stroll through the grove is just the thing,"
Drake interrupted.

She shook her head. "I don' know if you've been readin'
about the ghost cats people think they've been spottin' in
the swamps, but sometimes those things are more real than
we want them to be. I'd just feel safer if we stayed in town."

"Look at me." He kept his voice low, and she swore it
was almost a purr it was so soft and alluring, but it was
definitely an order.

Beneath her skin, she felt an itch. If she'd been a cat she
would have sworn he'd ruffled her fur the wrong way, but
before she could stop herself, her gaze jumped to his. Instantly she was caught by that commanding, focused stare.
His eyes were gorgeous, frightening and sexy all at once.

"You're safe with me."

His tone was just too intimate, too certain—so certain

that when she stared into his eyes, in spite of her brain telling her to be logical, she believed him. And how dumb was that when she knew there was a leopard stalking and killing people? Drake Donovan might be a powerful man in his world, and clearly everything about him shouted he could handle himself—but not with a killing machine like a shifter. Cunning and intelligent, the shifter used both man and beast to bring down prey.

She swallowed hard, unable to escape those piercing eyes. He'd locked in on her and there was no fleeing. It occurred to her suddenly that he was telling her something altogether different than she'd imagined. She frowned, but he was already turning her very gently but firmly back in the direction of the grove. Reluctantly, she took a few steps, confused by Drake, confused by her reaction to him.

She scowled. Drake Donovan threw her off balance. She glanced deeper into the shadows. Nothing moved. No eyes stared back. Whoever had been there had changed position. Still, she was uneasy and that wasn't a good sign. She dropped her hand very casually to the knife at her waist, unsnapping the safety flap with one thumb.

"We're fine," Drake said softly. "A man at ten o'clock and two more trailing after us."

Her scowl deepened. *She* was the guide. It was up to her to protect him in the swamp. This was *her* home turf and she should have spotted the others long before Drake became aware of them. He was messing up her warning system. She had the uncomfortable feeling he was setting off the alarms and she couldn't see beyond him. So why would she feel safe with him?

She flicked her gaze to the position he'd given her. Walking along the path merging with theirs was Amo Jeanmard, a man she'd known for some years. She glanced behind her and identified the Lanoux brothers, Robert and Dion. Twins, one was rarely seen without the other. They'd gone to school with Mahieu, but often dropped by the bar late at night to say hello. She liked both of them. She suspected

Robert flirted with her for fun, but that Dion was quite serious. From the look on his face, he wasn't happy to see her
with Drake.

She came from a society of people who were friendly
but very private. The men had long ago tried to point out
to her father that she was a wild child, but when he hadn't
responded, they all seemed to think they needed to keep an
eye on her, from a distance of course.

"They're neighbors," she announced, relaxing a little.
If a killer lurked in the grove, he wouldn't show himself
with so many grouped together. Once she got her charge
settled into the bed-and-breakfast, she'd go back to the
house and add to her supply of weapons. She wasn't going
to endanger anyone, but she had to make a living. Donovan was paying too much money and she needed it. She
refused to be dependent on her brothers for income. That
would give them some semblance of control over her and,
at this late date, now that she was grown, she wasn't about
to let them have any say in her life. She flashed a smile at
the Lanoux brothers. They had obviously quickened their
pace to catch up.

Beside her, Drake reacted so subtly she couldn't put her
finger on what he did, but the air charged with tension and
he seemed all at once dangerous, not at all the easygoing
man he had appeared. His gaze settled on the two men and
didn't waver. She *felt* the difference, felt him coiling in
readiness, and suddenly she wasn't so certain anyone was
safe with Donovan. His eyes glittered with menace and he
very gently but firmly lifted her by the waist and put her
behind him, leaving him to face the two brothers alone.

Dion and Robert were nearly as bad, splitting apart to
come at Drake from either side, looking like professional
fighters instead of the easygoing men she knew them to be.
She was fast losing control of the situation, the tension in
the air stretching so thin it could be cut with a knife. She
should have been afraid for Drake, but something, some
coiling tension in Drake, made her afraid for the brothers.

"These are my neighbors," she reiterated. "My *friends*." She curled her fingers around Drake's biceps as if that might hold him back. His body was warm; no, hot. She felt the ripple of muscle beneath his skin and an answering heat pulsed between her legs.

Drake hesitated and then, to her relief, she saw him flash a brief smile. His eyes were still as focused and she noticed that his body still shielded hers, but some of the tension in him eased. Not tension, she corrected herself—that was coming from the Lanoux brothers. But certainly Drake was coiled and ready should an attack come.

"Dion." Saria projected more friendliness than usual into her voice. "How are you? What are you doin' here?"

"I could ask the same question of you, *chère*," Dion greeted, stopping just a short distance from them, his gaze running over Donovan, sizing him up. Apparently whatever he saw he didn't like, because there was no friendliness whatsoever.

"I've got a guide gig." She willed Dion to understand it was lucrative and he'd better not blow it for her. "Drake, this is Dion Lanoux and his brother Robert. They're close neighbors. Dion, Robert, this is Drake Donovan. I'm going to show him around the swamp and bayou."

"Really?" Robert's eyebrow shot up. "Why?"

"Robert." Saria was appalled. "Mind your own business."

"You don' mind, Donovan, but I need to speak with Saria a moment," Dion said smoothly, and held out his hand to Saria.

She felt a sudden surge of power running beneath Drake's skin. Her eyes jumped to his face. He was looking at Dion, not Robert, and there was something very deadly in his expression. "Saria." His voice was very soft. "If you're afraid of them, you don't have to go with them."

He knew. She had thought she'd been so clever and careful. She'd hidden terror from her own brothers, from her neighbors, and yet this total stranger, within minutes of meeting her, knew. She forced a smile, a little impressed that he was obviously willing to fight off both brothers on her behalf. "No, even though they have clearly forgotten their manners, they're friends." Maybe if she said it enough times, both sides would stop posturing and play nice.

Ignoring Dion's hand, she stepped around Drake, or nearly did. He shifted his weight slightly, cutting her off. His fingers just barely trailed down her arm to her wrist, settling with infinite gentleness. "You're absolutely certain, Saria? I assure you, there's no need to protect me." He gave her a faint grin.

Her heart nearly stopped and then began pounding. He was so gorgeous. And the way he touched her, featherlight— she felt it all the way to her bones. Heat rushed through her veins and she swallowed hard, trying not to give in to sheer physical attraction.

"You're wrong about that," Dion said, glaring at the sight of Drake's fingers loosely forming a bracelet around Saria's wrist.

She followed his annoyed gaze and had to fight from blushing as she pulled away and very firmly stepped around Drake. "You could use the phone, Dion," she said, "if it is so necessary to get in touch with me." She walked ahead of him, but stopped where she could keep an eye on Drake and Robert. If the twins had planned some underhanded sneak attack on her customer, she was going to let them know once and for all that she could take care of her own.

"Do your brothers know what you're doin'?" Dion hissed between clenched teeth. "That man is dangerous, Saria. You're in over your head."

She tapped her fingers on her thigh, wholly aware of Drake's interest. She was careful not to look at him. "This isn't any of your business, Dion, nor is it my brothers' business. I'm a licensed guide. In case you haven't noticed in the last few years, it's how I make my livin'."

Dion shook his head, stepping closer to her and lowering his voice another octave. "Not with this man. If he wants a guide, I'll do it for you. You have no idea what you're dealin' with."

"So tell me," she challenged. "He didn't roll over and play scared when you and your brother tried double-teaming him." Fury burned through her. "If you know somethin' about this man, tell me now."

"I've been around men like him, Saria; you haven't. He's too still. He didn't even blink when we came up on him and believe me, *chère*, normal men fear us."

She believed him. Robert and Dion were built strong and could fight fiercely. Others left them alone, knowing that if you fought one, you'd be fighting the other.

She shrugged one shoulder. "Then I guess I'll be safe out in the swamp with him."

Drake could hear the whispered conversation rather easily, as could his leopard. His cat was already far too close to the surface, and once again he found himself struggling to keep the animal under control. Saria was surrounded by leopards. And if he hadn't known it before, he sure as hell knew it now: he didn't want *any* male in *any* form near her.

The Lanoux twins, as well as the man in the shadows, whoever he'd been—and Drake wouldn't be able to tell until he managed to get over there and nose around—were certainly leopard. The older gentleman—Amo Jeanmard, she'd called him—who was watching them from the path with interest was a leopard as well. Drake had stumbled into a real shifter lair, where not one but several families grouped together to form a loose coalition. He hadn't honestly known one existed outside of the rain forest.

He inhaled the scent of males in their prime, furious that another male had entered their realm. An outsider, possibly a rogue. He had no fear of them—both he and his leopard had been fighting since he was a child—but he hadn't shifted in a long while. The surgeon had been adamant that he take it slow and allow his leg to fully heal before he tried shifting again. That mattered little to his cat.

His animal raged, throwing himself at Drake. But Drake

had been an alpha for many years, running teams of male leopards in the rain forest, where their primitive natures often edged out the civility of their human sides. It took strength, patience, and discipline to control them—all of which he had in abundance. More than anything, he had to get Saria away from the males. If he read her correctly— and he was very good at reading people—she was as independent as they came.

Ignoring the others, as well as the older man coming up behind him, he sent her a small, taunting smile. "If your man objects to you showing me around, Ms. Boudreaux, perhaps you could recommend another guide."

Saria blushed as she turned toward him. He found it charming, even alluring, and, as color swept into her face, he felt a bit guilty for manipulating her.

Her eyes glittered, more amber than brown. "*Monsieur* Lanoux is *not* my man. *I'm* your guide, Mr. Donovan, and no one is takin' the job from me."

She pushed past Dion, stalking toward Drake, her shoulders stiff with outrage. She actually shoved against Robert as she passed him, her shoulder hitting his. She was a little thing but solid, and she had surprised, even shocked, the male. She rocked him, Drake saw with satisfaction. His grin widened, and he allowed admiration to flare for a moment in his eyes. He loved her accent and he noted it got stronger when she was angry, something well worth remembering.

Saria picked up his bag and pointed the way into the grove with it. At the same time, she glared at the brothers. "I'm quite capable of keeping us safe in the swamp."

"Your brothers . . ." Dion began.

"Mind their own business," she snapped back. "Good evening, Mr. Jeanmard," she greeted the older man as she continued walking down the winding path into the trees.

She was magnificent. Drake found himself smiling even as he confirmed the newcomer was definitely leopard. He followed Saria, resisting the cat's desire to roar his triumph to the other males. *Sometimes, my friend, using brains is far better than brawn,* he soothed his cat. *We're close now. It will be soon.* The swamp called to the wildness bred into his bones.

"What was that back there?" he asked, knowing she would wonder if he didn't. "Are they upset because you got the work instead of them?"

"I take customers into the swamp all the time," she said. "I don' know what got into them. They aren't related to me and we don' date, so don' worry about it."

Drake glanced to his right without turning his head. Dion Lanoux paced beside them several yards away, winding in and out of the thicker stands of trees. To his left, Robert Lanoux did the same thing. There was no doubt their cats had scented his. This was going to be one very interesting investigation. More than anything else, he needed to find out just how big the lair was, how many members it had, and if one of them had become a serial killer. He glanced at the woman leading the way through the grove. She walked with confidence, but she was nervous. Twice, her hand brushed the hilt of the knife and she sent several surreptitious glances into the surrounding trees.

"I don't want to make trouble for you," he said.

She sent him a small glance over her shoulder. Yeah. She knew the Lanoux brothers were in the grove, pacing along beside them, and she didn't like it one bit. She *had* to be the female his cat had reacted to. It made sense. *He* was reacting to the woman. The men were edgy with a stranger in their midst. That might be natural, but to actually challenge one wasn't—unless a female was close to the emerging.

The Han Vol Dan, the period of time when a female shifter's leopard as well as the woman were both ready to mate at the same time, was the most dangerous time for all shifters. The male cats became edgy and restless, combative and difficult to control. Drake studied Saria. There was no sign of a cat now, nothing that gave away that a female leopard could be hiding beneath all that glorious skin.

It took him a good few minutes before he realized everything in him—every cell, every muscle, everything he was—reached for her. Saria Boudreaux belonged to him and he was going to have to steal her right out from under the noses of every single male in what looked as if it could be a considerable lair. And he had to do it right in the middle of a murder investigation. No small task but there was no question, he was looking forward to it.

"What?" Saria glanced at him over her shoulder again.

He was grinning; he couldn't help himself. It felt damned good to be alive.

"Nothing. Just enjoying the evening—and the company. You live in a beautiful place, Saria."

She sent him a faint, pleased smile. "It is, isn't it? Not many people appreciate it."

He followed her contentedly, and with danger pacing close and the night closing in, he felt right at home.